WARNER BOOKS

A Time Warner Company

WARNER BOOKS EDITION

Cover design by Diane Luger

Warner Books, Inc.
1271 Avenue of the Americas
New York, NY 10020

Visit our Web site at
http://pathfinder.com/twep

A Time Warner Company

Printed in the United States of America

First Printing: June, 1997

10 9 8 7 6 5 4 3 2 1

PRAISE FOR AUTHOR STELLA CAMERON AND HER NOVELS

❧ ❧ ❧

"LUSH AND PROVOCATIVE . . . ANOTHER FINE, WICKEDLY SEXY TALE FROM THE TALENTED MS. CAMERON."

—*Romantic Times* on *Beloved*

❧

"HER NARRATIVE IS RICH, HER STYLE DISTINCT, AND HER CHARACTERS WONDERFULLY WICKED."

—*Publishers Weekly* on *Charmed*

❧

"A BEAUTIFUL, EMOTIONAL BOOK WITH A HAUNTINGLY LYRICAL QUALITY."

—Affaire de Coeur

❧

"A SENSUAL, ROLLICKING LOVE STORY ABOUT THE MISCHIEVOUS, MADCAP SIDE OF LOVE."

—*A Little Romance* on *Bride*

❧

"CAMERON LEAVES YOU BREATHLESS, SATISFIED . . . AND HUNGRY FOR MORE."

—Elizabeth Lowell

❧

"A MARVELOUSLY TALENTED HISTORICAL AUTHOR."

—Romantic Times

ALSO BY STELLA CAMERON

HISTORICAL:

*Dear Stranger**
His Magic Touch
Only by Your Touch

THE ROSSMARA QUARTET:

Fascination
Charmed
*Bride**
*Beloved**

CONTEMPORARY:

Breathless
Pure Delights
Sheer Pleasures
True Bliss
Guilty Pleasures

*PUBLISHED BY
WARNER BOOKS

To Peace and Justice, and to Honor.

Chapter One

England, 1848

"Do you suppose *all* men have mysterious parts?" Lily Adler posed the question as much for herself as for her companion.

With a hushed swish of horsehair petticoats, Rosemary Godwin climbed onto the pew behind Lily's. She stood on her toes to squint through clear sections in a stained-glass window overlooking the graveyard of St. Cedric's Church, Come Piddle, Hampshire.

"This is perfect." Lily pried up the rusted handle on her window and pushed. "An opportunity to observe without being observed."

"You shouldn't open it," Rosemary whispered. "He may hear us."

"Don't be a silly goose." Lily strained and managed at last to budge the heavy, lead-paned window a scant inch or two. "He is too involved in his own business. Look at him. A vain, self-important creature if ever I saw one. Besides, we are at some distance, and the walls are thick."

"Do keep your voice down," Rosemary implored.

Stretching as tall as she could manage, Lily succeeded

only in raising her nose to the level of the stone sill. "Give me my Bible. Put it where I may stand on it."

"Lily!"

Really, Lily thought, looking askance at Rosemary, there were times when having the local clergyman's sister as one's best friend could be most tiresome. All this pious nonsense did strain the nerves so.

"Well," Lily said, deciding not to mention using her Bible as a stepping stool again. "You have not answered me. The question is, *do* all men have mysterious parts?"

Rosemary mumbled so low, Lily couldn't understand a word. "Speak up," she said, aware of her sharpness, but not especially contrite.

"I said," Rosemary responded with more than her customary quiet vinegar, "that I'm moved to believe they all do. After all, why should one man be different from another in that respect?"

Lily considered. "Oh, I imagine that even while possessing similar arrangements, they probably are not created exactly the same. But we are agreed that they are all at least similarly burdened. That is something."

"Yes," Rosemary agreed. "Something."

"So one could choose any man to study. Or a number of them, in order to make comparisons."

"Shall you use him, perhaps?" Rosemary spoke of the tall, dark-haired man who, very inappropriately, leaned against the side of a tomb inside an enclosure surrounded by a low, iron fence. "After all, he is to be very conveniently placed for such an undertaking. In your own home, no less. Why, if you are clever—and we know you are—you may find endless situations in which to come upon him."

"I do not like him."

"You do not know him."

"I know what he intends." Lily felt a fresh twist of disquiet. "He plans to wheedle his way into my papa's trust. He has already done so."

"A very handsome man, though," Rosemary said, her light voice wistful. "And you will admit that Come Piddle cannot boast a surfeit of handsome men. Or eligible men of any variety."

"We cannot assume that a man's interesting face is an assurance of interesting other things. Why, he may be endowed with nothing of note for our purpose."

Rosemary rubbed grime from the panes immediately before her blue eyes. "He is singular, though, do you not admit? Large, but in a most . . . appealing way?"

"Arrogant, I should have said," Lily remarked, and sniffed. "In that manner of handsome men who know they are handsome. His eyes are the lightest of browns, you know. Rather eerie. He saw me when I was coming downstairs this morning. He stared at me. Not a smile. But then, we have not been introduced, and he is by way of being a servant."

"Oh, *Lily*."

"Oh, *Lily*," Lily said, mimicking her friend. "Well, it is true. Tall and exceedingly handsome, he may be. And possessed of eyes like that picture of a hungry tiger in Papa's study, but—Ooh, the thought makes me shudder."

"With what?" Rosemary asked.

Lily looked hard at her.

"Well." Rosemary was all innocence. The clusters of blond ringlets over each ear bobbed. "I wondered if he makes you shudder with excitement. I have heard it said that such reactions may be felt. I rather hope I shall feel them myself one day."

"Not, I hope, for a servant," Lily said severely. "At least, not a servant who is bent on usurping your position with your father."

"I do not have a father," Rosemary pointed out. "And neither do I have a portion worth a man's attention. He is not a servant, you know, Lily. He's a man of letters. Your father's secretary, now. And by all accounts a very educated man, so Eustace tells me."

The Reverend Eustace Godwin was Rosemary's much older brother and had his living at St. Cedric's. He was also a stuffy, overbearing, selectively obsequious, easily impressed boor, and Lily could not abide him.

Lily returned her full attention to the man dressed in black, who crossed his arms, and his ankles, and appeared completely absorbed with his own thoughts. Absorbed, and relaxed as he lounged upon some poor departed soul's final resting place.

"Oliver Worth," she muttered. "Of Boston. Can you imagine? Oliver Worth of Boston, suddenly at my beloved Blackmoor Hall. All over Blackmoor Hall. Examining, touching—when he thinks he is not observed, of course. But I know. I've seen him."

"He has only been there a few days, dearest Lily. You will have to speak with him eventually."

Oh, yes, she would have to speak with him. Papa had announced this very morning that he had lost patience with her refusal to be formally introduced to Mr. Oliver Worth of Boston.

"An *American,*" she said, resting her chin on cold stone, and wishing that gentleman could not take the pleasure from a warm, May morning.

"Well, I think he's mysterious," Rosemary said. "And

I'm just sure he will make a worthy subject for the Society's investigation."

"He has a strong body, doesn't he?" Lily replied. "Or so it appears. Why must he always wear black? Unfashionable."

"I think it suits him. And he does have a strong body. I've always found a gentleman's shoulders, if they are large, to be . . . well, they make me want to touch them." Rosemary ducked down. "Oh dear, do say he can't have heard me."

"He can't have heard you," Lily said, regarding the broad shoulders in question. "Another subject for deeper examination—the female response to dimension. Of course, as with all mysterious parts, we must devise a reliable method of measurement."

"Oh, dear."

"Please don't keep saying, 'oh, dear.' Mr. Oliver Worth of Boston has a very solid-looking chest, Rosemary."

"Oh, dear."

"Rose—"

"Sorry. Yes, I was thinking as much myself. He has a very solid-looking sort of chest. Lily, do come away from the window."

"Fiddle. I will not. You know perfectly well he cannot see me. Nor can he hear me—more's the pity. The poor, foolish creature would no doubt die of embarrassment."

"Because we say he is handsome and possessed of a large, strong-looking body?"

Lily wrinkled her nose. "His legs—"

"Lily!"

"How are we to deal with our study if you faint at the mention of a man's legs? He has . . . yes, his legs are inclined to please me. I like the upper—"

"Lily!"

"Hush, or he *will* hear. Lily, Lily, Lily. I am five and twenty. You are four and twenty. It has become evident that we are to remain spinsters. Thank goodness. But we are women of the world with an admirable determination to ensure that we are not denied all experiences available—even if some must be of a largely academic nature."

"Oh, dear."

Lily glowered at her dear friend. "How have you become so afraid?"

"I'm not really. It's just that this all seemed like such a good idea until we actually began to do something about it."

"What good would it be if we didn't do something about it? One can't conduct worthwhile experiments without getting one's hands on suitable specimens."

"Oh, dear."

Lily couldn't bring herself to chastise Rosemary again. "Sit down if you want to, dearest. I will report my observations to you. I do wonder why he stays there like that, though."

"Perhaps he's waiting," Rosemary suggested meekly.

"Waiting for what?"

"I don't know."

"A man's mouth is important. Mr. Worth's mouth cannot be faulted. I am a fair woman, and I must admit that of him. I find the small dimples where his lips turn up very intriguing. And the bottom lip, fuller than the upper—a clearly made, firm mouth. Excellent teeth, also."

"Perhaps they make all the men of Boston exceedingly large, exceedingly handsome, and very strong."

"And graceful," Lily added thoughtfully. "I observed

him from the gallery above the entry hall. He walks as if possessed of great energy, but with grace."

"Very interesting."

Oh, the man was interesting to look at, no doubt of that. And he had an interesting voice, too. Low and still—unless he laughed. Lily had heard him laugh when he was in her papa's study. Papa had also laughed, sounded quite delighted. And Papa did not laugh often, despite the wry wit he saved for Lily alone.

Lily considered how Papa seemed quite delighted with the presence of Oliver Worth, whom he'd engaged—without warning—as his secretary. Her father had returned from a business and lecture engagement in London and simply informed her that he'd had "the great good fortune" to find a man who was of like mind. In addition to his mostly silent partnership in a lucrative merchant bank founded by his grandfather, Papa was a philosopher of some note. Until now he had never expressed any interest in the assistance of anyone but Lily.

She regarded the usurper, and stiffened at what she felt. Jealousy. Never in her life had she succumbed to so despicable an emotion—until Mr. Oliver Worth of Boston.

"Can we go now?" Rosemary asked. "We had said we'd try to meet Myrtle—"

"Yes, I know. I don't think I shall be able to meet with Myrtle today." Abruptly, she longed for some time alone with Papa. She must make him see that he was being duped by an opportunist.

Mr. Worth took off his hat. Instantly, the breeze ruffled the thick, dark hair he wore overly long. He pushed back his jacket to rest his hands on his hips, and raised his face to the sun.

Lily pressed a hand to her breast.

He uncrossed his feet, and crossed them in the opposite direction. His trousers, though exceedingly plain, were finely cut and settled . . . well, they settled.

"I shall study him," Lily said, without deciding to say any such thing.

Rosemary said nothing.

"If he were not some stranger bent on taking advantage of my father, I should find him the most attractive man I have ever seen. Rosemary, his eyes are closed and he smiles a little at the warmth on his face."

"Mmm."

"When he smiles, he has dimples beneath his cheekbones, as well as at the corners of his mouth."

"Mmm."

"Of course, he is probably some sort of despicable devil."

"Lily."

Lily sighed. "Yes, of course. But, as I was saying, he is probably a devil or some such thing. What other kind of man would take his leisure on a tomb in the graveyard?"

"I have a terrible feeling about this."

So did Lily.

"Perhaps we should be making inquiries about him elsewhere," Rosemary said. "To find out more."

"Possibly," Lily said. She popped down, collected prayer books from their slot on the back of the pew in front of hers, and stacked them on the seat. Making sure they were secure, she climbed up again. "He is really quite beautiful," she said, again without intending to say any such thing. She so shocked herself that she gulped.

Rosemary was silent, and when Lily glanced down at her, she found the other woman's face upturned and troubled.

Drawing a deep breath, Lily studied him once more. "He will be my subject. Only for the moment, of course. And only until I know all there is to know about him that is of interest to us. Then I shall find another subject."

"You called him beautiful," Rosemary whispered.

Lily's tongue had an unfortunate habit of causing her deep trouble. "A figure of speech only. Oh!"

"What is it?"

"He is . . . That is to say, he has reclined on top of the tomb. Oh, my goodness. With his hands under his head and his coat flapped open. And his legs stretched . . . Oh, my goodness. He stretches like a very large cat. On a *tomb*."

"No," Rosemary whispered. "The idea. Well, I suppose this is exactly what we hoped for."

"Indeed," Lily agreed, unable to stop herself from staring very hard at Mr. Oliver Worth of Boston. "A man possessing some obviously interesting mysterious parts." He removed a hand from behind his head and covered his eyes instead. "Rosemary. Oh, Rosemary, do you suppose . . . No, of course not."

"What?"

"Well, I do find it suspicious, this sudden decision of Papa's to . . . No, no, it cannot be."

Rosemary sat on the very edge of her pew, her pink silk skirts rustling with her anxious fidgeting. "Tell me. Please."

The new idea blossomed rapidly and became horribly sensible to Lily. "Nothing. I shall do as I have now planned. Consider it done. By the next meeting of the Society, I shall hope to have a report containing solid statistics."

"Oh, dear."

She would not get angry with dear Rosemary, who, despite a great will to experience adventure, had the burden of her stifling only relative. But, yes, Papa could just have devised a most foolhardy plan. It would not work. It would not.

"I should like to go now, Lily."

Surely Papa was not so desperate? He knew as well as she that in Come Piddle, in the company of what society there was to be had, she had been pronounced "pleasant, but plain." And he also had heard comments about his daughter being "entirely too quick and assertive to engage the attention of any sensible man."

Lily regarded the too-fine, supine form of Mr. Worth. A secretary? Or a prospective husband for the daughter Papa had frequently informed he'd like to see "safely" married.

"I shall never marry," she said. "I shall never be subordinate to a man, to a creature who claims superiority because of his mysterious parts."

"Lily?"

"Yes," she said. "We shall go. Everything begins to make sense. Why did it take so long for me to see this. Oh, Papa, how could you?"

"Lily?"

"If you say that again, I shall change my name. I'll call on you soon to set a time for our next meeting. You can tell Myrtle. Oh, indeed, I can play this game well. I am well suited for such a battle of wits. Mr. Worth, you had best guard your hidden parts well. I intend to have at them."

"Lily! You are rash."

"Rash indeed." She laughed. "You do not begin to guess just how rash when the need arises—or should I say, the opportunity? He will not even know I am observing him until it is too late for him to hide. I shall be nowhere, and everywhere. My persecution shall be tireless, and relentless. Eventually he will flee Blackmoor. He will give up whatever plot he has entered into and rush to find a place where he may hope my eyes will not follow. Even then, he will constantly feel the need to cover himself."

"But this is only a scientific experiment for our edification and greater knowledge," Rosemary said, her voice trembling.

Lily calmed herself and stepped from her pilc of books. "And so it shall be. Off we go." She darted along the pew and hopped down to flagstones dappled by shafts of sun turned to jeweled hues by the windows. "I shall keep careful notes. Each tiny point shall be detailed, each obvious characteristic, every deviation. Come, Rosemary. I shall walk directly past the man. He will not expect that."

"I have to return to the rectory," Rosemary said in strangled tones. "I forgot Eustace said he needed me later in the morning."

That might be just as well. "Do go to him, then. I shall join you soon. Or you may come to me if you can." What she intended to do would be best accomplished alone. "I am going to consider an appropriate subject for your study. I know you are against it, but Witless might be sickeningly engrossing."

"Lord Witmore? Oh, Lily, don't even suggest that again."

She would not pursue the subject of their neighbor at Fell Manor—at least not until the next time she met with Rosemary. "Off we go, then. We shall part at the door. I'll give time for you to make your escape. Then I shall march up to Mr. Worth and tell him what I think of a man who takes his leisure on another's final resting place."

"You will not. You will not speak to a man to whom you have not been introduced."

"I shall introduce myself." Since she had every reason to suppose he had followed her to St. Cedric's, why not? "And I shall begin preliminary investigations."

"I can see I shall not dissuade you," Rosemary said in a small voice, still huddled against the wall at the very end of her pew. "Go, then. But I think I shall remain awhile to make sure the flowers have sufficient water."

Lily looked at her friend through swirls of dust motes. "As you wish. Please don't worry so about me."

"Oh, I know you are strong," Rosemary said. "You will do well enough. It's just that I am becoming uncertain of this adventure we have designed. Of course, I will not abandon it unless you should decide to do so."

"I won't," Lily assured her.

"Yes. I didn't think so. Oh, dear. If Eustace were ever to discover that the Junior Altar Society is really the Society for the Exposure and Examination of Mysterious Male Parts, I do believe he might have an attack."

Chapter Two

Clearly she was already besotted with him.

Ah, yes, the simple creature must be dazzled.

Oliver breathed deeply of the pleasant air with its scents of damp grass and early-blooming roses. England. At last he was about to make a place for himself where he'd always belonged.

Unfortunate he'd been obliged to agree to woo Lily Adler, but he was accustomed to making the best of a situation, and he'd make more than the best of this one.

His anger upon arriving in Hampshire had shocked him, shocked him with its sudden intensity. He hadn't expected any emotion other than relief that he would finally confront the past and make his peace with it. He'd believed he had already controlled his anger. For reasons he intended to unearth, he'd been robbed of his rights, but his task was not to try to regain those rights. The only purpose here was to find the truth.

He smiled a little. The hard stone beneath his back didn't displease him. There was something reassuring about stone—about its unyielding quality. A man knew where he was with stone.

Each time he encountered Miss Adler, she looked at him with the oddest of expressions. His smile widened.

The sight of him obviously befuddled her. Even as he rested in this pleasant spot, she was no doubt going about her pious business inside the church, secure in the notion that he had no idea how she pined for him. But Oliver was a man of the world. He knew when deeper meaning seethed behind a female's dour-faced silence, behind her feigned shyness.

Lily Adler might hope to intrigue him with her coy demeanor, but Oliver saw through it all. He would let her play her little games, then he would use her. Naturally he would be kind. He did not intend to hurt anyone—at least, not a simple young woman who meant nothing to him. In fact, he would do his utmost to bring her pleasure that would compensate her for any service she might perform for him.

Surely she would leave the church before too long. When she did, he would smile respectfully, and bow—respectfully—and murmur something respectful as he went into the church himself. Professor Adler had explained that his beloved daughter spent a great deal of time at St. Cedric's. Oliver would do well to impress both the father—whom he admired—and the daughter, with his own devout nature.

Tomorrow he would make an excuse to go to London, where he'd report to Nick Westmoreland. His friend, widowed brother-in-law, and now business partner, should be more than ready to accompany Oliver for a little entertainment.

The price of that company would doubtless be yet another diatribe about the foolhardiness of this venture.

Oliver frowned. He would not turn back, could not turn back now. Not until he'd done what he came to do. And he had a feeling that the silent Miss Lily Adler might be a great help in that regard.

He'd best stir himself and prepare to appear respectful, but interested. Yes, that should set her righteous heart fluttering.

"Mr. Worth, I presume?"

Oliver sat up so abruptly, his neck snapped. Lily Adler stood at the corner of the tomb, her gray silk bonnet slightly askew, and an expression of anything but prim shyness in eyes as gray as the bonnet.

"Have you no shame, sir?" She set her rather too-wide mouth in a firm line. Her pointed chin quivered. "Does nothing seem inappropriate to you?"

"Miss Adler." With all the dignity he could muster, he swung his feet to the grass and stood up. He reached to sweep off his hat, then realized he wasn't wearing it. Instead he smoothed back his hair and straightened his jacket. "What a delightful surprise to encounter you here."

"Fiddle," she said succinctly.

Oliver inclined his head. "I beg your pardon?"

"I said, fiddle. Surprised? Fiddle! I am no green girl, Mr. Worth. I know what you are about. Remember that, if you please. That"—she pointed a steady finger at the tomb—"is the hallowed resting place of someone gone to a higher reward. The Reverend Mr. Eustace Godwin would have something to say about your disrespect for his graveyard."

Oliver took a step away from the resting place in question. "Quite so. What can I have been thinking of?"

"Very little, I should imagine."

He studied her angry face. Plain, so he'd been warned, yet she was not plain—exactly. There was a certain fey charm to her large, clear eyes, to her rather sharp features.

Elfin, perhaps. Not that Oliver had ever been interested in women of less than obvious allure.

Miss Adler's tongue, however, was endowed with the most waspish quality. And he had yet to discover if she could fashion a smile. How bloody annoying that he must at least tolerate the chit while he went about the task he'd waited so many years to fulfill.

"My father is a good man," she announced. "The best of men. He is kind and honorable, and very, very wise. But, as with most men, he can be somewhat simple in his dealings with other men and the foibles of human nature. I believe a determined man possessed of sufficient intellect and cunning could trick him."

By God, she had twigged him. Not entirely, of course, but to some degree. "Professor Adler is a wonderful man." Honestly spoken. "I consider myself blessed to have secured a post with him. Your attack upon my motives for doing so shocks me, Miss Adler, shocks me deeply. I am wounded." He shook his head and averted his face as if too affected to meet her gaze. She must be diverted at any cost.

"How did my father secure your services?"

Oliver faced her again and smiled warmly. "As unlikely as it seems, Professor Adler and I have a mutual acquaintance. Don't you find it extraordinary how fate takes a hand in these things?"

"What mutual acquaintance?"

Gad, she was overly direct. "A friend of a friend, actually. A friend of your father's encountered a friend of mine. Mention was made that Professor Adler sought a secretary, and the man I knew was aware that I hoped to find a position in England."

She shifted from foot to foot, and set the belled skirt of

her gray silk gown swaying. Neither short nor tall, Miss Adler was a puny female. Oliver noted a tiny waist, and a bosom that made the slightest impression on a fine, white muslin chemisette above the neckline of her bodice. Slight, but . . . nice, in a tender sort of fashion. The suggestion of soft, gentle flesh not entirely hidden caused a stirring he had not expected.

A journey to London was essential.

"You are an American," she said, as if pronouncing sentence for some crime.

"I am." Another stirring, of anger this time, caught him as much by surprise as the other sensation.

"Why would an American choose to take up a menial task with a country professor in England?"

She was bent on deliberately baiting him. Dashed if he could imagine why. This was not at all what he'd expected of his first private encounter with her.

"Mr. Worth?"

"You have confounded me, Miss Adler. Your father is a successful, accomplished man. I do not regard my post as his secretary and research assistant as menial, yet if you regard it as so, I stand corrected." He would choke on this servile drivel. "As to being an American in England—this is my dream, dear lady. You see, I am an orphan. No, do not show me pity. I never ask for pity." He held up a hand.

"No pity," Miss Adler announced. She watched him with narrow-eyed intensity. If she felt the faintest twinge of compassion, she hid it well.

Did she ever smile—ever?

Oliver cleared his throat. "Yes, well, thank you. As a child I was cared for by good people who were of English stock. They spoke a great deal, and with fondness, of England. I formed an attachment for this country and determined to make it my own home. I cannot explain matters more clearly. I felt drawn to your fair shores, and to the nation responsible for those dear people who took in a boy of such humble beginnings."

In the silence that followed, Oliver reconstructed the speech he'd invented so hastily and managed not to wince at the puerile clumsiness of it.

Miss Adler didn't wince either.

Miss Adler stared again, and said, "How affecting. A poor child taken in by angels, who returns to the land of those angels of mercy to pay homage to their roots. Do all men of Boston speak as you do?"

"Speak?"

"Your accents are cultured enough, I suppose, yet there is a certain uncommon quality."

"Americans have American accents of various kinds," he told her, tamping down irritation. She was provincial, and arrogant. Amazing. Infuriating.

Her black hair was a stark contrast to her gray eyes. Her bonnet and gown, and fine paisley shawl, were of evident quality but well-worn. Oliver noted that she was without gloves, that a button had been lost at the waist of her bodice, and that several of the yellow daisies lining her bonnet brim were in danger of being lost.

She had no style. But, he concluded, since her father was wealthy she had no style because she was not concerned with such things. Dash it all, he couldn't remember encountering another female exactly like her—in any manner.

"So many questions, Miss Adler." He adopted a jovial tone and made sure his smile came from his eyes as well as his lips. "You'll know me well after today."

"I already know you well, sir. You are transparent to me."

Words failed him. She wanted him to lose his temper. She wanted him to fly into a rage, pack his wounded sensibilities, and leave.

"There is no shame in a man earning his living, Miss Adler, if he does so honestly. I cannot expect to be considered as other than a paid employee in your father's house, yet I can hope you will not despise me for that."

She regarded him fully, and so directly he found he could not do otherwise than look back. He saw her swallow, and the pucker between her brows. If possible, her natural pallor became more noticeable.

"Are you an honest man, sir?"

Wind caught at her bonnet ribbons and moved his own hair, yet the morning seemed airless now. She was a little thing, little, pale, and yes, plain in a way—but he felt her will and it was strong, vibrant, demanding.

Impulsively he reached to touch the crease between her eyebrows. "So serious," he murmured, surprised she did not start away. "Frowns will crease that pretty brow."

Then she did step back, and jerked her head aside. "I asked you a question, and you have answered it." Pink washed her cheeks. "Above all other faults I deplore deceit. In particular, deceit that is cruel in its intent. A pretty woman need not be told she is pretty to know as much. I assure you the same can be said for women like me. Good day to you."

Damn his eyes, but he'd made a hash of things. He retrieved his hat and set off after Miss Adler. Her back was straight, her head held high, and her skirts flipped rapidly about her marching heels.

He caught up with her easily and fell into step beside her.

The only sounds were of his boots on the stone path, and her soft shoes scuffing. She walked faster and faster until she all but ran. He heard her breathing, harsh in her throat.

"Miss Adler," he said when they'd left the churchyard and started along the main village street toward a wide lane that led toward Blackmoor Hall. "Miss Adler, please don't upset yourself."

"I—" She stopped, her face even more pink now. "How dare you presume to tell me how I should feel. Why—"

Two elderly ladies approached and entered the village grocery shop. In response to their greetings, Miss Adler nodded, then hurried on as soon as they were safely inside the shop.

He would not give up his quest to win her approval. He could not. In oppressive silence they carried on past the rows of gray stone cottages with their thatched roofs and gardens massed with budding flowers.

Carriage tracks rutted the lane that flanked part of the walled grounds of the estate at Blackmoor Hall. The previous night's rainfall had left puddles. Miss Adler nimbly avoided these. It seemed to Oliver that her every step was driven with a certain desperation.

Desperation to be rid of him.

"You are decided to despise me," he said. "May I know why?"

She hesitated, rushed on a small distance, whirled about and rushed back to stand toe-to-toe with him. Her position made it necessary for her to tip up her face to look at him. "I am confused by all this." She set her mouth in that singular fashion of hers.

"Please try to explain," he suggested quietly. In that moment he recognized the powerful part she could come to play in his life and struggled to suppress the agitation the thought caused him. "I have explained myself well enough. Why should you scorn me for what I am? And, in fact, your behavior suggests that you think I am something other than what I say I am." Because she was intuitive.

She gave her head a single, violent shake, detaching a yellow daisy almost entirely from her bonnet brim so that it hung before her eye. "Do you agree that gentlemen are taught the art of empty flattery, Mr. Worth?"

Barking, running circles around each other, two hounds scampered from a gap in a hedgerow and dashed toward Oliver and Miss Adler. The smallest animal, a shaggy, white creature, bounded at her, spraying muddy water in all directions. Oliver caught his companion by the waist and swung her from the ground.

She said, "Oh," and her mouth remained open.

The dog shot beneath her and fell into pursuit of its companion.

Oliver looked into Miss Adler's face and said, "You weigh nothing."

"I most certainly do weigh something," she retorted.

"Almost nothing." He frowned, and jiggled her a little to test his theory. "Remarkable. I am accustomed to quite substantial females." Not to scraps whose waists his hands enclosed. He liked the way she felt, liked her clean breath on his face, liked her mouth where he could study it with ease. Wide, but not too wide. And soft. And where the tips of his thumbs rested, barely touching the undersides of her breasts through the stiffened bodice, he felt—

"No doubt you are accustomed to more womanly figures." Her fine nostrils flared. "I would be obliged if you would put me down."

He did so hurriedly. "Of course. Forgive me."

"You are the most amazingly impetuous man, but I must thank you." She brushed at her skirts and made an ineffectual effort to straighten the bedraggled headpiece. A rub at her face deposited a smudge of dirt on her nose. Evidently her dress had not entirely escaped the dog's dirt. She said, "I should have been covered with mud. However, on the subject of flattery—"

"You are so unrelenting. In some matters there are no absolutes. If gentlemen are taught the art of empty flattery, it is by females who demand such flattery."

Her eyes took on a darker hue. "I do not demand flattery. I also know I am not a pretty woman." As he would have answered, she shook her head sharply. "No. No, I do not want you to argue with me on this. I merely use the truth as an example. You complimented me for some reason I don't understand. But I should not judge you so ill for that."

There seemed no appropriate answer.

"I ask you again, are you an honest man?"

He was an honest man. He might be prepared to use less than honest means to gain what he wanted in Come Piddle, but he would always consider himself honest.

"Mr. Worth?"

The most natural thing would be for him to ask her if he might use her first name. He stopped himself, remembering that he was that creature she abhorred, a hired man.

"Mr.—"

"I am an honest man." Steeling himself, he went on. "I intend to make a place for myself in England. Your father's trust, his decision to retain me, have started me on the road to my goal." Not lies, not lies at all.

Miss Adler turned away, then back, and looked up at

him, her head tilted. "Perhaps so. Perhaps I have misjudged you. I admire honesty and industry so very much. In fact, I cannot think of a single virtue I hold more dear."

Oliver made a noise of agreement. Sunlight touched her cheek, her neck, tipped her dark eyelashes. So earnest. So very sincere. She was supple. He'd felt how supple when he'd so impetuously held her.

Oliver would like to hold Miss Adler again. . . . He would like to discover how she would bend to even more intimate touches.

"What are you thinking, sir?"

He coughed, and bowed his face, recovering his composure. "I'm thinking that I would count myself a fortunate man if you thought well of me."

She made to walk on, and Oliver joined her. What he'd said wasn't a lie. He would like her to admire him, to . . . to trust him.

He needed her acceptance. Setting his jaw and clasping his hands behind his back, he walked with more purpose. There was no place in his plans for sentimental fascination with the type of female who could never hold his interest for more than a moment.

"Then," she said at last, "I shall apologize to you. Papa has warned me often enough that I am overly headstrong—and that I have an acid tongue."

"No—" The rules here were different. He must not employ the hasty platitudes most women expected and enjoyed. "Thank you, but there is no need for you to apologize to me. I was too flippant."

"You had no means of knowing me. I am, as you see, quite senior in years, and yet I have little experience with social niceties between men and women."

Senior in years?

Passing beneath an arch crowned with a handsome stone stag, they entered through the wide front gates of the main drive to Blackmoor Hall. "You do a great deal of walking," he remarked.

"As, evidently, do you."

"You are a female, Miss Adler, and not an especially robust one at that."

"I am exceedingly robust," she announced, turning on him once more. "And before you comment on my habit of going about alone, I am too old, and too . . . I am too old to consider my reputation at risk."

He clamped his teeth together to contain a retort that he knew her to be only five and twenty. Not a child, it was true, but not *old* either. And if she knew just how much at risk her reputation might be, she'd be running from him now.

The slightest of smiles appeared and disappeared so swiftly, he wasn't sure he'd seen it at all. "I was indeed wrong about you. You see"—she pointed at him again—"you were moved to flatter me again, weren't you? I saw it in your eyes. But you allowed honesty to prevail. Bravo, Mr. Worth, bravo."

He would strangle on his admirable efforts.

She shot out a hand. "Will you forgive me my rudeness?"

Slowly, he enfolded her hand in his and squeezed carefully. Such spirit in such an unsubstantial package. Why could she not have been a forward romp of a creature, glad of a diversion and unlikely to take long to forget that diversion?

"There is nothing to forgive," he told Miss Adler gravely.

She smiled again, not with her mouth but with her eyes.

They softened, and crinkled at the corners. "I would not wish to embarrass you, but I admire you for making your way against all odds." Her hand remained in his. "I should have honored my father's judgment in the matter of a trustworthy nature."

"Thank you, Miss Adler." He should feel triumph rather than dread.

He had no choice but to release her and accompany her toward the imposing, ivy-covered mansion with its crenellated turrets and parapets.

When they reached a broad walkway at the edge of the great lawns that swept down to the house, she stopped again, glanced at him again. "Some cannot understand why my father keeps such a great house when we are only two," she said. "He bought Blackmoor for my mother because she fell in love with it. After she died he could not bring himself to part with it."

"Your mother had remarkably good taste," Oliver said.

"Yes, she did. Welcome to our home, Mr. Worth."

"Thank you, Miss Adler."

She nodded. "There is no need to thank me. I am also an excellent judge of character, and I can tell you have right on your side. Honor and truth, Mr. Worth, shine in your face."

Chapter Three

Whenever Emmaline Fribble smiled at her, Lily expected vexation to follow.

Fribble smiled now.

"Come in, Lily," her father said, looking up from his deep, brown leather chair as she entered his study. "Your aunt will give me no peace until I speak with you."

Fribble slapped the voluminous skirts of her mint-green and purple gown. A beribboned cap erupted into clusters of multihued bows over braids of brown hair that looped around her ears. Her sigh gusted loudly. "Look at her, Professor Adler. Did you ever see the like in a young woman? True, she is no girl, but still there is a good prospect for a match that would suit perfectly well. If we can only *do* something with her."

Lily met her father's eyes, and the understanding they had always shared passed between them. Fribble and Lily's mother, Kitty Adler, had been stepsisters. Upon Kitty's untimely death, Fribble had rushed to care for "poor Kitty's" child. A widow, Fribble had spent the ten years of her residence at Blackmoor taking far more care of her dead stepsister's husband than of his daughter. Fribble aspired to becoming the second Mrs. Adler, a post Lily's papa showed no interest in filling.

"Come and talk to me," Papa said to Lily. "Sit where I can see how sickly you appear. Your aunt is beside herself with worry about you."

Lily advanced beneath the piercing scrutiny of her aunt and her father's kindly smile. A tall, stooped man, with little left of his hair but a gray circlet around a shiny domed skull, Professor Adler was a spirited man in his own right. Behind his spectacles, his bright blue eyes had the sparkle of a much younger man.

"Oh, I declare she makes me all of a twitter," Fribble said, her voice wobbling. Her hands fluttered before her pretty, round face. "Why will you do nothing to make the best of yourself?"

"Now, Mrs. Fribble, she—"

"No, Professor Adler, you must not be swayed by your too-generous nature. And I must do what my poor departed Kitty would want me to do. It is time—long past time—for Lily to be married. She cannot expect to remain a burden on our good nature forever."

Again Lily met Papa's eyes. They had long ago agreed that allowing Fribble to pretend a position she did not enjoy was easier than tolerating her fits of hysterics if Papa, even mildly, corrected the issue.

"Your hair, Lily." Leaning forward from the waist, her considerable bosom heaving above the lace-trimmed neck of her gown, Fribble tottered toward Lily. "Really, you reduce me to tears. Braids unraveled. Hair trailing like some unkempt peasant's. And that dress. Why, there is mud on the skirt. Is that a tear I see?"

"Yes, a tear," Lily said calmly, using a toe to raise the offending portion of her skirt. "I had an unexpected encounter with a dog on the way home this afternoon. I was about to redo my hair when you sent for me. If you will recall, the message was that I must come at once, so I did."

Lily caught her hair in one hand and held it at her shoulder—and she grew quite still. She felt another presence and glanced around.

Mr. Worth stood at a secretaire beside one of the room's three tall windows. Stood, utterly unmoving, the fingertips of one hand splayed on the surface of the table, his hard jaw raised while he studied her with those eyes the color of fine whiskey.

Embarrassment rushed blood to her face for the second time that day, the second time and for the same reason: Mr. Worth had the power to unnerve her. She was acutely conscious of her unbound hair, and of having been chided about the manner of her dress in front of him.

His regard did not waver. He did not smile, or show any emotion at all, unless it was austere, possibly disapproving reserve.

Papa cleared his throat. "Oliver and I have been working on my paper, Lily. The meaning of the increasing tendency for much to be said about very little is engrossing to both of us. I had thought that a full vessel, if struck, makes but a small sound. But in terms of excess—such as we enjoy—men and women are not simply satiated, they are filled to bursting. Yet they babble nonsense. Want, even a little want, builds thoughtfulness and character. We must explore this phenomenon."

Oliver, the grateful, honest man, was already sharing with her father the confidences that had been Lily's alone. She did not look at him then. "You are right, Papa, as always. I should like to return to my rooms now."

"Nonsense," Fribble said. "Chatter about broken pots

and the like must wait. Now, Professor Adler, to the matter I told you we should discuss with Lily."

The slightest movement returned Lily's attention to Mr. Worth. He now inclined his head and watched her openly, but with the same dark, brooding expression.

"What exactly was the nature of the matter, Mrs. Fribble?" Papa asked. "I don't believe you mentioned it."

"Oh, Professor Adler, you do vex me sometimes. I told you I should wait for Lily's attendance before sharing this wonderful news. Do stop tugging your hair, Lily. And sit down. You make me so nervous."

Lily tossed her hair behind her back. Nothing was to be gained from trying to restrain it.

"The Earl of Witmore called on me this morning." Jiggling on her toes, Fribble made the tops of her breasts, and her plump chin, tremble. "There! What do you think of that?"

"Witless," Lily muttered under her breath. Lord Witmore, their closest neighbor, was in the habit of arriving unannounced—and frequently.

"He called on you?" Papa said, frowning. "Why should he call on you in particular, Mrs. Fribble?"

Fribble's agitation gave her the air of a chubby hen in possession of a particularly promising egg. "His lordship came for you, of course, Professor Adler. As he always does. But I would not have you disturbed at your work, even by so elevated a visitor."

"Elevated," Lily mumbled.

"Do speak up," Fribble demanded. "Really, one would think you completely unschooled. That will have to change, my girl, if you are to take an important place in society. Just yesterday I was speaking of these frustrations with Mrs. Bumwallop. We both have grave doubts of the positive effects of you and Myrtle on each other. And what the Reverend Mr. Godwin is thinking, allowing that sister of his to run wild like a rowdy boy, I cannot imagine."

"Aunt!" This was beyond all. "Rosemary Godwin is my best friend and she is beyond reproach. If she has a fault, it is that she is overly timid. A better person I never encountered. And Myrtle is a gentle soul. How cruel to say otherwise of either of them."

Fribble seemed to think better of arguing.

"Why did Lord Witmore grace this house today, Mrs. Fribble?" Papa asked, sounding weary. "I cannot imagine that he had other than his usual reason for visiting. But I should greatly appreciate dispensing with this topic with all haste so that Oliver and I may continue our work."

Oliver, Oliver, Oliver.

"Lord Witmore"—Fribble shook her head and fanned herself with a hand—"I am overcome to think of it. Lord Witmore—he didn't say this directly, of course, but I understood—Lord Witmore is disposed to repeat his offer for your hand, Lily. What do you think of that?"

Lily feared she might disgrace herself by stating exactly what she thought of Lord Witmore. Instead she stopped herself from glancing at Mr. Worth and concentrated on her father. Despite Papa's kind tendency to be generous to all, she was certain he shared her low opinion of their posturing neighbor.

Papa took off his spectacles and fiddled with them.

"Papa?" Lily said. She did look at Oliver Worth then. His presence at this exchange proved how quickly her father had taken him into total confidence.

Fribble went to stand at Professor Adler's shoulder. She leaned close to him and smiled at Lily. "I think we have all known that a desire to visit the place where his father died could not be his only reason for coming so often all these years."

Still Papa said nothing. "Are you suggesting that Lord Witless fell in love with my charms when we first came here? When I was a little girl of ten, and even plainer than I am now?"

"*Witmore,*" Fribble said severely. "I have warned you—"

"You are not plain, Lily," Papa said sharply. "It may suit your purposes to pretend as much, miss, but it is not so. You are like your mother. You are not as obvious as most young ladies, but you are not plain."

She felt rebuked and touched at the same time. "We should not discuss this. There is nothing to discuss. Aunt Fribble, you are caught up in imaginings. Revolting Reggie . . . Lord Witmore has not asked for my hand, and neither will he." Please let it be so. He had approached her father when she'd been but fifteen. Fortunately Papa had firmly set the other man aside, pointing out Lily's tender years.

Fribble rested a hand on Papa's arm in a familiar manner he pretended not to notice. "You really must make her do what is best in this instance, Professor Adler. Lord Witmore is going to offer for her, I tell you. There will be no more chances such as this one. There will be no more chances!" She fluttered her lashes rapidly. "I have said it, and must hope you will accept my words in the spirit in which they are intended, Lily. A woman needs security. A woman alone is never secure." She produced a lace handkerchief and touched it to the corners of each eye. "Listen to me, my dear. I know about these things."

Lily dared another glance at Oliver Worth. He looked

back, unblinking. There was . . . She plucked the thread where she'd lost a button at her waist. There was an intimacy in his gaze. This was foolish. *Foolish.* He was a man interested in all things, including domestic matters. His steady perusal was no more than an academic study.

But when she looked again, heat gathered beneath her skin. A faint shudder climbed her spine. She must look away.

One of his dark, flaring eyebrows rose. A question? Was he silently asking her something? It was as if they were connected, and somehow she dreaded breaking that connection.

"Oh, she must not be allowed to spoil this wonderful opportunity," Fribble wailed. "Speak to her. Convince her. *Tell* her this is her duty."

"Lily?" Papa said at last.

She remembered to breathe. "I shall never marry," she said clearly.

"Professor Adler! You must prevail in this. She is determined to continue in that headstrong, quiet manner of hers. She has no sense of duty. Lord Witmore will offer for her, I tell you. Lily will become a countess. A *countess*. And she will be on our very doorstep at Fell Manor. Her life will be immeasurably improved, as will ours." Fribble frowned with deep meaning. "Such connections will be useful, Professor Adler. I need not explain the benefits of patrons in high places."

"Or of opportunities to attend endless, boring parties with incredibly boring people," Lily commented.

"Oh!" Fribble shrieked. "She is an ungrateful girl. After all I've done for her. I gave up my life to take her mother's place. Of course, I did not expect gratitude, one never gets gratitude from those who owe it most. But now she has an opportunity to do something meaningful for us, and she should be made to do it!"

"Calm yourself, my dear Mrs. Fribble," Papa ordered. "Rest, dear lady. We'll have tea brought to you in your rooms."

"I am perfectly—"

"No. No." Papa stood and took Fribble by the elbow. "Not another word. To your rooms at once. Rest. You are too selfless. Far too selfless. And you aren't strong."

Oliver Worth's sudden cough made Lily look at him again. He raised his brows owlishly.

Lily found her mouth had dropped open. She closed it.

He winked.

The urge to laugh all but undid her.

Papa ushered Fribble to the door, sending a lopsided smile in Lily's direction as he did so.

Fribble hovered a moment on the threshold before favoring Papa with a doleful glance and leaving.

Still at his post by the secretaire, Oliver Worth's wry amusement had disappeared. He seemed to have no need of movement for the longest periods.

Lily sighed, and examined her hands. She felt him staring at her—continuing to stare at her.

She raised her eyes once more. He was the most interesting man she had ever encountered.

Surely her blood stopped flowing in her veins. Her skin felt cold. But then it felt exceedingly warm. They regarded each other, and Lily thought she could have stayed as she was indefinitely.

He brought a closed hand to his mouth, dug his thumbnail into his bottom lip.

Such a mouth.

Lily's lips parted of their own volition.

He looked at her mouth.

The next breath she took went no farther than her throat. The cold, the heat, the trembling inside—so new, so thrilling.

"So, Lily," Papa said, resuming his place near the fireplace. "Lord Witmore is about to offer for you, hmm, my girl?"

Half-turned from her, shadow clung to the sharp lines of Oliver Worth's face. Without a word, or an overt act, he behaved as if they were the only two in the room.

"I spoke to you, Lily. Are you so overwhelmed that you cannot answer me?"

She managed to finish taking a breath, and to turn to her father. "I'm sorry, Papa. There really isn't anything to discuss, is there? Even if Witless . . . Even if Lord Witmore should ask to marry me—and I doubt he will—we both know any such arrangement would be out of the question."

"Do we?" Thoughtfully, Papa picked up a glass of Madeira that had been all but forgotten on the table beside his chair. "Why exactly should it be out of the question?"

Lily gaped, and sputtered, "Papa!"

"Do you not think I might like to indulge a grandchild or two before I die?"

She must be dreaming. No, having a nightmare. Her awareness of Oliver Worth became overwhelming. "You jest with me. I must return to my rooms. I have letters to write."

"Not until we have finished our discussion, my dear, if you please. I know I have never expressed any particular liking for young Witmore, but perhaps I have judged him too harshly. After all, if he considers you a prize worth pursuing, he has fine taste."

"Papa." Lily lowered her voice and whispered urgently, "Papa, please do not fun me in this."

"I'm not funning you," Papa said serenely." I have mentioned to you on more than one occasion of late that I am anxious to see you married."

Lily felt the unfamiliar sting of tears. "You would betray me by trying to give me to such a man?"

Setting down his glass, Papa ran a finger around the rim before answering, "I would never betray you. You are my dearest possession. And you know this. But I will not live forever, and if you will not consider your future, well, then, I must."

Still whispering, Lily told him, "I will not marry, I tell you. Never. There can be no marriage worth having without equality, and without love. I have never seen such an arrangement. Therefore, it cannot exist. Therefore, I shall not marry."

"Your mother and I loved each other," her father said mildly. "I wish I had treated her more as my equal."

She was chastened, and blinked to clear her eyes. "I'm sorry. I spoke thoughtlessly. I only wish I could remember more of my mother."

"You are very like her. Any man who marries you will be very fortunate."

The man behind her was at some distance, yet he might have been touching her. Lily wrapped her arms around herself. He might be holding her. She knew he had not, for an instant, stopped watching her.

"If Witmore does ask for your hand, I shall consider it my duty to entertain his offer." When Papa looked at her, his face was utterly serious. "And I shall expect you to entertain it also. You must learn to be more open, Lily. Once your mind is made up, you do not waver. This can be a fine trait. It can also be narrow."

She could not believe it. After the times they had chuckled together about the despicable nature of Lord Witmore, her dear papa had declared himself prepared to abandon her to the man. For the sake of convention, the convention that dictated that a woman was fulfilled only in marriage, her one true champion would sentence her to life with a man she despised.

"Think on what I have said," Papa told her. "I am not to be swayed in this."

"I cannot marry if I do not love," Lily murmured. She struggled against an urge to run from the room. "I will never feel otherwise."

"Most people do not love before marriage," Papa said, and coughed. "If they do, I know it is a fine thing. But with the will, love may soon follow. I urge you to open your mind and take time to examine Lord Witmore in a fresh light."

"Never."

"Stubborn behavior doesn't become you."

Her father didn't sound like himself, didn't sound as he had ever sounded before. "You cannot mean this."

"I can, and I do."

Lily started for the door. "May I please leave now?"

"Leave, but do not forget what I have asked of you. Open your mind and heart and grant Lord Witmore what you would wish granted to yourself—a chance to prove your goodness."

He meant it. Lily went to the door. She turned back and said, "It could never be, Papa. I could not bear it."

"Oliver," Papa said, beckoning his secretary. "Let me see where we were before this interruption."

Lily pressed fingers over her mouth. As she turned away, Oliver Worth carried an open book to her father. When the older man bent over the pages, his assistant raised his eyes to Lily's face.

He pitied her.

This stranger had taken her place with her father, and he pitied her.

Chapter Four

A fine debacle in the making.

Oliver closed the study door behind him. He approached the wide staircase that rose, bifurcated, and flared around a circular gallery above the handsome foyer.

She would go, not to her rooms, but to the north wing of the house, a wing rarely entered by other than Lily. So the professor had told Oliver moments after she'd left.

The agreement he'd made with Professor Adler had seemed both useful and essentially harmless. Useful, it had already proved. Harmless, he'd learned it could never be. As a result of Oliver's actions here, someone would lose. It would not be Oliver.

He strode to the gallery, made his way through several long corridors, and outside to a bridge leading to the north wing. In the center of the bridge he lingered, surveying Blackmoor lands to the west. Behind him was a view into the central courtyard, but to the west lay formal gardens ranged around a lake and backed by pretty woods. The woods gave way to hills that rolled on as far as he could see. All Blackmoor. All beautiful.

Here he might find the peace that had always eluded him.

But, he reminded himself, he was not here for peace—not that kind of peace.

Oliver reached a heavy, grayed oak door and pushed it open. This must be a game played with great finesse. Whatever happened, he must find a way to leave these people without causing them too much pain. The Adlers were no part of what had haunted him so long.

Where would he find Lily? He should have taken more detailed directions from the professor. This wing seemed older than the rest of the house, probably because the furnishings were sparse, as if consisting of items too good to be disposed of but not required elsewhere. Portraits lined paneled walls so dark they appeared black. Candles had not been lit. Pale sun through deeply recessed casements gave poor relief to the shadows thick in the hall. All the doors he passed were closed.

Music stopped him.

From somewhere not far ahead came the sound of a piano played with sure fingers. A gentle tune, a waltz he had never heard before.

He discovered Lily seated at a grand piano. The instrument occupied a wide, curved alcove in an elegantly proportioned room that might have been used for musicales. Lily's back was to him and her absorption flowed through each intense, swaying motion of her body. She had abandoned any attempt to restrain her hair, and it hung, heavy and shining blue-black, almost to her waist.

He smiled at her hair, and at the bedraggled appearance of her gown. She was unique, an *Originale,* though not of the type accepted by society.

Walking quietly, Oliver approached over a fabulous silk rug in tones of red and green and gold that put him in mind of a stained-glass window. Bloodred silk covered the walls, and damask of a like color was drawn back from the diamond-paned windows around Lily's alcove.

When he stood close enough to see her hands run over the keys, he stopped and grew still. The gift of stillness came naturally, but it had once saved his life at sea when a villain had him cornered. In the darkness the other man, dagger raised, had passed Oliver's unmoving form. He preferred not to dwell on what had happened afterward.

Miss Lily Adler was no villain with a passion for blood, but she held in her hands something almost as dear to Oliver as his life. She did not know, might never have to know, but she held his lone chance to save his family's honor.

She bent to her music.

Had Miss Adler ever danced? he wondered. Had she ever known a man's touch, in tenderness or even the beginnings of passion? Her father had protested that she was not plain. Oliver had observed her defiant face and known that her parent told the truth. If beauty could come from within, then Lily Adler was not plain.

Beauty from within?

This damnable waiting, and feeling his way when he wanted to rush forward, was thickening his wit!

The waltz faded in a rushing scale of high notes. With her head bowed, the lady settled her hands in her lap and remained so.

Oliver saw when she felt him behind her. Fearing he would shock her, he tried to retreat.

Too late.

She stood and whirled about, her eyes huge, a hand pressed to her heart. "Oh," she breathed, sinking back against the keys and jerking upright again at their discordant jangle. "I didn't hear you, Mr. Worth. You frightened me."

"Forgive me."

In her father's study he'd been unaccountably transfixed by her. Then he'd examined his feelings and decided they were caused by her oddly ethereal air. In the midst of a boldly drawn cast she stood as a small, delicately made creature who seemed almost otherworldly. She also exuded more energy and will than Professor Adler and the frightful Mrs. Fribble together.

Lily Adler fascinated him.

She was so singular, he wanted to know her, to really know her.

"I could see you were upset by what was said in your father's study." He did not relish this charade. "I thought perhaps you needed a friend? Or should I say the ear of someone who admires you, and wishes you well?"

If possible, she appeared even smaller. With her unbound hair and pathetic gown, there was about her such a forlorn aspect that Oliver wanted to gather her in his arms and assure her he would protect her.

Madness.

Indeed she was otherworldly. She had somehow bewitched him!

"Thank you, Mr. Worth, but there is no need for you to concern yourself."

In other words, do not presume to rise above your station. He bowed briefly. "As you say. But I am concerned. As fellow travelers in this world, if we do not care for each other, then who will care for us, Miss Adler? Answer me that."

She frowned a little and lowered her lashes. "No one, sir. No one. I do believe you are a very kind man."

A conniving man. Muscles in his back tightened. "I believe you are more than kind. You have principles." Without planning to do so, he closed the space between them and reached for her hands. "This Lord Witmore? You don't like him?"

Lily Adler put her hands in his and let him lead her from the other side of the piano bench. "I detest him," she said, and her mouth trembled. "In all the years since Papa bought this house from his father, I have loathed the Earl of Witmore. He has taken wicked advantage of my father's guilt. Not that he has any need to feel guilty."

Rather than press her, Oliver remained silent.

"It wasn't Papa's fault that the former earl died on the eve of leaving this house, but I know he continues to regret such an unfortunate happening. Mama was sad, too. She insisted Witless should be made to feel welcome here for as long as he wished to come." She sighed and pressed her lips together. "My father adored my mother. I believe he still does. In her memory he will continue to suffer that man."

"Perhaps the professor has come to like him," Oliver suggested.

"No, he hasn't. He is simply too generous to tell him to stay away from Blackmoor Hall, I tell you."

Oliver gauged his attack. He must be very careful here. "But the professor has urged you to consider accepting an offer of marriage from the earl."

"And I cannot understand it!" She clung to him. "Papa has allowed him access to the house almost at will. The previous earl, the present earl's father, died in this house the night before he was to have left. That gentleman had sold the estate to my father and planned to retire to Fell Manor, which also belonged to their family."

Oliver listened intently. "Why should that mean this Lord Witmore needs to come here often?"

"Because he says it eases his grief. In silence, and in solitude, he sits in the chamber where his father died. My papa tells me it is a sign that Lord Witmore has not healed from his loss. So he comes here. But I *hate* him."

She might never have known passion with a man, but she was passionate. Oliver looked down into her bright eyes and felt her vivid spirit. He looked at her lips and saw how soft they were. He looked at the gentle swell of her breasts and wanted to kiss them. She would be a lissome thing in his arms, all flowing black hair and white skin—and heat within.

"He has soft hands," she said.

Oliver raised his eyes to hers. "I beg your pardon?"

"Revolting Reggie has soft hands. Soft, and warm, and damp. Disgusting."

"He has touched you?" The tightening in his belly, his thighs, was unexpected and made no sense.

Miss Adler bowed her head. "It is too embarrassing."

"Then don't even think about it." The man had dared to put his hands on her. Rage flooded Oliver.

"He came into my rooms," she said. "He pretended to be lost and amazed to be there. Then he . . . He . . ."

Oliver waited. Very cautiously, he chafed her hands.

"He tried to kiss me, and I thought I should pass out from the horror of it." Her voice died to nothing.

Oliver took her hands to his chest and, gently, flattened and covered them there.

"He pushed me against my bed and . . . and his mouth was wet. There is nothing manly about him. Yet Papa thinks I should consider marrying him."

Moving both of her hands beneath one of his, Oliver

eased her face into the hollow of his shoulder and slid his fingers beneath her hair to smooth her neck.

She sighed.

Oliver stared straight ahead and set his teeth.

Her skin had the texture of satin. Her hair slipped over the back of his hand. When he looked down, it was at the shimmering lights in that hair, and at her pliant body resting against him. Almost expecting her to leap away, he stroked from her neck, to her back, and downward to her waist. He stroked and murmured small, meaningless words.

She didn't try to escape.

Oliver kissed the top of her head and settled his mouth there.

He knew the moment when she stopped breathing. Now she would pull away from him.

She didn't. Rather, she turned her head to nestle her cheek on the stuff of his coat. She sighed again, long and quiet.

"My name is Oliver," he told her. "I'd be a happy man if you could say it, even if only once."

She said nothing at all, but pressed closer to him.

This was the result of stress, of shock at her father's remarks—of disappointment at what she thought was betrayal.

Perhaps it had been wrong to leap at the opportunity Professor Adler had presented in the form of a post here, but Oliver was only a man, and the offer had been an unbelievable piece of good fortune.

That offer had led to this, this meeting in this room, with her father's approval and encouragement.

Professor Percy Adler had selected Oliver Worth to be his son-in-law and heir.

"Oliver?"

His heart beat hard. Surely he had misheard.

"Oliver?"

"Yes."

"Do you feel a certain . . . *reaching* within you?" As she spoke, she allowed herself to rest entirely upon him. Her slight weight pressed urgently, and she slid her hands beneath his coat and as far around his body as her arms could go.

He felt something. He felt things he ought not to feel, and the damnation of it was that he wanted to feel them. "I like the sound of my name when you say it."

"So do I. I cannot imagine what has happened to me, but I know I want to hold you, and to have you hold me. It is a little madness, but why should I not enjoy a little madness if it is offered? We shall go from this room today and it will be as if it never happened."

No, it definitely would not be as if it had never happened. He would make sure neither of them ever forgot. "You hold me because you're unhappy. And because you need comfort, and think of me as trustworthy." Which meant she was a poor judge of character, at least in this instance.

"I hold you because you first held me, and I liked it."

No woman of his acquaintance had ever managed to confound him as this one did. "I'm glad, Miss Adler."

"I should like you to call me Lily. You may call me Lily at all times, and I shall call you Oliver. If that is questioned, we shall simply remark that since we live and work in the same house and are of an age, we have decided informality is useful. And also, we consider it modern."

Singular. Bloody singular. "I hope the professor will

approve." He knew he would, but appearances must be maintained.

"I am too old not to make up my own mind on these matters."

"You are not old enough to say you and I are of an age. I am thirty-one."

"A wonderful age in a man. But then, any age would be wonderful in you."

Oliver screwed up his eyes. This was the very devil. Surely she must be dizzy with some sort of daring emotion.

"Should you like to leave now, Oliver?"

"No. I'd like to stay exactly where I am. In fact, the only thing I should like better would be to kiss you." He never spoke without considering what he would say. So why had he done so now?

Lily rubbed his sides through his waistcoat and shirt. "I like the way you feel," she said. Her pleasure led her to explore his waist, his hips, his thighs.

The jolt that struck jarred him to the gut—and other places. "Perhaps you shouldn't do that, Lily."

"Why?" She turned her face up to his. "Men are most interesting."

There seemed no end to her capacity for astonishing him.

"You don't dislike being close to me, do you?" she asked.

"No, Lily."

"In fact, you are stimulated."

Gad. "Yes, Lily."

"Should you really like to kiss me?"

Enough academic analysis. Oliver settled his mouth against her brow. She perplexed him. His eyes closed, squeezed shut. Rising to her toes, she brought her lips to his neck. Like a seeking kitten, testing, trying its way, she made a dozen grazing passes of her lips beneath his jaw, then against his cheek, and his chin.

Oliver held her with hands that shook at the force of his desire to crush her to him and claim her mouth—to claim all of her.

Taking her face in his hands, he held her still and studied her. Words failed him, all the pretty words he had intended to employ in the seduction of the woman he had been charged to woo. Need had made her abandon her nature and seek solace in the arms of a man who was all but a stranger. Need made that stranger seek to provide that solace—but it was his own need.

"Oliver," she whispered. "You quake with something mysterious."

Not so mysterious. "Yes, Lily," he said, and brought his lips to hers. Skin to skin, they touched. And Oliver felt what he had never felt before—a sensation of falling. The brush of his mouth against Lily's was so light it tingled, burned, yet that touch made him weak with desire.

He was a large man, and the effort to hold her as she must be held, like crystal he might smash, cost him dearly. But the cost only deepened the rage of his passion. Another instant and he would frighten her away forever.

"You are sweet," he told her, stroking her cheek with his, pressing his mouth into her hair and into the softness above the neck of her gown.

It was enough. More than enough. Now he must release her.

"You are like wine," she said. "I have drunk very little, but it made me feel like this. Almost."

"Almost?" He could scarcely breathe for the surge in his groin.

"Almost." She sought and found his mouth again and kissed him quickly before guiding his face to her neck once more. "The wine was not so strong as you. I do believe just a little more of you would have me foxed, Oliver." Her giggle was like no sound he had ever heard her make. Young. Happy. Enraptured by her own daring.

"Lily, I fear being found like this. For you, not for me."

"Oh," she said with laughter in her voice. "Of course. It would certainly be dreadful for an elderly spinster to be discovered thus."

"You are not elderly. And your reputation is of concern to me, if not to you."

"Will you be shocked if I tell you something?"

"Probably."

"Good. Then I shall tell you. I loved your kiss. I loved it so much that I should like you to kiss me again."

She was extraordinary. "We have been gone a long time, Lily."

"Not now, then," she said, straightening his cravat. "But at sometime perhaps. I think I have decided that I must take some matters into my own hands. I do not care to marry—especially since I would doubtless be expected to accept Lord Witmore. But I see no reason not to examine the mysterious parts . . . That is, I should like to sample the exciting elements of matters between men and women."

"Sample?" He had definitely misheard this time. "Surely you don't mean—"

"I most certainly do. We should return to the south wing. My father will be looking for you. And Fribble will be fluttering about my rooms readying herself to plead the virtues of Lord Witmore."

And he was to ready himself for whenever she decided to further sample the *exciting* elements of matters between men and women?

She turned about to close the keyboard. There was nothing of the coquette in her. So why did she send blood pounding through his body and throbbing into his manhood as if he were confronted with a naked opera dancer?

A naked opera dancer could never have this effect on him!

"Come, Oliver." Her sideways glance held speculation, and determination. "I begin to form a notion that could be very useful to both of us. But we must hurry back. And you will say nothing of what happened here. Do you promise?"

"Oh, I promise." He could scarcely contain a laugh. She enthralled him with her nonsense.

In the corridor leading to the outer door and the bridge, she walked with purpose. "These are portraits of Lord Witmore's family. All of the furnishings here were his. Fell Manor is not so large as Blackmoor. The former Lord Witmore wanted to sell some things he thought he had no room for. They are of historic interest, and quite valuable, so Papa bought them." She swept an arm up toward the paintings. "So the lords and ladies of Blackmoor remain at home."

Oliver slowed his pace and studied each face he passed. "A dour lot," he remarked.

"Depressing," Lily pronounced. "Some of them are handsome, but they do not appear to have a spark of humor among them."

"Does the present Lord Witmore resemble his ancestors?"

"Yes. Only, he is grown soft. And his mouth is red, which I deplore. And his face. Papa was quick enough to say that was because Lord Witmore is too free with spirits—before it was apparently decided that I should encourage the man's advances." She planted her feet and swung to face Oliver. "Why would Papa do such an outrageous thing? I thought he joked, but then he did not appear to do so."

Oliver cleared his throat and pretended to be engrossed in a painting of a frail-looking old lady with sharp eyes.

"That was Lord Witmore's grandmother. She lived in Fell Manor until she died."

Oliver made an interested noise and moved to the next oil. He grew cold. How could he not have noticed this as he passed?

"They don't talk about him," Lily said, standing at his shoulder. "He's the black sheep. The Marquess of Blackmoor. The late earl's older brother. Revolting Reggie's uncle."

"The black sheep?"

"Yes. I don't know why, but he was banished for something terrible. They say he put his family in grave jeopardy. No one knows where he is."

Oliver gazed at a narrow, clever face.

"We believe that was painted when he was only twenty-one," Lily said. "This would have been his estate. I like his face. I wish I could meet him."

"An interesting face," Oliver agreed, staring at the painted eyes of the man who had been his father.

Chapter Five

Nick Westmoreland was as fair as Oliver was dark. Thirty-two, and widowed by the death of Oliver's sister, Anne, Nick no longer laughed as much as he had when he and Oliver had met at a house party in Newport ten years earlier.

Facing Oliver across a heavy oak table in the dim interior of Come Piddle's tiny Faint Heart Inn, Nick's thunderous demeanor promised a grim encounter. He'd arrived from London only half an hour previous but bristled with taut energy.

The innkeeper placed tankards of ale in front of Nick and Oliver. "There you be, then. Fine night if you likes a drownin', hey?" The florid man rolled on his heels and hovered as if anticipating pleasantries, but withdrew, coughing mightily, when only silence greeted him.

"I left London within the hour of getting your letter," Nick said when they were alone. "I'd been expecting to see you. You should have come to me more than a week ago. What in God's name are you about?"

No part of Oliver's present endeavor had met with Nick's approval. Oliver said, "You know what I'm about. I asked you to come here because it didn't seem prudent for me to leave presently, and I needed to see you."

The evening was young. Several raucous young bucks were engrossed in matching each other drink for drink. Straight-backed, the Reverend Mr. Eustace Godwin stood at the bar. His glass had been refilled twice since Nick and Oliver arrived.

Evidently apprehensive, Nick glanced at another company, two richly dressed men and two equally richly dressed women. Seated at a table close by, this band was too involved in loud laughter and conversation to notice Oliver and Nick.

"I have to ask you to do me a great favor," Oliver said. "It won't be possible for me to return to Boston yet."

"Damn it all, man!" Nick leaned across the table. "We've got a business to run. Competition's heating up and we need to stand shoulder-to-shoulder."

"We are shoulder-to-shoulder," Oliver said, bringing a hand down on top of Nick's clenched fist. "Give me the time I need. I can make decisions as well here as in America. We have Gabriel there. I'd trust him with my life, as would you. If you will remain in London and keep me informed of matters while I complete my business in England, we'll do very well."

Nick fell back in his chair. Not anger but anxiety shaded his green eyes. He shook his head repeatedly.

Cigar smoke hung in a pungent haze, and the air reeked of old ale. The loud company of men and women grew louder still. Complaining in cracked tones, a parrot sidled back and forth on his perch beside a fireplace tall enough to accommodate a man upright.

"Nick, are you with me?"

"Could I change your mind?"

Oliver looked at the low black beams overhead. This was going to be even more difficult than he'd imagined.

Those intent on testing their capacity for drink broke into song, raising their glasses high as they joined voices for a chorus about merry maids.

Oliver lifted his tankard and swallowed some of the warm brew.

"You gave me your word you would satisfy your curiosity and return at once to London and to Boston." Abruptly, with his customary quick movements, Nick jerked forward again. "McInary wants an answer. Do we join our ships with his—time our passages to coincide, and to provide greater safety for our cargoes and his? We promised him we'd be ready to give him our decision a week ago."

"If you agree, tell him yes," Oliver said. "I've given it thought and I see no harm. There may be great good. The faster our clippers become, the less I fear piracy, but we cannot be too careful."

Some of Nick's black expression eased. "I agree. And, as you say, Gabriel's more than capable of overseeing matters while we're absent. But I don't like this intrigue of yours."

"There is no—"

"Bloody hell, Oliver! Don't toy with me. You are intent on playing this foolish—this dangerous game. You have always insisted your title meant nothing to you, yet—"

"It means nothing to me."

"Then why have you been in this godforsaken hamlet for more than two weeks? You've seen the house. You've walked on the land where your father was born—and where he was probably gravely misused—and it's time to move on."

Oliver tightened his fingers over Nick's. "My father *was* misused. Cruelly misused. I have no doubt of that.

And I intend to discover what happened. Nick, I want to clear my father's name."

"Oh . . . my . . . God." Pulling his hand from beneath Oliver's, Nick propped his elbows and buried his face. "I knew it." His voice was muffled.

"What did you know?" Oliver spoke low. "Or think you knew? I must do what I must do. There are things here I couldn't have expected—my own feelings in particular. My father was wronged. *I* was wronged. I have never turned my back on a fight I needed to win, and I won't turn my back on this one."

Nick's face shot up. "You ask me what I knew? There you have it. You don't have a reputation as a hard, unyielding man for nothing, my friend. Your father left this place, and—"

"He was sent away."

"Sent away. Does it matter?"

"It matters to me, as it mattered to him. He would not speak much of it. He would not explain except to say he had been wronged. That he'd been accused of risking his family's position. If my father said he was wronged, then I know it was so. They sent him away and he was forever divided from his family and from this place he loved. He thought he hid his love for England and Hampshire well. But that love was in his eyes with every word he spoke of it."

With fine, long-fingered hands, Nick revolved his tankard on the scarred table.

"She told me my father was the black sheep," Oliver said. "Can you credit how that made me feel? He was said to be the black sheep, to have done something terrible. And no one knew where he was. If he is mentioned here, it is as if he still lives. But they never knew or cared where he went."

"Who is *she*?" Nick's green eyes regarded Oliver's face steadily.

Damn, he hadn't intended to mention her. "Lily Adler," he said, offhanded. "Professor Adler's daughter."

The other man's gaze didn't waver. "And comely, no doubt. I know you, Oliver Worth. No pretty piece is safe within your reach."

Any ready retort eluded him. "Lily is safe from me."

"Oh . . . my . . . *God*."

"You are remarkably free with blasphemy tonight, Nick."

"Don't attempt to divert me. You have come to this damnable placc and bccome besotted with some female. The first was a shock I should have expected. The second is a shock I had hoped to see, but not here."

"I am besotted with no one." A week had passed since the encounter in the north wing. He'd kept his distance from Lily Adler afterward and would not even examine his feelings about her. "And you have nothing to fear. Fate made certain I was stripped of what should have been mine. I accept that. But I do not accept the smeared name of the most honorable man I ever knew."

Nick pushed his ale aside. "Your father accepted it. He made a new life, and a damned good life. He took what they sent him away with and built an empire, and he did it after taking your mother's name. It was his wish to forget what happened here."

"So you say." Emotion heated Oliver's blood. "He thought of you as a son, too. When you married Anne he welcomed you, and I'm glad he did. My greatest unhappiness is her loss, as I know it is yours. We have shared so much. My father and I had our differences, but in some things we were like one heart. And I know what my heart tells me in this."

"Then tell it to me," Nick said. "Admit that although your father chose never to acknowledge his title and roots once he left them behind, you can't accept that. Admit that although he made Helen Worth's name legally his own—so that no man would even remember who he had been—*you* yearn to find some means to announce to the world that you are Marquess of Blackmoor."

"It isn't so," Oliver said, but felt a coldness. "Professor Adler is a gentleman. A scholar. It was amazing fortune that I read of his lecture in Town. I took that fortune as a sign that I should come here. His offer of a position surprised me, but I could not have asked for a better disguise while I did what I had to do."

"Adler doesn't know who you are?" Suspicion sharpened Nick's tongue.

"He knows I am an American. No more."

"But he retained you as his assistant. An unlikely series of events."

"Unlikely, but true," Oliver protested. "We share a great many interests. And once I told him I wished to make a home in England, he—" Damn his hot head and too-ready tongue.

Nick gripped the edge of the table and made to rise. "You can't. Oliver, you can't, I tell you."

"I should not have said it." Guilt washed Oliver. "I don't know what I want. But I confess that I told the professor I wanted a home in England. I had to if I was to find a way into his house. My *father's* house, Nick. The house, the estate they denied him with their lies. And I will discover what his sin was supposed to be. I will not leave until I have accomplished that."

"How can I persuade you out of this."

"Don't try. Only give me what help I may ask of you."

His friend parted his lips and worked his jaw. Tension clung to his sharply drawn features. "There could be danger here, Oliver."

They looked at each other and Oliver admitted, "I know. If there was cause enough to destroy a man, there's cause enough to destroy the man's son. But rest easily, my friend, you know I am no stranger to matters requiring caution."

"You left London without fully explaining your actions." Once more Nick looked around the noisy room. "There is more to all this, isn't there? What else made this Adler take you into his employ? Besides your common interests, and your supposed decision to remain in England?"

Excluding Nick had never been simple. "There is another reason, but I ask you not to press me on it now. If it is ever necessary, I will explain." That reason had become a daily, and nightly, torment. Deceiving the father was bad enough—deceiving the daughter had become unbearable.

"I am an unhappy man," Nick said. "You know I will support you in any decision, but I fear I shall regret doing so on this occasion."

"Have I ever failed to win a fight, Nick?"

"Is this a fight?"

He had thoughtlessly betrayed his own expectations. "It may be." Why not be honest? "Evidently I have a cousin in the area. The son of my father's brother—he who inherited Blackmoor Hall. It was this uncle who sold the estate to raise money for his debts. If he was part of what happened, and if this cousin has any notion of it, I must make certain he is not made aware of who I am."

"You resemble your father," Nick said. "Is there any danger a family likeness might be noticed?"

"None," Oliver said, convinced he was correct. Lily had looked at the portrait of his father when Frederick, then Earl of Witmore, had been close enough to Oliver's present age, yet she'd shown no sign of comparing them.

"I don't like it," Nick muttered. "I shall set up in Salisbury. It's nearer."

"I need you in London."

"We are partners," Nick said, his mouth a grim line. "*I* need *you* with me. You choose to go your own way for your own reasons. I'll accept those reasons, but for the rest I must follow my instincts. Gabriel shall attend to matters in Boston. Wilkins is a reliable man ready for greater responsibility. You've said as much yourself. He can be our liaison in Town. If you need me, it will be quickly. Salisbury it shall be. You should have little difficulty getting away to visit me there. And the cathedral will make an anonymous meeting place."

The Reverend Mr. Godwin came their way. A stocky, ponderous man with too serious an expression for one who appeared no more than thirty-five or so, he saw Oliver and nodded.

"Be careful," was all Oliver had time to say to Nick, then, "Good evening, Mr. Godwin."

"Is it?" Godwin paused near their table and dolorously surveyed first Nick, then Oliver. His light blue eyes watered in a face reddened by drink. "It is a blissful man who finds joy in the evil world of men, Mr. Worth. Blissful indeed. Those of us who think deeply know the truth of it. *We* do not find joy in evil men."

"No," Oliver said, unable to fashion another response.

"I suppose you also find joy at the Hall?" Godwin asked, rocking a little and blinking deliberately. "Must say I was surprised Professor Adler took in a stranger. Most surprised. Shouldn't have recommended it meself, but God will protect the meek. And if he were to fail to do so, *I* should ensure the safety of Miss Adler, sir. Kindly remember that."

Leaving Nick and Oliver to puzzle over his comments, Godwin wandered away. He produced a scrap from his pocket and fed it to the parrot. The bird turned aside and regarded the clergyman with one black eye before amazing Oliver by butting the man gently with its head.

"Odd type," Nick remarked when Godwin had left the inn. "I rather think he's infatuated with your Miss Adler."

"My Miss Adler, as you call her, is interested in no man." Not entirely true, but a useful fiction nevertheless. "She is quite mature and leaves no doubt that she isn't impressed with the male of the species."

Nick laughed, a welcome sight and sound. "If I thought that were true after she's seen you, I'd worry for your reputation." He touched Oliver's sleeve. "I think we're about to get more company."

Guffawing, looking in Nick and Oliver's direction, a sandy-haired, paunchy man rose from the nearby table. He staggered toward them. "Come back now, Reggie!" was the cry of one woman, a lush, chestnut-haired creature in flounced green silk with a swansdown-trimmed, orange velvet shoulder cape. "Reggie." Her fulsome voice took on a petulant note.

Reggie's attention was elsewhere; on Oliver, to be precise.

"You know him?" Nick asked.

There was not time to reply before the man arrived, dragged a chair over uneven wooden floors, and sat down heavily. "Witmore," he said, looking closely at Oliver. "Lord Witmore. Believe we're neighbors—in a manner of speaking. You're the secretary. Am I correct?"

Waves of rancid, spirit-laced breath blasted Oliver's nostrils, and he winced. Lily had been right when she said his cousin was a man gone soft. And Professor Adler had been right in laying the blame for that softness at the feet of Witmore's excesses. Fine red veins mottled a thick-jowled but still-handsome face. Despite the difference in their build and coloring—Oliver's father had been a dark-haired, sharp-featured man to his death—despite the differences, Witmore bore an uncanny resemblance to the uncle he'd never known.

Witmore's fist slammed into the table with such force that the man wobbled in his chair. "Asked you a question, dammit," he roared. "Answer your betters straight, or you'll know the back of my hand."

"Oliver—"

Oliver signaled for Nick not to interfere. "Good evening, my lord," he said. "I'm Oliver Worth, Professor Adler's assistant."

"Bloody *assistant*, hey? What's your game, then?"

Oliver met Nick's eyes.

"Smart fella like you," Witmore said, slurring every word. "Don't tell me you're only interested in Adler's addle-brained notions. Think you see your way to getting your hands on the old fool's fat purse, d'you?"

Nick's boot, connecting with Oliver's shin, sent a timely message. His brother-in-law knew him too well. Now would be a disastrous moment to render this drunken popinjay unconscious.

"Who's he?" Witmore asked, squinting at Nick.

"An old friend."

"Servants dressed like gentlemen, with old friends dressed like gentlemen." Witmore raised his flaccid jaw and turned his head to focus on Oliver again. "I know scoundrels when I see 'em. Look, I've nothing against a man making the best of his opportunities. All I ask is that you come clean."

Oliver pushed his tankard in front of Witmore. "You look as if you need refreshment, my lord. Allow me."

Slobbering, Witmore obliged by upending the ale and gulping. As much of the brew ran down his chin and onto his coat and linen as into his throat. Oliver shook his head slightly at Nick. A meeting with Witmore had been inevitable if there was to be any hope of learning more about what had happened to his father. And the advantage of pitting a sober wit against a fuddled one was not to be discounted.

"I know a reasonable fella when I see one," Witmore said, setting the tankard down with exaggerated care and burping. "Can we trust your friend, here?" He jerked his head in Nick's direction.

"With my life," Oliver said without the faintest smile.

Witmore attempted a wink. Both eyes closed. "This conversation never happened, mind?"

Oliver placed his left hand over the right side of his chest. "On my heart," he said. "We never even met."

"And you?" The earl's attention found Nick.

Nick cupped his ear and shouted, "What did he say?" at Oliver.

"Doesn't hear well," Oliver said to Witmore, and grinned. He tapped his head. "Pleasant enough chap, too, but crackbrained. No need to concern yourself with him. He'll follow my lead." He'd hear more of this later.

Witmore drew himself up. "Been meanin' to take a look at you. Knew you must be the fella when Godwin came over and spoke to you. Pompous, pandering ass, Godwin, don't you know?"

Oliver made a noncommittal sound.

"Word has it old Adler's taken with you. Is that true?"

Giving what he hoped was a knowing smile, Oliver said, "I believe the professor trusts me." Now let him see how the land lay with this one's feelings toward Professor Adler.

"Pay you handsomely, does he?"

"One is never paid enough." Oliver's next knowing smile took in Nick, whose admirably vague expression slipped somewhat.

Witmore raised Oliver's empty tankard and shouted, "Drinks all around, Fuller. Hurry, man!" He ignored calls from his friends to return to them. "Well, enough said for now. But you might be in the way of deepening your pockets. Could be of some use to me. Need I say more?"

Oliver would like his dear, sickening cousin to say a great deal more. "I'll be ready if you need my help."

"Jolly good fella." Witmore clapped Oliver on the back. "Just keep your eyes open. Anything interesting—come to me at Fell Manor. Door always open, don't y'know."

"Perhaps you could give me a small hint about what you'd find interesting?"

"No need. No need at all. You'll know when you see it. Comings and goings from a place where there shouldn't be comings and goings. That sort of thing. S'there somewhere, I tell you. Pay handsomely. Man of my word where these things are concerned."

So engrossed was Oliver that he failed to notice that the younger of Witmore's female companions had left their table. She arrived at the man's shoulder. Auburn-haired and blue-eyed, the creature was a beauty. Over-round perhaps, and just possibly too bald in her manner of looking at a man, but sumptuous nevertheless.

Both Oliver and Nick stood.

Witmore remained seated.

"Reggie," she simpered, wrapping her arms around his neck. "Poor Drucilla is despondent. She thinks you have abandoned us because you no longer adore her." The lady lisped markedly.

"Don't adore her," Witmore announced, frowning. "She may have her uses to me at some time—nothing more."

"Oh, Reggie." The young lady's tongue remained between her teeth. "Introduce me to your new friends."

"Not a bit of it. Let me go. Get away."

"I'm Lady Virtue Beamont." Showing no concern at Witmore's rudeness, she smiled at Oliver. "Reggie's little sister. He's ever so nasty to me, but I still love him."

"You love every man," Witmore mumbled. "Damn liability to a fella."

"What's Reggie been talking to you about?" Her large, baby-blue eyes opened and closed lazily. To many men the effect would be alluring. Oliver saw hardness in her stare.

"This is Oliver Worth and his fool." The earl dismissed Nick with a flip of the wrist. "Worth's the man Adler employed to help with his affairs. Just asked him to keep an eye open for us. Could be useful."

So, he had not one, but at least two cousins. And a distasteful lot they were.

Lady Virtue stopped embracing her brother's neck. She

settled her plump hands on the hips of her striped peach silk gown and swayed. Lady Virtue had much to sway. "You mustn't take my brother seriously when he's—well, you know what I mean."

"No," Oliver said, all innocence, "I don't. What can you mean?"

Her smile disappeared. With the slightest narrowing of her eyes she continued to study him. "Have we met before?"

The smile Oliver bestowed all but hurt his jaw. "I assure you that if we'd met, Lady Virtue, *I* should never have forgotten the occasion." An uncomfortable tightening clamped his belly.

"A flatterer, no less," Witmore said. Grabbing a tankard from Fuller, the innkeeper, he drank thirstily. "Man of letters. Man of *affairs,* perhaps." He hiccuped and slapped his knee.

Lady Virtue's perusal of Oliver didn't waver. "How long have you been in Come Piddle?"

"Two weeks, Lady Virtue."

"With the Adlers."

"Indeed."

"As Professor Adler's lackey?"

Only with difficulty did he hold back a retort. "I am his assistant, and secretary."

"And that colorless little toad of a daughter? What is her name? *Lily?*" Lady Virtue shivered as if with revulsion. "A pious, churchgoing toad. I have not looked closely, but I imagine she even has warts."

"Steady on, Virtue," Lord Witmore said, frowning at his sister while turning his head from side to side to focus more clearly. "Lily's a charming girl. Different from you, of course, sweeting, but quite delightful in her own way."

"Do you think her delightful, Mr. Worth?" Lady Virtue asked.

He could not read what was afoot here. "I am employed by the father, not the daughter," he said, conscious that caution could be of the essence.

"So you regard her as unworthy of notice?"

"Whose got warts?" Nick asked, suddenly and very loudly, cupping his ear once more.

Oliver swallowed a bark of laughter. His old friend was displaying formerly hidden talents. "No one, Nick," he shouted back. "You drink your ale, there's a good lad."

"Whoops!" Tugging at the fastenings on his trousers, Witmore heaved to his feet. "Need to piss. Fuller, bring me a piss pot!"

At that, the other man at Witmore's table, a much older fellow, rose. Tall and cadaverously thin, with light brown hair and colorless eyes, he strutted, chickenlike, to take Witmore by the arm and guide him outside.

Lady Virtue Beaumont, showing no sign of embarrassment at her brother's crudity, sat in his chair. "Why are you here in Come Piddle, Mr. Worth?"

This, an inquisition by a stranger who might well suspect they were other than strangers, had never occurred to Oliver as a possibility. "I'm American. I've always wanted to make a home in England, and I finally decided to do so."

"And you chose to work for Professor Adler."

"He chose me to work for him."

Lady Virtue tilted her head and examined him from head to toe. "He pays you well?"

"Well enough."

"But you would consider a boon from my brother, if that boon were considerable?"

Oliver stepped away from the table. "Evidently you have misunderstood me. Now I must take my leave of you. Come with me, Nick."

Ever the prudent, detail-minded man, Nick said, "What did you say?"

"Come with me," Oliver shouted. "If you will excuse us, Lady Virtue?"

She got to her feet, and there was a moment when she seemed about to step in front of him again. Then she stood aside. "I'll excuse you for the present, Mr. Worth." Her smile was pure coquette. "I feel we shall meet again. Soon. You feel it too, don't you?"

He didn't answer her.

"I see that you do. We recognize each other, you and I. We know we need each other. Be glad. We must be sure to take time to enjoy each other as we use each other." She turned from him and swept back to join the other woman.

"Let's get out of here," Oliver said, throwing coins on the table. "I find the atmosphere doesn't suit me."

Nick had taken a room at The Faint Heart, but they went instead into the dark, rain-drenched inn yard where Oliver had left the horse Mr. Adler had placed at his disposal.

"Now, will you listen to me and give up this nonsense?" Nick asked, pressing against the inn wall in an attempt to escape the rain. "We'll spend the night here and make our way to London in the morning."

"No."

"Damn it, man, give it up, I beg you."

"I cannot. You heard that drunken fool. There's something he's trying to find out at Blackmoor."

"Perhaps. It doesn't have bearing on you."

"It may. It may very well. But even if it doesn't, his father knew why mine was stripped of all but a token inheritance, and sent away."

"So you think."

"So I know. My father as good as said as much. His brother wronged him. I will not leave until I know what happened."

"Oliver." Nick gripped his arm and brought his face close. "She knew you. That woman told you she *recognized* you."

"So she did." Oliver had noted the sharpness of Lady Virtue's gaze. "Surely she only referred to some imagined likeness of spirit between us." He prayed he was right.

Chapter Six

"Listen to me, Oliver Worth. Oh, I know you cannot hear, but I demand that you listen anyway—fool!

"You dismiss me. I am as nothing in your eyes compared to you. Soon you will wish you had considered what manner of enemy I am. It will be too late. You will look into the eyes of death before you take my measure.

"So fine, so strong, so sure. How long have I known this time must come? Too long. Too long wasted while what should be my due is held beyond my reach.

"Your ruin is a shadow at your back. Turn around!

"You don't see me, but I see you—I will see every move you make until you move for the last time.

"Are you enjoying your pretense with the pretentious, babbling professor, and his shrew daughter? Use them. I will also use them, use them both—use you all. They will rue the day you came into their home.

"Oliver Worth, so handsome and powerful upon your horse. Fearless. Your nostrils flare at the scents of smoke and sweat, but you are a man to be admired as you sit there. The horse shifts beneath you and you smile as you ponder how all the world is yours to take.

"Look! Look here and you will see me. In the shadows by the inn wall. Can't you see me? I am watching you,

Oliver Worth, interloper here. And I'm glad you have chosen this time to show yourself, for I am ready to make an end of it, an end of you.

"I will destroy you. Do you hear me? I am here. Oliver Worth, I am going to squeeze out your heart!

"You have cherished your power, and planned how you will grind me into the dirt. You dream of seeing me writhe there, of setting your boot upon my head and crushing out my pride, and my life.

"You do not know I discern your very thought, the way you plot against me. You cannot guess how I know the shape of your evil even before it is fashioned. But I shall extract my revenge, take everything you hold dear, laugh as you beg for mercy.

"Arrogant. So sure of what you intend. Look at you. You are blind to the threat. I am before you, yet your skin doesn't quiver at the sight of me. I have touched you, but you didn't know me. I set my hand upon that very horse you ride, but you will never know—unless I tell you how I had to resist temptation. I could have loosened the girth this night, shouted with the others when the saddle slipped. All would have cried out with horror. But you would not have died, and I want only your ultimate defeat.

"You don't guess it, but you are not so formidable an opponent as you might have been. If you had remained unfettered, with your skin alone to protect, you would fight to the death. I see that. Your death, or mine—if you should discover me. But now there is the Adler girl. Oh, I know that look in a man's eye. You laughed when you were asked about your intentions there, but I see through that, Oliver Worth. You would use her as you no doubt use anyone who can help you get what you think you should own. But I wager that your empty honor would lead you

to protect her from harm if it came her way through any connection to you.

"Ah! You turn toward me. Hello, Oliver Worth. See me? See my bared teeth? I would tear out your heart with my teeth. Bind you, and bite away an eye while you screamed, but leave you the other to observe how I mutilate you.

"It will be the sweeter if you come to care deeply for Lily Adler. Yes, I think I shall wait a little longer than I planned. I should enjoy seeing if you are vulnerable after all. I have learned your reputation with women. They say your appetites exhaust the most lusty of them, but that they cannot resist you. How delicious to observe you brought low by a simple creature who lays bare some spurious weakness in you. Weakened by the weak. Perfect.

"You will not win. You will surrender everything that is mine.

"Hate will keep me whole—it will keep me safe. With hate in my heart, my head, and at my right hand, and my left, I shall prevail.

"Hate will become your companion into hell—it will secure for me what is mine. And I will celebrate your pain with my triumph.

"The struggle has been too long.

"It is all but done. If you take her for your own, I shall take her from you, and use her in front of you. Then she shall witness your agony.

"But if you do not take her, well then, so much the better for you. You will die a little faster.

"I am beset! I am beset! Only your destruction can save me!"

Chapter Seven

"Lily Adler, you didn't!"

"I did."

"No. Oh, Rosemary, make her say she didn't." Myrtle Bumwallop opened her brown eyes and her small mouth as wide as they would stretch. "No! You couldn't have, Lily."

Lily sat on the edge of her floral chintz chair near Rosemary Godwin's parlor fire and tapped a toe irritably.

Given to theatrics, Myrtle flung the back of one hand to her brow. "You *didn't.*"

"I didn't, then," Lily said, and sighed.

Rosemary had stopped pouring tea. She clutched her hands together at her small waist, but Lily thought her timorous friend was close to laughter.

"I know you," Myrtle said, her pert nose all but twitching. "You did, didn't you?"

"Yes, I did."

"You are wicked, Lily," Rosemary said, giggling.

"Of course you didn't." Rather than relief, Myrtle's prettily plump person exuded disappointment. "You're mean, Lily. You revel in upsetting me."

The afternoon had grown chill. Lily raised her skirts a few inches to warm her ankles by the fire, and said, "I am known for the joy I take in torturing my friends." The Rectory tended to ornate but comfortable furnishings, and Lily enjoyed her cozy visits.

"Rosemary." With an expression of deep agitation, Myrtle took a few tottering steps toward their hostess and lowered her voice. "Do you think even Lily would invite a gentleman to one of our meetings?"

"Hard to say." Rosemary resumed pouring tea. Paris mint became her fair coloring and was delightful against the deeper shades of blush and green that dominated the room. "But I should think it possible."

"I am beyond vexed," Lily announced, feeling anything but vexed. Thrilled exhilaration warred with trepidation at her own daring. "Really, I always do my best to advance the studies of our little society. How can you chide me for my efforts?"

"We should be on guard for excesses of passion," Rosemary said mildly, carrying a delicate cup and saucer to Lily. "Certainly we are all committed to our cause, but we must not give in to exactly the thoughtless sort of behavior we hope to explore. In all its manifestations."

"*Male* behavior," Lily said, trying not to bubble at the thought of what was to come.

Fluffing her skirts, Myrtle turned her head at the angle she considered most suited to her features. "Well, I shouldn't like to suggest that all male behavior is thoughtless. There are times when they can be charming."

"When they have reason to be charming," Lily said darkly. "And we shall discover their most guarded secret: what exactly it is that drives their . . . drive?"

"And how," Myrtle added, momentarily diverted. Her smile became distant and beatific. "Oh, I do look forward to delving beneath that which makes them *so* male."

Rosemary tutted and said, *"Myrtle."*

"Bravo, Myrtle." Twitching her skirts even higher, Lily frowned at a large hole in one of her cream silk stockings. "That is exactly why I asked Mr. Oliver Worth to join us this afternoon."

Myrtle shrieked.

The door opened and the Godwins' housekeeper bustled in. "There's a gentleman come to see you, Miss Rosemary. Says he's expected."

"Show him in," Rosemary said, drawing herself up until the servant departed, then slapping her hands to her cheeks and whispering, "You *did,* Lily. What are we to do? What shall we *say*?"

Just then, the gentleman in question joined them in the drawing room.

"Good afternoon, Oliver." Lily's heart thundered as it seemed determined to do at the briefest sight of him. "We're so glad you could join us." She found she couldn't do anything but savor the sight of the man.

Somberly dressed as ever, Oliver bowed over first Rosemary's, then Myrtle's hands, and murmured his greetings. When he released her, Myrtle remained where she was, fingers suspended.

"Good afternoon to you, Lily." A slight frown replaced the warmth in his expression. If she did not know the nature of the man, she'd be reminded of the very devil by his flamboyant handsomeness. He advanced to stand beside her but didn't take her hand. "And a cool afternoon it is. Fortunate the April showers already did their work, although I find the flowers in this room more than a match for any I've seen outside."

Made speechless by this unexpected poetry, words failed Lily. With visible reluctance, Oliver looked away from her face—to her ankles. Her very exposed ankles. Her very dilapidated stockings.

Lily also looked at them.

Oliver cleared his throat. "I see you are cold."

She released her skirts and leaped to her feet. Covering her mortification with severity, she pursed her lips.

"Should you care for tea, Mr. Worth?" Rosemary asked.

He continued to study Lily. "No, thank you, Miss Godwin."

"Something, er, a little stronger perhaps?"

"No, thank you, Miss Godwin."

Lily didn't think she had ever seen eyes quite the light gold shade of Oliver's. And even when he did not smile, the dimples by the upturned corners of his mouth remained.

"Please don't be reticent, Mr. Worth. I know gentlemen do like spirits now and then." Rosemary's pale-green skirts swayed at the edge of Lily's vision.

"Thank you," Oliver said, his expression softening. Slowly, he smiled. "But I am more than happy as I am, Miss Godwin. What could a man desire more than the company of an enchanting woman?"

He meant her? No, he was being polite, nothing more. Yes, something more. Noddycock that she was. He was being *male*. This was part of it, a huge part, the part she'd mentioned this very afternoon, and only minutes earlier. She would concentrate harder. They used words to advance the design that occurred to them whenever they were in the company of females.

Charm for the sake of getting what they wanted.

And she had fallen for that charm instantly!

"And there we have the start of it," she told the room. "Exactly what I have observed."

He appeared puzzled. "What have you observed?"

Myrtle's face—a study in mock horror—bobbed behind Oliver's left shoulder. Her ecstasy at the wonderful diversion radiated in her every wiggle.

"I have observed that despite the inclement weather for the time of year, the flowers have not suffered," Lily said. "Thank you for coming. I hope we shall have a spirited discussion."

Evidently Rosemary was in such a twitter that she'd forgotten he didn't want tea. She brought him a particularly tiny cup and waved him to a delicate gilt chair with the slenderest of legs. In his well-tailored trousers, Oliver's strong legs were extremely interesting.

"Papa mentioned how it is often a good thing to observe the habits of foreigners," Lily remarked, noting with some concern how the chair creaked when Oliver settled on the petit point cushion.

"Professor Adler is a very innovative man," he said.

"Yes, well, I found myself considering his remarks about how rarely we have the opportunity to discuss domestic arrangements with those of other cultures."

"How true."

"Naturally Papa did not have anything like our humble society endeavors in mind"—in fact, her papa would be horrified if he knew of her forward behavior in inviting his secretary to a ladies' meeting—"but he spoke of his theory on the value of comparisons at such length that I decided this was an occasion not to be missed."

"Indeed," Oliver murmured.

How beautifully his black coat settled on his considerable shoulders. Against his white linen, his skin bore a tan rarely seen on English gentlemen. The tan made his teeth very white. Lily glanced at his hands. Not soft in the manner of so many men, but broad, long-fingered, and strong. And she had felt those fingers on her face, her neck. He had kissed her, and she had kissed him. . . .

"You did not exactly name your society, Lily." When he bowed his head, the flared angle of his brows became dramatic.

She felt a flush on her body. "We are the Junior Altar Society," she said firmly, not daring to look at either Myrtle or Rosemary.

"Because there's an old Altar Society," Myrtle said breathlessly. "I mean, a Senior Altar Society. My mama is the president. They are such fuddy . . . Well, you see, they are *senior*, of course, and would not welcome our youthful vigor and enthusiasm. So we meet to—um—practice. We—"

"We consider the responsibility of becoming full Altar Society members very weighty." Rosemary interrupted in a faint voice, but still surprised Lily. "So we're preparing ourselves for the duties we'll be required to perform by becoming as . . . informed as possible."

"Well said," Lily announced heartily. "Just so, Rosemary."

"And you think studying the domestic habits of another culture will assist you in becoming informed for your duties?"

She observed his face, searching for either suspicion or amusement, but found neither. "Just so, Oliver. We can learn from others. Papa has always made certain I was attentive to different opinions on every subject. I should imagine attitudes are very different in America."

The cup handle presented some awkwardness in Oliver's large hand. "How exactly do you expect to incorporate knowledge of American domesticity into the duties of St. Cedric's Altar Society?" He was not a clumsy man. He took the cup to his mouth and drank.

Lily had returned to her chair. This time she kept her ankles well covered. "Our deepest area of interest is in the attitude of the male toward the female." She had not intended to sound so strident.

"To help with Altar Society duties?"

He was too clever. "Forgive me. I should have explained our theories and concerns."

Rosemary and Myrtle huddled together on a puce velvet couch behind the tea tray. Myrtle studied Oliver with open admiration.

Lily frowned at her friends. They were no help at all.

"Our pleasure is to serve," Myrtle said in a rush. "And understanding is the cornerstone of service, isn't it, Lily?"

Good heavens. "Of course it is. Yes, of course."

"We live to serve," Myrtle said.

Oliver drank more tea. "Admirable."

"To serve adequately, we must have understanding."

"Yes. The cornerstone of service. So you said."

"More tea?" Rosemary picked up the silver pot.

Oliver set down his cup and saucer on a round marquetry table. "No, thank you, Miss Godwin."

There was no help for it but to take charge of this conversation before all was lost. "My thought was that you could discuss the philosophical aspects of the attitudes of American men toward women."

"Philosophical aspects?"

"Of their attitudes toward women. From a spiritual point of view, that is."

His failure to answer filled Lily with apprehension. This had seemed such a delicious idea. To actually have a specimen present for examination. Now she couldn't think how she'd intended to get to that examination.

"Since the man is the head of the household, and the household pivots on the relationship of those within it to their religious life. You see how it would seem that the man's relationship with the woman is a parallel, Oliver?"

His nod was not at all emphatic.

"Oh, good," Myrtle said gaily. "You were right, Lily. A most insightful and *charming* man. Little wonder you are so taken with him."

An appalled silence followed. Lily yearned to flee. Rosemary's face turned red. Myrtle's blissful ignorance of the discomfort she had caused showed in her smile.

"Thank you," Oliver said, his eyes so intent on Lily's that she had to glance away. "Your approach to your topic is novel. Ask away. I shall do my utmost to help."

"You have a family?" she asked. "In Boston?" How personal that sounded. He would think . . . oh, my, perhaps he was even a married man!

"Alas, I do not." His serious demeanor suggested the fact didn't please him. "As I thought I had explained, my parents are both dead. I had a sister, but, sadly, she died some two years ago."

Lily felt his unhappiness and regretted being the cause of his having to mention personal tragedy.

"And you have no wife?" Myrtle inquired.

Horrified, nevertheless Lily held her breath waiting for him to answer.

"If I had a wife, Miss, er—"

"Myrtle. Myrtle Bumwallop."

"If I had a wife, Miss Bumwallop, I should not feel free to wander the world in search of a place I wish to make my home."

"Sterling," Rosemary said. "I do believe our ultimate happiness depends on attitudes such as yours, Mr. Worth. The family is the foundation of society—of successful, satisfying society."

"And the foundation of the family is the harmonious arrangement between man and woman," Lily put in, grateful for Rosemary's sensible intervention. "As husbands and wives. We would like to know if, in America, this is seen as the case."

He considered. "Husbands and wives are the foundation of the family? True. Family is the foundation of society? True." His chair creaked. "After all, Lily, without family there would be no society—not as we know it, that is. And without husbands and wives there would be no families—as we know them."

"There, you see?" Myrtle's cry was triumphant. "Just the same in America. I know you are about to say that without men and women there would be no husbands and wives—as we know them!"

Rosemary closed her eyes.

Oliver smiled at Myrtle. "No, I'm sure there wouldn't."

Before the inevitable uncomfortable silence could follow, Lily said, "In America, do men behave toward women as they do here?"

"In what way?"

There would be no simple way out of this encounter. What had seemed a splendid idea threatened to become a disaster. "We—that is, the members of the Society for—The members of the Junior Altar Society have noted the tendency for there to be less understanding between men and women than we might hope for."

"And you consider this more the fault of the male than the female?"

"Yes." Honesty should be allowed to prevail. All would be well if she expressed exactly what she believed. "Since men consider themselves so incredibly superior—and since society has pandered to that opinion and allowed them power over women—men definitely set the tone for relationships."

"That may be so in some cases. In many even. It is not so in all cases."

"We tend to wonder why men want women at all, since they frequently let us know they consider us trivial."

"I cannot speak for all men, Lily, but I assure you many of us do not consider women trivial."

Aha, progress. "Because you have particular needs which only we can meet?"

Amazingly, a slash of red appeared over each of Oliver's cheekbones.

"Lily always puts things so well," Myrtle told them all. "We are of the opinion that there should be no mysteries between men and women."

Rosemary pushed a fresh cup of tea into Myrtle's hands and frowned, a frown Myrtle showed no sign of noticing. "In your own experiences with family structure and the church, Mr. Worth," Rosemary said with the determination Lily recognized as driven by necessity, "in America, that is. Is there satisfaction and comfort in the manner of things?"

"I believe so." He didn't sound certain.

"Probably in America—being a newer and I expect more modern-thinking country—men are more comfortable making the secret mysteries of their desires known." Myrtle's tea went untasted. "How useful it would be to understand the dark turnings of a man's mind when he thinks about a woman. Those thoughts—and sensations—that lead him to pursue her."

Never given to the vapors, nevertheless Lily wondered if pretending that condition might be a relief at this moment.

"What makes you think the turnings of a man's mind are dark, Miss Bumwallop?"

"Well, they are, aren't they? I have seen how there is much deep, very deep, dark rumination in a gentleman's eyes when he looks at a woman. A woman he considers comely. Tell me. Is that because he somehow knows she has a soul that will please him?"

Oliver coughed. He coughed violently and turned his head aside.

Suspicious, Lily watched him closely. If she didn't know him to be a thoughtful man, she'd almost wonder if his coughing was designed to cover laughter.

It could not be.

"Should you like water, Mr. Worth?" Rosemary asked.

He shook his head.

"The deepest question," Myrtle continued, "is what exactly does his attraction to her soul create? Perhaps I should say, *stimulate.*"

Another fit of coughing shook Oliver.

"Are you sick?" Ever the caretaker, Rosemary left her seat and poured a glass of lemonade from a carafe. "I do believe you have taken a chill."

"The lemonade will help." Once caught by a topic dear to her heart, Myrtle was not easily diverted. "What happens when you are attracted to a female, Mr. Worth?"

It was Lily's turn to close her eyes. This was all her fault. She should have rehearsed this meeting with her friends. No, she should not have brought the meeting about at all.

Oliver drank some of the lemonade. "What made you think American women could be more modern in their thinking than you, Miss Bumwallop?"

Myrtle, her body erect in its tight corset, glanced from Rosemary, to Lily, and back to Oliver. She was finally, and blessedly, at a loss for a reply.

"It is only that America, being foreign, seems exotic to us," Lily said. "We are probably wrong, but we thought conventions might be more advanced."

"Men are very secretive," Myrtle announced. "Oh, I am not criticizing, you understand, just observing. We know they speak among themselves about women, because we've seen them doing so. But they guard those conversations."

"Much as women speak among themselves about men, perhaps?"

"Oh, yes," Myrtle said blithely. "But, you see, we make no secret that we gain enormous pleasure from speculating about gentlemen."

"You think gentlemen make a secret of the pleasure they gain from speculating about women? Not so, Miss Bumwallop."

Myrtle leaned forward. "Do tell us the kinds of things they say. And how they make you feel. And is there any—*physical* manifestation from those feelings?"

"Physical?" Oliver mused, swinging his glass between finger and thumb. "Oh, yes, quite physical. And you ladies? I suppose there must be some physical reaction. If there weren't, you wouldn't be curious about how those reactions feel in the male."

"Exactly!" A radiant smile made Myrtle even prettier. "How insightful you are, Mr. Worth."

He looked not at Myrtle, but at Lily. He didn't smile at all when he said, "Is that what interests you most in this discussion, Lily? My physical reactions to an interest in a particular female? In her soul?"

She would die. But first she would find an opportunity to tell Myrtle she was the cause of that death.

"Lily?" Oliver persisted.

"I find all elements of human relationships engrossing," she told him. "I should be glad to discuss whatever would most please you to discuss."

He inclined his head so that only she could see his face. Free from the scrutiny of her friends, he made a deliberate survey of Lily. Of every part of Lily, from her hair, to her face—with a long pause at her mouth—to her bosom! Another disgracefully long pause, not that there was much that would interest him. Her entire person received his assessment, and so serious did he find the project that it took a great deal of time. Didn't it?

He deliberately tortured her.

Lily glowed. She burned. He must see how overheated she had become.

"You would be glad to discuss whatever would please me most?" he asked, the dimples at the corners of his mouth deepening.

"Yes."

"How very modern of you, Lily. There is something I had in mind."

"We'll all be glad to discuss whatever it is," Myrtle said.

"Thank you." Oliver's eyes didn't smile. "I'll look forward to meeting with you and Miss Godwin again. Soon, perhaps. But in the meantime I do believe my needs will be best served by a more intimate comparison of feelings."

Lily thought her heart must have stopped beating.

Oliver rose and offered her his hand. "Thank you for inviting me. I wish I had more time to enjoy the company of the Junior Altar Society. Very stimulating."

She watched him take her fingers to his lips.

His mouth lingered there—lingered, and lingered.

Myrtle and Rosemary sighed loudly, and in unison.

Oliver looked into Lily's eyes. "Our emotional and physical reactions, hmm? With emphasis on the differences between men and women? A discussion? Oh, I shall look forward to that."

Chapter Eight

Oliver had behaved as if their meeting of the previous day, at the Godwins', had never taken place. Each time he'd encountered Lily since leaving her at the rectory, he'd smiled politely but shown no inclination to linger.

She ought to be glad.

Lily wasn't glad, she was agitated beyond endurance.

He hadn't done more than nod at her during dinner this evening. Afterward he and Papa had hastened away to the study, leaving Lily with another dull night ahead.

What had Oliver meant when he'd spoken of wanting to have a private discussion with her?

Handwork bored her. She rose from the window seat in her sitting room and tossed her embroidery hoop on the floor. Foolishness. The stuff of empty convention. The cobbled mass of colored threads would be of no more use than any previous piece she had attempted.

Restlessness overtook her and she paced about the room Fribble had insisted must be "girlish." The result wasn't entirely displeasing. True, Lily would have chosen fewer frills, but the dominating shades of yellow, from sunshine to rich butter, satisfied her well enough.

"Lily? Where are you?" Aunt Fribble sang out her arrival as she rustled into the room. Resplendent in bow-trimmed violet, with pleated epaulets at her shoulders, she closed the door firmly behind her. "There you are. My dear child, we must talk. Haven't I done my best to be a mother to you? Not that I could ever take dear Kitty's place, but I have done my best. When I meet my maker he will say that of me. Emmaline Fribble did her best for her poor, dear stepsister's child."

"Yes," Lily said when Emmaline paused for breath. "I'm sure he will."

"And now you have to give me credit for having your best interests at heart. Our best interests at heart. You must trust me, and help me."

"You are agitated, Aunt Fribble." Sometimes stating the obvious was the best that could be done.

"Agitated?" Stays creaking, she retrieved the embroidery hoop. "Our future success is in your hands and you can only remark that I am agitated?"

Further mention of Lord Witmore had been inevitable. Lily had expected the topic to be pursued days ago.

"Ooh, you can be so vexing." Fribble's bosom swelled. "And that dress. Oh, you will be the death of me. *Brown*. Brown, old, and very shabby. And it does not suit you. Why a plain woman would choose such plain clothes I cannot fathom. Why, Lily? You are pale, and will not do anything to give yourself more color. And that dark hair. Becoming on a man. Oppressive on a woman. And your mouth—so large. No, no, we must do something with you, I say."

"Thank you, Aunt." These diatribes usually had little effect, but today Lily felt the cut. "What would you suggest I do about my ugly face?"

"Draw attention elsewhere."

"To my ugly body, you mean?"

"Well." Fribble pushed out her rouged lips and considered. "A great deal may be accomplished with padding."

"No."

"And bright colors. Rich fabrics. Flounces. Beads and the like. I do not approve of excesses for the young, but this is a time when we must make the best of you."

"No."

"What do you mean, no?" Her aunt's already pink cheeks grew more pink. "I'll thank you to show some respect. And you are to attempt an air of grace, my girl. Grace and poise. We must work together in this. And your deplorable habit of appearing so . . . so, *untidy*, must be corrected. Mrs. Bumwallop mentioned how you are never well put together. Most embarrassing."

Mrs. Bumwallop's opinion mattered not one jot to Lily. "If our conversation is over, I should like to prepare for bed."

In a mighty swish of flounced skirts, Emmaline brushed past Lily and plopped herself on the window seat. "I have told you there is something we must determine to bring about together."

"And you have explained it."

"No, I have not. I came to discuss that horrid Mr. Oliver Worth."

Lily looked at her aunt. "Oliver?"

"That is the first thing that must stop. Such familiarity. What can you be thinking of? Encouraging first names with a servant."

"He is Papa's assistant. Papa thinks very highly of him."

"Rubbish."

"It is not rubbish," Lily protested. "Papa is already entrusting his confidence to Oliver. You must have seen how they spend so much time closeted together." The thought of the way her father had begun to exclude her from discussions they had always shared continued to pain her.

Fribble's mouth all but disappeared. "Yes," she said at last. "Yes, you are right. I believe you may already understand what I understand. The man is a menace."

"Aunt—"

"Do not interrupt me." Aunt Fribble frowned at Lily's handiwork and set it aside. "We have to be united in this. Clearly the dear professor is too trusting to see through the man's schemes. We are not."

Lily stared at her own distorted reflection in the night-dark window and puzzled what her aunt could mean.

"We know Mr. Worth thinks he's found himself a fat pigeon. He intends to insinuate himself deeper and deeper into your father's confidences, and his *affections,* and find a way to line his own pockets. There! What do you say to that?"

Oliver, plotting to take advantage of Papa? Such a thought had never occurred to Lily. "No. No, of course not. Why would Papa fall for such an intrigue?" Now that she had evidence that Papa was actually considering an offer from Revolting Witless, Lily knew she'd been wrong in her momentary suspicion about Oliver as a prospective husband. "What do you mean by affections, Aunt Fribble?"

Holding her chin high, Fribble rose to her feet. She cast a knowing, deeply meaningful look at Lily. "A man wants a son."

"A man wants a son," Lily repeated. "Men do want sons. True. What has that to do with this?"

Fribble's bosom rose hugely and she let out a long-suffering sigh. "It wounds me to tell you this, but I must. Naturally I have always known your father's disappointment in not having a son. My poor, dear stepsister knew it before me. I will not use pretty words. The professor has suffered quietly all these years. But now he has found a man he wishes were his son, and the scoundrel knows as much."

Words failed Lily. She took the seat Fribble had vacated.

"If we do not act, Mr. Oliver Worth of Boston will find a way to get his hands on what should be . . . yours."

"Aunt Fribble, what nonsense. Only a fool would fall for such a scheme. Papa is an exceedingly intelligent man."

"Intelligent men have weaknesses, too, you know. I have seen how things are, I tell you. I would not put it past Mr. Worth to engineer a marriage to you if necessary. There! Now do you begin to see?"

Lily didn't see at all.

"Oh, fie, you force me to be blunt." Sweeping her skirts around, affording Lily a profile of an exaggerated bustle the lady didn't need, Fribble laced her fingers together. "I detest Mr. Oliver Worth, but I would lie if I said he was other than an extremely handsome man. Handsome of face and figure. *Now* do you see?"

Lily shook her head.

"A man like that wouldn't look at you, would he?" Fribble's voice rose to a cracked soprano. She cleared her throat. "Yet we have both seen that he fawns upon you. Lily this and Lily that. And he has persuaded you to call him Oliver. Why, he is transparent. He courts you to gain your father's pleasure. He would marry you for the same reason and no other."

"He isn't going to marry me," Lily said, her heart beating too hard. Of course, Fribble was right. A man like Oliver would never be interested in a woman such as Lily. Yet she had entertained notions that he found her desirable. She felt sick, and foolish.

"An *American*, mind you," Fribble said. "Probably the product of some thief, or worse—some *murderer.* No doubt his family, if you can suppose such people have families, no doubt they were forced to flee England. Why else would anyone leave this fair land for a wild place populated with savages. Can you imagine the horror? Our impeccable reputation soiled by the offspring of criminals? He would want things his way, too. He'd bide his time until you inherited, then find a way to rid himself of everything but his newfound wealth."

The narrowness of this woman disgusted Lily. Her own stupidity more than disgusted her. She knew her place in the way of things. She knew she must make the best of a good mind and a kind heart. True, she had desires, but she must never allow them to blind her to her own shortcomings.

"Are you listening to me, Lily?"

"I'm not going to marry anyone."

"Yes, you are. You're going to marry Lord Witmore. He will add to our success, not sweep it away. But we'll speak more of that once this is dispatched. You are to help me get Oliver Worth out of this house. If you plead your case well, your father will listen to you."

Distress made Lily chilled. "I'm sure I have no idea what all these imaginings of yours are, but I'll have no part of them. Why would you so hate the idea of my marrying Oliver, but think it perfectly lovely for me to marry Witless?"

"Witmore," Fribble shrieked. "I am beside myself. And do not use that man's first name again. It isn't suitable. Of course I would rather you marry Lord Witmore than a penniless nobody, a nobody with no position that could possibly be of use to any of us."

"I'm tired." And light-headed. And weak to her soul. She got up again and started for her bedroom. "Please excuse me. I'd like to sleep."

"I will not excuse you. We have to work together in this. If we don't, Mr. Worth will ruin everything I've planned for, I tell you."

Lily didn't trust herself to argue, or to point out that her relative's plans were selfish, and her treatment of Lily cruel. "Calm yourself. We'll speak of this again soon."

"Lily!"

"Soon," she said again. "Good night."

"Very well. Good night. But I shall have my way in this, and the American will not suit me at all. If you will not help me, I shall have to find another way to get rid of him. But I *will* get rid of him."

Lily heard the longcase clock at the top of the great staircase strike two and gave up on sleep. She slipped from bed, donned a robe, and left her rooms. She would make her way to the north wing and hope music would calm her unhappy thoughts.

From the time of her mother's death, the north wing and the piano only she played had become Lily's haven. It was the one place Fribble would never go, since she insisted it was ominous. She had repeatedly begged Professor Adler to dispose of the Witmores' effects from rooms above the lowest floor, and to seal the door from the bridge. Papa had promised the former Earl of Witmore to maintain the wing exactly as it had always been, and Papa kept his word.

Fribble hadn't minded that Witless continued to keep the key to a lower entrance to the wing, the entrance to his late father's rooms. Those should continue to be available, Fribble insisted, for poor, dear Lord Witmore's solace.

Lily arrived at the juncture of three corridors. The south wing lay behind her. Ahead rose steps to another floor and the bridge. To her right was a long passage that flanked the entire east wing.

The rooms Oliver occupied were reached from this passage.

But for a faint glow from a lamp some distance from where she stood, all was dark.

Now do you see?

Yes, she saw what Fribble had meant all too well. No explanation should have been necessary. He was handsome, forceful, a presence no one would fail to note even before he spoke. And when he spoke, he would draw any audience under his spell.

She had been absurd. She would not be absurd again.

Surefooted, Lily climbed the stairs. By necessity she'd learned to move through near-darkness with the aid of very little light. She made certain she caught no one's attention and that she returned to her room before dawn.

Her heart was heavy. Every child of God deserved to be valued for that which made them unique. No man or woman should be considered less than any other, yet chance, the chance that made a face and form either beautiful or plain, had the power to grant more importance to one than another. She had known from childhood—Fribble had made sure she did—that she was not a well-favored person. So be it. For a short time she had forgotten. Now she remembered well.

What could Oliver have meant when he said he wanted a private discussion with her?

Words, mere words.

Could he have designs on tricking Papa in some manner? If he did, she must make certain he failed. Oliver hadn't attempted to make his employer consider him as a future son-in-law. If he had, and if Papa thought that a good plan, there would have been no question of entertaining an offer from Lord Witmore.

Oh, she had chased these patterns a thousand times in her mind.

Nothing would be lost by confronting the accused.

Lily spun around. She hesitated only an instant before hurrying back the way she'd come.

At the junction of the three corridors, she sped to the left and rushed on, her white robe and gown billowing behind her.

If she paused now, she'd turn back forever.

These rooms hadn't been used in years, not since Mama died and Papa no longer cared to have visitors. Oliver had been told to choose his quarters and had taken the green suite, so Fribble had remarked. Fribble thought them ugly and harsh, but too good for a servant.

The lamp Lily had noted rested on the flat head of an ornamental elephant fashioned of leather and brass.

The elephant stood opposite the open door to the green suite.

Lights shone inside the room, a large, masculinely appointed sitting room.

He was also awake, then.

There was still time for retreat.

She had never, never been a silly, shy ninny, and she

would not become one now. Confront the foe, confront and show your own true colors. Show strength.

Her tap on the dark wood of the door wasn't particularly strong.

No voice suggested she either advance or go away. Lily knocked harder, but still received no response.

She took a step past the threshold and said, "Oliver," but more softly than even she had intended.

Ebony and brass gleamed with a soft patina, all furnishings of the early Napoleonic origin her father favored. Green silk striped with narrow gold hung the walls, and silk carpet in shades of green covered much of the aged oak floors.

"Oliver." This time she was a great deal more firm. Emboldened by her own voice, she said, "It's Lily. May we talk?"

She glanced toward a door to her right, open again, but with not even the faintest of illuminations beyond.

Lily frowned. That would be his bedroom. She was instantly reminded of the hour, and of her absolutely unsuitable mode of dress. And the very idea that she had decided to call on a gentleman in such circumstances was shocking. She might be a woman no eligible man would look at, but she was aware of proprieties.

At least she had come to her senses before he could discover her presence. She rose to her toes and made to creep away—and smelled an acrid scent.

Burning?

Coals in the grate had gone out. Not even a wisp of smoke rose to account for the smell. But it was there, quite strong and unpleasant.

A great thud of her heart stole Lily's breath. He smoked

a cigar with Papa after dinner each evening. Perhaps he'd smoked here.

Did gentlemen smoke in bed?

Abandoning caution, she darted to the bedroom and flung the door wide. Light from the sitting room showed a massive four-poster heaped with a tangle that must be Oliver wound in his disheveled covers.

Lily's eyes stung.

Something burned in this room. She flew to the side of the bed and shouted, "Oliver! Oliver, wake up! Oh, please wake up!"

She cast wildly about. He must respond. Leaning over the mattress, she tore at the covers.

Light flickered into the room. "Lily? What the—What are you doing here?"

Oliver's voice sent a shock to her toes. "Burning. I smelled burning. I came to wake you."

"Did you?" With a candleholder in one hand, he came toward her. "All the way from your rooms?"

At first she didn't catch his meaning. Then she shook her head, no. "No, of course not. I . . . Of course not. I was passing by and the door was open."

"Passing by?"

Oh, mortification. They were both fully aware that she would not simply pass by his rooms in the early hours of the morning. She would not pass them at all. The only reason to come into the corridor that led here would be to visit his suite.

When he stood beside her, he raised his candle and looked from her to his bed. He sniffed. Instantly his brows drew together. "I'm dashed. You're right. Burning, by God." He flung back the overs, dragged the closest pillow from the mattress, and exclaimed.

A blackened area marred the white linen. Black, with a hole burned in the center and brown singe marks at its outer edge. Soot streaked the underside of the pillow. The whole was wet.

Oliver put his fingers to the ruined linen. "What do we suppose was the reason for this?"

Shudders overtook Lily. "I don't know."

"Don't you? Oh, but you do if you will think about it."

"Perhaps you left a cigar alight," she suggested.

"You have a quick mind, but no. Do you see any sign of a cigar? No. I asked what the reason for leaving such a message might be."

"A message?" She couldn't imagine what he meant.

Oliver stooped and picked up a candle Lily hadn't noticed. He held it out to her. "The weapon of warning, I believe."

It had been used but barely. "Ah." She let out her breath. "You must have knocked it over."

"I didn't knock it over. I'm carrying the candle from beside the bed. Notice that there is no holder there."

She took note.

"Where is your candle, Lily?"

"I know my way. I have been comfortable in the darkness since I was a child."

"Unusual."

"Fribble says it's contrary of me."

He studied her again. "Do you dislike me, Lily?"

His eyes, gold in the wavering candlelight, mesmerized her. Why would he ask her such a question?

"At a loss for words?" he asked. "Never. Not you. If you wanted me to leave Blackmoor, why didn't you say as much?"

"I . . . I don't understand you."

He went to a ewer and basin on his washstand. "You waited until you saw me leave, then you came to deposit your little warning. Neat. Burn my bed and put out the fire with water from this." He tapped the ewer.

"No," Lily protested.

"What did you want me to think? That you would be prepared to burn me alive in my bed if I don't go away? Or perhaps this was just the first of the unpleasant surprises you had planned for me. Hmm?"

That was it. The final straw. "Oliver Worth, you are a noddycock!" She marched past him and into his sitting room where the door to the passageway remained open. This she closed. "Come in here and face me like a man."

Smiling faintly, he strolled to join her. Dressed in his trousers and shirt, without a coat or waistcoat, he lounged nonchalantly against a massive bureau. His shirt unbuttoned almost to the waist, his cuffs hanging loose about his forearms, nevertheless he seemed perfectly comfortable.

He said, "Face you like a man, hmm?"

"Take back your accusations, sir. At once."

"Why should I?"

"Oh, men are so abominably thickheaded." She pointed toward the passageway. "I waited for you to leave? What excellent powers of deduction you have. I must be certain to ask your help when I have a puzzle to unravel. Naturally I waited for you to leave because, of course, I knew you might just choose to leave at such an hour on this particular night."

"I often leave my rooms in the night."

"Yes, well, I knew that. But this was the night on which I chose to burn a hole in your mattress. To make you leave

Blackmoor." She grew still. "Oh, Oliver. Oh, my. Someone did do that, didn't they? Someone did . . . They did."

"Yes, they did." He smiled suddenly, brilliantly. "And I thought you liked me, at least a little."

"I do." *Fiddle.* "Did."

"Did?"

"Do."

"Good."

He had tied her neatly, easily, in the kind of knots she'd vowed to avoid. "I like a great many people. I dislike almost nobody." There, an admirably cool note. "We must consider what has happened here calmly. Who could have done this thing?"

"I know who didn't."

She grimaced at him. "You, I suppose."

"True. But I was going to say that you didn't do it. I already knew as much. You'd hardly have cried out like some crazed creature if you hoped to deliver an ominous warning without my guessing your identity, would you?"

"I would not."

"I thought you wouldn't."

Lily shivered afresh. "Lock the door."

"You think I should?"

"Absolutely. Lock it, and keep it locked. I think you have the right of it. Someone wants you to leave Blackmoor Hall."

"Would you say this someone intends for me to think they would take my life if I should remain?"

Murder? She felt for the nearest chair and sat down hard. "You make light of it, but they could mean that, couldn't they?"

Oliver strolled to lock the door. His overlong hair and flaring features, together with his mode of dress, put Lily in mind of a pirate. If she hadn't been frightened for him, she might have laughed. How would he respond to such a comparison?

He faced her. The grim set of his mouth showed that he found little humor in the situation. "You happened to choose this evening to come in search of me."

Her face glowed. "That was not my intent."

"You would have no means of knowing that I often go to the library when I can't sleep. But someone else has obviously taken good note of the habit. Someone who wishes me ill. Or who is afraid of me for some reason, perhaps."

"How could anyone be—" Lily stopped, and made much of ensuring that the ribbons on her robe were tightly tied. "No one has reason to be afraid of you, do they?" Fribble would never stoop to something like this. She was a frightened, grabbing woman, but she was no criminal.

Oliver watched her; she felt him do so even without looking at him. "Yet," she continued slowly, "I agree that we have cause for concern."

"We?"

He sought to trip her at every turn. "You are in my father's house. Your safety here is my concern."

"Yours, rather than your father's?" he asked softly.

He considered her bold and presumptuous. "Should we go to my father?"

"You imagine I need your protection, that you should speak to the professor on my behalf? Do I seem incapable of dealing with such matters?"

Her embarrassment blossomed. "I should have said that I think you should go to my father."

"So that he will view me as a liability who could cost him his home?"

"I should leave." She should never have come.

"You ask me to lock the door and speak with you. Then you say you must leave." He shrugged and added, "You're right, of course."

Lily rose awkwardly to her feet. "You must think me impetuous." She was impetuous, and wrongheaded. "Forgive me. It was only that I—I was going to play my piano when I remembered that you'd mentioned wanting to discuss something with me."

"Did I?"

If he had any thought at all about her, it must be that he considered her ridiculous. Her attempt at a lighthearted laugh stuck in her throat. "Obviously I was mistaken. Again, forgive me."

"Consider yourself forgiven." His yawn suggested disinterest—boredom even—and that he wished the meeting terminated. "I would appreciate your help in one matter."

Already on her way to the door, she stopped and faced him again. "Anything." Why must she sound so desperate to please him?

"Perhaps it would be best not to mention this night's events to anyone." He walked around her and unlocked the door, evidently all too anxious to be rid of her. "After all, no real harm was done and it could have been an accident of some kind."

"I suppose it might have," she agreed. "Naturally I shall say nothing."

"Good." He smiled and opened the door wide. "Good night, then."

Dismissed. Oliver had dismissed her.

Where there had been a man she thought she'd begun to know, a stranger stood, a stranger who didn't want her company.

Lily turned from him and said, "Good night," as she fled.

Chapter Nine

He had to protect himself. He had to. He could not risk jeopardizing the single-minded dedication he'd honed for this business by flirting with the unthinkable: sentiment.

She threatened him.

Closing the door slowly, Oliver leaned his back against it. Confound this madness. There could be no question of becoming deeply involved with anyone here.

Lily Adler? Audacious, yet subtle, Lily Adler? The antithesis of Oliver Worth's well-known and definitely obvious taste in females?

Impossible. She had come to him with that damnable honest openness in her gray eyes. And for a moment he'd been charmed—more than charmed, perhaps. Her simplicity had reached a part of him that was better left as it was—suitably toughened.

That honesty of hers, her lack of guile, had touched him from the moment they'd first spoken in St. Cedric's churchyard.

Now—in an effort to protect himself from becoming vulnerable—he'd wounded her, made her feel foolish. He might forgive himself for finding his attraction to Lily unnerving. Allowing her to suffer humiliation on his account was unforgivable.

Oliver tore open the door and strode into the passageway. He took up the lamp from the leather elephant's head. She would run to the sanctuary of her rooms and hide.

Most women would. Lily wasn't most women. He might well find her with her piano, with her music.

Urgency drove him. He didn't know what he would say, only that he must find her.

He did find her, and quickly. She stood in the center of the bridge to the north wing. With her face raised to a star-encrusted sky, she showed no sign of hearing his approach.

Her robe fluttered in the breeze. Moonlight through fine lawn showed her body in silhouette. A diminutive creature. More vulnerable than she could possibly know.

She deserved his chivalry, not his violation of her person, even if only visually.

Oliver left his lamp behind and concentrated on her upturned face. "Lily. I'm sorry."

Her start was so violent, he silently cursed his own clumsiness. "It's cold out here," he told her. "Come back inside."

"It's beautiful. And not at all cold."

Her voice was as he should have expected—remote. Before him stood one of the few truly strong women he'd ever encountered. "You may be right, but you aren't dressed for the night air."

"I am not a child." Her hair was wound into a single thick braid that had swung forward. She tossed it behind her shoulder. "Thank you for your concern. Good night."

Why would she not need to gather her pride? "May I stand with you?"

She shrugged.

"I'll consider that your agreement." Nevertheless, the few steps to her side were some of the least comfortable he had taken. "The moon paints a different picture than the sun."

"Or the wind, or the rain—or snow."

"Indeed. All beautiful, I should imagine. But moonlight on a clear night may be my favorite condition for viewing from this bridge."

She wrapped her arms around her middle. "You could almost be an Englishman, Oliver."

At least she hadn't reverted to formal address. "I think I should regard that as a compliment. But how so?"

"We English are experts at discussing the weather. We resort to it at the least provocation—or with no provocation at all. And we invariably find the weather most interesting when we are confronted with an awkward situation we'd rather avoid. You show promise in that area."

"You know how to hurt a man."

"And you know how to hurt a woman." She drew in an audible breath. "Careless. I can speak so carelessly."

"But honestly, I wager."

"Self-pity isn't pretty."

Neither was arrogance, or disregard for another's heart. "We should go in." At this moment he scarcely knew himself.

"No. Please. You go. I must stay, at least a while longer."

"Then I'll stay with you." He wanted to stay with her, wherever that might be. "What I did—how I behaved—it was because I am unsure of myself."

She looked at him then. "Unsure? You? Surely you're funning me."

"In most instances I'd be flattered to be told I'm a hard man. From your lips the suggestion becomes a reproach."

"I have no right to—"

"Yes." He raised a hand and would have touched her, but didn't dare. "Yes. You do have a right. And you have the right of it. I cannot change who I am, but I can regret that I am not different. I should be so glad if I thought . . ." A rash man could do himself great harm.

Lily didn't prompt him. She waited, and when he didn't continue, she returned her eyes to the stars.

"Thank you for caring about me," he told her. "Thank you for risking your reputation by rushing into my rooms because you thought I was in danger."

"We know my reputation isn't an issue."

Oliver narrowed his eyes. And he did touch her. He settled his hand lightly on her back, beneath the heavy braid. "A single woman's reputation is always an issue."

"When I said I was on my way here but changed my mind, I told the truth. I also told the truth when I told you I decided to come to see you. But when I said it was only because you'd mentioned wanting to discuss something with me, I lied. I did think of that, but only because I was searching for an excuse to see you."

Her skin, through the thin robe and gown, was cool, her flesh firm. He stroked downward to her waist, and back up to rest his fingers at the nape of her neck.

Lily shivered and hunched her shoulders. "Perhaps it was as well that I made myself a fool—"

"You did not! How could you? How can such honesty be less than honorable?" He was not himself. This fullness in his breast, the welling of feeling. He should see her to her rooms and withdraw before he had even more to regret. "Lily, I must insist that we get you safely back. If someone were to learn we've been together like this, and alone, well, you would be ruined."

Her abrupt laughter was the last thing he'd expected, but laugh she did, sad, mirthless laughter. As abruptly, the sound ceased and she said, "There is nothing to ruin. Don't you understand? I know this. You don't have to worry about my tender feelings. Women like me never have to protect their precious reputations, because no one believes there's any need. In fact, as a woman I am invisible."

She rendered him speechless.

"You are kind, Oliver. And I confess that I have entertained silly notions about you. You are very beautiful. Perhaps that is an odd thing to call a man, but it's true, and the world is more beautiful because of you. Your kindness led you to be courteous to me, but I am returned to my senses. I know your attention has been no more than a wish for pleasant relations in this household."

"Lily, you steal my breath." Her frankness stunned him, made him feel mean of spirit.

"Don't worry. Now I see what a goose I've been. I will not embarrass you further." She turned her face to him again. "I'm very glad my father found you. You are already a great comfort to him, I see that."

My God, he was despicable. Her father would be cast to the depths if he had any idea how their actions had injured his beloved daughter. "Please, let me speak. How you could think yourself invisible, as you put it, escapes me." There could be no turning back from his course, but surely he could obtain his goal without injuring this woman. "I assure you that what I feel for you at this moment means you are anything but invisible to me. What I feel should make you run from me."

Wisps of hair fanned her cheek. The question he saw in her night-darkened eyes let him know she did not understand. "You are subtle, Lily. Do you know what I'm saying to you?"

She shook her head, and her lips parted a little. He heard the faint sound of moist skin separating, of her tongue moving within her mouth when she swallowed. And he heard her softly expelled breath.

He held his own breath, then pressed on. "The women I have known have been . . . Do you comprehend what I mean when I say *known,* Lily?"

"Women who have been—whom you have been close to? In the manner men become close to women?" She pressed her steepled fingertips to her mouth. "I feel stupid. I have not led a life that would allow much knowledge of these things, other than what I have been able to read and observe. Then, naturally, there is the gossip. But I do know the type of relationships you refer to."

But not, he would wager his life, in any detail. "Very well. The women I have known are not like you."

Her strange laugh turned his stomach this time. "That is unfortunate. For them and for me," he told her. "They have been—obvious. I cannot think of another means to describe them. They have amused and entertained me. And, in turn, they have gained from me. To say otherwise would be to lie. But you are different. For that you should be glad." He was glad.

"You are a good man. Good inside. Don't concern yourself with my feelings. I am a practical woman in the manner women like me learn to be practical. We learn to settle for what cannot be changed. I am not sorry for myself."

"Why should you be?" The anger that smote him was unexpected, and unexpectedly violent. "Because some malign creature has insulted you? Jealousy, I tell you. Such an insult could only stem from jealousy at your sweet, innocent loveliness."

"I am *not* lovely!" In the moonlight, tears stood, glistening in her eyes. "But that is not a tragedy. It is the way of things. And we should not be having this conversation. You must be exasperated with such nonsense."

The tightening of his fingers on her neck was involuntary. When she didn't object, he smoothed the skin there and his gut contracted with the power of the emotion he felt. He had lost his mind, and was glad of it!

"You are toying with danger, Lily Adler."

She snorted and muttered, "Fiddle," but in a subdued manner.

"Look at me," he ordered. "Look at me now, miss."

When she ignored him, he took hold of her braid and tugged gently until she did turn her head. She said, "How am I toying with danger, sir? Don't threaten my tender reputation again, please. Not only does no one know we are here, but I assure you the fact would raise no particular interest."

Oliver released her hair; he had to. The urge to pull her close and kiss her overwhelmed him. He had kissed her once before. That had been wrong, a liberty not deserved. The next kiss—and he very much wanted there to be a next kiss—would not only be right, it would be the beginning of other things he desired and that must not take place at all unless she understood their meaning.

With her head held high, she offered him her hand.

"We are not strangers. Only strangers shake hands, or

those who are afraid of intimacy." But he did take her hand, and raise it to his lips, watch her face as he tasted her knuckles, slowly, thoroughly, and the places where one finger met the next, and her palms when he turned her hands over—and the sensitive skin at the insides of her wrists.

"Oh," she said. It was all she said as her eyes drifted closed and squeezed tight shut.

"You are a woman meant to be loved by a man. And I intend to be that man." He no longer cared that he stepped onto dangerous ground. There were ways for a man to have everything he desired, and he would find those ways here.

She closed her hands into fists and averted her face. Clouds passed over the moon and echoing shadows dappled her skin, her hair, her scantily clad form.

"Will you allow me to—" What should he ask? How far could he go without fear of risking her happiness, or his own? "Would you allow me to court you? To try to show you who you are in my eyes?"

"I am a miserable creature."

He leaned to see her face and waited until she opened her eyes and looked back at him. "A miserable creature? You? You are fire and spirit, my courageous friend. There is nothing miserable about you."

"You will not say that when I tell you that since you arrived I have entertained all manner of despicable theories about your motives here."

"Doubtless. You are, after all, a despicable girl."

"I am five and twenty."

"A despicable old woman."

Her fleeting, there-and-gone smile enthralled him. She

said, "I have thought that you were here for some covert plan of which my father knew nothing."

Oliver's blood stopped moving in his veins. Was she testing him?

"There. Now you see the depth of my devious imaginings? At first I decided Papa, who has been anxious to marry me off, had chosen you to be his son-in-law."

His own laugh had better sound more amused to her than it did to him.

"See? Foolish, but malign, because my suspicion rose from jealousy of you. I felt you had taken my place with my father, and I resented you for it. No, I hated you for it. And then it seemed possible that my father might have been able to buy you as a husband for me."

If she had delivered him a blow, he could not have felt more exposed.

Her wrists were still within his grasp, and she tried to twist them free. Oliver would not release her.

"I am an unhappy woman," she told him quietly. "Trust is the only foundation upon which to build . . . a friendship. I should like to have counted you my friend, but I have not trusted you. For that I am sorry and I ask your forgiveness. I do not expect you to forget."

Every word she spoke was a bitter-tipped arrow. Tossing caution away, he wrapped an arm around her shoulders and drew her against his side. "I know you aren't a child. And I'm sure you'll stamp on my toes, or pinch me when I insist we go back inside, but I insist anyway."

She did resist, but only for an instant. Then she let him lead her into the south wing and made no protest as he guided her along the corridor to his rooms. Once inside the sitting room, he closed the door, put her in a chair, and set about rekindling the fire.

"You are a capable man," she said. "Accustomed to using your hands."

"And my back," he said without thinking. It wouldn't do to mention the hours he'd spent under sail unless he pretended to have done so as a member of a crew. He'd told enough lies, both by what he'd said and by what he hadn't said.

Flames crackled to life and he stood again, brushing soot from his fingers. With her hands clasped between her knees and the filmy white night garments settled about her, Lily looked very young, and very defenseless. They were both aware that this circumstance was extraordinary.

"It will not go away," she told him. "We—you must confront what someone did here tonight, Oliver."

"I had not forgotten. I have just chosen to put it aside. I would rather speak of other things now." Do other things now.

"It was no accident. The candle."

He shook his head. "No. But you are not to dwell on the event. I have it in hand."

"How?" she asked with the familiar upward tilt of her sharp chin. "Do you have some notion of the culprit?"

"None. That's the damn . . . That's the rub. But I shall be on my guard."

"And I shall be on guard for you." She sat straighter. "Anyone who persists in trying to hurt you will not find me an easy foe."

Rather than the desire to laugh that he might have expected, he wanted to take her in his arms and hug her. A fierce little spirit. "Thank you. I shouldn't like you to be my enemy."

"You have nothing to fear. I shall never be your enemy."

Never? How he wished he weren't almost sure she wouldn't be able to keep that promise. "You have a singular effect on me, Lily Adler." With her irreverent wit, Anne, his sister, had shown him how to grasp the joy of the moment. Now he must see if he'd learned the lesson. "Do you hear me, miss?"

She cocked her head. "I hear you. You are forceful, sir, and demanding."

"So I've been told. Does my manner upset you?"

"Nothing about you upsets me."

Already she had confessed her attraction to him. And she had bared her conviction that she thought herself of no interest to him.

"Wait." He swept up the coat he had tossed on a bench and spread it around her shoulders. "There. I should never forgive myself if you took cold."

"Because I chose to go outside? Gallantry is affecting, but unnecessary here." But she didn't attempt to stop him from drawing the garment together beneath her chin.

Dropping to his knees by her feet, he regarded her. "I have lived, Lily. I have lived considerably."

"You are sophisticated, you mean? I know. Your sophistication excites me."

She surprised him almost every time she spoke. "Why?"

"Because my life has been simple, and narrow. My horizon rarely presses beyond Come Piddle. As a child I went to London for Queen Victoria's Coronation. It was all a wonder. Bath intrigued me. But even travel—in the company of family and friends—does little to expand one. I have longed to spread my wings. Not to go far away, I suppose, but to know more. Knowing isn't just reading in books and remembering, it's the experience of being with people who can bring you where they've been because those places and experiences are part of who they are."

"You are complicated," he told her with a short laugh.

"So are you. And I like it that you are. In you I also feel the other sophistication, of the world, rather than about the world. In matters of—what you term experience, I think. Worldliness. You inflame sensations in me. Is that shocking?"

Oliver worked muscles in his jaw. Shocking? "Yes, in a way." He laughed again—to cover his need to think, rather than out of amusement. "The way one is shocked by the pleasantly unexpected in this instance."

She tucked his coat around her neck and settled her chin on her chest. "I shouldn't stay any longer."

"I thought you said you weren't afraid for your reputation."

"I'm not."

"Again—yet again, you should be."

"I feel bold."

He sat on the floor and put her cold, satin-slippered feet upon his thigh. "I am prepared to deal with the bold Lily Adler."

"I do have one regret about not being pretty. It is that if I were, although little might change, at least I would not feel so silly for wanting you."

There was no doubt that she did not seek his compliments. Neither could she as much as guess or imagine the effect on him of what she said so carelessly. What she told him, she told him with complete honesty, as she might explain that the flounce on the hem of her robe had become unstitched from the garment. It had—and the satin slippers were so old as to be worn over her toes. She constantly and in so many ways caught his entire attention.

"Lily, I want you to listen to me. Then I shall ask you a question, and ask you to answer me thoughtfully. Will you do this?"

She brought the collar of his coat to her cheek and rubbed lightly back and forth. "I will do it."

"I find you compelling. When I look at you I have feelings—feelings men get when they are confronted by a woman who attracts them. Physically, and in this case, emotionally. Your face and your body are pleasing to me. And you, who you are, appeal to me."

Pink stole over her pale cheeks.

"Do you understand me?"

"Yes." Her fingers curled into the dark stuff of his coat. Her knuckles were white.

"Does what I say frighten you?"

"No."

He didn't quite believe her. "Do you think I say these things to further some design of my own—for my advantage?"

A downward sweep of her thick eyelashes was her only response.

"Do you, Lily? If you do, I can't blame you."

"No, I don't think that. I think you an honorable man who is making his own way in the world, an educated man who has found a place that pleases him. Is that true?"

True enough, but far from all of it. "It's true. And what of you and me? Would you consider . . . ? Would you accept my friendship?"

She contemplated him, her expression one of deep concentration, for so long he almost repeated the question. Then she said, "Yes. Your friendship would be very dear to me."

Her intensity, the sensation that she thought his offer

the most important in the world, brought a wide smile to his lips and a leap to his heart. He raised her right foot, tossed the slipper aside and kissed each of her toes, rested his head on her knee, and rubbed her bare ankle.

Hasty fool!

Oliver gritted his teeth and held still, waiting for her to scream and run.

When she touched his hair, so tentatively he felt her shake, he kept his eyes shut. Emotion washed him. He breathed through his mouth and didn't trust himself to move or speak.

Lily stroked his hair, stroked to his collar. She leaned over him and settled the side of her face on his temple.

She kissed him there. Kissed him, and nuzzled him with her cheek again. Her soft sighs caressed his skin.

Oliver Worth was a rake and a hard, driven man. Oliver was a man of whom it was said no one woman could satisfy him for long. They were wrong, dammit, all of them. This one woman could satisfy him—perhaps forever.

"You are a large person," she whispered. "Very different from me."

"Mmm." Very different. Wonderfully different.

"I am not ignorant, you know. I'm aware that men are also different in their . . . appetites?"

He set his teeth. Now she'd decided to assure him that she was no innocent—and appeared all the more innocent for her effort.

"Is it true that men are affronted by women's bodies?"

"What?" He sat up and turned until he could settle his hands about her waist and see her face. "What drivel is this? Men affronted by women's bodies?"

Her eyes were huge. "I merely asked. Since I've heard

it said that husbands prefer their wives to be dressed at all times, I assume there must be some reason."

"Old wives' nonsense," he told her, his attention focusing on her mouth. "When I kissed you before, I was wrong. Many would say I should be wrong to kiss you now, but I'd like to do so. That and a great deal more."

"So should I."

He tried to respond, but shook his head instead.

Lily leaned forward, closed her eyes, and touched her mouth to his.

Chapter Ten

They kissed.

He'd told her it would be wrong, but that he wanted to kiss her and do a great deal more. And she had said, "So would I."

Amazing girl.

Wait. Don't rush this. Give her time. But her lips opened a little so that he felt the moistness within. A rush of heat overtook him, heat and tension in his skin, and beneath his skin. Brushing, brushing, he tilted his lips over hers, back and forth, urging the way a little wider but not daring to go too far.

Her fingertips were like moths at his jaw, then beneath the open neck of his shirt. Eager, seeking fingers that explored—and drove him wild.

A pale, plain little mouse of a creature.

Nick would laugh.

Her tongue slipped along his bottom lip.

No man who held her, looked into her dove eyes, would do other than send up prayers of gratitude.

She drank him in without knowing she drained him.

His shirt parted company with his shoulders, pushed aside so that this quiet miss could *expand* her knowledge. The cool air in the room did nothing to lessen the burning in his gut, and in his brain.

He sprang hard.

Aroused by a church mouse, no less.

Her mouth left his but her eyes remained closed. "I certainly am not offended by your body," she told him. "In fact, I should like to see much more of it."

Oliver held her face in his hands and kissed her lips repeatedly, firmly. "There are those," he told her and kissed her again, "who would consider that request very forward."

Her eyes flew open. "Oh! No. No, I am . . . Fiddle. I am forward, then. After all, I am a spinster and I am alone in a man's room in the early hours of the morning. How can I be other than forward?"

"You are fabulous. A fabulous, miraculous creature. And you frighten me to the marrow."

Disbelief fashioned her frown. "I couldn't possibly frighten you."

Little did she know. "Very well. You test my ability to absorb your mercurial curiosity. Will that do?"

"If it means you're considering my request, it will do very well."

"Good lord, what do you think Her Royal Highness would think of this behavior?"

She smiled, smiled with a genuine delight he had never seen in her before. The result curled to uproot any reserve that might be left to him. Her eyes shone and a single dimple showed in her right cheek. The black braid had surrendered its bonds, and her hair tumbled loose about her shoulders.

"The thought of our Queen amuses you?"

"I do not give a jot what the Queen might think. *That* amuses me. I feel different than I have ever felt. If that is a sin, then I am a sinner. And sinners obviously find the most pleasure in the world. I don't believe in lies. I have told you as much. Therefore I cannot say your skin, touching it, doesn't send little tremblings into places . . . into places I know I must not name."

"Is that a fact?" If he could maintain the jovial manner, it would be for the best. Safer. "Aren't you tired, Lily?"

"I've never been less tired in my life. One of the places is in here"—she indicated her stomach—"but it does go elsewhere."

"Does it?"

"Do you . . . Of course you don't."

"Do I what?"

"Well. Do you have any *unusual* sensations anywhere?"

God. "Yes. Unusual would be one description for them, I suppose."

"Put your hand on me. Where I showed you. I'm sure you will feel something."

"Oh, I'm sure I would, too. I'll just believe you."

"But . . . Oliver, I want you to do it."

Restraint, he reminded himself. Restraint and moderation in all things. She'd asked him to touch her. He spread his fingers wide over her flat belly.

He felt her hold her breath.

He felt a need to be rid of his torturous trousers.

"Also here," she said, lifting his hand. "Do you feel burning here, as if it grows full, perhaps?" With fingers that shook, she pressed his hand over her breast and held it there.

"Lily?"

"What do you feel?"

"Desperation."

Instantly she made to draw back, but he rose to his knees over her, opened the robe, and covered both of her soft breasts through the flimsy gown. Her nipples stiffened against his palms. He pulled the tapes that closed the gown undone and spread it wide.

A gasp escaped her. She watched his face as if expecting a reproach.

Oliver smiled at her, leaned to kiss her brow slowly, lingeringly. He must be very careful with her. "Your body pleases me more than I can explain. There are things—within my mind, and within my body—that I cannot describe. Some I can show you, but you will not see how I feel. You must believe that you bring me great pleasure."

Oliver Worth, gentle man. And he liked it, dammit. The war within him grated, and he wished it gone.

"Show me, then."

Startled, he remained with his mouth on her brow and his hands on her breasts. He wanted to kiss them. She wanted him naked!

"Oliver. Would it embarrass you to share your most mysterious parts with me?"

"You are incredible," he murmured, making circles with his palms over her budded nipples. Gently, he took each one between finger and thumb.

Lily cried out. A small cry of pleasure, and he released her.

When he stood, she attempted to cover herself.

"Don't," he urged her. "I should like to see you as you are."

Silently she tipped her head against the back of the chair and left her gown and robe as they were, open to the waist, revealing her high, pointed breasts, her slender waist and the beginning flare of her hips.

The fire burned bright. Quickly, Oliver snuffed the lamps and returned to stand before her. For an instant he knew disquiet, but it departed just as quickly and he shed his shirt. He hardly thought of himself, of his own body while he looked at hers.

"You torture me, Lily Adler. You are like no one I have even dreamed of." He saw understanding in her eyes.

She sat forward and reached for him. When he came close, she touched his belly, watched his muscles contract. "Oh, I do like the feel of you," she said.

"And I like the feel of you. And the look of you. And the sound of you."

Her smile came from within. "There is so much I want to learn. About you."

Oliver set his teeth together and pushed aside thoughts of those things he must keep from her if he hoped to keep her respect.

"Should you"—she met his eyes—"should you feel comfortable sharing all of yourself with me?"

The miss had the damndest queer way of expressing herself. Queer and irresistible. "If you're comfortable sharing yourself with me, then I'm comfortable sharing myself with you." But he must gauge her readiness for him, and the appropriateness of his own actions. No easy tasks when his blood pounded in his temple—and in his groin.

"Will you share everything? All of you? Those parts you keep hidden?" she asked.

Such a singular manner of expression. Singularly singular! "You are such a curious female."

"I believe I am a normal female," she retorted. "Have you read Viscountess Hunsingore's illuminating work?"

Gad.

"*Illuminations for, and Advice to the Modern Female on the Subjects of Courtship and Marriage*?"

He had indeed read the volume. The shockingly direct material it contained had been much discussed at parties in Newport.

"Of course, in most respects it would not apply to me, but I'm sure there would be a great deal that is of interest."

Relief flowed through him. "I doubt it." She had not read it. "Not at all the thing for you. Allow me to be your guide in these matters." Oh, yes, indeed, allow him to be her guide.

Lily pressed her palms to his ribs and tested the texture of the hair on his chest. Her total absorption inflamed him. Holding still took inhuman control.

Her exploration moved to his hips, his buttocks. She pressed her lips together in fierce concentration. "What are you thinking, Oliver?"

That he wished to dispense with her pure white garments and show her how *mysterious* the body could be, the body with another body that was so different, yet so incomplete when alone.

"Why are you silent?" she said, but didn't stop her journey of discovery.

"I find it hard to speak when you touch me like this, Lily. That is something you must learn about men. Their bodies respond to the touch of a woman." To the very presence of a woman. What she did to him was beyond description. His legs were weak, his skin hot, his mind a turmoil—his rod bursting. Oliver trembled with the effort to restrain himself from bearing her up and thrusting himself inside her. She would have no defense, because she did not know what she should defend against.

"This is the most male part of you." Without warning, she slipped a hand between his thighs and supported him.

Wonder washed her features. "A throbbing thing restrained by your trousers."

"God, Lily," he breathed. "You are blunt in a manner that makes me helpless in your hands." And in ecstasy in her hands. He panted; he couldn't stop himself.

"I should not touch you so?"

She started to withdraw, but he stopped her. "You should touch me so. Now you must touch me so, I beg of you. I need your touch."

"Should you prefer me to deal with your needs without the interference of your trousers?"

He laughed shortly. "You ask such questions! And in such forthright terms. I could not stand to frighten you. Already you have experienced too much for one night."

"No!" In her fervor, she squeezed him. "Not nearly enough. There is much yet to be revealed."

Oliver almost sank to his knees. "Wait, little one. Please wait or you will be the death—and the shame—of me. A moment." He rested a hand on her shoulder and bent to remove his boots.

Each time he moved, to even the smallest degree, she used his vulnerability to her advantage. Audacious! A short nail scratched one of his nipples lightly, and he gasped. The hair on his body definitely compelled her. She smoothed it, combed it with her fingers.

"Torturer," he protested when the boots were discarded. "Now, you will put your hands in your lap and allow me to finish."

The dip of her head, her upward glance, sent his gut into a fall. With a shrug she let her robe and gown slip down about her hips. She removed her arms from the sleeves. Her hips were fully revealed. The hair at the apex of her thighs was lustrous and dark, and that was where she demurely folded her hands.

Oliver shouted with laughter. "You are a demon in angel's clothing."

"A demon who has discarded an angel's clothing, you mean."

Swiftly, he leaned down and kissed her hard. Her arms went around his neck, and she clung. Order in all things. He must be the one to conduct this dance. Giving her no warning of his intent, he fastened his mouth on a nipple, but gently—suckled firmly enough to grin at her shout of incredulous pleasure.

She tried to stop him from taking his mouth from her. He tweaked her other nipple, drawing another cry, and pressed a thumb into the slick folds between her legs. She caught his arms and held fast. Trepidation filled her eyes.

"Hush," Oliver told her, kissing her lips again. "This is what a man and woman can bring to each other."

She gulped and said, "I'm not bringing it to you. Oh!"

Dropping beside her, he surrounded her body in one arm, drew her against him until her breasts pressed his chest. He flinched at his own need. He stroked with his fingers, played her with his thumb, watched sweet pain, and passion, fix her features. He drew gasps from her.

She writhed, bucked against his hand. "What is this?" Her voice was weak and breathy. "What is it, Oliver?"

"It is a making ready of the way for other things, sweet."

Her neck arched, and her breasts. Each pink peak invited him, and he accepted, using the very tip of his tongue to drive her to the edge of discovery.

"Oliver." Her eyes opened wide and she drove her fingertips mindlessly into his flesh. "Oh, Oliver." Spasms

shook her, rippled through her. Her heels on the floor, she bent backward over his arm, abandoned in giving herself up to climax, and in opening herself to him.

When the assault on her flesh and senses began to fade, he settled her amid the discarded tangle of her night robes, caressed her upturned face, kissed her reddened lips. There was so much more he longed to share with her, but he must be patient.

Lily drew up her knees and wrapped her arms around her limbs. "That was beyond all." Disbelief clung to her voice. "Now I insist upon doing for you what you have done for me."

Oliver closed his eyes and shook his head. He ran his tongue the length of her thigh.

"Enough," she said, sucking in a breath. "Off with them, sir."

Off with them? "What do you mean by that, miss?"

"I am a weak woman, sir. Do not sap my energy further by insisting on being obtuse. Remove your trousers. I am no ninny. I have eyes. I see that these events have had a noticeable effect on you."

"Do you indeed?" He should feel something other than amused delight. He didn't. Unless it was the most intense passion he ever recalled.

"Up," Lily ordered, pointing an imperious finger. *"Disrobe."*

Grinning somewhat sheepishly, Oliver stood and undid the fastenings on his trousers. He paused. "I don't believe it. You have embarrassed me! I'm not accustomed to presenting myself as a show in this manner."

She made a *hmph*ing sound and said, "Let us not invent a fiction here, Oliver. Perhaps you have not acted in precisely this manner before. But do not fun me that you've never removed your clothes for a woman before, because I shall not believe you."

"Lily!"

"You already knew that I was forward. Come along. Don't hold me in suspense or I shall think you have something to hide."

"You, my girl, are outrageous."

"Perhaps so." Her attention was fixed on the region that seemed of most interest to her. "I have always had a manner people said was too quick. But I have never been considered outrageous—that I know. The thought pleases me."

He found he hesitated to finish undressing. "My dear, it does grow so very late."

"Not too late," she said distinctly. "We have more to accomplish, don't we, Oliver?"

Did they? Or should he insist they had accomplished all that should ever be accomplished?

"Shall I help you? I very much want to make you feel as you have made me feel."

The rush of voluptuous desire pounded him. He stripped his trousers down and stepped out of them, threw them aside, and stood before her. Planting his feet apart, he settled his fists on his hips and barely restrained a laugh at the expression on her face.

She took far too long to say, *"Oliver!"*

"Yes, Lily?"

"Well. So that's what it's all about."

He frowned, and tilted his head.

"I must say," she continued, "that a sensible approach to these matters would be so much more appropriate. After all, it's very straightforward, really."

Oliver scrubbed at his face.

"I mean . . . Well, the topic is straightforward, not the . . . the . . . Well, actually, it's straightforward, too, isn't it?"

"At present," he said, hearing his own strangled tones. "That's because I am aroused by you. Do you understand what takes place between a man and a woman in these circumstances?"

"In moments of passion, you mean. Oh, yes, I think so. More or less, anyway. I think I shall enjoy it quite well."

Oliver moaned.

"Are you ill?"

"I am beside myself. I ache, Lily. I throb for the need of release. I am mad with wanting you."

She touched him before he realized she'd left the chair. Her hand, closing around him, punched the air from his lungs and brought his hips jutting toward her.

"Wonderful," she murmured, watching him slide back and forth within her hands. "What strength. How does this feel?"

He shook his head.

She paused. "Not good?"

"Wonderful," he managed to gasp. "But you'd better stop, or I'll shock you."

"Nothing about you could shock me."

The lady assumed too much. "Lily, I cannot remain standing."

"You said you weren't ill."

"I'm not ill." He covered her hands upon him and sank slowly to his knees, taking her with him. "I am transported. You are . . . Don't stop."

"I won't." She frowned in concentration. "I should like to explain how you made me feel when you . . . well, when you did. It was—"

"Lily."

"What is it?"

"Please don't speak. Just do what you're doing. Don't—stop. Don't—stop. Aah." His release flowed through him, power and surrender, the only surrender that made a man more of a man.

She said not a word. Instead she eased him to the carpet, on his side, and stretched out facing him, pressed to him so close there was no place where he ended and she began.

Sighing, she rubbed his buttocks, the tense backs of his thighs, and when he wrapped a leg over her small hips she shifted to thread a knee between his.

Heavy lethargy made its visit, and almost at once it ebbed again and he felt the surge of desire once more. He smiled against her hair. "So, Lily, what have you to say about all this?"

"To think I might have lived my whole life without such a splendid experience. Oh, I will have so much to tell . . . so much to talk about to myself, to think about."

"Tell me what you will think about."

"You. I shall think about you, and about how you make me feel. And I'll see you as you really are. From this moment on I shall look at you and see you standing before me naked."

A calming thought. "Shall you indeed?"

"Oh, yes. Now that I know exactly how you are made, I shall visualize every part of you. And this"—she cradled his quickening rod in her hands—"I will be able to see if you're thinking about such things, too. Won't I? All I'll have to do is look."

"You shall do no such thing, miss! A young lady doesn't spend her time staring at a man's . . . You will not stare at me."

"At a man's supreme scepter?"

Oliver shouted with laughter and clasped her to him. He buried his face in her hair. "I don't know if you're an innocent humorist or a designing devil."

"I am truthful only," she said, sounding prim. "This part of you is proud and beautiful."

"Stop." He tickled her and she let him go, fought to capture his wrists. "You are no match for me, sweet Lily. Am I to take it you are well satisfied with the night's events?"

"I cannot say that." She managed to clutch one wrist, but only in time for him to carry her hand with his to her breast. "Oh, certainly, this has been most enlightening, but I am by no means completely content."

"What?" He turned her to her back and arranged himself over her, careful to support his weight on his elbows. He was a pleased, but far from satiated, man. "Am I to take it that you are greedy for more?" There was much more to the adventure, and he intended to follow every new path with her.

She grew still, and very serious—and wetted her lips as she stared up at him. "I don't think I could ever feel I've had enough of you. But I do know I shall have to savor this night in my mind and be happy."

Oliver let his lips meet hers and kissed her long, softly, but urgently. Her arms tightened around him, and he felt the fullness of her strength in the embrace.

"There," he said when he put a quarter inch or so between their mouths. "That is the seal of my promise to you."

Her eyes were luminous. "Promise?"

Careful. He could not see the road ahead. So many potential hazards littered the way, there was no hope of guessing his own future. To attempt to visualize that future with another was impossible, even more impossible when that person would surely reject him when she truly knew him.

"What promise, Oliver?"

"My promise to be your champion."

She smiled, only the second such smile he'd seen. And she was radiant. "We are friends, then? Different than most friends, it's true—because we have known this." Her heels rode the sides of his thighs and she wrapped her legs around him.

Give me strength. She tried him without knowing the danger she toyed with. "Yes. Different. Even closer." Much closer, and what hope remained of making sane decisions would be gone. Already she was compromised, but not so much so that all was lost—or gained. The thought cooled him.

"We shall care for each other? Confide in each other?"

This way lay danger, but he would not, could not draw back. "That we will."

"Kiss me again. And show me other things."

"I don't think there's much you haven't seen," he said wryly.

"You mean there is nothing more?"

Ah. "Not now, sweet one. I have been indiscreet with you as it is. For the rest we must wait and see."

She went to speak, but closed her mouth and tilted up her chin, begging for a kiss.

Oliver obliged gladly. She learned so quickly, this sparrow girl of his.

A mighty slam jarred his every nerve. Oliver raised his head.

Lily cried out and clutched him. The shatter of porcelain or glass burst the quiet air.

The door had flown open and smashed against the wall so hard, a Chinese porcelain urn had shot from its ebony plinth to the floor.

"What is it?" Fear had made Lily strong. "What, Oliver?"

When he tried to rise, she remained wrapped around him. "It's all right. Nothing but the wind, I'm sure," he whispered.

"There is little wind tonight."

"Lily," he said firmly. "Please be calm."

"I am calm. I will not let you face some danger alone."

Oliver made himself laugh. He got to his feet and deposited her in the chair. "I'm going to close the door."

The only light in the room came from the fire. He could see the lamp's glow in the passage.

"Lily—"

Flame, streaking into the gloomy room, froze him. Flame that was brilliant, then extinguished. "Who's there, dammit?" He started for the door, but Lily threw herself at him and wrapped her arms about his waist. "Let me go," he insisted. "There's someone out there."

"And you will not confront him."

"The lamp. For God's sake!" Roughly, he tore her from him. "Someone threw the lamp. They are deadly, I tell you."

"Deadly!" A voice, high and full, sang out from beyond the door. "Lily! Oh, Lily, for shame. Flee. Flee or he will destroy you."

Lily screamed.

Scrambling, casting about the room to be certain nothing had caught fire, Oliver rushed to the door and into the corridor.

He took only one more stride before he tripped, fell, and sprawled his length over the back of what was obviously the damnable leather elephant.

The sensation of Lily's soft hands on his back made him angry. Someone had said he was a threat to her. "Gone," he said. "I won't catch him now."

"No. Please get up. We must be very sure we understand each other now, Oliver."

He pushed to his feet and drew her back into the room before locking the door. "Put on your clothes. I must see you safely back to your rooms." He should never have allowed lust to overcome logic.

"Very well. But we have made a pact. You and I shall care for each other, remember. We are friends of a special nature now."

"I am a danger to you. I feel that. Whoever did this thing doesn't want me near you. So be it. I must be certain of your safety."

She turned on him, stood with her back straight, her lovely breasts heaving with the power of her emotion. "You, sir, are a noddycock."

"Lily—"

"Do not 'Lily' me. You are for me, and I am for you. And we shall stand together. You shall be the keeper of my mysterious parts, and I shall be the keeper of yours. And that, sir, is that!"

Chapter Eleven

"Now I have what I wanted most—next to justice. I have knowledge that will make you impotent.

"And I have power over you.

"Everything is changed now, Oliver Worth. A wise man makes certain there is no crack in his armor. There is a chasm in yours. And you have guided me, you have shown where I must deliver my fatal thrust.

"Have a care—although it will make no difference. But I should enjoy a little spice to the chase. I need to see your sweat, your fear.

"Now I know what I must do. Every step you take, you will take with me. And I will be designing our finale.

"The girl makes it perfect, don't you see? I had thought her a simple diversion—something to enjoy for but an instant. But now I know it is she who will draw an exquisite suspense into our drama. I know how men like you are. At the base of the reputation you guard—'Oh, he is a rakehell, a man among men, no woman can hold him'—at the base of it all lies the truth of your weakness. Pathos. You have the bleeding heart of a mawkish female who swoons over love, whatever that may be.

"You have been snared by love. I see it now. And I shall use it to make my victory the sweeter. When you turn on *me and know my face, rage will raise your hand. For the moment, perhaps many moments, you will think you can obliterate me. But then I shall use Lily Adler. You will give all to save her.*

"She will be your nemesis. And you will be hers."

Chapter Twelve

Witless was coming

Lily ran down the curving staircase to the hall. She cast about. Fribble would be close behind. Puffed up with excitement, she had come to Lily to inform her, "You are to be honored. You are to have a chance to honor us all." And with a wagging finger she'd delivered what she considered should be the most welcome words in the world. "Lord Witmore has sent word. He is to visit shortly, and he has asked an audience with the dear professor. Oh, Lily, such formality can only mean one thing. Hurry, child. I'll send Hilda to you. Have her help you change that ghastly frock. And do something with your hair. Rouge, for goodness' sake. Put color in those cheeks. Get ready at once." Then Fribble had sailed from Lily's rooms chattering about her own toilette.

Three days. Three days since the wonderful events with Oliver, and he had, once again, fallen into a silence with her. Pleasant enough, it was true, but silent nevertheless.

Where was he now?

She sped to Papa's study. The door stood open and the room was empty.

The same was true of the library, the two small salons and the parlor where they took breakfast.

Beyond the drawing room where Papa preferred to receive was a conservatory filled with palms so tall their crowns touched the glass dome. Lily caught sight of movement.

Oliver. She watched him, and her heart stood still. With his hands clasped behind his back, he wandered, apparently without purpose, back and forth between the brick-lined plantings. When he reached the end of one bed and turned to trace its opposite flank, the dark concentration in his features alarmed her.

But his face was so dear, his face and form.

Oh, what she had felt at his hands.

She opened the door and stepped down into humid air. Nearby sprays of waxy, white stephanotis blooms gave their subtle, sweet scent.

Perfume could not hold Lily's attention. Unsure, she walked slowly toward Oliver, but stopped when he saw her. Only anger could fashion such a frown.

He did not want to encounter her.

She turned to leave him.

"Stay, dammit."

Lily's breath caught in her throat. Anger was too weak a word for the emotion she heard in his voice.

"Come here."

Tears sprang into her eyes. Her feet would not move.

"Hell and damnation, girl. Come here, I tell you."

He spoke as if she were a naughty child. "How dare you?" She spun toward him again. "How dare you speak to me like that?"

"I dare," he muttered, closing the space between them and grasping her wrist. "I dare because I cannot drive you from my mind. You torture and haunt me, and it will not do. I will not allow you to interfere with what must be most important to me."

Gasping, her lungs burning with the effort to smother sobs, she stumbled in his wake. He pulled her behind him to a far corner of the conservatory where they were hidden from the drawing-room windows.

"Now." Jerking her before him, he spread his feet and jutted his jaw, then fixed her with narrowed eyes. "What is it you want? Haven't you interfered enough with my peace?"

Lily couldn't speak. She gulped and swallowed, and blinked against the burning in her eyes.

"Speak. Are you mute, as well as a nuisance?"

She tore her arm from his hand and did what she had never in her life done before. She struck another human being. So hard her fingers tingled, she slapped Oliver's face.

He did not flinch.

Cold to her bones, she stared at him. "I am afraid for you. There is evil here, yet you behave as if—"

"*Silence.*" He raised a single finger.

Lily covered her mouth. The tears wouldn't be stemmed now. She retreated backward, but he shot out a hand and restrained her.

"I am . . . broken." She bowed her head. "I am wrong. I don't know what is happening to me. Violence is not part of my nature. I regret my actions. We shall not speak again. Please let me go."

"Forget me."

The strange, deep stillness in his voice made her shudder. "Yes. Yes, I will forget you. Of course I will. Good day to you."

He shook her. "I have work to do. Can you understand that?"

What had she done? How had she caused him to change in so short a time?

"There are things I should tell you," he said. "I can't now. Perhaps I shall never be able to. But I am sorry. I have been very wrong. I have wronged you—but not, thank God, irreparably."

She wanted only to be alone. How would she bear to look at him each day? "You have done nothing to me."

"If you stay away from me you will not be harmed. Please forget what passed between us."

The flare of fury in her breast stole all caution. "Forget?" Flinging her arm aside, she broke his grip. "Forget what passed between us? Oh, I shall forget, sir. And I shall forget you. After all, why should I remember something of so little importance? Trivial, sir, so very trivial. Why, I find I cannot even recall what it is I'm supposed to forget." She clapped a fist to her breast. "Not at all. Nothing to forget."

"I am beside myself," Oliver said. The rage dissolved, replaced by something Lily couldn't understand. Disgust? "You are right to put me in my place, Lily. I am not for you."

Trembling, she told him, "It is I who am not for you. I wish it had been I who turned you aside with vicious words."

"Lily—"

"If I were beautiful and sought after, and clever, and a toast, I should revel in turning my face from you as if I did not see you at all." She lied, she lied, her heart was breaking.

"You are lovely," he said softly. "Clever and lovely.

The brightest star in any sky I shall ever see. Wherever I go I shall see you as I saw you beneath the stars on the bridge."

"Then why must you hurt me so?"

"I must hurt you to save you. What you want can never be."

She would not make herself a fool again.

A raised voice reached them, and Oliver put a finger to his lips.

"Lily!" Fribble. "Lily, where are you? Come here this minute."

Oliver's face became blank. The respectful employee, her father's most trusted assistant—a stranger.

"Lily! Are you out here?"

"Yes, Aunt Fribble." She made herself smile at Oliver. "Please excuse me. I understand Lord Witmore is about to pay us a visit. He may have arrived. He has requested an audience with my father."

Oliver's expression didn't waver. He bowed, and presented her with his back.

Her heart pounding, Lily left him and met her aunt on the steps into the drawing room.

"Oh, my goodness. Oh, what am I ever to do with you." Fribble kept her voice low, leading Lily to assume their company was, even then, in the drawing room. "I told you to change that frightful dress. Drab green. It does not become you at all. Why must you defy me in all things?"

"There wasn't time," Lily said. Not time to change, and to find Oliver. "I didn't want to keep anyone waiting." Now she was a liar.

"You look dull and unfashionable." Fribble sighed. "But I can do nothing about that. Lift up your head and smile, girl. A great deal depends on you."

Her own sumptuous gold silk skirts trailing behind her, Fribble led the way into the red drawing room and waved Lily beside her. "Here she is," she trilled. "Lily is so very accomplished. Her interests are positively without number. She is an expert on exotic plants and must frequently be routed out from study of our conservatory specimens."

With difficulty, Lily managed to stop herself from protesting this shocking untruth.

Witless fixed her with his bloodshot brown eyes and made no attempt to hide his opinion of her, or her green dress. Clearly, he thought her person distasteful.

Uneasiness settled between the occupants of the drawing room.

Standing as close to the door as possible, Lady Virtue stared vacantly ahead. She wore a gown of rich cherry color and a matching bonnet with pleats beneath the brim, and satin rosettes at her ears. A pretty creature, Lily was forced to admit. Pretty, but vacuous, and mean. Lily had observed the small unkindnesses Lady Virtue Beaumont visited on those she considered unimportant.

Hovering beside a thin, considerably older man was Lady Virtue's companion. This was Drucilla, Baroness Allcombe, a widow who had made herself as disliked as Lady Virtue in Come Piddle. The baroness favored garish clothes and far too much paint.

The exceedingly thin man, whom Lily didn't know, could boast tastes similar to his companion's. Purple velvet coat, yellow and black check trousers, a floppy pink satin neckcloth, and peach satin waistcoat made him an elderly clown. His artificially red lips and high colored cheeks forced Lily to swallow a giggle, as did the careful arrangement of his thin, light brown hair.

Much clearing of throats, and *hmm*ing, and shuffling of feet ensued.

"Laycock," the scrawny popinjay suddenly announced. "Dashed rude of me. Sir Cecil Laycock at your service. How d'you do?"

"How do you do," Fribble said, bobbing a curtsy, her eyelashes batting so fast, Lily wondered how she saw at all. "We're honored by your presence."

"Yes, well," Papa said shortly. He wore his favorite plum-colored coat, and the breeches he refused to give up. "Lord Witmore has come to visit. We're delighted, aren't we, Lily?"

"My lord comes frequently," she said, unashamed to be graceless. This day was already too much. "But I wish him good health."

Fribble's cross anxiety permeated the room. Lily saw how her aunt longed to chastise her for unrefined behavior.

"I wish you good health, too, Lily," Witless said. He swayed ever so slightly forward. "May I say that you look quite fetching in that dress. I do believe green shows off your eyes to advantage."

She could not, would not thank him for such transparent and forced flattery.

"Isn't that lovely," Fribble said when it was evident her stepniece intended to ignore Witless's comments. "And Lord Witmore has brought his sister, and her companion—and a friend—to visit us also."

"I noticed there were others with him," Lily said, ashamed of her childish conduct but helpless to turn back from this course.

"Oh!" The baroness exclaimed loudly and pressed herself to Sir Cecil's side. "A cat, Cecil. A *cat*. I declare I cannot abide the things, and they always seek me out. Get rid of it at once."

Lily looked around the room and located the object of the baroness's horror. "There you are," she said, spying a small but sinuous black cat with round yellow eyes. "Where have you been, Raven? I was beside myself looking for you." She had never seen the animal before.

"Lily," Fribble said. "When—"

"Oh, last night," Lily interrupted. "She must have got out of my rooms and come to tuck herself in a cozy corner here. Come to me, Ravcn."

"I shall swoon," the baroness warned, flapping a lace handkerchief before her face. "Cecil, I am overcome."

"Shut up," Witless said succinctly. "Virtue, take Drucilla outside."

"No," Virtue said, all petulance and pout. "I came to be with you for the event. Drucilla must take care of her own foolishness. Keep the animal away from me also, if you please."

The cat strolled across the red and gold carpet and made directly for the baroness.

Had she not been thinking about Oliver, Lily might have found great sport in the situation.

"You see," the silly woman squealed. "Malevolent, they are. It knows I don't care for it, so it torments me."

"It really is very nice of you to visit," Lily said, retrieving the cat, who climbed to her shoulder and draped itself around her neck. "I can't bear my cat to cause such discomfort, so I'll leave you all to enjoy each other. I have pressing matters to attend. I'm sure you understand."

"Speak to her, Professor," Fribble gasped.

"Dashed rude," Sir Cecil said, putting one toe forward

and posing with his hands on his hips. "What could possibly be more pressing than entertainin' your betters?"

"I've ordered tea," Fribble announced. With tiny, hip-swaying steps, she fussed over a chaise, arranging cushions just so. "Come, Lady Virtue, rest. We insist, don't we, Professor."

"I should say so," Papa agreed dutifully. "Wouldn't want you overexerting yourself. Perhaps you'd like to go to bed."

Lily recognized Papa's contrary sense of humor and suppressed a laugh.

"Go to bed?" Lady Virtue flounced to the couch and allowed Fribble to help her settle among the cushions. "We are come to support my brother, not to go to bed, sir."

"Quite," Sir Cecil agreed, executing a small shuffle that ended with the opposite toe extended. "Some damn appealing pieces you've got here, Adler. Must be blunt in chamber pots, what?"

"Chamber pots?" Papa said.

"Isn't that what you said the fella made his money in, Witmore?" Sir Cecil asked as if Papa weren't in the room. "I'd swear you said it was chamber pots."

Witless had the grace to color. "And I'd swear you misheard. The professor has some sort of banking connections. But he is a philosopher."

"A *philosopher*." Sir Cecil raised both palms. "A country thinker, what? Tell me, how does a man become so bloody rich sittin' in the country and thinkin'?"

"Professor," Witless said loudly. "Thank you for receiving us. I've no doubt you realize there must be some weighty reason for this visit."

Mutinous and with the cat still about her neck, Lily sauntered toward Baroness Allcombe. That lady was too intent upon Witless to notice she was about to become close neighbor to a dreaded animal.

"I expect you would like to see the professor alone, Lord Witmore," Fribble said, breathless. "I should make us all comfortable elsewhere."

"We're comfortable where we are," Lady Virtue said shortly. "Do get on with it, Reggie. After all, there's hardly any reason to dally with niceties."

Lily maneuvered close to the baroness and smiled privately when the cat leaped at the woman, landing on her shoulder. Much shrieking ensued, and Sir Cecil was called upon to "save" Lady Virtue's companion. The cat retreated to a corner, leaving the painted pair to lean upon each other and whisper, while sending venomous glares at Lily.

"Have we disposed of these little diversions?" Lady Virtue asked. "*Please,* Reggie. I have an appointment with the modiste."

"And I must return to my rooms," Lily said. "I am determined to finish a gift an acquaintance will need, and time grows short."

"What gift?" Lady Virtue asked.

"Oh"—Lily made an airy gesture—"I am embroidering a scene."

"She is ever so accomplished," Fribble said. "Quick, too. I have never seen a girl so quick with a needle. Why, I'm constantly forced to insist she leave her gentle labors to at least take a little sustenance, and to walk in the fresh air."

Lady Virtue didn't bother to cover a bored yawn.

Lily discovered she could still be amazed at Fribble's power of invention—and that she didn't care what the silly female said.

"Admirable," Witless remarked. He smiled at Lily, a dreadful sight, and motioned for her to come closer. "I should like you to have the pleasure of hearing my plans, my dear."

"Oh, I am very aware of my place, Lord Witmore. My parent has taught me well the importance of humility. I shouldn't dream of intruding on your personal affairs."

"I insist," Witless said. "In this case my personal affairs are inseparable from yours, dear girl."

Just then, Oliver, his tall figure dressed in black, took a seat on a bench in the conservatory—just outside the open door to the drawing room. He would be certain to hear every word uttered inside.

Lily looked away from Oliver Worth's back as he opened a book on his lap.

He had no interest in events here. The bench was merely convenient.

"What do you say to that, Lily?" Fribble asked, her agony at waiting evident in her strained posture. "Lord Witmore considers you of the utmost importance to his personal happiness."

"That so, Witmore?" Papa asked.

Witless ran his tongue over his lips and said, "I should say so. Now I don't want you to thank me, Lily. I'm glad to do this for you. Your father has been a good neighbor to us, and joining the two families for the good of all is more than appropriate, don't you know."

"I don't," she muttered.

Leaning forward, his elbows akimbo and his hands on his hips, Sir Cecil moved around the room on his toes. His ridiculous gait fascinated Lily—or it would have fascinated her had she not been both terrified and sickened by Witless's suggestions.

"Don't see any point to waitin'," Witless said. "She's not gettin' any younger. Might as well get on with it. After all, it's time to get started on securin' things for future generations."

Lily felt her face turn pale.

"Get on with it, Reggie," Lady Virtue begged.

And she was supposed to as much as consider an alliance with these people? Death would be preferable. Lily looked at Oliver's back once more. If she could not at least see him, she would as soon not see anyone at all.

He hated her. He regretting having . . . he regretted their time together.

"Here we have it, then," Witless said. He extended a hand toward Lily. "Stand with me, please. Seems appropriate."

Fribble let out an excited squeak and pushed Lily, none too gently, toward the earl.

Witless picked up Lily's hand from the folds of her skirts and held it in his clammy fingers. "I know you'll do your best. But I insist you accept what cannot be changed. Your beginnings are humble. We accept that, don't we, Virtue?"

"Hmm? Yes, I suppose we do."

"There you have it, then, Lily. We shall make allowances."

"Damn handsome of you," Papa said. "Damn handsome, wouldn't you say, Lily?"

She couldn't believe what she heard. And Papa's behavior was more horrifying to her than Lord Witmore's.

"The girl's overwhelmed, you see," Papa said, his head inclined and bowed in a respectful manner toward Witless. "She couldn't have hoped for the attentions of so great a man."

Witless flapped a hand in a patronizing gesture. "Least I can do for a man me own father thought so highly of. Settled, then, is it?"

"Oh, I should think so," Papa said.

Lily gaped.

Fribble bounced on her toes and clapped.

Lady Virtue leaned against her cushions and closed her eyes.

The baroness checked to be certain enough of her bosom was revealed.

Sir Cecil used a glass to peruse hallmarks more closely.

"Very well," Lord Witmore announced heartily. "Let's take a glass on it, then. And will three weeks from tomorrow do? Yes, of course it will. I can see you're all overcome. Understandable."

"Understandable," Lady Virtue said.

Sir Cecil and the baroness intoned, "Understandable," in unison.

"Glass of what?" Papa asked.

"Champagne," Lady Virtue said promptly, suddenly alert. "And some little cakes. I do enjoy little cakes when I'm peckish."

"Brandy for me," Witless said. He squeezed Lily's hand. "No need for you to stay now, m'dear. Might as well get about your watercolors."

"Embroidery," Lily corrected. "I'm making a shroud."

"A shroud?" The baroness fell back as if wounded. "A shroud for whom? Surely such a thing takes a long time."

"No longer than possible under the circumstances," Lily assured her. "After all, you can imagine the problems that can arise. I've heard it said that when bodies become too ripe, all manner of dangerous situations occur."

Papa coughed, and coughed, and fell back. He hurried

to pour brandy into several glasses and proceeded to hand one to all present. "A toast," he roared, uncharacteristically rambunctious. "Exactly what shall we drink to?"

"Should have thought that was obvious." Witless raised his glass. "To good sense and generosity. To the rightful order of things. To the support of what God would choose to smile upon."

Papa smiled upon all and said, "A man of words and not of deed is like a garden full of weeds. Suzanne Simmons said that. Wise woman. They thought she was a man, of course, supposedly Samuel. But Suzanne was discovered, and her words are a treasured heritage."

Lily barely made herself stay in the room. All the world had gone mad, and her beloved, calm father with it.

"Lily," he said, waving his glass wide. "Have I not spoken to you of Lord Witmore's good heart? Have I not told you that this man has hidden depths? Leave a dog in the water as long as you like: it will never be a crocodile. Or was that wine? Perhaps it should be that the log *will* become a crocodile if you leave it in wine long enough. Simmons also, I think. But it could have been Quick." Papa tapped his chin, shook his head, and didn't appear to note how the company had grown still and silent. He tutted thoughtfully. "Wrong quote. A fool's mouth is his destruction. That's what I meant to say."

"Damn me," Sir Cecil remarked, his all-but-invisible brows raised. "Is this the nonsense that buys other fellas houses? I think he's insultin' you, Reggie."

"Rubbish," Witless said, grinning. "He's overwhelmed, aren't you, Adler?"

"Entirely," Papa agreed. "Lily and her little group will be forever in your debt."

"Ooh," Fribble wailed, in evident agitation. "Ooh, dear."

"What do you mean by that?" Witless asked, his expansive smile wavering. "What group?"

"You cannot fool me with humility, Witmore," Papa said. "You've obviously heard how Lily's industrious Junior Altar Society is looking to bring about extensive renovations to St. Cedric's. Your promise of patronage is beyond generous. Far beyond generous, isn't it, Lily?"

Only by extreme strength of will did she neither laugh nor stand speechless. "Yes. Beyond generous." She did love Papa. Quiet, inclined to separate himself from simple matters, nevertheless his wicked wit chose the perfect moments to appear.

"How much did you say the carpets for the altar steps will cost?"

She cleared her throat. "Several hundred pounds."

"Junior Altar Society?" Witless exploded. His already ruddy complexion became purple. "I've no interest in any bloody silly female gossip group. Damn it all, Adler, I've just told you I'm prepared to take your daughter off your hands."

Fribble moaned and fell into a chair.

The baroness all but staggered to sit beside Lady Virtue's knees on the chaise.

With a limp wrist extended, Sir Cecil appeared close to collapse.

"I've decided to marry your daughter," Witless continued, and drained his glass. He held it out. "More. My nerves are quite destroyed."

"Why didn't you say so?" Papa got the decanter and filled his guest's glass to the rim. "Well, well, would you have countenanced that? And I thought this was all about a donation that would draw us all together for a good cause. Well, well. A proposal of marriage."

"To take place in three weeks," Witless plowed on. "Of course, there are formalities to be dispensed with—settlement, and so on. You won't have difficulty there. Things will be straightforward."

Lily detested him. She was beneath his notice except as a source of getting his hands on the estate his family had lost through careless excess.

"What do you think of all this, Lily?" Papa asked. "A proposal of marriage."

"She'll be a countess," Fribble said weakly.

"Indeed she would," Papa agreed.

"London parties," Fribble went on, her eyes glazed. "Streams of titled people."

"Are we done here, Reggie?" Lady Virtue asked.

He swallowed his second glass of brandy. "I should think so. Call on me tomorrow, Adler. I'll have the papers drawn up by then."

"We're honored, aren't we, Lily?" Papa said. "We shall certainly have to discuss these matters."

The hope of salvation Lily had momentarily embraced was quickly destroyed.

Lord Witmore set aside his glass. "Nothing to discuss. And no need to thank me. Come along. I see we've overcome these people, and we have other matters to attend to."

"Well," Papa said. "Thank you for sparing time for us."

"Think nothing of it. Until tomorrow, then. Shall we say noon?"

To Lily's misery Papa said, "Noon," and drank more brandy.

The garish entourage assembled, and followed behind

Witmore. They passed through the door with no attempts at pleasant farewells—until Sir Cecil took his first prancing step onto the black and white marble tile in the great hall.

From somewhere about his person fell an item that glittered, then clattered on the marble. When he seemed not to notice, Lily moved forward to retreive Papa's gold figurine of King Henry VIII. The piece was old and treasured.

"Sir Cecil," Lily said. "You dropped this."

He stopped, drew up his hands as if burned, made his eyes and mouth round, and said, "*I* dropped it. *I?* No, no, I assure you not. I know nothing except the fact of my ignorance."

"And there," Papa said when the company had left, "goes a man with complete understanding of himself. He is a fool."

"He is Lord Witmore's friend," Fribble said, quivering with some emotion. "As such, and since Lord Witmore is to be a member of the family, we must respect him."

Papa took the figurine from Lily. "I suppose your aunt is right, my dear. We shall just have to learn tolerance of Lord Witmore's silly friends."

"Papa!"

He patted her hand. "Excuse me, my child. I need time alone to think about the matter of settlements."

Lily stared aghast as he made his way down the hall to his rooms.

Chapter Thirteen

A shadow fell across the moonlit path, across Lily's own shadow.

She stopped her solitary walk and waited, knowing who was about to overtake her.

"Lily, may I accompany you?"

To refuse would sound childish. "If you wish." Her desperation had grown since the visit that afternoon of Lord Witmore and his dreadful entourage. She needed to be alone, to forget that Papa seemed determined to give her to such a man. And she needed to put Oliver Worth out of her mind. He tormented her by his very presence.

Oliver said, "Where are you going?" and fell in beside her on the trail that wound around the lake.

"As far as I can," she told him. She told the truth, but it would have been better to lie to him.

"I should prefer not to have to follow you to make sure you're safe."

She paused. "I beg your pardon?"

"You understood me, I'm sure. Would you please avoid walking alone in the darkness? Particularly here, where a slip could land you in the water."

"No, Oliver, I shall not avoid walking in the darkness. Although with such a moon it isn't dark."

He touched her cheek.

Lily averted her head and settled her cashmere shawl more closely around her. "I'm safe. Thank you for worrying about me, but I have walked these grounds since I was a little girl. There is no inch that is unknown to me."

"Perhaps so. But we're both aware that there may be other elements to consider now."

"Oliver"—she turned to him but kept her eyes lowered—"I believe you are a kind man. I do not believe you planned to hurt me. After all, you didn't ask me to invade your rooms in the dead of night—or for me to throw myself at you." How grateful she was that the gloom hid her blush.

"There is no regret for that episode on my part." He sounded so formal.

"Thank you," she said, equally formal. "Nor on mine. So we shall consider the incident forgotten, and you may go about your business without another thought of me."

"That's as if you told me to cut off a hand and forget I once had it."

Intense quiet set in, broken only by the rustle of the breeze in tall grasses and the gentle lap of water at the bank. Two swans, their feathers a luminous glow, glided by.

"Do you understand what I'm telling you, Lily?"

"You confuse me. This afternoon I came to you for understanding and you were angry. Now you'd have me believe I am necessary to your happiness."

"My happiness, and my misery," he said. "I was angered by my own feelings, by their implications. I have tried to deny those feelings, but—oh, you will be puzzled by such a statement. Don't think about it."

"I won't." Of course she would. "Please don't let me

keep you. As I've told you, I'm very accustomed to taking my exercise out here."

"I did not happen upon you, little one. I've watched you all day."

"You could not have!" She had heard it suggested that men could not bear to consider that a woman wasn't flattered by their attentions. "I have been in my rooms."

"And I've made certain I knew you were in your rooms, and whenever you left your rooms. I intended to find a time to speak with you."

"To be certain I am not prostrate at your treatment of me? I am stronger than that, I assure you. Now, please, allow me to continue on my way."

"By all means. Shall we make a complete turn around this very large lake? Or had you another destination in mind?"

"I did not have it in mind to have company." In fact, she had a plan, a necessary investigation to perform—alone.

"If you choose to return to the house, I shall leave you there."

Lily snapped a stalk of feathery pampas grass from the clumps lining the water and brushed it beneath her chin. Could she trust Oliver? And, if she could trust him, how far? If her suspicions were correct, the suspicions that had grown stronger by the hour since Witless left, then she might need an ally.

"I'm not returning to the house, not exactly. There are some matters I must consider carefully. And I have an idea to pursue in the—in a certain place. I came this way because I often do so and no one will suspect my destination lies elsewhere."

"You are a mystery," he said. "Lily, do not forget that two troublesome incidents occurred the other evening."

"Only two?" she said without considering her retort well enough. She continued her walk.

He easily resumed his long strides at her side. "I was referring to the matter of the candle in my bed, and the intrusion that occurred later. For the rest, I scarcely think *troublesome* an appropriate description."

"No description would be appropriate. It should never be spoken of again."

"Oh, I doubt that will be possible. But I must warn you that there is a malign force at work here. I have no doubt the aim is to rid Blackmoor of my presence. But I doubt this person would balk at bringing you into his stew if I fail to do his scurrilous bidding."

"How will he bring me in?" She swung her skirts a little. "To do so would be to reveal himself as a mischief-maker. And anyway, we should deny any such accusations."

He laughed abruptly. "You are wonderful. That sharp mind of yours is a dangerous weapon."

"I am going to the north wing."

This time it was Oliver who stood still. "From this route? I thought the lower floors were locked, except to Lord Witmore."

She waited for him to join her again and said, "They are. I appropriated a key from the butler's pantry."

"Why, in God's name?"

"Witless has no heart and no conscience. He is a despicable, puffed-up, self-indulgent, lascivious popinjay."

"You don't like him," Oliver said with laughter in his voice.

"Don't make sport of me. I am not amused. And you and I are definitely not on terms that allow for friendly repartee. I do not believe, for one instant, that he goes to his dead father's rooms—his father who has been dead these ten years—to commune with the spirit of the deceased."

"Why, then?"

Lily pursed her lips and thought deeply.

"I should like to discuss the situation between us," Oliver said. "If you would allow me."

"I wouldn't," she said curtly. "I think . . . Why would I take you into my confidence? I know almost nothing about you."

"You know a great deal about me, miss." No amusement entered his voice now. "I cannot imagine there is another alive who has made a better study of me."

Or one who could have found him more pleasing than Lily.

"It's unsafe for you to be abroad alone," Oliver said. "I ask you again if you will do me the kindness of being cautious. You have only to ask and I shall be glad to accompany you wherever you want to go."

For how long? Until her father packed her off to Fell Manor? She shook her head.

"Stubbornness doesn't suit you."

He thought she had denied his request. "Since I am stubborn by nature I must always be unappealing." This fencing match was shallow. They both sought to avoid the anger that had passed between them—and the passion they had shared. Lily was grateful to reach the place where the path forked. She went to the right, toward the dark north wing.

"Will you share your idea with me?" Oliver asked. "On my honor, you may trust me. With anything. I should never betray you, Lily Adler."

She would not consider how tenderness seemed to hover in his voice. "Come if you will. There is no need for me to share the meanderings of my mind."

The rise to the north wing was steep. The castellated roof walks stood black against the silvered sky. Lily climbed the slope with Oliver's hand at her elbow. Even so light a touch set her nerves jumping, but a sign that she thought anything of it one way or the other would give him yet another advantage over her.

Tall yews, clipped to form a long tunnel, made an eerie way to the door at the base of this part of the building. A subtle shiver brought goose bumps out on Lily's arms and legs. Silliness, nothing more. If Oliver hadn't tried to frighten her, she'd have come confidently enough.

She was glad he was with her.

The place was utterly creepy.

With a screech, an owl left some perch and its wings flapped over the yew tunnel. Lily held her breath and barely restrained herself from reaching to take hold of Oliver. Instead she produced the key and felt until she could insert it in the lock.

Oliver had fallen silent. He was a large, solid form behind her, as encompassing as the yews, and, oddly, seemingly as firm-rooted.

The door creaked inward, so heavy that Lily had to push with both hands.

"Stand still," Oliver said. "Let me go before you and see about some lights."

"No lights," she whispered. "Someone might see. Where I'm going we can light a lamp. There are no windows. Or none that have not been sealed over by Witless."

"We shall break our necks on the way."

Lily rolled in her lips and considered. Maturity must

lead her in this. She closed the door firmly and sought Oliver's hand. "Do as I tell you and you will not fall. It isn't far. Up these two steps here." She guided him. "Now. This way."

"Well, if I hadn't already considered you above deceit, I certainly do now. You spoke the truth when you said you see in the dark. You are like a cat."

She didn't respond to that. "We will turn right here." Promptly he stumbled against her and swore. "You are in too much of a hurry," she said. "God is not responsible for that."

"You have an acid tongue, miss."

"And you are pigheaded. Left. Now wait a moment." She produced a second key and inserted it in another lock. "This is the room where the old earl died. Witless comes here to commune with his spirit."

Oliver followed her silently into the hushed sanctum where the present Lord Witmore spent a great many hours. Lily found a lamp and lighted it. Instantly a glow spread over the extraordinary Oriental furnishings.

Wordlessly, Oliver took the lamp from her and held it high. He surveyed the room with minute care. Tall chests of black lacquer, and inlaid with gold and jewels, stood by the walls. Near a vast, gray marble fireplace was a chair covered with the skin of a leopard, and with gold claws at the ends of its legs. Before the chair, a footstool fashioned of three jade dragons supported a red velvet cushion on their twined tails.

"Gad," Oliver whispered. "And Witmore likes to come and sit in here?"

"Who knows what he does here," Lily said darkly. "But I intend to find out."

"The bed is a fabulous thing. Why would your Witmore not take it with him?"

Pure rage made Lily all but blind. "He is *not* 'my' Witmore. If he ever is, it will not be for long."

"Oho! And why will that be?"

"Never mind." Her careless tongue must be controlled. "These furnishings were among those bought by my papa to please the old earl. As I mentioned before, he was in dire need of funds.

"The bed belonged to an emperor of China, so Papa told me once. The former earl paid a fortune to have it brought here by a ship commissioned especially for the purpose of making a safe transport of it."

"Gold," Oliver commented. "At least, coated in gold. All the way to its crown canopy. Perhaps your Witmore is systematically chipping bits from inconspicuous places and bearing them away."

She would not remind him again that Witless was not hers. "Well, you have seen that I am quite capable of looking after myself here. I'm sure you're anxious to be about your own affairs."

"I *am* about my own affairs."

In the yellow lamplight, she looked into his face, into his tiger's eyes. "Lord Witmore wants something," she said, never intending to say any such thing.

"I rather thought you believed he did."

"Am I so transparent?"

"To me, perhaps. It can be the way of things between people who are of a mind."

She would not argue, or concede, the point. "I have puzzled and puzzled the problem. Now I think I am sure. Lord Witmore wants two things. Blackmoor Hall—which he intends to get by marrying me and waiting for my father to die. And an excuse to spend as much time as he wants here without raising any particular interest. There is talk about his visits to this room being extremely odd, and I'm sure the talk has reached his ears. After all, he is a gossip who counts the greatest gossips in the county among his closest friends."

Oliver glanced around the room again. "Must be worth a fortune." Carrying the lamp, he sauntered to the bed and climbed upon its high mattress.

"Oliver," Lily scolded, faltered, then hurried to his side. "Please don't do that."

He stretched out on his back and settled the lamp on his stomach. "I've always been partial to grand beds. These hangings are among the most dramatic I've ever seen. Cloth of gold, no less. Excessive, but damnably striking. I'd like to have seen the rest of the emperor's hovel."

"Oliver," Lily hissed. "Get off the bed."

"Why? Are other guests expected?"

"Do not fun me."

"I'm not funning you. Lie beside me."

Lily took a step backward. "I should like you to leave now."

"No. Not possible." He patted the mattress at his side, smoothed the red cover with its design of gold dragons. "We must talk, and you know it. One of the most pleasant ways for a man and woman to talk is side by side on a comfortable bed. This is exceedingly comfortable."

"Absolutely not," Lily said.

"Then I shall stay here until you agree."

"I'm not going to agree."

"What are you embroidering a shroud for?"

Lily stuttered, then said, "It's rude to eavesdrop."

"Undoubtedly. But a man can hardly be accused of

eavesdropping on a conversation so loud the entire district might have heard. Whose shroud?"

He could be infuriating. He *was* infuriating. Almost all the time. "No one in particular. Whoever needs it next, in fact. One has to work constantly to make sure these things are ready when required."

"You made it up."

She had to smile. "Then why did you ask me about it?"

"Because I enjoyed your little joke at the expense of those frightful people."

"Those frightful people my father would have me count my family."

That silenced him.

"I think there is something in this room that Witless has been looking for these ten years."

Oliver's head snapped toward her. He raised himself onto his elbows. "Something?"

"Something, or a clue to something. He comes and goes with such a thunderous expression. If he finds peace here, it certainly doesn't show."

Oliver frowned and peered into dark corners. "Surely he'd have found anything there was to find by now."

"One would think so. But I refuse to accept that he spends time here mourning his dead father. Lord Witmore is not a deep fellow. And there is gossip in the village about his debts. The tradespeople don't like to press for payment. They don't say much, because that's the way of it with people of his class. Or so I'm told. They pay when they feel like it. But I think his coffers are shallow and he's casting about for a means to fill them."

"You," Oliver said. "He's going to use you to fill them."

And he didn't care, she thought with despair. Lily held the ends of her shawl tightly.

"Come here," Oliver said softly. "Just lie beside me. I'm troubled, Lily, and only you can ease my unhappiness."

Her stomach turned. She struggled against her desire to do exactly as he asked. "This mood is unlike you," she told him. "I am not amused."

"Good. Neither am I. Tell me what you think Lord Witmore can possibly hope to find here."

"It's a puzzle. Surely if some treasure existed his father would have used it to save himself from financial ruin."

Oliver put the lamp on a high chest beside the bed. "I do believe you have a point there," he said.

"But you think me a silly female with too much time to invent stories."

"On the contrary, I think you an extremely intelligent female who may have stumbled upon something of great importance." His voice had become distant, as if he scarcely considered her presence. He eased himself to sit up. "I do not like your Witmore any more than you do."

"He is *not* . . . You deliberately torment me."

"It's one way of dealing with what is truly on my mind."

Her stomach felt strange. "I don't believe in avoiding unpleasant matters."

"Oh"—he rolled his head to look at her—"not unpleasant in this case. Just dangerous. Would you allow me to assist you in trying to discover if your neighbor has a hidden motive for visiting here?"

She still held the pampas wand and touched its soft tip to her chin. "I am nothing that would ever interest him."

"Fool."

Lily looked at Oliver.

His jaw flexed. "I know what I'm saying. Any man who could fail to be interested in you is a fool."

She dared not speak.

"Are you prepared to marry the man?"

"No!" In a rush, she scrambled up the steps and onto the bed. Heedless of consequences, she curled against Oliver and tucked her face into his neck. "I will not, I tell you. First I would die, and I'm entirely too fond of life to embrace that notion."

His laugh, or the rumble of it beneath her breast, surprised Lily. She raised her head to peer into his face. Narrowed, glittering gold eyes looked back at her.

"You are amused by my dilemma?"

"I am cheered by your spirit when I know you are troubled."

Lily made to remove herself, but Oliver wrapped her in his arms so tightly, she gasped. "I have you, Lily Adler. You shall not leave until I decide to release you. I do not anticipate doing so for some time."

When she started to protest, he shifted until she was secured beneath him. Then Oliver kissed her. He kissed her fiercely, desperately, turning her head from side to side with his ardor. Again and again, he drew her lower lip between his teeth and sucked, and bit gently, then slipped his tongue deeply into her mouth.

Lily's body flamed. She pushed her hands beneath his coat, seeking to get closer to him.

A rain of softer kisses fell on her mouth, her jaw, her neck. He pulled away the shawl and dropped it on the floor. The neck of her gown was high but wide, and he found what skin he could to taste.

No reason, she had no reason left where Oliver Worth

was concerned. But she did know what she wanted, and there might never be another opportunity to tell him.

She pushed hard at him.

His face tightly drawn, the nostrils of his straight nose flared, he stared down at her. There was a darkness in him, something dangerous that ignited the slightest fear. Fear that fascinated and drove her.

"Please, Oliver," she said, her own breathless voice a foreign sound in her ears. "I should like to be naked with you again."

His breath expelled, low and long. She saw sweat break at his temples. "You will haunt me every moment of my life," he told her. "You are strong liquor to me. The finest liquor to me. I think I must . . . Oh, my God." He sat up and buried his head in his hands.

Lily knelt. She made no attempt to touch him—yet. Rather, she went about the task of unfastening her gown.

Oliver moaned. "Lily, I beg of you, do not torment me."

"It was you who insisted upon coming with me," she reminded him tartly. "Now you must bear the consequences. I shall attempt to save you from too much unpleasantness."

He moaned again.

The gown wasn't easy to remove on her own, but she accomplished it and spread the serviceable green garment on the bottom of the bed. "Perhaps you would consider taking off your own clothes," she said, aware of the heavy beat of her heart. "I find I am anxious to remind myself of certain aspects of you."

"Oh . . . my . . . *God.*"

"Really, I shall have to arrange for you to attend another meeting of the Junior Altar Society. You are in need of spiritual guidance."

"I'm in need of guidance? I doubt you and your charming friends are qualified to minister to me."

Lily loosed her petticoats and balanced on the mattress to step out of them. She let them fall to the floor, stood in her stays and chemise, and looked down into Oliver's face. His lips parted. Muscles flexed beside his mouth. He held his hands out to her.

Lily cocked her head and said, "What is it?"

"You cannot know what you do to me. Come here. I will deal with the rest of those provocative articles you probably think of as simple."

"My chemise? My drawers? My stays?"

"You are shameless, miss. Even to speak of such things is unheard of."

"I know"—she also knew her smile was smug—"I take delight in being outrageous. There, I confess my own eccentricity."

Before she could react, he bent forward and brought her tumbling astride his lap. "Sit there, minx. I find I am too warm." With that he worked off his jacket and waistcoat and removed his shirt.

"Oh," Lily said, helpless to hide her ecstasy at the sight of his broad chest and powerful shoulders. She combed her fingers through the shiny dark hair on his chest and said, "Oh," again, but more breathlessly. She dared to use a forefinger to follow where the hair grew in a line toward the waist of his trousers, and beneath.

He caught her hand. "You are unbelievable. But I'm glad to make myself believe in you."

"Your fault, Oliver. Just to look at you in any circumstance is to feel I may faint from wanting to touch you. But seeing you unclothed sends me into a frenzy. Oh, I must kiss you here." Here was first one nipple, then the other, and he writhed and clamped her to him. Then he used one hand to cup her bottom—and to slip inside the divided center seam of her drawers to stroke where she'd never considered being stroked. She let out a little cry, but it was of delight.

"Now," he said, sitting her up firmly. "I know we have business to conduct."

She raised her brows. "Business?"

"We will get to that. First, I want to spend time as it should be spent between you and me." With sure fingers, he unlaced her chemise and slipped it from her shoulders until her breasts were revealed.

Lily attempted to pull the chemise over her again. Oliver would have none of it. "You are going to learn more about yourself. And about me, what you do to me. See how beautiful you are?"

Her stays pushed up her breasts. With the chemise fallen away, she felt brazen, as if she offered herself to him, for his pleasure, for his feast. And she did.

Oliver played with her breasts. He stroked the white flesh, and beneath her bottom, his hips shifted. She felt that wonderful part of him grow full, and hard, and hot, and then there was an answering throb in the moistening flesh between her thighs.

With fingers and thumbs, he rolled her nipples, pulled them, smiled as they peaked. She watched what he did and grew so hot, she pulsed. Panting, she placed her hands beneath her own breasts and leaned toward him.

"An able student," he said before he suckled. He drew firmly on each, and an answering spasm pulled in her belly.

He rested his cheek on one sweetly aching breast and lifted her up until he could undo his trousers. Lily braced herself on his muscular shoulders and saw with wonder how he sprang free.

Once more he settled her, resting that part of him against the white stuff of her drawers.

"You enjoyed what we shared the other evening," he said. "Should you like to enjoy it again?"

Lily couldn't speak. She took his smooth flesh into her hands and squeezed.

Oliver all but tore her hands away. "You will end all before it is begun, sweet. Let me lead you in this."

He lifted her to sit leaning against his raised knees. She hung her head forward, conscious of her naked breasts, her disheveled hair, of the wanton picture she must make.

"Another pleasure to show you," Oliver said, and opened her drawers. She had no time to protest before he buried his mouth in the hair he'd revealed. He curled his tongue into wet folds and licked at her while she filled her fingers with his hair and cried out.

For a moment she was desperate to stop him. "No, Oliver. No, you cannot." But he made no response. He sucked, and laved, and nibbled, and then the burning mounted, and she would have begged him to continue forever.

Her body was not her own. She fell over his back, scratched him mindlessly, bit the unyielding muscle in his shoulders.

And the marvelous, pumping spasms broke.

His voice came to her dimly: "You are my love. You are my heart." Passion made fools of men. That wisdom was already known by her small group.

She did not care if he spoke foolishly. The blackness, tinged with red, centered in her brain and she drew her being around it, and embraced it, and treasured it.

And before the wildness ebbed she raised her head and looked into Oliver's eyes. He smiled at her, his features ruthless, violent in some manner that excited rather than frightened her.

Her drawers were open wide. With his attention still on her face, he settled his manhood against the slick hair he'd revealed, and explored. Lily stroked him there, rubbed him against her.

"You know what I want," he said. "You are an amazement to me."

He tipped his head back, exposing the distended veins in his strong throat. Lily tested the broad tip of his rod and shuddered when he cried out. "What do you want?" she asked him. "Please, Oliver. Guide me."

"You don't know what you ask, little one. You test me beyond what any man should try to resist. You are all you should be. It is enough."

"To hold you to me like this?" Massaging his distended flesh against hers caused fresh ripples of sensation. She gasped.

"Perfect," he said, falling on the bed. "Don't stop, sweet Lily. Don't stop."

She continued, rising to her knees again to press the end of him against the bud that seemed the center of all feeling. And tension mounted, and pleasure, and Oliver all but sobbed aloud, and his hips rose from the bed.

Lily worked over him, and over herself, gave herself up to delight so exquisite her body grew bathed in perspiration.

His great shout echoed about the exotic room, and his juices filled her hands and flowed over her, and she threw herself on top of him. There was magic in feeling him give up something of his body's making to her.

Together they grew quiet.

Later, and she knew it was much later, for the lamp had burned low, Oliver drew the rich bedcover over them and wrapped her close in his arms. "I did not ask to find you, my Lily. It would have been better if I hadn't. But I would not change one moment with you."

"I would only ask for many more moments with you," she told him. "Tomorrow Papa is to go to Lord Witmore and discuss a marriage settlement."

"So I understood."

Of course he did. He'd heard. Her happiness grew cold in her breast. Desperation made her tremble.

"I would like to take this thing from you, this thing you don't want."

"Then take it," she told him impulsively, rising to an elbow. "Help me."

"How?"

She must dare to say it. "Tell Papa we wish to be married."

"Lily!" His eyes snapped open.

"I know you have no interest in taking a wife, but you would confuse everything. You would divert Papa from this dreadful course. I do believe his only thought is to see me married."

"Not to his assistant."

"Why not? He likes you." Her desperation shamed her. "I'm sorry. I am a disgrace. Please forgive me."

"You could never be a disgrace. Nor could you need forgiveness." Absently, he stroked her breasts with the backs of his fingers. "What we have done together, Lily, it is not entirely . . . That is to say, we have not completed the *act*. Do you understand?"

She puckered her brow. "We haven't?"

"No. You are certainly compromised by anyone's standards, but you are not entirely violated."

She didn't care for his cool manner of discussing these matters. "Whatever you have done to me could never be a violation in my eyes. But if you say there is more, well, then, I must wait for you to reveal it to me."

"You must *not* encourage me to reveal it. And I must endeavor to make certain I control myself in the future. Not easy when I am near you. You must help me."

Lowering her lashes, she decided she could be forgiven a little coyness just this once. "You will be near me on other occasions, then?"

He gave her nipples another delicious tweak. "I have a suspicion that may well be the case. And you have extraordinary appetites, my dear girl. In fact, you are a prize for any man. But I find I can't tolerate thinking of another man being with you like this."

"They never shall be," she told him with honesty. "For my life I shall remember the times I have spent with you."

"But there is Lord Witmore."

She felt sick at the thought. "Please help me, Oliver. Please do not consign me to that horror."

"We should return to the south wing."

"Oliver?"

"I'll help you dress."

Lily's throat burned with the effort to hold back tears. He enjoyed their times together, but nothing more. Although he spoke of not wanting her to be with another man, he would not do anything to avert such a situation.

In silence he assisted her into her clothes, avoiding too intimate a contact with her body. He clothed himself quickly, with economical movements, and set about smoothing her hair as if he were practiced at the matter of a female's toilette.

She stood before him like an obedient child but with her heart turning in her breast.

"You will do, I think," he said at last, retrieving her shawl and wrapping it around her shoulders. "I find you beautiful in whatever you wear. Your simplicity pleases me greatly."

"Thank you. I'm afraid I have no style."

"You have your own style."

"As you say." She found she hadn't the energy for spirited conversation.

Oliver held out his hand. "I'll blow out the lamp. You'll have to guide me, since I don't share your wonderful vision."

She knew she held him too tightly, but did so anyway. When the lights went out, she took him to the door and into the passageway, where she locked the door behind them.

They'd only gone a few steps when he removed his hand from hers and put his arm around her shoulders.

Willing back stinging tears, Lily moved toward the main door.

"Stop," Oliver said as they turned the final corner. "I closed the door, didn't I?"

"Yes," Lily said, wishing she didn't feel the strong breeze on her face, or see the distant arch of pale light at the other end of the yew tunnel. "You closed it and I slid the latch into place very deliberately. The latch cannot raise itself. It has been opened."

"Damnation!"

She trembled. "Someone is watching us, Oliver."

"Because they want to make sure I stay away from you," he said, almost under his breath.

"We will not allow them to frighten us."

He drew her outside and waited for her to deal with the lock. Keeping her behind him, he walked forward until he emerged into the moonlight and searched around. "He is a coward. He seeks to do battle without risking his skin, because he knows he would forfeit that skin to me."

His flat conviction brought an icy ripple to Lily's limbs. "It's possible I am the cause of this. Probable. Surely it must be something to do with Lord Witmore. He is the only one who is desperate to use me for his own ends. The possibility that you might foil that would be enough to make him try to get rid of you."

"Yes," Oliver agreed. He took her hand again and started along a path that led directly to the front of Blackmoor Hall. "You may be right. So we shall beat him at his game. I shall speak to the professor first thing in the morning."

"And what will you say?" Lily asked anxiously. "I want to be with you."

"I shall say that we wish to marry."

But he didn't want to. He was driven by honor and decency. "You are too good. I cannot let you do this."

He hurried her on.

Sadness swelled. Lily tugged him to a halt. "You are an honest man. Honest to your heart, and too honorable not to want to save me. We have shared . . . we have shared pleasure, and I am glad. But I know my part is the greater in that. You would never have come to me."

"I came to you tonight," he said quietly. "You didn't ask me to follow you."

"You've been afraid for me. We both know this."

"My mind is made up. Unless you are horrified at the idea, I am going to ask your father for your hand."

Lily couldn't bear it. He offered what she wanted more

than anything in the world, but only because he thought he must. She pulled her hand from his and turned away. "I will not agree, Oliver. I should never have suggested such a thing. If I am destined to marry a man who doesn't love me, it would be better if I didn't love him either."

"Lily—"

"Forgive me for being emotional when you've been so kind. I shall recover. And I shall manage. I'm strong."

He took her by the shoulders and turned her to face him. "Will you promise me one thing?"

In the moonlight, his face was slashed with shadow. "I would promise you anything," she told him.

"Even that you will try not to hate me should I ever disappoint you?"

A puzzling man, a marvelously puzzling man. "I could never hate you."

He dropped his hands. "God forgive me, but I shall do it."

She waited, and when he didn't speak again, she rested a hand on his cheek.

Oliver seized her wrist and kissed her fingers, her palm. He groaned softly, deep in his throat.

"What is it?" Lily stroked his hair. "You are pained."

"Pained with longing. I shall try to do this as it should be done. Will you marry me, Lily?"

Her heart stopped. Her blood stopped moving in her veins.

"Lily?"

"Out of duty? You would do this because I was impetuous and because you would help me out of a sense of duty."

With her hand clasped in both of his, he kissed her

cheek, slowly, rubbed his jaw against her brow. "Marry me, Lily."

"And watch you come to hate me?"

"Never, silly girl. Never. It's no use. I must take what I want and hope fate will smile on me. I want you, Lily. I love you."

Chapter Fourteen

"*How* big are they?" Reginald Beaumont, Earl of Witmore, asked as he pressed his ear to his friend's mouth. "You don't say." He made exaggerated gestures before his chest and laughed. A rivulet of Madeira ran down his chin.

Sir Cecil Laycock wrinkled his nose and turned his face from his companion's drink-fouled breath. "I'd assumed you'd had a sampling by now, old chap," he said. "I say, Virtue, didn't I tell you Drucilla's jugs were as big as marrows?"

Virtue ignored him. She rifled through rich but old-fashioned clothes in shabby wardrobes pressed into alcoves beneath the sloping roof. Cecil had found the room by exploring forsaken areas at Fell Manor.

Virtue missed London and the racy salons of her daring friends. She hoped this evening's entertainment would be less boring than the last effort Cecil had presented for his hosts' edification. However, she felt an unfamiliar disquiet. There was something almost wild in Cecil's grimly determined countenance. Wild and unfamiliar. He'd made it clear to her that this interlude was intended to accomplish more than their amusement. In fact, he'd held her arms so tightly that she was bruised, and he'd told her their future, his and hers, might depend on what happened tonight. But why this sullen determination? They always got what they wanted, didn't they?

So engrossed was she that she didn't spy Cecil's approach until his bony hands snaked beneath her arms. He pulled the bodice of her gown beneath her breasts and jiggled them.

"Stop!" She tried to smack him away, but Cecil was stronger than he appeared. He lifted her from her feet and swung her around. "Reggie! Stop him at once."

"Not my problem," Reggie said, yawning, and making no attempt to hide his interest. "I say, Virtue, you've grown into a big girl yourself."

"Not as big as Drucilla," Cecil commented. "But worthy of a man's note, what?"

Virtue preferred to take her pleasure in more private ways. That is, ways of her own design, although she wasn't especially particular about the composition of the players. Only Cecil's frightening cautions had led her to come this evening. Already she began to doubt the wisdom of her presence.

"Bring her here, Cecil. I—"

"Shut up, Reggie," Virtue said. "I find I'm growing impatient with your behavior, Cecil. Kindly put me down. We'll discuss what we must do at another time."

"Rubbish," Cecil said. "About time you understood the way of things, m'dear. Enough foolishness. And I prefer a little something extra with business. Makes it so much more pleasurable, don't you know?"

Virtue's feet continued to swing inches from the ground, and Cecil had made her nipples harden. What did it matter if she couldn't abide the man? In the absence of more suitable swains, he could do her a service. She reached back to rub him, and wriggled when he grunted.

Cecil dropped her and turned away. "Patience," he said with a coolness that angered her. "I've got more on my mind than your appetites."

His words stung her. Then she caught Reggie eyeing her breasts. She bounced them briefly for his benefit and slipped her bodice back into place.

"You're mean to me, Virtue," Reggie said. "Least you could do would be to comfort me a little. Just a feel—nothing more, of course. Wouldn't hurt anything, and nobody would ever know. After all, it isn't as if we were related, not really. Step, and all that."

Reggie's father had been her mother's second husband. Virtue had been the product of Mama's first marriage. "Why should you need comfort?" she asked, titillated nonetheless at the prospect of dallying with her step-brother. He did not stir her juices, but there was the almost-forbidden aspect.

"I need comfort because I am to marry the woman you refer to, correctly, as a toad." Strolling toward Virtue, he pouted. "Imagine it, darling. I am to suffer that skinny little creature until her prattling father dies."

Virtue darted out of Reggie's reach. She lifted the lid from the top of a pile of leather hatboxes and swept out a tricorn complete with trailing white feather. "I declare this place is a veritable treasure trove. How did you come upon it, Cecil?"

Cecil stretched out on the couch and rested the back of a hand on his brow. "*Ennui*, dearest. Pure *ennui*. With nothing to divert me but the serious business that lies ahead, I have wandered the rooms and corridors of this inadequate little place of yours. I found all this." He gestured with his free hand. "And I decided it would make a splendid spot for an unusual party."

"I don't see why," Virtue said.

Cecil closed his eyes. "You will soon enough. Drink up, Reggie, old chap. Pour one for me."

Dutifully Reggie downed another glass and filled it again. He ignored Cecil's request.

Virtue settled the dusty tricorn on Reggie's head and tugged the feather under his nose. "A white mustachio. How dashing, Reggie. Ooh, I bet you could tickle all kinds of things with that."

"Why not let me show you how many?" He made a grab for her, but she evaded him. "Can't we get on with it, Cecil? I'm quite tired."

Virtue waited for Cecil's response. He was a man who adored building anticipation. And he was inventive, she must give him that. "It's late," she told him. "Almost one in the morning. And Reggie and I have some matters to discuss in preparation for the potty professor's visit."

"Hah!" Cecil pointed at her. "Your fault. You were the one who led me to believe the old fool made chamber pots. Then I discover he's a partner in one of the biggest bloody banks in the land. It's fortunate he's also a sentimental fool who abides by his dead wife's wishes. Dashed convenient he still gives you endless visitin' privileges, Reggie."

"Virtue's right," Reggie said, unsteady on his feet, and showing signs of waxing maudlin. He upended his glass and refilled it yet again from one of half a dozen bottles lined on top of a scarred sea trunk. "Right. She's right. There can't be any mistakes in what must be done when Adler comes. My whole future rests on our success. I've got to marry the toad and get her with child. That'll stop any tongues wagging. Then I'll hope the old man makes a speedy departure."

Virtue caught Cecil's eye. He gave her a knowing stare, and at last understanding passed between them. They had work to do with Reggie, who gave frequent hints that Virtue and Cecil could not be assured of sharing the fortune he would acquire by marrying the Adler girl. They had vowed to use Reggie's fear of public exposure of the depth of his dissolute nature to secure comfortable futures for themselves. Evidently Cecil had decided to force the issue here—tonight. Virtue shivered anew with arousal. What exactly could Cecil have in mind?

"Of course," Reggie said, waving a bottle in one hand and raising his glass in the other. "These pale misses can be quite diverting. Kissed Lily once, y'know. I knew from the start I'd have to have her. Tried too soon, but I remember her hard little tits. Divertin'."

"A toad," Virtue muttered.

Reggie was still contemplating his fresh angle on Lily Adler. "She might fight. I should like that. And her father's fat coffers will sweeten my wedded bliss."

Cecil shook his head, warning Virtue to have a care what she said. There were things they spoke of between them, things they knew that Reggie must never know—unless they had to force him to do as he was told.

With his flamboyant hat still in place, Reggie staggered to one of the open wardrobes and groped for a scarlet satin gown with a pearl-encrusted stomacher. What there was of the top of the bodice came to a point in the center and dipped down on either side as if it would frame the undersides of the breasts.

Reggie studied the dress. "Bit drafty, wouldn't you say?" He snorted, and snuffled.

"Worn over another garment," Virtue told him.

"Like to see this without anything underneath." Reggie wavered, and blinked slowly. "What d'you think of that, Laycock?"

"First-rate idea."

"Want a ruff," Reggie said. "Wonderful things, ruffs. Clothing that doesn't cover anything." He guffawed. "Know what I mean?" Reggie's head disappeared inside one of the wardrobes as he shuffled about inside.

Cecil came to stand beside Virtue. "He's past reason," he whispered of Reggie. "We've got to have a care he drinks enough, but not too much."

"He'll do as he's told regardless."

"Maybe. Maybe not. He's got to remember what happens here. As long as he does, his spurious concerns with public opinion should help. Praise be that the fool doesn't realize the world already considers him depraved."

"You go too far," Virtue said. She looked at Cecil. "Don't forget you insult a member of my family."

Cecil snickered unpleasantly.

She tossed her head. "We've dallied enough. I thought you said we should make sport for ourselves while we entangle him. I take it you have plans toward that end?"

"What are you saying?" Reggie asked loudly, emerging from the wardrobe. "Don't whisper, damn you. Speak up."

"Be quiet," Virtue told him, growing edgy again.

"The devil I will," Reggie said, truculent. "What's got into you? Take off your dress. Your marrows are every bit as nice as Drucilla's, I'll warrant. I want to look at them. Give me a show, Virtue."

"Reggie's right, " Cecil said, narrowing his eyes at her. "But even better, put on the red dress, darling. For Reggie.

After all, he chose it, and I think you're the only woman who could do it justice. That old Chinese screen will give you a place to prepare."

Virtue examined the dress and went back to the wardrobe to look among the other clothes again. Cecil slipped beside her and whispered, "Give him his bloody show. Give him the ultimate. Or make him think he's *taken* the ultimate. That's my plan, dear thing. Then, with the threat of exposure, he'll do whatever we tell him after that."

She batted him and said, "No. Absolutely not. You're sick, Cecil."

He whispered again. "We won't debate who among us is the sickest. It will only be a fiction, I tell you. Close enough for him to think he took you—when he's sober again. And I'll be the witness to his treatment of you. Don't tell me the prospect doesn't excite you."

Virtue grew hot, and jumpy—and excited. With a last glance at Reggie, she went behind the cracked Chinese screen.

Cecil stood where he could watch her. He raised his shoulders and rubbed his hands. "The nature of this game is blackmail of a sort," he told her in low tones. "Your fool of a stepbrother will not dare to cross us for fear we'll expose him for the depraved libertine we shall make him out to be. Drucilla also knows what she must say if called upon to do so."

"This is dangerous," Virtue said, deriving pleasure from the lust in Cecil's eyes as she stepped out of her dress and slipped free of her chemise. Her breasts must be bared for the outrageous gown she prepared to don.

Cecil's words didn't entirely quell Virtue's disquiet, but

she agreed they must move to make certain they got what they deserved, what was right.

Reggie adjusted his crotch. He leaned forward from the waist and peered toward Virtue. "Hurry up," he said, his face growing red and sweaty.

She struggled into the stiff gown, fiddled with the boned bodice, and called, "Are you ready to decide if the costume will do, Reggie?"

"We're ready," Cecil told her, moistening his lips. "We're breathless with waiting, my beauty."

With mincing steps, Virtue sidled from behind the screen. She wore the once-fabulous red gown that left her breasts naked. She relished the strangled groan that escaped her stepbrother. Swaying, kicking forward first one, then the other foot, she held her hands behind her back and came to the center of a worn rug that had been spread on dust-gray boards. "Shall I do? I think I should make quite a stir at any gathering, don't you?"

"Gathering?" Reggie said pettishly. "What gathering? Dashed secretive nonsense."

"You know we talked about it," Virtue told him. "After your wedding, Reggie. A special celebration—probably at the Hall where we belong. We'll hold a costume ball."

Reggie sniffed and smacked his lips.

"I shall be the mystery woman in red," Virtue said.

"Not once they see those," Reggie shouted, pointing at her bosom. "They'll pick out those pumpkins easily enough."

Virtue bit her lips to redden them and turned sideways to show off another view of her big breasts. She revolved, and posed at the opposite aspect. "I shall wear a mask," she told them, smiling, and feeling the luscious prick of arousal.

Cecil refilled Reggie's glass, watched him empty it, and poured another big measure. "The door's locked, Reggie," he said. "Why not do what you want to do. Have Virtue. She's begging for it."

"*Cecil,*" Virtue said, afraid, but thrilled by that fear.

Bleary-eyed and sagging, Reggie turned his head from side to side in an effort to focus on Cecil. "I fancy that," he said. "Make her keep still for me."

Virtue played with the rims of her nipples, making sure Reggie saw.

"Look at that," Cecil squealed. "Come on, Reggie. Give her what she wants."

Virtue breathed rapidly. She knew a moment's disquiet. "Have a care, Cecil," she said. "Don't go too far."

"I want her to rape me instead," Reggie bellowed. "Come and rape me, Virtue. Now! I order you to rape me now."

"The man's a fool," Cecil said through his teeth. "But we need him, and we need him in the palms of our hands." He raised his voice. "We'll make sure she does, Reggie. Better help her, though. Get ready for her."

Reggie undid his trousers and pushed them down around his ankles.

"He really does want to be raped," Cecil muttered. "Fortunately he'll remember very little in the morning—other than the things we make sure he remembers. And in the way we want them remembered."

"Lot to be said for a party," Reggie crooned. "Brothers together in the sport, hey, Cecil? When's she coming for me, then?"

"She's coming," Cecil told him. "Lean on me, old chap, while she gets ready for you." To Virtue he whispered urgently, "Look at him. Incapable, dammit. This will be a piece of invention."

Virtue hugged herself. "Is this necessary?"

Reggie tripped over his trousers and landed on all fours. Scuffling, he crawled to Virtue and lifted her skirts. He groped at the crotch of her tights until he ripped them asunder.

"Well, I'm damned," Cecil said. "The fool will make things easier for us yet. Won't go down well that the Earl of Witmore forced himself upon his stepsister."

The sight of Reggie's bare buttocks disquieted Virtue. She took her pleasure with strangers, not with relatives—even if their relationship wasn't by blood.

A glass, thrust into her hands by Cecil, caught her off guard and she all but dropped it. "Drink," he ordered. "You're pale. I don't have time for mewling female nonsense now."

Reggie fell back on his heels and announced, "Rape, I tell you," appearing close to passing out. "Force me, Virtue." He contrived to stretch out on his back.

Virtue's womanly places ached. She hadn't known Reggie's considerable proportions. The drink had rendered him flaccid, but he was built like a horse.

"Sit on me." Reggie's words blended into a fuddled stream. He reached for her.

"Get on with it," Cecil ordered, and gave her a push. When she made no move to obey, he lifted her, spread her legs, and forced her down on top of Reggie. "Make it quick before we lose this one entirely."

Through the wash of heat and lust, she struggled with fear at what she was about. Reggie quickened against her.

"It's enough," she told Cecil thickly. "What we say will be enough."

"Not to ensure my hold over *you,* dearest," he told her, baring his teeth. He dropped to his knees and reached to thrust Reggie's pulsing rod inside her. Cecil laughed, and held her still while Reggie heaved his hips off the floor.

"It's *enough,*" Virtue insisted, desperate now. "Let me go. We have what we want."

"You have what you want," Cecil said. "I'm making very certain I have what *I* want."

His head lolled, but Reggie drove into her once, twice, three times, and with the fourth invasion she felt the warm rush of his juices—but only an instant before her own release shattered into her belly, into the places she couldn't name, into her breasts.

Virtue burned. She throbbed. But when she looked into Cecil's cold eyes, horror unfurled. He intended to use this against her. He intended to control her, and Reggie. She clambered to her feet.

"Whassat?" Reggie opened his eyes and promptly cast up his accounts on the carpet.

Cecil turned his head aside and dragged the other man to lie on the couch. "Sleep it off," he told him before turning to Virtue again. "He had his way with you," Cecil told her. "Of course, if it becomes necessary, I shall recall that you instigated the proceedings. Let's hope it can remain a secret, a secret between the three of us. As long as I get what I deserve, it will. Good enough?"

Virtue nodded, her head falling forward. She began straightening her gown.

"Don't bother," Cecil said. "Take it off. All the way off."

She ignored him and continued to brush down the ruined skirts.

"We're partners," Cecil told her. "Partners make sure they please each other. It's time for you to please me."

"I'm tired," she told him, feeling sick.

Cecil began taking off his clothes. "Not too tired, my dear. I am now in command. You will all do exactly as I say."

"You have no more hold over me than I have over you."

Shortly he stood naked, a spindly, flaccid creature, but with a rod that stood surprisingly erect for a man in his condition. "Some things are never acceptable, my dear. How will you explain if I reveal that you rutted with your brother? You will both pray I say nothing, and I will say nothing as long as you are both very, very good to me. No, Virtue, you hold nothing over me. We shall work together as I have planned, but always as I see fit. Take off the gown or I shall tear it off. Of course, that would make things the more pleasant. The choice is yours."

Trembling, but with rage rather than anxiety, she stripped down to her chemise, stays, and drawers. The latter were wet from Reggie's ministrations.

"Now, while we enjoy ourselves, we shall make sure we both understand what is to take place. Three weeks to that sot's marriage to the Adler creature, and then we will be close to our prize. Come here."

"Reggie will marry the toad and I shall make her sorry she was ever born," Virtue said with a flare of vicious anticipation. "Her narrow world will be shattered. She will creep into whatever space I allow her here and pray to be left alone."

Cecil reached for her. He set about unlacing her stays. Frustrated before he finished, he sat beside Reggie's feet on the couch and pulled her astride his lap, pushing inside her without preamble. He sucked in a breath and squeezed her arms until she cried out.

"Now to our understanding," he said, moving within her.

Virtue's flesh responded, and she panted. "We have our understanding. The Adler female will be subjugated. When her father dies, Reggie and I will return to our rightful home and regain possession of all we lost. We will also gain possession of the professor's considerable fortune."

She disliked Cecil's hands on her breasts, his slack lips fastening on her nipples, but she closed her eyes and pretended excitement. It was easier than dealing with one of his unpleasant moods.

With loud grunts and many groans, Cecil finished his business but kept her on his lap when she longed to get away from him.

He smiled, showing discolored teeth. "Very nice, my dear. I shouldn't have waited so long. I'll arrange to move to the room next to yours."

She contained the urge to protest.

"Now, you have the way of things almost right."

"Entirely right by my lights. I begin to doubt that there was any need to use Reggie so cruelly. He is as determined to reclaim our birthright as I am."

"He thought to keep everything for himself and get rid of us," Cecil said. "But he is a fool. You are also a fool. But now I have you both where you will not be tempted to oppose me."

"But everything is already arranged."

"So you think. Do you believe I am prepared to wait for Adler to die before taking possession of what I need?

What I will have. I have lived long enough without benefit of any fortune. That will change, and soon."

"It is *our* fortune," she pointed out, and she did feel terror. Quickly she added, "Although we shall always be grateful for your friendship and you will, of course, gain the advantage of our good fortune."

His hands, closing around her neck, shocked Virtue to silence.

"You must learn how it will be," Cecil said serenely, while he tightened his grip on her throat. "It is you who will be grateful for whatever I choose to toss you. You and your brother would never manage alone. Fortunately you are not, and will never be alone. With me, all will be accomplished, and in short order."

Virtue's teeth chattered; she couldn't stop them.

Cecil grinned. "The morning approaches, a most important morning. It will begin our new lives, our new and complete happiness."

"I wish to get up," she told him.

"Not until I'm sure you understand exactly what will happen very soon. Immediately after the marriage, Professor Adler will meet with a sad accident. He will die and, as Lily Adler's husband, Reggie will inherit."

Virtue stared at him, the import of his words slowly becoming clear. "It is dangerous."

"It is essential. Leave it to me. There will be no questions afterward."

She smiled, gradually smiled wider. "Then the little toad will be completely at our mercy. Presuming to live in our home, to order how it shall be run, to receive *me* as a visitor! Oh, yes, she shall suffer for the insults I've borne."

"Indeed she will, my pet."

"She must be sent away. She can live here. Yes, I should like that."

"Adler's assistant must be quickly dispatched."

"Ah." Virtue thought of the darkly silent, exceedingly handsome Mr. Worth. "Perhaps he need not go too quickly."

"At once," Cecil said, his face twisted. "That shall be our first task as soon as the old man is disposed of."

She disguised her regret. "As you say, Cecil."

"Then there will be but one matter to deal with."

"Only one?"

"The girl. Lily Adler will also die."

Chapter Fifteen

"Silence is the wisest argument," Professor Adler told Oliver from his place on the opposite side of the breakfast table. Absently, he stroked Oliver's cat, who had curled on his lap.

"As you say, sir." Oliver was not always certain of the professor's reasoning. "But you do approve of my plan to ask for Lily's hand?"

"We are born toward the inevitable," the other man said. "Eat, man, eat."

Oliver found he had no appetite for the fresh serving of kidneys and eggs his employer had served from the sideboard, but he swallowed a forkful of the eggs. The parlor where the family—and Oliver—took most of their meals pleased him. Whimsical murals of maidens dancing among flowers covered fluted ceiling panels. Similar depictions decorated ovals in a white plaster fireplace. Gilt-framed paintings of fruits and flowers relieved rose silk-covered walls. Even the furniture was of a light, feminine nature. Not a man's room, yet the professor favored it and chose to linger there each morning after his meal, which was served at five sharp. Oliver had been present for almost two hours while Professor Adler had managed to say much about very little, and nothing that directly addressed the question Oliver had posed.

"One may regret speaking, but rarely does one regret having kept silent."

Oliver nodded sagely. The professor was rarely in full philosophical mode so early in the day.

"If a man keeps his mouth closed, he cannot be damned by his words."

The message became clearer. "Your wisdom will be my guide." In other words, in the upcoming encounter he was supposed to examine every word before speaking and, even then, speak very little.

"Men must bear the emotional excesses of the female bravely."

"Indeed."

"There *will* be emotional excesses," the professor said. He selected a piece of toast from the silver rack and set it upon his plate. He fed a crumb to Raven before saying, "I used to breakfast later, Oliver. When my dearest wife was alive, we breakfasted together and I found much joy in our companionship at the beginning of the day."

"She liked this room," Oliver said. Of course, a woman's room, the late Mrs. Adler's to be precise.

"She did indeed. This was her house, her choice. It's too big, of course, but she planned to fill it with people. Since I lost her I've had little interest in social affairs, but I take pleasure in being where Kitty loved to be." The toast took the other man's attention, toast and thoughts that made his blue eyes distant in expression.

Little sleep and heavy calculation—and exertion—had left Oliver anxious to settle what must be settled. Unfortunately there were some matters that would remain, and which might ultimately make him a most unhappy man.

He drank coffee and set down his cup. "I believe you may expect little opposition from Lily in this matter. In fact, my dealings with her led me to believe she will be very sensible." He did not dare to let his mind wander too far into the dealings he mentioned. The professor would view his assistant in quite a different light if he knew of the hours Lily had spent with him in the night.

Oliver held himself erect and would not dwell on the reactions of his body to very vivid images of those hours.

"How are your nerves this morning?" Professor Adler asked, leaning back in his chair and hanging on to the bottom of his waistcoat. "Perhaps a nip of something would be in order."

"My nerves are in fine form." In fact, they were shredded. "Sir, I am aware of the great trust you have—"

"Think nothing of it. I made no secret of my hopes. I am delighted you see things my way. Lily is a delightful girl, and will make a splendid wife."

At last the professor chose to speak of their conspiracy directly. "You have never explained why you chose me."

"Why?"

"We met casually enough. You still cannot say that you know a great deal about me." A powerful understatement. "When we met I was a stranger who came to a lecture, nothing more."

Professor Adler looked at him sharply. "I do not think I could fully explain myself to you this morning, perhaps not for many mornings, if at all. But I am, and have been, a good judge of character. I know an honest man when I meet one."

Oliver pushed his plate aside. He had no stomach for more food. These upright people had been fooled by him, and he did not admire himself for the deception.

"You are a good man, Oliver. I don't suggest you have nothing you would not prefer to forget, but your heart is fine. And you are exceedingly intelligent and learned. A quick, well-exercised mind is a gift to be treasured above all others. These are the things that made me choose you when I had no intention of choosing anyone at all."

"Thank you, sir," Oliver said quietly. Whatever happened, there must be a way to do as little harm as possible to the Adlers.

"I have an acute intuition," the professor continued. "I followed that intuition in what most men would consider a reckless fashion. Prove me right, Oliver. Prove me right."

He rose and went to the fireplace to pull the bell. Within moments Gambol, the Adlers' antique butler, arrived. Stooped so low he must look up to see his master, his wizened face lighted with the good humor he invariably displayed. "Good morning, Professor."

"Gambol," Adler said. "Please arrange for Miss Lily and Mrs. Fribble to join us."

"Mrs. Fribble?" Oliver said.

The professor's eyes twinkled. "What did you think I was talking about when I spoke of emotional excess? Not Lily, surely. The sooner, the better, Gambol. And please ask Mrs. Willis to provide fresh tea and so on."

Gambol left.

Oliver and the professor had spent only moments trying to think of some discussion to fill the silence when the door opened and Lily entered.

As Oliver stood, she smiled at him, and only him. She waved him back into his seat. The strands of braids looped at her ears were loosely executed, but she had tucked white rosebuds into each and the effect was charmingly young and fresh.

"You are pretty this morning," Professor Adler said, too heartily. "Fresh as those flowers in your hair, my dear."

"Thank you, Papa."

"Very pretty, Lily," Oliver said quietly. "Roses become you."

She blushed a little, but that wasn't enough to disguise that she was tired. Dark smudges underscored her expressive eyes. A morning dress of yellow muslin spotted with white had about it a limp quality. Not for the first time Oliver had the impression that Lily's clothes had seen a great deal of duty.

"That dress," the professor said, as if he heard Oliver's thoughts. "Have I seen it before?"

Lily fiddled with a width of blue lace tied around the waist. The lace did not at all complement the dress. "Myrtle was giving it away. She very kindly said I might have it. I do so hate all the fuss of dressmakers and so on, Papa. So I gratefully accepted it." She fingered the lace at her waist. "This was my idea. Something a little bright, I thought."

"Quite so," the professor said. "No doubt you will be the envy of all the young ladies hereabouts. What do you say, Oliver?"

"No doubt." What she wore was of no interest to him, other than as a measure of her nature. She was without vanity.

A thump preceded the appearance of Mrs. Willis, the housekeeper. She steadfastly refused to allow any of the younger maids to wait upon her employer at breakfast.

The thump had been the result of her leather-shod toe connecting with the door to fling it open. She was dressed in black from her silk cap to her shoes, and her plump face appeared gray, the expression sour.

She smacked a laden tray upon the sideboard and removed a large silver pot of tea, fresh toast, and two covered dishes to replace those grown cold.

Without a word, Mrs. Willis departed once more, pausing outside the door to hook it shut with a foot.

"There," the professor said. "Hot tea. You must keep your strength up, Lily."

"Why?"

"Um. Because you must. You are an energetic young woman and must feed that energy."

Lily's eyes met Oliver's briefly and passed on. He knew she was thinking what he was thinking: that they had *both* been extremely energetic early in the morning.

"Oliver tells me he has something to speak to me about," Professor Adler said. "Apparently it concerns you, and he asked that you be present."

He had asked no such thing, but this was not the time to argue.

"Me?" Lily carried a cup of tea to the table and sat down facing Oliver. She contrived to look completely innocent. "What could concern me?"

The charade must be carried out. "I know this is abrupt, unexpected—possibly even outrageous—but I have an idea I'd like to put forward."

"Oliver is a man of inspiration, Lily. He keeps me in constant suspense."

She kept her eyes on Oliver's face.

"He joined me early for breakfast and has done nothing but hint of some plan ever since. But he will not divulge this plan unless you are present."

"How mysterious," she said.

Oliver cleared his throat. He marveled at the professor's capacity for subtle theatrics. The man showed no sign of anything but sincere interest.

The door was opened by Gambol, who stood back to allow Mrs. Fribble to enter. Yawning, shoulders sagging dramatically, that lady trailed to the table and sat down. A rouched pink cap covered her shiny brown hair. She was, in fact, a study in pink bows and flounces. She rested her cheek on a palm and allowed her eyes to all but close.

"Good morning to you, Mrs. Fribble!" the professor boomed, sending Raven fleeing for a corner. "My dear, you look absolutely blooming."

At that Mrs. Fribble rallied somewhat to favor him with a wan smile. "Thank you, professor. Since I feel so poorly I can't imagine why I should appear blooming, but if I do, I'm delighted. I had hoped to sleep late in preparation for this important day. Of course, your summons meant I came at once."

"Tea, Aunt Fribble?" Lily asked, and, when the other woman only sighed, poured tea anyway and put it before her aunt. Lily also served a heaping plate of eggs, kippers, bacon, sausage, and potatoes.

Poor, poorly Mrs. Fribble set about demolishing the meal.

"Well, Oliver?" Professor Adler said. "We're in suspense, aren't we, Lily?"

"Indeed, Papa." That she was in suspense was in no question. It was not, however, lighthearted suspense. Her pale, worried face testified to her anxiety.

"That silly Myrtle Bumwallop called yesterday afternoon," Mrs. Fribble mumbled around a mouthful of food. "I told her we were in the midst of exceedingly important and private family business. Sent her packing."

"Aunt Fribble!" Lily started to rise, but dropped back

into her chair. She set her lips in a straight line. "I shall go to her today and apologize."

"Bit harsh, weren't you, Mrs. Fribble?" the professor asked mildly. "Nice young thing, Myrtle. Straightforward and unassuming. Her father's a good man, too. Sea captain, y'know."

Mrs. Fribble ignored the topic of the Bumwallops and turned her attention to Lily—and dropped her knife and fork with a clatter. "What are you wearing? Oh, Professor, I really must protest and ask for relief with her. She is a disaster. Oh! You have no shape. There is little to be done about that, but some artful arrangements would help." She leaned closer to Lily. "The material is quite gone in places. Worn through."

Lily raised her chin. "I'm going to sew on blue rosettes to match the belt."

Mrs. Fribble slapped a hand to her brow. "You will be the death of me. Immediately after breakfast you will give that thing to me and it shall be used as blacking rags."

"Your matter of importance, Oliver?" The professor sounded weary.

"Importance?" Mrs. Fribble said loudly. "The only matter of importance today is the sealing of Lily's betrothal to dear Lord Witmore. Oh, happy day. At last we are to secure the connections we deserve."

Professor Adler leaned toward Oliver. "Could you tell us now, please?"

"Yes." He coughed, and eased his collar with two fingers. "Sir, I have a request to make of you. That is, I wish you to consider a suggestion I'd like to make. There is something that has been on my mind and which is in your power to assist me with. If you were to find my idea has merit, you could facilitate its execution."

Lily knocked her cup over, spilling tea on the highly polished cherry table.

Mrs. Fribble cried out and used her napkin to mop up the mess. "There is no hope for you," she informed Lily. "We must make certain to achieve our ends before the dear earl discovers how devoid of grace you are."

"Oliver?" the professor said with desperation in his eyes.

"I should like . . . That is, it would give me the greatest pleasure if you should decide to look favorably upon my request to present a request." Dammit, he sounded like an idiot.

"Ask."

"Servants at the family table," Mrs. Fribble said, her mouth a pinched bud. "Never would have been tolerated in my parents' home."

"Professor Adler, I should like to ask for your daughter's hand in marriage."

With the delivery of the word "marriage," the black cat leaped up beside Mrs. Fribble's plate and the woman screamed.

The animal had attached itself to Oliver only days after his arrival in Come Piddle. She usually spent her days curled on his bed, and her nights stalking elsewhere.

"Ring for Gambol," Mrs. Fribble demanded, pressed to the back of her chair. "Have this creature disposed of."

"That creature is mine," Oliver said. "Ignore her and she'll go away."

Mrs. Fribble looked at him and all color drained slowly from her face. "What did you say?"

"I said the cat is mine and that if you ignore—"

"Before that. What did you say before that?"

"I asked the professor if he would consider allowing me to offer for his daughter's hand."

Mrs. Fribble's mouth slackened and fell open, then she pressed her hands to her bosom and looked from the professor to Lily, and back to the professor. "He wants to know if you would allow him to offer for Lily? He wants . . . Professor? Oh! I knew no good could come of taking a stranger into our midst and allowing him to have ideas above his station. Send him away. Send him away at once."

While she ranted, the cat calmly set about stripping flesh from the kippers on her plate.

"Calm yourself, Mrs. Fribble." Professor Adler regarded Oliver with profound seriousness. "You wish to marry my daughter? Is that what you have finally asked?"

"Yes, sir."

"Oh!" Mrs. Fribble moaned. "The world is gone mad."

"Lily, what have you to say about this?"

Any help from Lily was not to be forthcoming. She trembled visibly and stared at Oliver as if he could put words into her mouth.

"I know this is a surprise," Oliver said. "But if you think about it, sir, you'll see the idea has merit. Lily and I share a great many interests. We are both deeply fascinated by your work—and by the exploration of subjects that encourage debate and experimentation." His mouth would undo him entirely before long. "Isn't that so, Lily."

She nodded.

"That is enough," Mrs. Fribble said. "More than enough. Send him packing, Professor. Today of all days. I will not have him take the joy out of so great a celebration."

Speaking as if he neither heard nor saw Mrs. Fribble,

the professor crossed his arms and frowned deeply. "This is a matter to which I must give a great deal of thought. Marriage, hmm? To my daughter? Not often a man gets two offers in two days. Goes to show what a desirable baggage you are, Lily Adler."

Lily smiled at that.

"Yes, well," the professor continued, "I shall go away and consider this request of yours, Oliver. I must say, you amaze me."

When the older man rose, Oliver stood also, and remained standing until the door closed behind the professor.

"Well!" Mrs. Fribble slammed her open hand down on the table, making her plate jump. The cat also jumped, but quickly continucd taking advantage of the situation.

"Please don't excite yourself, Aunt," Lily said, so softly her voice was barely audible. "May I pour you some fresh tea?"

"You may go to your room at once and get ready. I'm certain your father will want us to accompany him to Fell Manor at noon. Since that is but a few hours away, you'd best get started, although I'm sure I don't think it will be enough time to make anything of you."

Oliver made fists in his lap. He longed to tell this carelessly cruel creature his opinion of her.

"And you," Mrs. Fribble said, pointing at Oliver. "You have shown your true colors. I warned the professor that you were an opportunist, but he wouldn't listen. Now you have helped me prove that I am right. If you've any sense you won't wait for him to come and tell you to leave, you'll start packing of your own accord."

"Aunt," Lily said. "Aunt, please don't insult Oliver."

"Lily—"

"No," Lily told the woman firmly. "He is my friend and I respect and like him—very much. When you insult him, you insult me."

The door opened again and the professor reentered. "Yes," he said.

Oliver rose to his feet. "I'm sorry, sir?"

"I said I must go away to consider. I went. I considered. My answer is yes, you may marry my daughter."

Mrs. Fribble screamed.

With that, the cat dropped a kipper carcass into the woman's lap.

Chapter Sixteen

Within the hour the Reverend Mr. Eustace Godwin arrived. With him came Rosemary, who was so excited as to be even more silent than usual. She entered the drawing room where Lily waited with distraught Aunt Fribble, and rushed to clutch Lily's hand.

"Mr. Godwin," Aunt Fribble said in a weak, high whine. "I cannot tell you how relieved I am to see you. Finally a voice of reason in the midst of . . . Oh, Mr. Godwin, I can scarcely bring myself to speak of the unspeakable that has occurred here."

Papa followed Mr. Godwin, and Oliver followed Papa.

Lily looked at Oliver and could only just draw a breath. He had actually taken this step for her, to save her from Witless. He'd told her he loved her, yet she didn't dare believe it could be true. Regardless, he had assured her that he would be a happy man to marry her and spend his days at Blackmoor Hall, where he said he had found contentment.

He had said he loved her.

She felt light-headed and closed her eyes.

"Are you well, Lily?" Rosemary whispered. "I am so excited. He is the most handsome man I have ever seen."

"He is the best man in the world," Lily told her quietly. "The most honorable, and the most honest. He makes his heart and his conscience open to me, and he is determined that we shall have a good life together."

"I just knew it," Rosemary said, clutching Lily's arm. "From the moment I saw him I was certain there was something singular about him. For a while I almost thought I knew him, although I couldn't think from where. But now I know what I felt. I felt his goodness and had a premonition. Oh, do not ever tell Eustace I had one of those. That would not please him at all. But I did. I had a premonition that he would become very important in your life. Perhaps it was because you protested so much that you did not like him. They do say such protestations often lead to quite the reverse."

Lily regarded her friend with amazement. In all the years of their closeness, Rosemary had never made such a long speech.

"I asked Mr. Godwin to join us," Papa said. "We shall wish to proceed with all haste."

"Haste?" Aunt Fribble flopped onto the chaise and covered her eyes. "Where is my hartshorn?"

"Is there some reason for haste?" Mr. Godwin asked, his tone all suspicion. "Is there, perhaps, something I should know?"

"Not at all." Papa slapped the man on the back. "I simply mean that when two young people are in love, there is no reason to delay. Am I right, Oliver?"

"Right."

"We'd be obliged if you'd have your little talk with the happy couple, Reverend. Then, if you please, we'll ask you to announce the banns. Today is Saturday. That means we can plan for the wedding, hmm, three weeks and a day from tomorrow. Perfect."

Lily's thoughts revolved wildly, and refused to be complete in any way. Three weeks and a day and she was to be married to Oliver? And then she would be safe from Lord Witmore forever?

She would be Oliver's wife.

"Will that please you, Lily?" Oliver asked. He smiled at her, that smile that was part devilish, part gentle, part questioning.

"It pleases me very well," she told him.

"Then we'll proceed, Mr. Godwin. I believe there are formalities to be completed."

Rosemary's brother set a Bible upon the mantel, turned his rear to the fire, and lifted the flared skirt of his shiny black coat. Despite the approach of summer, the weather was still chilly, and Papa insisted fires should be lit every day until it grew warmer.

"Reverend," Aunt Fribble said. She rose laboriously from the chaise and stared beseechingly into his face. "There is a great deal that needs to be examined here. Oh, yes, indeed, a great deal. I . . . That is, we must look into this man's connections. He has none."

"In which case," Papa said without expression, "there's no point in looking into them, is there?"

Not to be silenced, Aunt Fribble continued. "There must be no question of posting banns without a great deal of careful investigation. He's an American, you know."

"His adoptive parents were English," Papa said. "Oliver has returned to the home of those good people and intends to make this his country."

"And the manner in which he came to Come Piddle is exceedingly strange." Fribble puffed up and trembled with agitation. "I have thought it suspect from the start. Now I am sure. He is a fortune hunter, nothing more. Why else would such a man be here a matter of weeks, then ask for the hand of someone like Lily?"

"Mrs. Fribble," Oliver said with a coolness that would have stopped Lily from further discussion. "I must ask you to consider what you say before you open your mouth."

"What? You dare to—"

"Mrs. Fribble," Papa said. "You and I will discuss matters later. Perhaps I have been less than fair in not taking time to speak with you alone. We shall do so later in the day."

"But we must leave for Fell Manor!" Fribble said. "Now. Or we shall be late."

"Heavy indeed is the burden that will not be moved," Papa remarked. "Mr. Godwin? Can we proceed?"

"Lily?" Mr. Godwin concentrated his pale blue eyes on her. "I would not be doing my duty if I didn't point out that your views on the married state are well known hereabouts. You have frequently been heard to say that you hold men in low esteem and that you would never consider marrying."

She smiled a little. "I have said as much many times." Now she looked at Oliver, whose dark brows were raised in question. "But that was before I met Oliver. Now my feelings are changed."

"Would you care to explain how he changed your mind?"

"None of your damn business," Oliver said, drawing gasps from Mr. Godwin and Fribble. Rosemary giggled, then looked embarrassed.

Lily sought to rescue the moment. "In my dealings with

Oliver I have found him intelligent, charming, and considerate. We share a great many interests—including a deep desire to reveal our mysteries to each other."

This time Rosemary snatched a pitcher of water and poured a glass, which she drank noisily. Lily waited until her friend had stopped drinking before sending her a secret and deliberately wicked grimace.

"Mysteries," the reverend said, sniffing. "One hopes those mysteries will be found pleasing to you both."

"We're assured they will," Oliver told him. "Now, if you would inform us of our responsibilities in these events, we won't keep you further."

"First I must dispense with all of my responsibilities, sir. And it is my responsibility to mention that there may be more to you than meets the eye."

Lily felt Oliver grow still. She studied him closely. He seemed to hold his breath and wait. Her own heart made a revolution.

"A man is judged by the company he keeps and by the places in which he keeps that company."

"Spit it out, man," Papa said.

"Probably nothing of importance," Mr. Godwin said, but he folded his hands and turned the corners of his mouth up in an expression of malicious anticipation. "Your friend, Mr. Worth. I assume your employer knows and approves of your friend?"

There was a short silence before Papa said, "What friend would that be?"

"Ah." Mr. Godwin raised his head and looked down his long nose. "Perhaps it's as well I thought to mention the matter. An exceedingly richly dressed man. An arrogant manner. Evidently in some position to command a great deal of respect from Mr. Worth. Or was it fear?"

Lily held her breath.

"Speak plainly," Oliver said. "You make no sense."

"Don't toy with me. Kindly give the identity of the fellow with whom you were drinking large quantities of ale at The Faint Heart."

"Nick?" Oliver said. "You mean Nick Westmoreland?"

"If he is the man who so troubled you, and caused you to abandon caution in the matter of sobriety, then yes, he is the man. I would ask you to explain your connection with him."

Mrs. Fribble wrung her hands and bobbed on her toes. "A drinking man," she babbled. "And he has a conspirator. I told you, Professor. He is not to be trusted. He has a conspirator in this plan of his."

"What plan would that be?" Oliver was deathly cool now.

"Why, to find a way into our pockets, of course."

"Your pockets, Mrs. Fribble?" There was menace in Oliver's light brown eyes. "And how exactly would my marriage to Lily gain my access to your pockets?"

"Ah," Papa said. "Logic grows weary of lofty depths."

Lily looked for some sign of offense in Fribble but found none.

"The matter of this Westmoreland," Mr. Godwin said. "Do you deny a clandestine meeting with him?"

"We met at The Faint Heart, and in full view of any who chanced to be there—including yourself, sir."

Godwin cast about the company. "Is Mr. Westmoreland known to all of you? Did Mr. Worth bring him to meet you?"

No one spoke.

"As I thought."

"Nick Westmoreland is a very old friend," Oliver said.

A white line formed around his mouth. "In fact, he was my brother-in-law. My sister, Anne, was his wife until her sudden death from a fever."

Propelled by her longing to comfort him, Lily went to his side and threaded her hands around his arm. She whispered, "Dear Oliver. Don't."

"Nick is in England on business," he continued. "In fact, he is staying in Salisbury and, if the professor will allow it, I should like to ask him to come and meet all of you."

Papa came suddenly and forcefully to life. "Of course, old chap, of course. I'm sorry to hear about your sister. We all are. Have this friend come and stay with us. Anytime. For as long as he likes. Any friend of yours is a friend of ours, right, Lily?"

"Oh, yes," Lily said, wishing she could reach into the place where Oliver hid his pain and soothe it away. "Send for him at once, Oliver."

"There's to be a wedding," Rosemary said. "Your wedding, Lily. Oh, happy day."

"A day to be rued," Fribble muttered. "A day to be rued if it cannot be averted. But do not listen to me. Only ask me why I didn't manage to stop it after it has occurred. Ruination will follow. Mark my words, ruination will follow."

"Can we rely upon you to attend to the formalities, Mr. Godwin?" Papa asked. He did not appear amused. Lily knew him well enough to recognize one of his rare, but contained, angry moods.

"Mr. Godwin?" Fribble said, a plea in her voice and in her eyes. "Our future is in your hands."

"Trust, my dear." Taking his Bible, Godwin tucked it beneath his arm and executed a deep bow to Fribble and another to Papa. "It is well you summoned me here today. You will need my help in the days to come more than you can know."

"Godwin," Papa said. "Stop this drivel. Either make yourself clear, or go about your business. And don't forget to whom you owe your living."

Papa had never been a man to hold matters of finance over the heads of others. That he did so now proved the depth of his disgust with Mr. Godwin. Lily could not bear to look at Rosemary, for she knew her friend would be mortified.

"It is because I owe my living to you that I would be doing less than my duty if I didn't protect your interests, Professor Adler."

Oliver's eyes narrowed on the clergyman's face, but he held his peace.

"I have no proof as yet," Mr. Godwin said. "But I have my suspicions."

"Godwin!" Papa roared.

"I shall excuse your harsh treatment of me because you are upset," Eustace Godwin said. He pointed a short forefinger at Oliver. "Beware of this man. And before you give him your daughter, be sure he is not marrying her to use her . . . *and* that he is who he says he is."

No one moved.

"Or perhaps," Mr. Godwin said in echoing tones, "that he is *not* someone whom he has not said that he is."

If there'd been time—and a graceful manner to arrange such a thing—Oliver would have visited Nick alone in Salisbury before descending with Lily on his arm. But since he'd felt obliged to leave Come Piddle immediately after Eustace Godwin's barely disguised comments against his character, Oliver had not had time to warn Nick of the visit. As it was, he could only pray his friend would show his customary quick comprehension of a new situation.

With Rosemary Godwin as chaperone, Professor Adler had gladly dispatched Lily and Oliver to visit the friend about whom Eustace Godwin had made such ominous suggestions.

Traveling in the Adlers' burgundy-colored barouche, drawn by a serviceable pair of grays, Oliver did his best to appear interested in Rosemary Godwin's occasional comments. That she only spoke to relieve Lily's tense silence, and his own, was obvious.

"See the poppies," Miss Godwin said to Lily. She was blond, blue-eyed, and birdlike, and her hands fluttered incessantly as she glanced from one to the other of her companions in evident high anxiety.

"Poppies are a favorite of mine," Oliver said when Lily failed to respond. "You seem to know a great deal about wildflowers, Miss Godwin."

She turned almost as red as the profusion of poppies spread like a carpet across the field before them. "A little," she said.

"The countryside here is beautiful. In America many landscapes are on a larger, perhaps a harsher scale. Beautiful, certainly, but without the softness of England's vistas."

"I should like to see America," Rosemary said.

At that Lily gave her entire attention to her friend. "You should like to see America, Rosemary? Why, you amaze me. You have never expressed interest in going even as far as London."

Rosemary's fair skin glowed brilliantly under Oliver

and Lily's scrutiny. "It was just that Mr. Worth made it sound interesting. I'm sure I shouldn't really like to make such a great journey."

The coach bowled on through a fine, sunny day. Oliver watched the names of villages come and go with a growing sense of foreboding. Middle Wallop followed Nether Wallop, but they made a westward turn before reaching Upper Wallop. From his conversation with the coachman he knew their arrival in Salisbury could not be far off.

"Cuckoo flowers," Rosemary remarked, her voice strained. "I've always liked their delicate pink. They grow by the hedges in the churchyard."

Perhaps Nick would be out.

Desperation made a man grasp for desperately frail hopes. In a town the size of Salisbury, although many times larger than Come Piddle, locating Nick could not be an impossible task.

In the coming days, Witmore might make some move that would help Oliver reach his goal.

Could Witmore be looking for something in his father's rooms? Could whatever he might be looking for be a clue to the reason Oliver's father had been banished from his family's bosom, and from England?

"The spire!" Lily pressed close to the window, and the rare sight of an unguarded smile lighted her face. "Just. I just see the top of it. How exciting."

And the threat grew nearer and nearer. He did love to look upon the marvel of the face some called plain, but which he could not see as other than radiant. When Lily was animated, her gray eyes became very dark and shining—and her wide mouth was all curves, curves that brought memories of how they felt when he kissed them.

Some might consider the path he'd chosen reckless. In

the absence of anyone who remembered his father, and the events surrounding his departure from England, his own investigation might lead to nothing. By marrying Lily, a permanent attachment to Blackmoor would be formed. He studied her. Once taken, this step could never be reversed. Would he be able to live among the trappings of his father's beginnings and find peace—whether or not he accomplished what he'd come to accomplish?

Witmore, that sickening man he'd as soon never have met, let alone be forced to recognize as a relation, didn't want Lily because he felt any affection for her. He wanted Blackmoor, of that there was no doubt. But—and here he was certain of his reasoning—the man also wanted complete freedom of access to the Hall.

Oliver could not shake the conviction that he and his cousin might well be searching for the same thing. Oliver wished to find some means to discover and reveal a truth that would clear his father's name. Witmore's aim was bound to be different. Could it, in fact, be the reverse? Could Witmore fear a revelation?

Hell and damnation, he was adrift. At least Witmore must know what it was he sought. Oliver's task was to search out someone who had been in Come Piddle in his father's time, someone who knew something, and who would be prepared to speak of it—someone who might not even exist.

"I suppose all the staff are new?" he asked, so suddenly he was aghast at his own clumsiness.

"What staff?" Lily said. "You mean our staff?"

Oliver forced a chuckle. "I can't imagine what made me think of that."

"Probably because there is such a feeling of things having been in place forever at the Hall," Lily said. "The staff has been with us as long as I remember. I believe they were retained when Mama and Papa bought Blackmoor. Why do you ask?"

"I was thinking how very taxing it must be to run such an establishment." He must watch his tongue. "There. Now you can see it. The cathedral. A jewel in this light."

"A star," Lily said. "See how it glitters gold. How much labor it must have taken to build such a thing."

"No doubt." He'd told Nick he would visit days ago. The first order of business would be to head off any angry outburst his old friend might make.

Salisbury was a large town, a market town. Fortunately today was not market day, though, and the bustle in the busy streets was no more than would be expected in any township of its size. Gigs plied in and out between hand-drawn carts, wheels and horses' hoofs settings up a grind and clatter. Rows of shops showed off their wares in windows that sparkled in the sunshine.

"A prosperous place," Rosemary remarked, referring, Oliver presumed, to the well-dressed people of Salisbury.

They approached the close that surrounded the cathedral, and drove, in fact, toward St. Anne's Gate, but the driver remembered Oliver's directions well and turned off at Vestry Lane.

"What is Mr. Westmoreland's business?" Lily asked.

The only surprise was that she hadn't thought to ask earlier. "I should like you to ask Nick that yourself. He will appreciate your interest in him."' *Coward.*

"How pretty it all is. I love the little gardens. So many daisies. And peonies! Such beautiful peonies and snapdragons."

Oliver ceased to listen to the young ladies' rhapsody of the beauty of Salisbury's gardens. The coach ground to a halt before a house somewhat larger than the others, and the driver jumped down to place the steps. He helped Lily and Rosemary to alight.

"Wait here, please," Oliver told the man.

He followed Lily and Rosemary through the front gate of number ten Vestry Lane with a sense of doom. Reaching past them, he raised the brass knocker and let it fall once.

Godwin's innuendoes had shaken him. There could be no way for the man to know Oliver's true identity, yet he certainly behaved as if he knew something.

Oliver recalled Godwin's threat if anyone were to threaten Lily's happiness, he, Godwin, would protect her even if God failed to do so. Pompous ass.

But what would happen when Oliver was unmasked? And he must eventually be unmasked. What would Lily think of his honor and honesty then? How would she tolerate that she'd married a man guilty of what she abhorred—lying?

No sound came from inside the house. Lily said, "Perhaps Mr. Westmoreland isn't at home? We didn't send word."

"Foolish of me," Oliver said, thinking that he should be grateful. He would take the ladies home, then return and prepare Nick.

Hurried footsteps halted his planning. The door was opened by a woman who appeared to be in her thirties. In her thirties, with a body no man would fail to speculate over, and a face any woman would envy.

"Good afternoon," she said, her voice cultured. "May I help you?"

Taken aback, Oliver checked the number of the house

again. But it was still ten. "We're looking for Mr. Nicholas Westmoreland."

The woman immediately took the measure of Lily and Rosemary. Oliver saw her decide there was no competition there. "He didn't say he was expecting guests."

So, Oliver thought, after so short a stay, Nick had already found himself a companion in whom he confided his comings and goings. "He must have forgotten. I'm Oliver Worth, his oldest friend. From Boston. This lady," he indicated Lily, "is my fiancée. And this is her friend."

"I see." The woman relaxed and stood back. "I'll tell Nick—Mr. Westmoreland you're here."

She'd barely ushered them into an adequate hall in tasteful shades of green and cream when heavy footfalls sounded. Nick descended. In shirtsleeves and waistcoat, but without a coat or cravat, he appeared disheveled.

At the sight of Oliver, he halted and his expression became one of fury. "Where in God's name have you been, man? Our whole bloody world is falling apart, and you're busy dallying with more of your never-ending supply of doxies."

Oliver groaned aloud.

Chapter Seventeen

Fell Manor was pleasant enough, Emmaline Fribble supposed—if one was forced to live in reduced circumstances. Having lived in as grand a home as Blackmoor Hall, any abode would be reduced.

Of gray, ivy-smothered stone, the facade was plain. A square block of a place with a great many ugly and crumbling gargoyles—and a line of stone urns that should be filled with flowers, but weren't, on either side of the uncompromising front door.

Oh, dear, there were probably no more than twenty bedrooms in the house. Three stories of windows not much wider than arrow slits in a castle's battlements. Well, not everyone could enjoy the best.

In the Beaumonts' time—Emmaline considered their time to have been before they were forced to sell Blackmoor Hall—in their time Fell Manor had been the dower house. The present Earl of Witmore's mother had died when he was a small child. That arrogant Lady Virtue's mother, already widowed once, had been the old earl's second wife, but she, too, had not lived long enough to take up residence in the dower house. Fell Manor had been empty and in poor repair when dear Lord Witmore had moved in.

Lord Witmore. Emmaline closed her eyes and shivered deliciously. If only she, rather than Lily, could further his ambitions.

"Emmaline Fribble, your future is in your hands today," she said aloud, standing beside the shabby buggy she'd been obliged to use since that ungrateful wretch, Lily, had taken the barouche to Salisbury. To Salisbury with that man! "In my hands, and I shall not fail."

"Remain," she told Leonard, the truculent wretch of a groom she'd pressed into service to drive her here. "And see what you can do to improve the appearance of this conveyance. It is a disgrace."

Leonard turned his insolent face toward her and smiled. He *smiled*! He had sun-bleached curls grown far too long, and a face considerably too comely for his station.

He winked at her!

Emmaline raised her chin and marched toward the manor. Such audacity. Really, one couldn't rely on the quality of servants these days.

She tossed her head and stalked up the front steps of the manor. A pull on the bell produced a hollow bong from inside. A huge man opened the door.

"I'm Mrs. Emmaline—"

"Fribble."

"Yes, well, I've come—"

"T'see themselves. They said ye would. Close the door after ye."

Left with her mouth open, Emmaline took a while to remember herself and step inside. The great, rude creature shambled away. He wore a green velvet coat so old it shone at the elbows.

And a kilt!

His knees showed!

His legs resembled the strong trunks of elm trees.

Emmaline pressed a hand over her heart. So many strange events in so short a time. This must be some relative of the Beaumonts—nothing else could account for his behavior.

"Excuse me," she said, hurrying to catch up. She must know all about the Beaumonts. "Which branch of the family are you—"

"MacLewd's the name. I'd not known ye were acquainted with my family."

"No," Emmaline said, trotting sideways beside him. "Of the Beaumonts, I mean. Which branch of the Beaumonts—"

"Am I related to? None." He frowned at her, drawing down impressive, shaggy brows as red as his shock of hair. "I'm a Scot, madam. The Beaumonts are no part Scot—more's the pity for them. I'm the butler."

Amazing. Outrageous. "I'm—"

"The female who lives over at the Hall with the Adlers."

"Yes. Mrs. Emmaline—"

"Fribble. So we said."

Emmaline felt quite faint. "There has been a slight change—"

"In plans. Aye, we know. I've listened t'his lordship settin' up such a racket for hours now. Ever since the professor himself dinna come."

"Oh." Suddenly afraid of facing poor Lord Witmore's wrath, Emmaline paused. "Is Lord Witmore more composed yet?"

"No."

"You mean he's still in a less than pleasant mood?"

"Aye, ye could say that. Here, see for yoursel'." Without bothering to knock, MacLewd flung open a door into a parlor made murky by a haze of pungent smoke. "Good luck t'ye. Ye'll need it."

The next moment Emmaline was left with Lord Witmore, Sir Cecil Laycock, and Lady Virtue. The three lounged on purple velvet divans, Sir Cecil and Lady Virtue on the same divan. Emmaline drew a shaky breath and advanced. The impropriety of the scene shocked her, but she smiled, filling that smile with as much sympathy as she could accomplish.

"Good afternoon," Emmaline said, executing a deep curtsy. "I don't know what you must think of us, but I am come to assure you that there has been a most unfortunate complication, but that it will only be a matter of time before it is corrected."

Sir Cecil sucked on an odd tube attached to a tall brass bottle of some kind. Emmaline had never seen such a smoking device before. While she watched, Lady Virtue took the tube and sucked before leaning on Sir Cecil in a most intimate and undignified manner. The two appeared relaxed. Lady Virtue was in disgraceful *dishabille*. Emmaline saw where Sir Cecil's hand rested, and averted her eyes.

"Do you remember what I told you, Mrs. Fribble?" Lord Witmore said. There was nothing relaxed about him.

Emmaline swallowed nervously. "I came because I knew you would be wondering what could have occurred. Despite the professor's note, I'm sure you cannot be other than confused by current events."

"I asked if you remembered what I told you."

She swallowed again. "About what, exactly?"

The speed with which he closed the space between

them brought a shriek to her lips. The earl promptly pinched her cheek—hard.

Tears filled Emmaline's eyes and overflowed.

"That was a warning," the earl said. "Do not trifle with me, or you will suffer. And I remind you that you and I have already had certain conversations. It would not be difficult for me to report those conversations as having been initiated by you. The result would be the end of your comfortable arrangement at the Adlers'."

"Why?" Emmaline whispered. "Why are you treating me like this? I came to offer you my help—and to comfort you."

"Help?" He made an insolent assessment of her from head to toe. "Comfort? You are nothing. How can you help? And what is it you think I require help with?"

A flare of defiance straightened her back. "With getting what you want. You aren't doing too well on your own, are you?"

"Aha!" Lord Witmore fell back a step and posed with his hands on his hips. "Is this spirit I see? Well, you may be of some use to me after all. I told you, Emmaline, that if you assisted me in my quest to marry Lily Adler, and to secure ownership of Blackmoor Hall, you would be well compensated."

"Yes. And you shall get what you want, your lordship. That's why I'm here, to assure you that if you are patient, this present inconvenience will be disposed of."

"Inconvenience? What do you mean, inconvenience?"

She trembled. "The, er, matter that has precipitated the present situation. That man."

"*Man?*" Lord Witmore stood over her, stood so close she must raise her chin to see his face. And a very red and angry face it was. "What man? What are you talking about?"

"The, er—"

"Leave the dowd be, Reggie," Lady Virtue said. She waved at Emmaline. "Come and have a little something for your nerves, dear. Come and sit with Cecil and me."

Emmaline drew her paisley shawl about her and clung to her velvet reticule with both hands. "I think I'd better go," she said, taking breaths through her mouth. "I came to do you a service, Lord Witmore, but my efforts are not appreciated."

Lord Witmore shocked her yet again by draping an arm around her shoulders in a most familiar fashion and guiding her to the door. Then he led her into the foyer—where the giant, MacLewd, stood with his arms crossed and a watchful expression in his dark eyes.

"Mrs. Fribble and I have business to conduct in the black boudoir," Lord Witmore told his butler.

Emmaline's heart beat so fast and hard, she feared she might expire on the spot. "Really, Lord Witmore, I should return to Blackmoor. They'll wonder where I am."

"Something tells me that is a lie. I believe you made sure your absence would not be noted."

At a leisurely pace he took her into a small boudoir bedecked in black damask. Silver etchings relieved black silk-hung walls. Tasseled silver cords edged cushions heaped upon a chaise. Similar cushions were tucked into plushly upholstered chairs and stacked before the fireplace. Even the floors were of such dark wood as to appear almost black.

"Sit," Lord Witmore instructed, indicating the chaise. "We have much to discuss, you and I. And we shall take as long as we have to take."

There was no escape. She would remain until he decided she might go. "Yes," she said faintly.

"*Sit,*" Lord Witmore ordered, but he didn't wait for her to do so. Rather, he grasped her by the waist and plunked her on the chaise.

He was so forceful. So *manly*. Emmaline arranged her skirts and blinked rapidly at him—she'd always been told she had particularly fine eyes.

Lord Witmore laughed. "You're a very handsome woman, Emmaline. May I call you Emmaline?"

Her heart fluttered. He was courting her. "Of course." She straightened her back and let the shawl fall about her elbows. After all, he was right, she was still a woman to make men's heads turn—regardless of what that horrid Lady Virtue said.

Lord Witmore rested a hand on the back of the chaise and looked down at her. "I have been forced to hide my true feelings, Emmaline. Expediency is a cruel taskmaster. But I cannot deny myself further. You and I are sophisticated adults. We will find a way to have it all, my dear, everything we want. And I want you."

She grew hot again and lowered her lashes. When he loosed the ribbons that secured her bonnet, she jumped. He set the bonnet aside.

"A man, you said." He gazed into her face. "Back there when we were speaking of matters at Blackmoor. What man would that be?"

"With my help, he can be stopped. Eustace is on our side. All we have to do is find some proof that the creature isn't what he says he is. Perhaps that he's a criminal, which he may well be. Then the professor will send him packing soon enough."

"Look at me, Emmaline."

She did so.

"Dearest, I want you to concentrate long enough to tell me exactly why the professor sent a message canceling his appointment with me."

Emmaline nodded her head.

"Do so," Lord Witmore said.

"I do believe Professor Adler apologized, didn't he?"

"Yes."

"And said he would come to you for a discussion?"

"Yes."

She played with the fringe on her shawl. "But if we wait, it will be too late."

"It will not be too late, because it can't be," he said. "If I do not get what I want, I might as well be dead. Neither of us wants that pass to come, do we, especially since someone might accidentally reveal your part in the affair?"

"No. I mean, yes. Oh, dear."

His hand, settling softly on her shoulder, brought a soundless gasp to Emmaline's lips. Slowly, exquisitely, he bent until his mouth all but touched hers.

She raised her chin and closed her eyes, and waited.

He would kiss her.

Emmaline sighed—and waited.

"I mustn't," Lord Witmore said.

Her eyes opened. "What?"

"I mustn't, must I?"

"Oh, yes. Oh, yes, you must."

"You insist, Emmaline?"

"I do."

She nodded wildly. Absolutely, she wanted him to.

"Tell me. Say it aloud. I want you to love me. *Say* it." His eyes were so close to hers, they looked fuzzy.

"You need me. Remember that," he told her.

"I need you," she panted.

"Say that you want me to do this."

"I want you to do this."

"Louder. You want me to make you my own."

"I will do anything if you will make me your own. Oh, Reginald, I am yours."

"Good. Now, concentrate if you can. What man is this you speak of? This man who can thwart what I must have."

"Oliver—Worth. The servant. The American nothing."

He kneeled beside her and inclined his head to gaze deeply into her eyes. "What has the secretary to do with me, dearest?"

"He asked to marry Lily."

The earl's attention shifted to her mouth. He passed his tongue over his own lips. "He asked to marry her? And Adler sent him away, of course."

She began to shake with longing.

Rising to his elbows, he studied her with narrowed eyes. "Adler sent him away?"

"No," she whispered. "He gave his permission."

"That is impossible. He had already agreed to come to me to make a settlement."

"Not exactly," she said. "I think you assumed he had."

The earl smiled, and Emmaline wasn't certain she cared for that smile. "You and I have an agreement," he said. "I told you that if you made sure there was no resistance to my marrying Lily Adler and regaining what is rightfully mine, you would become a rich woman."

"Yes, you did."

"What I didn't tell you was that if my plan fails, I will

be destroyed. And you, my dear one, will be destroyed with me."

"Why?" she managed to ask. "All I can do is my best. I promised I'd do my best and I have. And I will."

"Good. You say Godwin is on our side. He doesn't like me. Why should he be on our side?"

"He's on his own side," Emmaline said, all discretion gone. "He desires to have Lily for himself."

"Godwin wants to marry Lily Adler?"

"He wants to inherit Blackmoor."

"How do you know this?"

"He told me." Really, she did wish they didn't have to speak of these things now, when Reginald had only just revealed his true feelings for her. "He considers me a confidante, and I have encouraged him to talk to me in case he may become useful to us. To you and me, Reginald."

Reginald gave another of his strange smiles. "Very wise. But I would ask you to avoid any reciprocal confidence."

Emmaline relaxed a little. She took a daring step and rested her brow on his shoulder. "You may trust me in all things."

"I'm sure I can. We will not concern ourselves too deeply with Godwin. He will be easily enough controlled. I take it the wedding date has been set?"

This, Emmaline thought, was how true bliss felt. "Three weeks and a day."

His jaw flexed against her temple. "The longest time Mr. Worth may hope to remain in England. How sad. And he does appear to like it here. Where is he now?"

"In Salisbury."

Witmore frowned. "Salisbury? For what purpose?"

Emmaline raised her head to look at him. "To visit a friend. Eustace saw him with this man at—"

"The Faint Heart." A vicious grimace twisted the man's features. "Of course. I was too foxed to know what I was about, but I remember. I met the friend that night. And I let Worth know I was onto him. Not that I thought he had designs on getting the girl—only a way into the old man's purse. Damn."

"You should not overset yourself, my lord," she ventured.

He ignored her. "So that was the way of it. And Lily? Where is she, and what does she think of this?"

"She is glad. She's with him in Salisbury."

Lord Witmore framed her face with hard fingers. "Her father allowed her to go to Salisbury with a man—unchaperoned?"

"Rosemary Godwin is with them."

"Praise be for that. At least the opportunist cannot claim to have compromised her. But there is no time to waste. You will do exactly what I tell you to do. Do you understand?"

"Yes."

"If you do, I shall make sure you want for nothing."

"Thank you. How will you get rid of Mr. Worth?"

"By finding and revealing his weakness. Every man has a great weakness, and his will become clear to me. His very presence here is a mystery which may give me what I need."

Emmaline could scarcely breathe. "What if you don't find this weakness?"

"You had best pray that I do."

He kissed her. His mouth covered hers with the commanding strength she would have expected. Emmaline grew weak and trembling.

Then the kiss was over, the wonderful, masterful kiss that held so much promise. At last a man of position and importance had recognized her for the boon she could be to him, and for the passion that waited in her breast, had waited there for this moment, and to be set free.

She kept her eyes shut and sighed, allowing her smiling lips to show him the depth of her satisfaction.

"There, my dear. You have had what you so wanted. And you must help make very certain I am not thwarted in what I *must* have. If I am, you will be in a most unenviable position. You will be revealed as a woman of loose morals."

"No!"

"Imagine what the professor would think about this little interlude. He would throw you out if he knew you'd been with the man who is to be his daughter's husband."

She tried to get up. "You wouldn't tell him."

Lord Witmore held her still. "Oh, but I would if I had to. But I won't have to. You are my ultimate ally, sweeting. I only mention these things so that you will not forget how important they are."

Relief made her giggle. "I know you would never tell anyone about us." She was such a cake sometimes. "After all, they wouldn't believe you, would they?"

Lord Witmore laughed and stood up. "You heard everything Mrs. Fribble said, didn't you, MacLewd?"

The red-haired beast lounged inside the room, his features impassive. "Aye, m'lord, I heard. And I saw."

She screamed, and pressed her hands to her cheeks.

"Quite a sight, too, m'lord, if I may say so. A fiery piece ye've there."

"Fiery indeed, MacLewd. You can go now."

Once they were alone, Emmaline scrambled to her feet and pulled her shawl about her shoulders.

"I expected you to come, Mrs. Fribble. In fact, as soon as I received the professor's note I knew you would. I knew something must have occurred to threaten my plans, and that meant your plans were also threatened. I planned what just occurred. And I enjoyed it almost as much as you did. It's a good thing that I find you so predictable."

She gifted him with a haughty stare. "And I find you delightfully satisfying. I'll look forward to our next encounter." He would not cow her, and anyway, she had every intention of enjoying his delightful kisses again.

"It will be your task to help me isolate this man, Worth," Lord Witmore said. "Then I shall discover what he fears most and use it against him."

Emmaline snatched up her bonnet and crammed it on her head.

"You agree that you have no choice but to assist me?"

"No choice." And she would do what she must to protect herself and further her interests.

"Good. Go now and wait for my instructions. Oliver Worth will leave Hampshire before three weeks and a day have elapsed."

"He cannot be allowed to marry Lily," she said, fumbling with the bonnet ribbons. "If he did, we'd never see a penny of the professor's money."

Lord Witmore caught her arm and held it painfully. "You didn't listen to me. Worth will leave before three weeks and a day have elapsed. If he cooperates, he will leave alive."

Chapter Eighteen

"Doxies," Rosemary whispered into Lily's ear, "are women who are no better than they ought to be."

The two of them sat in the carriage outside number ten Vestry Lane, waiting for Oliver to take his leave of his rude friend.

"Indeed it does," Lily said, smarting from humiliation even as she prayed her faith in Oliver was not misplaced. "But more offensive than the suggestion is the idea that Mr. Nicholas Westmoreland thinks we are too stupid to know what he called us."

"Hush," Rosemary implored, peering anxiously from side to side.

Lily patted her hand. "There is nobody to hear us. Imagine, if we hadn't set about informing ourselves on these matters, we should have been ignorant of that man's meaning. I have a good mind to tell the coachman to drive off without Oliver Worth."

"Oh, you cannot!"

"Why? A man whose best friend assumes any ladies in his presence are no better than they ought to be?"

"You can be so harsh, Lily. Mr. Worth is a good man. I feel his goodness—as do you if you will allow yourself to be honest."

Lily poked a finger through a very small hole in the dress Myrtle had given her. "I'm going to sew blue rosettes on this," she said. "Blue satin. Bright blue. Don't you think they will be dashing?"

"I think you're changing the subject. Just as you always do when you know you must confess you are wrong."

Was she? "Why do you suppose Oliver found it necessary to dispatch us back to the carriage so that he might speak with his friend alone? Could it be that he was afraid Mr. Westmoreland would make some even more revealing comments about Oliver's nature and reputation?"

"Of course it could be," Rosemary said, frowning. "You can be such a Fribble-head about some things."

"A *Fribble*-head?"

Rosemary clapped her hands over her mouth. Her eyes sparkled. "I am wicked, but it did seem an appropriate comparison. It means being rather haughty and saying perfectly obvious things as if you invented them yourself. There! Now you know what a mean spirit I possess."

Despite her anxiety, Lily laughed. "You have invented a new word. How clever of you. But I must guard my heart here, Rosemary. I may love him—and I confess I do—but I am not so lost to myself as to sacrifice self-respect."

"No." Somber regard replaced Rosemary's humor. "You are sensible. But you have said you love him. I already knew as much. And I will be steadfast in helping you see the good in Mr. Worth, for love is not a plentiful thing, Lily."

"You are wise," Lily said quietly. This sharing of emotion in such a detached manner discomforted her. "I shall remember everything you've said. Don't worry, I will not be hasty. Blue rosettes? What do you think?"

"Um—perhaps not blue?"

"They wouldn't lend the dress style?"

"Oh, it already has quite singular style, Lily."

Her friend's approval pleased her. Rosemary had wonderful taste. Everyone said so. "Thank you! I shall have to get about the business of a wedding dress. And quickly—if I don't decide I won't marry Oliver after all."

"You will marry him. And here he comes. With Mr. Westmoreland. Lily, Mr. Westmoreland has a valise—he is coming with us! Oh, what shall we say to him? What shall we talk about?"

"Absolutely nothing," Lily said grimly, drawing into a corner against the soft leather squabs. "I have no intention of speaking to such an abominable fellow."

Mr. Westmoreland handed his valise up to the coachman and got in while Oliver held the door open. Since Lily and Rosemary sat side by side, the two gentlemen settled facing them, their hats on their laps.

Oliver knocked on the trap and the coach trundled off, leaving Vestry Lane and the pretty gardens behind. Not that Lily actually saw anything clearly while she stared through the window with such concentration.

Lily didn't have to look at Oliver to know he stared at her. Well, let him stare. And let him invent some clever words to get himself out of this pretty pickle.

"A beautiful day for a ride in the country, wouldn't you say, Nick?"

"Indeed, I would. Very good of Miss Adler's father to invite me to visit."

"The professor is a generous man. He has certainly been generous to me. But how can I not admire a man with such a daughter?"

"I would have said exactly the same thing," Mr. Westmoreland agreed. "You are fortunate—"

"That is enough," Lily said sharply, moving to sit on the very edge of her seat. "Kindly have the sense to deal with this difficult situation like men. Like men who know they are with women of the world."

"Forgive—"

"And," she continued, cutting off Mr. Westmoreland, "I do not mean the sort of women of the world you suggested we might be, sir. I am embarrassed for you."

Mr. Westmoreland reddened, but his green eyes didn't swerve from their regard of her.

Oliver smiled. He actually smiled at her, and leaned forward as if they were alone in some conspiracy.

"Miss Adler," Mr. Westmoreland said. "Miss Godwin. I am mortified. I had my reasons for being annoyed with Oliver, but those reasons were no excuse for my careless tongue."

"You are wonderful," Oliver said to Lily. His dimples were very much in evidence, and she could not look away from his mouth. "You surprise me. I shall never grow accustomed to your wit, or your good sense. Your directness is a delight—it will be the delight of my life."

He stole her breath, and her wit—and her words. She would not smile at him. He should not escape so easily as that.

"I admit," he said, "that I have seen a good deal of the world, and enjoyed a good deal of it. I have not lived the life of a priest."

"Very good," Lily said tartly. "I believe you have come as close to a point without actually arriving as it is possible. You have not lived the life of a priest?"

His smile died. "Hmm. No. In fact, there have been times when I had a reputation as quite the lad."

"Lad?" Then she did laugh. "What perfectly ridiculous

terms you men insist on using to make light of your natures."

"Very well. I used to be very fond of the ladies."

A muffled chuckle came from Mr. Westmoreland, who earned a scowl from his friend.

"When did you cease to be very fond of the ladies?" Lily inquired.

"Dash it all, you are overly direct," Oliver said, still glaring around the coach. "If you must know, it was you who changed my nature in that regard."

"I caused you to stop being fond of ladies? Dear, dear, and yet you insist you are fond of me."

Mr. Westmoreland laughed aloud. "She has you there, Oliver. You've found yourself a bride who'll be your match, old man. Congratulations! And to you, Lily, if I may call you Lily?"

She nodded.

"To you, Lily, I say that you are a fortunate woman. This man has been my friend for ten years, and a better man never walked the earth."

Rosemary tapped Lily's hand and murmured, "Ask him why he was so angry with Mr. Worth, if Mr. Worth is so good."

"Rosemary wonders, as we both should—"

"Because I had asked him to come to me and advise me on a business matter. I was anxious and he did not come soon enough for my liking. As simple as that, Miss Godwin. I am an architect who specializes in . . . designing places of worship. At Oliver's suggestion I decided to spend some time in Salisbury studying the cathedral."

"Oh, how wonderful," Rosemary said, sounding very earnest. "My brother is a clergyman. He has his living at St. Cedric's in Come Piddle. Through the patronage of

Lily's father. I know Eustace would be interested to discuss American places of worship with you."

Mr. Westmoreland nodded, and kept on nodding.

"How did you meet?" Lily asked Oliver.

"At a party," Oliver replied and winced.

"Naturally. And then Mr. Westmoreland met and married your sister." She added, "Please accept my condolences on the loss of your wife. How very sad."

"Yes." He turned to the countryside.

With rapid movements, Rosemary adjusted her gloves. For a girl who could be silent for long periods herself, she was remarkably uncomfortable with the silence of others. "It's a wonderful thing when friendship remains and grows. It can be such a comfort in difficult times. What did you do before you came to England, Mr. Worth?"

Mr. Westmoreland laughed. "Tell them, Oliver. They'll never believe it, of course, but tell them."

Oliver didn't look nearly as delighted. "I . . . studied."

"Yes, he studied. But of course you know he must have studied. A great deal. Man of broad knowledge, Oliver. Your father will already know that, Lily. Please call me Nick. Professor Adler gives lectures, so Oliver has told me. Said that's how they met. At one of your father's lectures. Astronomy. Oliver was always gazing at the stars."

A frightful pause followed in which the sound of the coach wheels grew unnaturally loud.

Oliver turned to Nick and, to Lily's horror, fell upon him. He knocked the other's hat to the floor of the coach and proceeded to pummel him until Nick threw up his hands and begged for mercy.

Rosemary gave a little shriek and huddled against Lily.

"You devil," Oliver cried. "You will be the jester. Astronomy, is it? My stars, you shall suffer for that joke."

"Enough," Nick bellowed. "I surrender. I'm sorry for my sins."

"Like boys," Lily said, bewildered. "Horseplay—like *lads*."

"This is what I must tolerate," Oliver said, red-faced and panting—and pointing at Nick. "He constantly embarrasses me with his games. Philosopher becomes astronomer—and all for the fun of his addiction to wordplay. And so he may confound me by revealing how I told him I shall never look at you and not see you beneath a star-filled sky."

Pretty words. She smiled at him, and thought how much joy she found in looking upon his face and hearing his voice. But had Nick really been joking when he'd mistakenly called Papa an astronomer? Or could it be that Nick really didn't know Papa was a philosopher? And the sudden, uncharacteristic, and rather silly scuffle? Young men simply being young men—or one man finding a way to draw attention from an uncomfortable gaffe? If Nick and Oliver were close friends, Nick would know what Oliver's deep interests were. A man suited to be the assistant of an astronomer might be expected to have a less close acquaintance with philosophy.

Oliver continued to pay a great deal of attention to items around Blackmoor. Lily frequently came upon him examining a piece of furniture or a picture—even running his fingers over the frame of a painting. As if assessing the value . . .

"Lily?" Oliver said, shifting to the front of his seat and taking her hand. "So pensive. Share your thoughts with me."

She looked at his hand, at the long, blunt-tipped fingers, and thought, not for the first time, that Oliver Worth had not always lived the genteel life of a man of letters.

"I am thinking that"—*that she did not know nearly enough about this man she had agreed to marry*—"that men take pleasure in guarding their little mysteries."

Rosemary choked, then coughed until Lily had to produce her hartshorn.

Chapter Nineteen

"I will do what I must do. Already I have delayed too long, but part of me relishes watching how you sink deeper into my trap.

"At the beginning I told myself I would find a way to spare you. I would show mercy, though your kind showed no mercy to mine. Even recently I considered how I might step back from this course I have chosen, but I cannot, I will not.

"I thought I had all the time in the world, that I would play with you, bait you. But you have forced my hand.

"Lily Adler? Marriage?

"Oh, no, that cannot be. A dalliance would have amused me. I saw the way of that. Play with a creature who would adore you even more—so much more—than the beautiful ones. A creature who would see only you, want to please only you—forget herself for you. That's the titillation, isn't it?

"But you cannot marry her.

"No, that would ruin all my plans.

"How much time is there? Little. Little for you, Oliver Worth—man of opportunity, man who would take what I must have.

"I must stop you now."

Chapter Twenty

He was a desperate man. Desperate men must sometimes employ desperate measures.

Lily Adler, looking at her, listening to her, the marvelous prospect of *touching* her, had become burning necessities. Oliver needed her, and not for any of the reasons he'd so blithely thought he might need her when they'd first met.

He loved her.

Oliver skulked in the shadows of the corridor outside her rooms.

Skulked? Oliver Worth, a man of wealth and success who had often grown tired of beautiful, fawning females? But, yes, he skulked like a thief waiting for an opportunity to make off with what he desired. An appropriate comparison.

Light footsteps sounded and he pulled back into a doorway. He didn't have to see Lily to feel her approach. Damn, but he was bewitched.

He slipped rapidly from his hiding place and accosted her in front of her rooms—and covered her mouth when she made to cry out.

She mumbled against his palm, but he continued to muzzle her while he pulled her inside her sitting room and closed the door. "I cannot bear it," he said into the hair at her temple. Holding her against the wall, he kissed her brow. "At every turn there is someone waiting to interrupt us. Three days we have been engaged and I have had less time with you than ever before."

She bit his palm, and when he howled and withdrew his hand, she pummeled his chest with both fists. "Oliver Worth, you are outrageous. Irrepressible. A mature man of the world? Hah! Hiding and jumping out—and frightening me out of my wits."

"That was hardly the passionate response I'd hoped for, my love. I thought you were a woman who thrilled to surprises."

Despite their closeness, she managed to cross her arms between them.

"I must be alone with you, Lily. *We* must be alone. I've waited in that damnable, drafty corridor an hour, hiding from your wretched stepmother, from your father, from Nick, from Eustace Godwin, from servants, from your hovering, twittering friends. I don't want to see anyone but you, do you understand me? *Do* you?"

Her eyes were huge. She nodded, and he stroked her jaw with his thumb. "You undo me, minx. I can't stay angry with you for a moment—even when you abuse me." He kissed her, gently. If he kissed her with the force of this moment's passion, he would surely render her unconscious from lack of breath.

A giggle startled him and he raised his head. Lily gazed at him with stunned concentration, then slowly her eyes regained focus and she shook herself slightly.

The giggle sounded again and Oliver spun around. The maid, Hilda, whom he gathered Lily shared with Mrs. Fribble, stood in the corner of the room. His precipitate arrival had cut her off from any means of escape, either to the corridor or to the bedroom. A pleasant-looking, well-padded young woman, she looked at Oliver and Lily with a mixture of avid fascination and awkwardness.

"Hilda," Lily said. "I didn't send for you."

"No, miss. Mrs. Fribble sent me. She said I was to arrange a bed in this room so you wouldn't be alone."

"I am accustomed to being alone, Hilda. I have been alone in these rooms since I was ten."

Hilda lowered her eyes. "Mrs. Fribble said—"

"I don't care what Mrs. Fribble said, I—"

"I shall deal with this." Oliver whisked Lily into the crook of one arm and rushed her from the room. "Miss Adler and I are going for a walk, Hilda. You may go to Mrs. Fribble and inform her of that, if you will. Tell her I requested that you do so."

He didn't stop hurrying Lily along until they reached his own rooms and were safely closeted inside. "You see," he said, pointing in a vague direction, but with a forcefully jabbing finger. "*They* shall not be allowed to intrude. Do you understand me, Lily? I will not tolerate their interference for another second. It's a bloody circus—I mean, it's a circus in this house. And I only want to be with you."

She frowned at him, frowned deeply and breathed deeply—and evaded his reaching arms. "Just a moment, if you please, Oliver. There are one or two questions I've been wanting to ask you for several days."

"Ask."

"Are you hiding something from me?"

The abruptness of the question locked his tongue. *Careful, she can't know what you're afraid she may know.* "I'm hiding a great deal," he told her easily, but his throat was dry. "I must hide it all or you would never marry me."

She showed no hint of amusement. Circling him, watching him pivot to keep her in his sights, she drove her teeth into her lower lip. Her energy reached him, almost tangibly. Every step she took was sure. She had no need to examine what she thought or said, because she didn't act impulsively—or not often. God, she did suspect him.

"If I told you I eat liver stew in bed at midnight, would you marry me, Lily?"

She continued to circle.

"This is bad." He felt sweat between his shoulder blades. "You are horrified by liver stew. Well, perhaps I can give it up. But there's the matter of—"

"Do not jest about this, Oliver. My question was simple. Are you hiding something from me? Something important?"

"Why do you ask such a thing?" If he told her the truth now, would there still be a future for them, or would he lose not only the chance to complete his quest but Lily herself? He couldn't bear to give up either, but the loss of Lily would destroy him.

"I know so little about you, Oliver."

"I've told you what I can." Lies, on lies, on lies.

"And there isn't anything you're hiding that may hurt us both after we are married—when we've taken that step that I never intended to take at all?"

He drew a breath. "No."

"Do you want to marry me because you want my inheritance?"

"You are blunt, my girl!"

"*Fiddle*. I am honest. I do not hide my concerns behind pretty posings."

"I don't want to marry you for your inheritance." It was true. He hadn't come to England to claim any fortune, he already had one. "What I want is you. And you know more about me than many young women approaching marriage know about their fiancés."

He saw the moment when her doubts fled. Her shoulders dropped, and the anxiety in her eyes turned to soft brilliance—to the promise of her intense feelings for him.

"Lily—"

Quickly she pressed her fingers to his lips. "Hush. Please let's be quiet awhile. Let's just *be.* I regret the doubts, my love. They are because I cannot truly believe you care for me. Or perhaps I believe it, but I'm afraid something will happen to steal the joy I find in you."

Oliver held her hand and closed his eyes. He rubbed his cheek against her palm, kissed each fingertip, the places separating each finger. "Perhaps these annoying people know what they're doing when they try to stop me from being alone with you," he murmured. "I have thoughts that would scandalize them all. I am dangerous to your virtue, Miss Adler."

"My virtue belongs to you, Mr. Worth."

"And I am dangerously close to taking possession of it."

"You mean—" She cleared her throat. "Oh, you do mean that, don't you?"

He opened his eyes and said, "I most certainly do."

"We are to be married in—"

"Two days less than three weeks. A lifetime. I shall wither, and shrivel, and blow away by then."

She looked at him with earnest horror. "Oh, I do hope not. If you do not feel able to tolerate . . . If waiting will cause you some deterioration of mind or body, then it is my duty to offer myself to avert such a disaster."

Offer. Ah, yes, a delightful word that drew arousing pictures in his mind. "I must contain myself," he told her.

Did she look disappointed?

"Not if it puts you in danger of shriveling. No, I will not allow that."

He held up a hand. "Fear not."

"You have already introduced me to some of the basic elements required for your well-being—and my own—but I admit that although I am aware of the . . . *Act*, I am not at all certain how it is accomplished. Not exactly."

Oliver felt an unaccustomed heat in his face—and a more pressing heat elsewhere. Then the damned, unaccountable tenderness blasted him and made him want to pick her up, cradle her, rock her. Lily, and only Lily, had ever made him feel this protective urge toward a woman.

"I see I have embarrassed you," she said, all serious concern. "Unforgivable of me. I am really most inept at expressing these things. Oliver, I should very much like to perform the Act with you. All of it. If you feel in the mood, or whatever."

For the second time in less than an hour, she rendered him speechless.

"Oh, my. Oh, *fiddle*. I'm botching this horribly. If you don't want to deal with teaching me more about the matter tonight, I understand. I'm sure that for an experienced man such as yourself, going through the mundane ins and outs of these things with me will be taxing."

Oliver moaned; he couldn't stop himself. And he pulled her into his arms and held her. He held her, ran his fingers into her hair until the looped braids unraveled. Through the silk stuff of her high-necked mauve gown he felt the heat of her body. He must not take advantage of her charming offer.

Must not.

"Are you at all tired, Oliver?"

He was afire. He throbbed. His every muscle and sinew ached with tension, the tension of holding her but not holding her as he longed to. "I'm a little tired."

"Could we rest, then? I thought your bed—on the night when I saw it—looked inviting. We could lie in each other's arms and consider our future, our wedding. And you could discuss with me what I should do to prepare to please you as a wife. In wifely matters. That is, the *Act.*"

He remembered the previous occasion on which they'd "rested" together. "Lily, I'm not sure that's a good idea." It was a wonderful idea. He could hold a discussion complete with practical application. "You must be tired, or you wouldn't have mentioned needing a rest. I should return you to your rooms."

"No."

"I shouldn't have brought you here. Everyone will talk."

"Let them talk. I'm not tired. And if you were to tell me, point by point, what happens in the Act, I should be ever so much less likely to be clumsy. I should imagine that clumsiness might cause something to get hung up somehow. After all, there must be some complexity to the execution of these things, and if I could make a list of the steps, things would be bound to go more smoothly."

She would be the death of him. "We will lie, side by side." Damn his weakness. "Just to feel you beside me—that is a dream, Lily. I don't know how I could be so lucky as to find you, and have you care for me."

"It is I who am lucky. Rosemary told me she felt you

were interesting, and she was right. I am always much too quick to make decisions about people, and I was too jealous of Papa's regard for you to consider how I felt about you."

With that, she took his hand and drew him toward the bedroom.

This way lay danger. He hung back.

Lily pulled harder, and smiled at him over her shoulder. When Lily Adler smiled, and the smile was filled with audacity and promise, she was beautiful. More beautiful. Hers was the most beautiful face in the world to Oliver.

"Come along," she urged. "Or send me away if you must."

Oliver went, and as he went he loosened his cravat and tore it off before it could choke him as he felt sure it shortly would.

She released him and went to light the lamp beside the bed—and Raven shot, hissing, from atop the mattress, to disappear into the sitting room. "Oliver!" Lily said, surveying the room and then looking at him. "The servants must be reprimanded. What a frightful mess. Did they put the room to rights yesterday, even? I cannot believe so much clutter is the product of one day."

Oliver gaped. His bed might have been kneaded like bread dough, and wound into a braided loaf, with trailing ends. Every drawer hung open and spilled its contents. The wardrobe door sagged wide. His clothes had been pulled out and dropped on the floor.

"Now I understand," Lily said, laughing. "You didn't want me to see how carelessly you deal with your personal possessions. My, we shall have to see about putting this to rights."

He narrowed his eyes to survey the damage, and went

directly to his trunks, stored against one wall. Each had been opened and rummaged through. Going to his knees, he removed what remained in the one on the right. Putting his back between the trunk and Lily, he pressed corners to release the false bottom, lifted it, and bowed his head. Gone. Whoever had searched his room had found what they were looking for—or so he had to think.

"Oliver? What is it?"

"Don't concern yourself."

"Oh, Oliver, this isn't—This is the work of thieves, isn't it? Someone came and went through your things. Oh, dear, we must go to Papa at once."

"No, that won't be necessary."

"It most certainly will. There must be an investigation at once."

"No, Lily, please." He pushed the bottom of the trunk until he heard the clasp snap. "Mischief is all I see here. There doesn't appear to be anything missing." Further exploration showed the efficient culprit had opened the bottoms in the other two trunks, not that it mattered except as proof that he'd known where to look, and probably had some idea what he was looking for.

Someone knew who he was. Oliver was certain of it.

Sinking to kneel beside him, Lily brought both a gentling, trembling desire, and desperation.

"Mr. Worth! Are you here, sir? Mr. Worth."

When Oliver would have leapt to his feet, Lily dragged on his arm, holding him beside her. "Stay," she said. "It's only Gambol. We're in here, Gambol! In the bedroom."

Oliver winced. There were times when Lily's forthrightness was overwhelming.

The old man came hesitantly through the door, craning his bent head to view the room in all directions. "Oh, my," he said. "Oh, dearie me. Such a commotion, then, Mr. Worth. I declare, you've had a visitor, haven't you? A thief. Oh, dearie me. What's missing, then?"

"Nothing," Oliver said. "Seems to have been a nasty prank of some sort, but the prankster didn't take anything, thank goodness."

"We must tell Papa," Lily said, leaning against Oliver and gazing up into his face. "He will want to know."

"I don't think that would be a good idea, Miss Lily," Gambol said. He shuffled forward. "This is in the nature of a violation, you see. A Trojan Horse, as it were. Attacked from the inside of his very own house. The shock wouldn't be good for him. Your father's not as young as he used to be."

Oliver looked at Gambol. Eighty if he was a day—certainly a good twenty years older than Professor Adler.

"No," Gambol continued. "I wouldn't risk causing the professor any worry. Well, if there's nothing I can do to help, I'll be on my way, then."

When the old man had left, Lily tapped Oliver's shoulder until he looked at her. "That was very odd," she said, sinking to sit on the floor beside the trunk. "Don't you think so?"

Oliver was too busy thinking of the ramifications of the thief's little haul to be concerned with one dotty old butler. "Not especially," he said.

"Well, it was. Why did he come here? He never said. And what was all that about not shocking my father? Papa is as calm as a poached egg."

"You do have a unique manner of expression," he said, distracted.

"Do you know what I think?"

"Hmm?" He needed to discuss this with Nick. A plan

must bc made—possibly to remove Lily from the house, since it was entirely possible it could be dangerous here now.

"I think Gambol already knew what happened."

Her words slowly took shape. He brought his face closer to hers. "With all this, you mean?" Spreading his arms, he indicated the shambles surrounding them.

"Of course with all this. And he came to see how you were affected. Why, Oliver? I've always liked Gambol. What can have led to such behavior?"

"You are too hasty with your story, my dear."

"No, I'm not. Listen. He came to . . . No, he came because he doesn't want Papa to know, and not because he's afraid for Papa's health. That's nonsense. If Gambol didn't do this, then he knows who did. That's much more likely. And he's protecting them." Her lips pursed and turned white. "*Well,* if that doesn't beat all. Someone's trying to make you leave, and Gambol knows about it. And he's protecting them."

"What a very tidy deduction." And how possibly logical. "But we have no proof. Confronting the man is out of the question. But on to other matters. Miss, would you accompany me to a place where, if we are careful not to be observed as we go, we may hope to be alone?"

Lily popped to her feet, stumbled, and bent over to unhitch the hem of her dress from the toe of her slipper. "Too long," she said. "Another of Myrtle's. She's taller than me. Come along, Oliver. I will accompany you anywhere—and we shall secure ourselves away from the world while we consider what to do next about this nonsense."

In any other circumstances, that promise would thrill

him. "Very well. The north wing?" He caught up his cravat and tied it hastily.

"The north wing," Lily agreed. "We can make sure it's as empty as it's supposed to be and lock ourselves in."

They walked into the sitting room, and were confronted by Mrs. Fribble. Her face glowed with umbrage. "I have caught you," she said, glowering at Oliver. "I've told the professor you are not to be trusted, that you have designs on Lily for reasons other than those you give, but he will not listen to me. Well, after this he'll have to."

"Mrs. Fribble, I assure you—"

"You are wrong," Lily said, planting her feet, plopping her hands on her hips. "Shame on you, Aunt Fribble."

"Well!" With a hand pressed to her bosom, Mrs. Fribble took a step backward. "After all I've done for you. Well. I must overcome any concern for my pride in this. Your welfare comes first, Lily. Always. I owe that to the memory of poor, dear Kitty. You are an innocent and cannot possibly be expected to know that this man is putting your reputation at risk."

"This man is going to marry me."

Even Oliver smarted at the dangerous edge to Lily's voice.

Fribble didn't have the sense to smart. She said, "Because he wants this estate and all that goes with it. If you think for a moment that a man who looks like Mr. Worth would be interested in you if you were poor, then you're even sillier than I thought."

Oliver's blood pumped hard. Such small, mean cuts were not worth his consideration, except that they were bound to hurt Lily. "Madam," he said. "Whatever can you mean? Are you suggesting that your poor, dear sister's daughter is unworthy of love?"

"Bosh," Mrs. Fribble declared. "Don't seek to tie me up in clever knots, sir. You don't love Lily. You love yourself, and might love a flashy creature or two for a while if it suited you. You've bewitched Professor Adler, and you've bewitched this foolish girl. But you have not bewitched me. Come, Lily, we will not stay a moment longer."

Lily threaded her arm through Oliver's and marched past her step-aunt. "You need not fear that being here will besmirch your pristine reputation," Lily said. "Oliver and I will leave. Stay if you wish—or go, and carry whatever unpleasant tales you wish. What I don't understand is why. Why don't you want me to be happy?"

"But I do," Mrs. Fribble said, trotting in Oliver and Lily's wake along the corridor. "You aren't listening to me, Lily. *Lily*. Don't you dare turn your back and walk away when I'm talking to you."

To Oliver's amusement, Lily proceeded to spin around, push her hand beneath his arm from the opposite direction, and walk backward. "I cannot help but hear you, Aunt. You shout. Go on your way, please. Oliver and I have plans to be alone."

"Oh!" Mrs. Fribble's cheeks were an interesting shade of purple. "Utter disrespect. But what can one expect of the young nowadays? You've been spoiled, had too much. And you appreciate nothing. I shall go to your father at once and tell him how you have treated me—and how inappropriate your behavior is."

Oliver pulled Lily aside to allow Mrs. Fribble to bustle away, her head held high.

"She intends to make Papa come in search of me," Lily said. "Oh, if she thinks I don't know what she's about, she's much mistaken."

Before Oliver could pursue that topic, Lily set off after Mrs. Fribble. When he said, "Lily?" she responded by pressing a forefinger to her lips and shaking her head. And she motioned for him to follow.

At considerable speed, she slipped to the end of the corridor. Rather than turn right toward the north wing, or return to her own rooms, she made for the way to the south wing.

Tempted to urge her to stop, Oliver strode at her side as far as the steps leading down to the gallery above the foyer.

Lily halted abruptly, and stepped back so sharply her heel landed on his toe and he gasped.

"Hush," she whispered urgently, clapping a hand—none too gently—over his mouth. "I do not believe what I see. Oh, my. Oh, dear. Oh, how wonderfully, awfully—*wonderful.*"

She bobbed on her toes, and set her teeth, and pointed with short jabbing motions.

Very carefully, Oliver leaned just far enough to see around the corner. Less carefully, he withdrew, shaking his head and grinning.

Lily hopped from foot to foot and mouthed, "Now!" before composing her face into a serene mask, and proceeded with gliding steps, taking Oliver with her.

Before them, braced against a recessed door, stood Lord Witmore. "You're certain?" Oliver heard the man say to Mrs. Fribble. "You will have no difficulty planting doubt in the professor's mind?"

"None, Reginald," the woman said breathlessly. Her arms were wound around Witmore's neck. "They have given me what I need. Come to my rooms now."

"You'd best go directly to the professor."

"He's not at home. A meeting with the Come Piddle Society of Thinking Men."

Witmore guffawed. "I say. An oxymoron, what?"

"Reginald," Mrs. Fribble finally managed to gasp. "This is so daring. I am quite breathless from excitement."

Oliver pushed Lily behind him.

Immediately she popped out again.

He scowled at her and put her on the other side of the corner.

Lily darted out of his reach and positioned herself for a clear view of the passionate pair.

"Let me hear you make the promise again," Lord Witmore said. "You will make certain Worth doesn't marry her."

"Oh, yes," Mrs. Fribble said. "Oh, yes, Reginald."

"You will discredit the man and make certain he's sent packing."

"Oh, yes, Reginald."

Reginald bent Fribble backward over his arm to bestow a closed-mouth kiss on her lips. He released her quickly and she fell against the door, giggling and fanning herself. "Oh, Reginald," she warbled. "Oh—" She looked past Reginald's shoulder, and directly into Oliver's eyes.

Chapter Twenty-one

Lily flew in Oliver's footsteps through the north wing. She ran, and laughed until she had to sag against a wall to catch her breath. "They looked so ridiculous," she said, watching Oliver throw open another door and enter with his lamp held aloft. "They looked absolutely foolish," she called out. "And sounded even more foolish."

"You should not have watched," he said severely, returning to take her hand and pull her along behind him. "You defied my authority, Lily."

"*Fiddle.*" She drove her heels into the carpet and leaned away from him. "I defied your authority? What authority?"

Oliver turned to stare down into her face. "You are to be my wife. It is my responsibility to care for you. That means it's my responsibility to make sure you are not exposed to unsuitable displays."

"*Perhaps* I'm going to be your wife."

"Let's not do this now, Lily. We—"

"Oh, no, sir. Oh, no. I'm aware that this is the way of it between many married couples. The wife must await her lord's pleasure to *blow her nose.* Not so with me, sir. If you must have a meek, subservient wife, then you'd best look elsewhere."

He threw up his hands and paced back and forth, pausing to send her a glare with each change of direction.

"Oh, stop it, Oliver, do. I have a strong mind. It will not suddenly turn to blancmange because I become Mrs. Worth. Is that unsatisfactory to you?"

"I like your strong mind," he said ferociously. "I like your strong will. You please me in—in almost every way."

"Almost isn't good enough." Trying not to smile, she observed his stalking progress. "Obviously we are ill-matched."

He paused and brought his face closer to hers. "In every way, then. But you will have to change."

It was Lily's turn to throw up her hands. "*Men.* They are impossible. I do believe some bright soul—a brave woman—will one day announce to the world that men are impossible to live with, or without. How frustrating."

"May I finish making certain we are alone here, miss?"

"May you finish?" she mimicked. "May you finish making certain no one will interrupt you having your way with me."

That stopped him entirely.

"Well, isn't that what you intended? You told me you had to be alone with me."

"I have already said that I think it a poor notion to, er, to pursue . . . whatever, before the wedding."

"The Act," she said, enormously pleased with the way color rose in his face whenever she mentioned the subject. "So you said, but I believe you were simply complying with the conventional rules of gentlemanly behavior. You were saying what you thought ought to be said, when in fact you wanted to bring me here so we wouldn't be disturbed."

"We shall change the subject." Oliver pointed toward the rest of the house, toward wherever Fribble and Witless might be. "That was an inappropriate display."

"Awful," she agreed.

"You thoroughly enjoyed watching them."

She nodded. "Thoroughly."

"Young ladies do not enjoy watching such things."

"You've been a young lady?" she inquired, all innocence.

"I"—he frowned, then closed his eyes—"I love everything about you, Lily Adler. How could I have suffered such a foolish lapse in thinking I could ever control you in any manner."

"I can't imagine. May I assume there won't be a similar lapse at some future time?"

Nodding wearily, but grinning his incredible grin, he said, "You may. Please God let these days to our wedding pass quickly. I must have you. I cannot wait to have you with me at all times."

"*Yes,*" she said, seizing his wrist and leading him to the top of the stairs that descended to the lower floors of the wing. "And you shall have me with you all the time. And I shall have you. And Fribble will not dare to say a cross word about you, Oliver. Oh, I shall never forget the look on her face when she saw us."

They clattered to the bottom of the stairs and set about another search. "Witmore brought me the most pleasure," Oliver said, no longer sounding amused. "He will have a care what he says and does in future. He did not even have enough courage to stay and defend that woman."

"He ran," Lily said. "He actually ran away. Frightful creature. Can you credit that Fribble has always fawned upon Papa? And she pretended she wanted me to marry

Witless because she thought he would be a good husband for me, and a good connection for our family. The only connection she wanted was for herself—to Witless."

"Lily."

"You know I'm right." She took the lamp from him and peered into a small, empty storage room. "She actually *desires* him."

"*Lily.*"

Two more bedrooms and a salon all revealed no sign of life.

"I do wonder about Witless's mysteries. All men have them, you know."

"How kind of you to enlighten me."

"There isn't anyone on this floor. We can lock the door at the bottom of the next flight and that'll leave only the ground floor."

Oliver kept an arm around her waist as they went down the final stairs, and shot home the bolt on the door.

"I'm trying to imagine Witless without clothes."

"*Lily!*"

"What? Why do you keep saying *Lily*? Rosemary does that."

"No doubt she does it if you shock her as you shock me."

"Far more, I assure you."

He groaned. "We're alone here. Good. At last we can do what has to be done."

Lily's heart pounded. "Yes, Oliver," she said, so much more meekly than she wanted to. "Whatever you say."

"I'm glad you can at least be led in something."

"I know when it's to my advantage to bow to your superior expertise."

"Good. I suggest the old earl's bedroom."

"My thought exactly. I find it so exotic and intriguing."

His dark hair had grown even longer, and it glinted in the lamplight. There were shadows on his face, drawing bold slashes about the sharp angles of his cheekbones and jaw, beneath his firmly set lower lip. His eyes held singular purpose that flipped Lily's stomach and caused a twinge of sharp feeling low inside her.

"Poor Fribble," she murmured, never intending to say any such thing.

Oliver raised his expressive brows. In the narrow confines of the corridor he towered over her, and Lily thought she liked the way that made her feel very much.

"Poor Fribble because she must content herself with Revolting Reggie rather than with marvelous you." She shuddered again. "I recall when he pressed his wet lips upon me. Sickening. Think how much more disgusting it would be to have him remove his clothes."

"Enough," Oliver said, grabbing her hand. "I will not listen to a single word more of this salacious speculation."

Rather than ashamed, Lily felt rather smug at having disquieted him. "As you wish." She went with him to the room where gold drapes shimmered, and jewels winked in black lacquer, and jade dragons supported their red velvet cushion in readiness for important feet.

Oliver crossed the room and pulled aside a drapery to inspect the casement.

"Witless had those boards nailed over the windows," Lily said. "To keep his beloved father's room as it had always been, so he said. So nothing would fade."

"Hmm," was all Oliver said.

"So we need not concern ourselves that there is any risk of being observed." They were entirely alone. Together and alone. Lily hugged herself.

Oliver surveyed the room. "Fabulous, isn't it?"

"Fabulous," she said dreamily. *He* was fabulous.

Stripping his coat, he dropped to his knees to look beneath the bed.

Lily laughed. "Oh, Oliver, don't. No one is hiding there."

"No," he agreed, sounding distracted. He glanced at her and tossed the coat aside. "Something tells me we shall have a long night here, my love. We'd best be very comfortable, hmm?"

"Oh, yes." The drumbeat of her heart must be loud enough for him to hear.

He removed his cravat and threw back the gold bedcover at the same time.

His haste excited Lily to trembling. "What should I do?" she asked.

"You will know," he told her. "Watch me, work with me. And as we advance I shall try to bind you to me forever, Lily. I must believe that by fully knowing my heart you will find it in your heart to love and accept everything about me."

The fervor in his voice, the intense way he concentrated on her, made it impossible to swallow, or even to breathe.

"Lily?"

"Yes, Oliver. Yes, of course you are right. Lead me where you would have me go and I'll follow willingly."

His smile, gentle yet filled with passion, brought tingling warmth to her flesh.

"Thank you," he said simply. "I don't deserve you, but I'll never let you go."

Hesitantly, Lily walked over the beautiful old carpet to the bed. Oliver turned his back and seemed engrossed in his surroundings.

To give her time to compose herself, Lily thought. He was the kindest, most considerate of men.

She took off her slippers and climbed the mahogany steps to the high mattress. On her hands and knees she moved to position herself in the center, and rested her head on one braced hand.

"Damn, this room is warm," Oliver said, glancing at her. He undid several buttons on his shirt and rolled up the full sleeves. "Be comfortable, my love. We shall take our time. All the time we need."

Already her hair streamed over her shoulders, and she found she liked the feel of it there. "All night," she murmured, and dropped to lie against the pillows. "I'm not at all tired."

"Nor I."

Should she remove her own clothes? The stays were no simple matter, but Oliver would help. She blushed wildly at the thought, but pulled undone the small satin bows that closed the high neck of Myrtle's old dress.

"This piece has captured my attention," Oliver said, going to a black lacquer secretaire with a raised bank of small drawers at the back of its leather-covered surface. "Incredibly fine workmanship. Intricate. A veritable puzzle of nooks and crannies, too." He commenced to pull drawers entirely out and feel in the spaces behind. When he'd examined every one, he eased the piece of furniture from the wall and looked behind, ran his hand over the back, crouched to look closely at the legs and test the gold clawed caps at their bases.

Lily rested a hand on her breast. Impossible as it seemed, Oliver was also nervous at this moment. His fierce activity showed his anxiety. "It isn't as if we haven't shared . . . special experiences before," she said.

"In this very room. We are already close, Oliver, and shall only become closer."

"Indeed," he said, pushing back the secretaire and approaching the bed. "You distract me, witch. I do believe you take pride in lying there like a wanton."

"I am only wanton with you," she said, hearing the husky quality of her own voice. "You make me feel wanton."

"Three weeks minus *three* days," he said, leaning to place a fleeting kiss on her lips. "It is after midnight. I have never been more grateful to see the passage of days."

With a sigh that raised his big shoulders, he turned from her again and stood with his hands on his hips. Slowly, Lily unbuttoned the rest of her bodice and undid the length of orange satin she'd found to use as a striking belt on the mauve silk gown. In the rise and fall of lamplight and shadow, she could see the outline of Oliver's broad back through his shirt, the way his body slimmed to a narrow waist. His bared forearms were muscular and tanned.

"One wonders exactly where to start," Oliver said. "If we are to be successful, there must be a plan."

"Oh, I just know your instincts will be perfect. Proceed in whatever manner pleases you. I am your willing assistant in these things."

He shook his head slightly. "Thank you. I pray to God I will preserve my honor in your eyes."

She grew restless. "You couldn't do otherwise." Once more she lay back on the pillows. The tape at the top of her chemise untied easily and she loosened the wide neck until it fell low over her breasts.

Wanton?

Yes, she felt wanton, and she loved it.

Oliver approached the chair with its leopard-skin seat.

He smoothed the fur, lifted the chair from the floor, and turned it upside down.

Lily wiggled and tried to settle. She could not. In deep places, and even beneath her very skin, a searing ache demanded attention. It demanded satisfaction.

She stroked the linen beside her and said, "Come here, Oliver. We will do this together, lead each other." The soaring canopy claimed her attention. "Beneath our very own golden sky. Why, there are even stars. Or the cloth seems to hold stars. Let us begin here and now."

"I do not think we shall find what we seek there, my love."

"No?" Lily sat up again.

The jade dragon footstool had claimed his attention. "We must be methodical. No part of this room will be left unexamined. We shall probe every crack and crevice."

"Oliver? What are you talking about?" She grew chilled, yet hot at the same time.

He looked at her. "I've told you. We're going to take advantage of the opportunity to search this room at our leisure. All night, if necessary. Every inch. If Witmore had found whatever it is that brings him here, he would no longer come. There may be nothing, but if there is, we shall find it."

Chapter Twenty-two

Why couldn't women be like men? Predictable and sensible? Oliver observed how Lily dragged the red and gold bedcover over her—over her head, even—and proceeded to rest! She was totally still and didn't make a sound. Yet only moments before she'd insisted she was anxious to assist him.

He set about searching one piece of furniture after another. A tall cabinet took considerable time. When he opened the doors he was confronted with at least fifty tiny drawers with red silk pulls on each gold handle. And he took them out, one by one, to check their bottoms, and the spaces into which they fitted. Tedious, but necessary if only for the process of elimination.

"You are beyond all, Oliver Worth."

At the sound of Lily's voice, he jumped. "I beg your pardon?"

"I *said*, you are beyond all." She sat with the bedcover pulled up to her neck and looked delightful with her black hair mussed around her face.

"And why, may I ask, would you make such a statement?"

"You don't know, do you? Even more amazing."

"Then enlighten me, dearest. It's important that we understand each other. I thought you wanted to help me in this task."

"I had no idea you intended to perform such a task, Oliver."

He frowned. Hadn't he explained? "No," he said thoughtfully. "No, I didn't really tell you, did I. That's a fault of mine. I tend to rush ahead assuming others know what I'm about. Forgive me."

"I don't think I shall. Not immediately, anyway." There was something in her eyes. Hurt? Surely not.

"You do agree that Witmore has probably been coming here to look for something?"

"I agree he may have been. It could be an explanation."

"I'm certain of it." But he hadn't told her what he thought Witmore might be looking for. Not that he knew himself in more than general terms. "I have made a leap in becoming convinced that he searches for something that could endanger his position."

This time Lily frowned. "What do you mean?"

Too soon. He swallowed. He'd decided to use this time together, alone, to reveal the truth about himself. Oliver longed to remove any misconceptions between them. But it was too soon. If he told her now, he might lose her.

"Oliver, what do you mean?" she repeated.

"Only that for Witmore to be so tenacious—for years—and even to try to force a marriage with you, suggests to me that more than simple greed motivates the man."

"I don't understand."

Of course she didn't. And perhaps she need never understand. After all, his own father had severed connections to his life here and had insisted he never wished to resume them. Father had begun a new and successful life.

To return to England in an attempt to right an old wrong had been Oliver's idea. Finding Lily had not been part of the plan, but it was wonderful and he could not lose her now. What harm could there be to putting the past behind him, especially if it might harm their union—or stop their union, even? He scrubbed at his face.

"Oliver?"

"I simply mean that I think Witmore believes there's something in this wing—very possibly in this room, since he concentrates so much time here—something that he must get his hands on. And to be so single-minded in this I can only wonder if it is something that might be damning to him if it came to light."

"You don't like him. Neither do I. But I do believe your conclusions rather far-fetched."

Because she was clearheaded and sensible. "Perhaps." And perhaps she was right, but he had nothing else but instinct to follow. "You do believe he's looking for something, don't you?"

She considered. "I've said I think he may be. When he's here no one is allowed to disturb him, and he always leaves in an angry mood and looking rather disheveled."

"Exactly!" Oliver said, triumphant. "Angry because he has found nothing. Disheveled because he's been trying to find something." And the need that had driven Oliver to England, and found him a lovely girl he adored, still had to be dealt with.

Lily rested her brow on her drawn-up knees.

"Oh, I am thoughtless," he said. "You're tired, poor girl. Rest, love. Sleep."

"I'm not sleepy."

He didn't know what else to say. "Well enough, then. I must continue my search. Help me if you wish. I know we'll find signs of Witmore's efforts. Like this"—he displayed the back of the skin-covered chair for her to see—"this has been pried loose. To allow him to feel inside, no doubt."

"You're right," she told him, but in a small, unenthusiastic voice.

"Of course I'm right," he said, gaining confidence. "And he has put his hands over the surfaces of the furnishings." He did so himself. "So many times that there is never any dust. He touches and feels everything."

"Yes, I see that."

"Every picture and frame." The ornate gilt matting on a painting of a Chinese warrior in battle dress claimed his notice. He examined it closely, then lifted the picture to look behind. "Everything. He searches constantly."

"The way you do."

Holding the painting, Oliver stood still. "The way I do?"

Her small features tightened and a sharp light entered her gray eyes. "Yes, Oliver, the way you do. Ever since you came to Blackmoor you've been assessing its contents."

He swallowed.

"Rather as if *you* were looking for something."

Slowly, he replaced the painting, taking the time to think how he would answer her. Now was not the time to reveal all; he felt very sure any such announcement would destroy her faith in him before he'd had enough time to bind them together.

"I regret if I've shown more than academic interest in this beautiful house. I'm afraid I may tend to become lost in my fascination for such things." An acid taste assailed his tongue. He detested lying as much as Lily detested lies, yet he'd trapped himself.

"I thought your area of expertise was philosophy. But, then, perhaps it's astronomy."

"You have a cruel tongue, Lily. I already explained how Nick is a rattlebrain in some areas. He both forgets what he's told and adds an element of mischief to his dealings. That was the cause of his irritating comments in the coach, nothing more."

"So you say. Where is he now?"

Composing dispatches to Gabriel in Boston. Nick had made no secret that he considered Oliver's plans foolish—possibly dangerously destructive, even. The events of the evening could only increase Nick's agitation, and make him more determined to persuade Oliver to leave Blackmoor, Come Piddle, Hampshire, and England behind. Permanently. And Lily with them.

"I asked where Nick is," Lily said.

Oliver ran a hand around his neck and approached her. "He's in his rooms. Writing." The closer he could come to the truth, the less foul he felt. "Nick is a quiet man. He prefers to keep to himself."

"An architect."

Damn Nick's hide for concocting such a fantasy. "Hmm."

"Eustace intends to invite him for a discussion."

Gad. "I'm sure Nick will find that stimulating."

"I'm glad someone is to be stimulated."

He stared at her, but she was engaged in accomplishing some task beneath the bedcover.

"What are you doing?" he asked her.

"It's rude to ask personal questions." With that, she

pulled the cover entirely over her head. He made out the movements of her elbows.

Oliver strode to her side and whipped away the cover.

She looked up from an evident attempt to fasten her chemise, a vain attempt, and clasped the thin fabric to her breasts.

"My love, what . . ." Oh, hell's teeth, he was a fool. "Lily, dearest. My dear, dear, wonderful girl."

"Stop it!" Holding the chemise together beneath her open bodice, she scrambled away and clambered down the bed steps. "Don't you dare patronize me, Oliver Worth. Don't you dare feel sorry for me."

"I don't."

"Oh!" She stood on the opposite side of the bed, shaking visibly, but not, Oliver thought, from cold. "Oh, you are horrid. You humiliate me. Reject me. And then you say you don't care."

"I didn't say . . . Let me hold you."

She drew herself up. "Thank you for the offer, but you have a room to search."

He started around the bed. "There is nothing more important to me than you."

Lily hopped from foot to foot, replacing her slippers. "How generous of you to say such a thing. I wish you good luck in your labors."

"Lily, please. I didn't realize what you . . . Damn it all, I didn't notice you were taking your clothes off."

"How complimentary."

He swung on his heel and crammed his fingers into his hair. "Impossible! No matter what I say, you are determined to bend my words."

"I've decided I'd rather not stay, Oliver. Please excuse me."

"You," he said, turning to her, "will go nowhere without me. Do you understand?"

"I am not your child, sir. Good night."

Bickering. They were bickering when they could be in the throes of passion. "Will you please stay with me?" he asked, approaching her, a hand outstretched.

"No. I don't want to be snappish, but how can you expect me to want to stay with you when I am so embarrassed? I thought you wished to . . . well, that you wished to."

"I *do* wish to."

She backed away. "You wish to so much that you didn't even notice I was removing my clothes."

"I was distracted, for God's sake."

She blinked rapidly, too rapidly. "Well, of course that explains it. How utterly demeaning."

"Lily, don't."

"Oh, I won't." With that, she flung away and ran from the room.

Grabbing up his cravat and coat, Oliver followed. "Damn it all," he muttered. "Damn coat. On and off. On and off. Damn woman."

Lily sped to the staircase, unlocked the door, and dashed upward.

One or two strides and he could stop her if he wished. To do so in anger, and while she was so overset, would be a mistake. Instead, he stayed a step behind all the way to the top floor.

There she finally looked back at him. "Another thing," she said. "Blasphemy becomes no man."

He opened his mouth to answer, but she was already speeding away again, in the direction of the music room.

More slowly, Oliver followed once more. Lily went directly to the piano and lighted a branch of candles. "I find it calms me to play," she told him, sounding so reasonable he rejoiced. "Alone. When I am finished, I shall find my way back."

"I cannot leave you."

"You can, and you will," she said. "This has been my home for many years. I am very comfortable here. I have never needed anyone to escort me."

"I wager you've never observed evidence of a thief in this house before either. Or been endangered when a lamp was thrown by a creature who threatened you in the darkness. Have you forgotten these things?"

"You make too much of them. You said nothing had actually been stolen. And anyway, it must have been Witless. He won't bother any of us again. He'll be too embarrassed to show his face here."

Oliver wished he was as convinced. "You may be right on all counts."

"Of course I'm right. It's obvious."

He considered. "Yes, I suppose so."

Lily had closed her bodice. Now she began to play, softly, but with great feeling. Within moments she seemed to forget him. Bending to her music, her fingers passed fluidly over the keys.

Oliver didn't recognize the piece. Drawn by the speeding notes that ran like a silver river, clear, over polished stones, he stood behind her. The composition had a quality that suggested happiness to Oliver, happiness and longing at once. Lily played as if possessed, but content in that possession.

With a final run, she stopped, and raised her hands from the keys.

He looked down on her hair where it curved over her

shoulders and on the wrongly buttoned bodice of her gown—and he smiled. Such a free spirit. So unconcerned with the things most young women spent their lives worrying about.

"What is that called?" he asked.

"You heard a little of it before. *Grace*. It is supposed to be the composition of some young German, or Russian, I cannot recall which. But it's said that in truth a Scottish nobleman—the Marquess of Stonehaven—wrote it about his wife some years ago. Music of love. The way he saw her in music. How special to be loved so."

Oliver bowed his head and thought about the other man, the man of whom she spoke. And he thought about Lily playing the piano he was almost certain had once been his father's. Frederick Worth had mentioned a piano with cloisonné panels.

His father would have approved of Lily.

"When I play *Grace* I see a woman dancing on sun-warmed grass," Lily said. "And she's laughing, and beckoning for a man to join her. It's the marquess, of course."

She folded her hands in her lap and turned her head away.

His throat constricted. He stroked her hair and let it slip through his fingers.

Lily didn't move.

There was a connection here. To his past, and from his past to his present and, through this woman, to his future. Carefully, he stepped away and went to the opposite end of the grand piano. By resting his elbows on the shell, he could watch her from beneath the raised lid. Candlelight danced over her pensive features.

"I should prefer to be alone, Oliver."

He had behaved badly. "Let me stay."

She raised her shoulders.

Oliver approached her again until he stood beside the keyboard, looking down at her.

Her sigh raised the bodice of her dress. A small woman in every way, yet more alluring to him than any other had ever been.

"Tell me what I should say, Lily?"

"I'm afraid."

He felt pain, as if from a blow. "I have made you afraid?"

She shook her head, and he saw that her eyelashes glittered. Tears, dammit. His fault. He said, "It is simple, but foolish, to become so involved with unimportant things that one doesn't realize there is a risk of losing what matters most."

"You didn't make me afraid. I've always been so—since I met you."

"Then how can you say it's not my fault?"

"Because it's mine." What he saw in her eyes, when she raised them, clenched his gut. The fear she spoke of was there. "My fault, Oliver. I hid my feelings for you behind sharp words and sham self-confidence. But all the time I . . . I was *interested* by you."

He ducked his head to make her meet his eyes. "Interested?"

"Interested," she repeated, and the stubborn set of her pointed chin almost made him smile. "I didn't think you could possibly be interested in me. Then, when you seemed to be, I dared to hope."

"And then you discovered I was in . . . interested in you, and now you know I always will be."

"Do I?"

"You doubt because you prepared to—to love me and I

didn't respond. I am a fool, my love. My only excuse is that a great deal has happened very quickly, and very unexpectedly." No excuse at all. "But it has also happened to you. If you wish it, I will go. I understand that you may need time alone, to consider what occurred this evening."

When she didn't answer he made to leave, but she caught his hand and kept him at her side.

She sat where she was, one hand in her lap, the other twined in his. If he could have held her, dared to take her in his arms, he would. He felt she might fly away at any moment and all but held his breath.

Seconds ticked past.

Neither of them moved. Oliver felt they did not breathe, and that their blood no longer pumped through their veins. They were frozen in time and place.

He could not bear to be so close yet not touch her, not when he knew he'd hurt her, not when he now carried her pain within him. Bending, he moved her hair and kissed the side of her neck.

She let out a shuddering breath.

Oliver kissed her again, long, and slow, and soft. He took the lobe of her ear in his teeth and bit gently.

Lily sighed, and her eyes drifted shut.

"Forgive me," he whispered.

"Forgive me," she echoed. "I am silly. I rush ahead without thinking—without really listening. Then I am mortified when I embarrass myself."

"You have nothing to be embarrassed about. I want to hold you, Lily."

"Because you are sorry for me."

He raised his head. "Sorry? Oh, no, my dear, not because I am sorry for you. Because I desire you as a man desires a woman." He should not pursue this tonight. The proper time would come and it was not now, not before she was his wife.

"I am confounded," she told him, rising abruptly from the bench and closing the keyboard. "Confused. You don't want me. You want me. You don't want me. You want me. I—"

He gripped her arm and swung her to face him. "I want you. I always want you. Do you understand me?"

Her lips parted, and he saw he'd shocked her.

"You talk glibly of knowing about men—about their mysteries, or whatever. What you do not know is the working of the mind of a man who desires a woman from the core of his being. The way I desire you. In such situations that man wants this woman all the time. Every moment. He falls asleep sweating, restless, and *ready* for her, Lily. And he awakens thinking of her. He turns in his bed to draw her into his arms and feels bereft when he discovers she isn't there."

All color had left her face. She said, "I see," but he knew she didn't see at all.

"Every time he looks at her, he cannot simply study her face, he must explore all of her." And he did so, from the top of her head, past her breasts—where he lingered—to her small waist and onward. "He sees whatever he looks at. Her smooth shoulders. Her breasts, high, pointed, small and sweet when they fit into his hands—when he takes their tips into his mouth."

She made a little sound and trembled again.

"Her waist is slender, and he can pass his hands around it in his thoughts, and feel it beneath his fingers. And her belly, flat and firm. Her thighs, and the place between where her womanliness is hidden, and where moisture forms, and heat, and swelling—and the searing, throbbing sensations that make her cry out for—"

"Don't!" She sank to sit on the keyboard cover. Her head hung forward. "Please, don't. It isn't seemly."

"An odd word on your lips, dearest. You push the walls of convention a thousand times a day."

"You make me weak."

He smiled. "I hope so. Weak, then strong. Strong when you are with me, for you will need to be strong. Your legs are pretty. Long for a small woman. Long and well made. I have touched them. I should like to touch them again."

"Now that you are not so distracted?" She tilted her face up and the glitter in her eyes was all anger. "Now that you are not inspecting my dowry?"

She was contrary, wrongheaded. "I shall have to find a way to gentle you, miss. To gentle your tongue before it wounds me."

"You will never gentle me, Oliver Worth. I have been shamed by my own reactions to you. But I am in command of myself now, and it shall not happen again."

"That you lose command of yourself?" He laughed. His own drive to command flowed hot once more. "But I think you will, dear Lily. I think I can make you lose yourself entirely to me."

"You think too highly of yourself, sir."

"Not at all. I think you seek to bait me—and you have succeeded. I have decided that it's time I sealed our bond." Without taking his eyes from her face, he moved in to stand with his thighs pressing her knees apart. "Yes, it's time."

She tried to edge away but only pressed into the piano. "You will not force me."

"No," he said. "I will not force you. Undo your dress, please."

Oliver removed his coat and dropped it, and the damnable cravat, and his shirt.

Still Lily made no attempt to unfasten her own clothing. She watched him with wide-open eyes and moistened lips.

He untied the bows at the neck of the ugly dress and made a vague note of the need to take her to London for gowns—many gowns. They would all be beautiful, and when she saw herself in them, she would feel beautiful.

The buttons down the front were next, and the outrageous length of orange satin around her waist.

With each move he made, she flinched but didn't try to stop him.

The dress was too big. Sliding the bodice from her shoulders and down her arms was simply accomplished. He regarded her narrow form encased in ridiculous but provocative stays. They held her pert breasts high, although they needed no help. Her nipples poked at the thin stuff of her chemise. And below, where the dress fell about her hips, the tapes on her petticoats were too long and fashioned in overlarge bows.

Oliver released these, and pushed down the petticoats until he could slip his hands beneath her firm, round bottom.

She grasped his shoulders for support, and he lifted her until he could allow the dress to fall at her feet.

"We can't, can we?" she murmured. "Here?"

"We can't what here?" he asked, allowing her no quarter now.

Lily pushed back her hair and Oliver feasted on the way her breasts rose inside their flimsy covering.

"Well, we can't do what you want to do like this? We have to lie down?"

He tipped back his head and laughed.

His laughter stopped abruptly when she ran her fingers through the hair on his chest, and said, "Why do you laugh at me? Am I so amusing all the time?"

"No," he said, and meant it. "You are not amusing all the time. Always seductive, but not always amusing. It is my place to teach you everything, Lily. Should you like to see how well you can do following instructions? If I tell you how things should be accomplished, would you enjoy guiding me, dear one?"

Her fingers closed painfully in his chest hair. "Yes, I should enjoy that," she told him formally.

"We have no need to lie down. When we are together in our own bed, no doubt we shall . . . No matter about that now. There are many ways to make love, many ways to join our bodies. Whatever, and wherever, and however we choose is as it should be. Whatever brings us pleasure."

"Yes, Oliver."

"I find you irresistible dressed as you are. It excites me. Give me your hand." When she did so he pressed it between his legs and felt satisfaction at the widening of her eyes. "Looking at you alone does that to me. Squeeze me, Lily."

"Yes, Oliver." With rapt concentration, she squeezed, sighed at the answering pulse of his flesh, and squeezed again. "I should like to kiss you there."

His knees all but buckled. He managed to say, "And so you shall. In time. I'd like to kiss your breasts."

She fumbled with the chemise until it was loosed and fell down around her arms, revealing her swollen breasts.

"How do they feel?" he asked.

She frowned.

"Touch them. Tell me how they feel then."

Keeping her eyes on his face, she quickly skimmed her fingertips over her nipples.

"No," he said. "No, dear one. Linger. Touch and pinch a little. Close your eyes and *feel*. I want to watch you."

She did as he asked. Her head fell slowly back and she supported her breasts, caught her nipples between fingers and thumbs and moaned.

With the tip of his tongue, Oliver flicked over the nubs of flesh she held, and locked his thighs when her hips pushed toward him.

"Is this as it should be?" she asked. "Oliver . . . Oh, Oliver."

He suckled, and placed his hands beneath hers, pushing her tender flesh higher until he rested his cheek on one breast and laved the other.

"Oliver?"

"Does the feeling please you?"

"Yes. *Yes*."

"Then all is as it should be." Or it would be soon.

"I'm wet, Oliver. Why do I grow wet?"

The furious swell of his manhood tore away Oliver's control. "You grow wet for me," he breathed. "To make our way easier."

"Then come to me and use it."

"Hush," he begged. He could not do this, not anymore. His restraint was cracking. "Lily, oh, Lily."

His trousers resisted long enough to drive him close to madness. He tore them down, spread the divide in her drawers, and drove into her slick flesh. He held her thighs while he pushed inside her, then ripped the white lawn apart to sink his fingers into her buttocks.

Her cry penetrated his brain, but faintly. Blackness and heat broke over him, and his body made its own pace. She felt like a warm, soft, pliant creature molded as a receptacle for everything of him that was male. Oliver felt the hammering of his maleness, the thud and pulse of his taking of this woman.

"Oliver!" she screamed.

He opened his eyes but was helpless to stop the rhythmic surging of his body into hers. Sweat burned his eyes. He dragged in great gulps of air.

Lily's mouth stretched in a grimace. She clutched his shoulder and he felt how she met him, thrust for thrust, cries jarring from her throat.

When his seed spilled—when release seemed to rip from his body, to tear him and make him long to be torn forever—he enfolded and held her, and she wound her arms around his neck and kissed his cheek, his eyelids.

He felt her spasms. Small, strong muscles when he was so tender he wanted to fall on her and beg her to stop, even while he begged her not to stop.

The storm ceased.

They held each other, panting out words neither needed to understand. When he could move, Oliver lifted Lily. Still inside her, he wrapped her legs around his hips and went with her to a sheet-draped chaise.

He fell, turning as he did so to bring her down on top of him.

"I didn't know," Lily said, almost brokenly. "I could not have guessed how it would be. I . . . To be with you—part of you—is true bliss."

Oliver settled her face beneath his jaw and stroked her tangled hair away from her brow. "You are my breath, my blood, my bone, Lily. You are wind in my hair, and song to my ears, and a poem to my heart. You are sun on my skin. And you are stars in the sky of my dreams. You are my life. You are my only love."

Hours had passed when they finally dressed. Lily searched Oliver's face again and again, seeking for some key to the mystery he had revealed to her—the mystery that she became with him.

She would find a way to ask him about the mystery, but not now.

"Let me," he said when she was dealing with the fastenings on her dress. And he tied tapes, buttoned buttons, fashioned bows with his capable, wonderful fingers. Concentration drew his fine brows together, and only when he must have felt her eyes on his did he look back at her.

"Thank you," she said. "Am I a very wicked woman?"

One brow rose. "Wicked?"

"Oliver, I am complete with you. There is nothing I would not do with you. And I love doing it!" She giggled into a hand and felt young and marvelously silly. "So I am that wanton thing, aren't I?"

"You, my girl, are that wonderful thing. And I shall not sleep again until you are my wife."

"Yes, you will. If you don't you will not be able to marry me, because you'll fall asleep at the altar."

"Always literal," he said, sighing. "Come, I'd best get you back to your rooms, although how I shall bear to let you go I cannot imagine."

She wanted to tell him to stay with her, but knew she mustn't.

Holding hands, they strolled toward the door to the bridge, each aware that they dawdled to delay the parting.

"I love you," Lily said shyly.

Oliver used a knuckle to tip up her face. And he kissed her softly before carrying on. "I know you love me," he said. "Almost as much as I love you."

She didn't argue, but she smiled a secret smile, certain he could not possibly love her nearly as much as she loved him.

Through the dim corridor they progressed, reluctant to bid their night goodbye.

Oliver glanced at the paintings as they passed, and Lily looked from face to face also. "Do you think they disapprove greatly?" she asked.

"I think they're jealous," he responded. "We have stirred their painted hearts." He came to a halt.

Lily frowned and followed the direction of his starc. "Oh, Oliver. My goodness. How can that be?"

"I should have expected it," he said quietly. "Another sign, damn him."

Lily couldn't imagine what he meant. In the morning she would have to tell Papa that the painting of the banished marquess was missing.

Chapter Twenty-three

"Mr. Nicholas Westmoreland to see you, miss." Hilda stood just inside Lily's sitting-room door and bobbed a curtsy.

Lily stepped away from the modiste who was working on her wedding dress and didn't care that the woman rolled her eyes. "Have him come in, please, Hilda." Never mind that the last person she expected to see in her rooms was Mr. Westmoreland. He could save her from the modiste's ridiculous fussing—even if only for a short time.

"Good morning, Lily," Nick said, coming in without waiting for Hilda to admit him. "I'm here on a mission."

Hilda gave Mr. Westmoreland a sly glance before departing and closing the door.

"Good morning," Lily said. "I hope you're enjoying your stay with us." She liked the closeness she'd observed between Oliver and Nick.

"Mademoiselle," the modiste implored. *"S'il vous plaît."*

"Madame," Nick said to the modiste. "I also bring a message for you from Mr. Worth. I believe he spoke to you about a certain something he wanted you to do."

"Oh!" Lily plopped her fists on her hips. "You are a

thespian, sir. Or an accomplished liar. You said you didn't know anything about it."

His serious expression didn't change. "But I can't be sure we're talking about the same something, can I? Mr. Worth would like to see you before you go, madame."

Rather than leave, Nick hovered while Mme. Sportes continued pinning and tucking, tweaking and tutting.

Nick's appraisal made Lily uncomfortable. She glanced at him and smiled.

He nodded but didn't return her smile. "Very fetching. You are different from Oliver's other women."

Oliver's other women. Lily stared at him. "Does he have so many?"

The man laughed. He was more than attractive, with very green eyes and thick brown hair. Tall, he imparted an air of impatient energy. He moved restlessly, his hands behind his back. "Oliver is a different man now, Lily. He obviously has eyes for no one but you."

She shouldn't feel such relief.

"You have changed him."

"And he has changed me," she said, revolving slowly while the hem of the white satin gown was pinned.

Still Nick showed no sign of leaving.

"I shall overlay the bodice with Belgian lace, *mademoiselle.* And there will be many pearls."

Lily waved a hand. "Whatever you want. But I should like some color."

"Color?" The woman gestured widely. "What color? What can you mean?"

"I mean color. My wedding is to be a celebration. Color. I am particularly fond of rosettes."

Mme. Sportes pushed out her lips and frowned. "Yes,"

she said uncertainly. "It could be. White satin rosettes. Perhaps at the hem."

"Lily," Nick said. "I promised I'd rejoin the party in the garden."

"What party?" Lily asked, frowning at her reflection in a mirror.

"Your father and Oliver. And Lord Witmore and his sister—and their friend."

Lily forgot the pins beneath her long, tight sleeve and dropped her arm to her side. Immediately she squealed and raised the arm again. "Witmore? Here? I can't believe the man's gall." She knew Oliver had confided previous events to Nick—some previous events. "What does he want? How can he possibly show his face?"

"He's a pompous ass," Nick said, and cleared his throat uncomfortably. "Excuse me. I mean he is not a man of deep character. I know Oliver would like you to join him as soon as you can."

"Hurry," Lily told the modiste. "We can finish later. I must hear what Witless has to say for himself. Is Aunt Fribble there?"

"She wasn't when I left. May I be frank with you, Lily?"

"Of course."

"A frank question, then. Are you certain you and Oliver are right for each other?"

At first she wasn't sure she'd heard him correctly. The question in his eyes assured her she had. "You have taken me by surprise."

"I believe you to be an honest, thoughtful woman. And I want the best for my old friend. I also believe that you are a delight and I understand why he is so taken with you. I will only ask you this once. Do you think he is suited to living his life in a small English village?"

She could not say what she wished to say: that she was certain Oliver would never regret deciding to make a life here. "How may we know for sure what our hearts may decide at some future time? I know I love him, and that will never change. And I believe he loves me as much."

"A good answer. But what if he should come to miss his homeland? His homeland isn't England."

Lily ran her teeth over her bottom lip. The yellow room no longer seemed so bright, and her heart was no longer so light. "I don't know," she said quietly. Would he welcome her into his life in America?

Nick bowed and retreated. "Thank you. All I ask is that you be sure this marriage is the best thing for both of you."

She laced her fingers together tightly and held them against her stomach. "I know you only ask because you care for Oliver."

"Yes. And—although we are newly acquainted—I also want the best for you, Lily. You are a very special woman. But perhaps it will all be for the best and my worries will be proven wrong. I hope so. May I at least tell Oliver that you look ravishing in your gown?" His sudden smile transformed his serious face. He became boyishly charming.

Lily smiled back. "You may tell him that. And I will join you shortly."

"Good enough. By the great oak in the rose gardens." He saluted and was gone.

And with him went the last vestiges of joy Lily had found in the day.

"Rosettes at the hem, then, *mademoiselle*?"

Would she make Oliver happy? "Yes," she said, distracted. "I have some suitable material for the purpose."

She could not turn back from Oliver. Even if she was being selfish in letting him marry her, in encouraging him to make his home here, she couldn't do otherwise.

"I must obtain fabric from the same lot," the modiste said.

"I told you I wanted color," Lily said, feeling fretful. "Wait." She ran to the bedroom, rummaged through a box in her wardrobe, and returned. "Here. Use this."

"This?" Mme. Sportes looked from the satin ribbon to Lily. "But—"

"It will do very well. And it will mean there is less money spent on a dress to be worn once."

The woman held the ribbon aloft and let it unroll. "It is striped, *mademoiselle*, striped purple, and green, and pink."

"Yes. And there is a great deal of it. So make the rosettes very large."

Oliver's attention strayed repeatedly to the doors at the back of the house. Any hour spent without Lily was an hour wasted. Nick emerged and ran down the steps.

"A handsome man," Lady Virtue remarked, her blue eyes narrowed on Nick. "But a tradesman. How unfortunate."

"Mr. Westmoreland is an architect," Professor Adler said. "Very interesting man."

"Very interesting," Lady Virtue murmured. Oliver made note to warn Nick to watch out for his honor.

With Sir Cecil Laycock snoring on a blanket beside him, Lord Witmore lounged in a white wooden chair, a glass of champagne—champagne he'd brought with him—balanced on its arm. "Well," he said, raising the glass. "I'll do it again once the little lady arrives. But here's to you, Worth. Congratulations to the best fella and all that."

"Mr. Worth is hardly a better fellow than you, Reggie, darling," Lady Virtue said without taking her eyes off the approaching Nick. "He merely caught Lily's eye. No doubt she's taken with his being a foreigner. Something rather like girls who fall in love with men in uniform. We all know about that."

Another figure approached, a large man with red hair. He wore a green velvet jacket and a kilt, and his big knees showed above socks of red, green, and yellow. He arrived with a large hamper, set it down, and threw open the lid.

"Ah, jolly good, McLewd," Witmore said. "Another little peace offerin'."

"I'm sure you don't need to bring peace offerings," the professor said. "After all, you wanted to marry Lily but she didn't want to marry you. Seems simple enough. Who can know the depth of a woman's intuition? If she sees beneath the skin to the soul and finds an onion, well, there you are, aren't you?"

Oliver was close to laughing aloud at the intent concentration on Witmore's face. The man actually thought he'd just heard a philosophical pearl.

"Cecil!" Witmore roused himself. "Wake up, Cecil. Pâté, professor? Game pies? Caviar? Potted salmon? Jellied venison? McLewd will serve us."

"Are you well, McLewd?" the professor asked, a trifle stiffly, Oliver thought.

"Aye," the giant said. "Well enough, sir. Will ye try the poached pigeon hearts?"

"McLewd used to work for me," Professor Adler said to Oliver. "Before Lord Witmore lured him away."

Nick ambled up and stood a small distance from the others. Silent, as only he could be silent—in a manner that caught the attention of all—he returned Lady Virtue's coquettish smiles with an indifferent nod.

The sight of Lily running down the steps from the house distracted Oliver. He went to meet her. Before they were closer than a hundred yards he saw the breadth of her smile. She held out her hands and he strode to take them.

"Eleven days," he told her. "Have days ever passed so slowly?"

She shook her head and bobbed to her toes to kiss him lightly. "Never. I declare we should have gone to Gretna Green, Oliver."

"We'll go now, then," he told her. "At once."

"Hmm. I think my papa would have something to say about that. But tell me, what does Witless want? I am beside myself with curiosity. Oliver—can you countenance that he would show his face here?"

"He's showed his face and is about ingratiating himself with all who come near. The man's amazing."

"No wonder Fribble's nowhere to be seen," she said with narrowed eyes. "He shall not ingratiate himself with me."

Hand in hand they joined the party beneath the wide branches of an ancient oak surrounded at a short distance by beds of billowing roses.

"Here's our little bride-to-be," Lady Virtue said in a tone one might use when speaking to a very small child. "Oliver said you were being fitted for your wedding dress. Do be certain it is as simple as possible, dear. Very small people must do whatever they can to overcome the impression of immature stature."

"I'm sure the dress will be delightful," Oliver said. "Your neighbors came to wish us well, Lily."

"And to bring a picnic," Lord Witmore announced in booming tones. "This calls for a celebration, what?"

Lady Virtue rose from her chair. She frowned at Lily. "Are you well? You're very pale, my dear. And so thin. Why, you're little more than a bundle of bones." Her upper lip curled with distaste. "Not at all healthy-looking. Marriage is taxing, dear girl, you must be more robust if you are to survive."

"I'm very strong, thank you," Lily said.

"Reggie and I came to offer you our support," Lady Virtue said. "After all, you aren't exactly proficient in the area of social niceties, are you, Lily? Since the entire neighborhood will expect your wedding to be an impeccable affair, you'll need help. Reggie and I will give you that help."

Sir Cecil Laycock made a chomping noise, snored so loudly he almost wakened himself, and turned on his side.

"Where is Aunt Fribble" Lily asked, looking at Witmore.

"Indisposed," Papa said promptly.

Fribble had been generally indisposed since That Night.

Oliver felt Lily move restlessly beside him. She said, with no attempt at civility, "I'm sure Papa will be glad for you to enjoy your picnic here, Lord Witmore. But I'm sorry to say we Adlers have some pressing matters to attend."

In other words, the lady had no wish to spend time with her detestable neighbors.

Professor Adler promptly rose. "As you say, my dear."

Cross petulance didn't suit Lady Virtue's features. "You are absolutely right, Lily. Of course you have a great deal to do." She stood on the other side of Oliver from Lily. "You and Cecil have your picnic, Reggie. Lily needs someone of her own age to share this special time with her, don't you, Lily?"

"Well, I—"

"Of course you do. I want to know everything about your wedding gown. And you will have other matters you need to discuss. Not that I would know a great deal of help, since I am also unmarried." She slanted Oliver a seductive glance. "But talking about intimate things can make them so much less fearsome."

Oliver was so angry, he simply ignored Virtue. "If you'll excuse us," he said to Witmore and his distasteful sister, "we'll leave you to your picnic."

"I wouldn't hear of it," Lady Virtue persisted. "Reggie and I came to offer whatever assistance might be useful. I have a particularly beautiful diamond necklace. I'd thought Lily would enjoy wearing it at her wedding."

Oliver did not trust the woman.

"That's kind of you," Lily said. "But I'd rather not."

Lady Virtue laughed. "Oh, don't worry, they'll be the focus of attention, but sometimes that's as well, don't you think? Everyone will look at the necklace, and afterward they will think you must have been lovely wearing them." She clapped her hands and laughed.

Oliver ground his teeth.

"I have an even better idea." She slipped her hands around Oliver's elbow and clung. "Let us allow the rest to remain here, Oliver. I want to share a perfectly wonderful inspiration of mine with you. We both know how receptive you are to inspiration."

The woman's beautiful blue eyes were so cold, Oliver felt a chill run down his spine. For the purpose of unsettling Lily, she sought to suggest some connection between them. Clearly, Oliver mused, desperation made these people determined to continue their mischief.

"I cannot imagine," Oliver said, removing her hands from his arm, "that you and I could ever share anything of interest, Lady Virtue. Now, if you'll excuse us?"

He turned from her and took Lily's hand in his. It was only as he passed the man that he noted how Sir Cecil Laycock continued to snore while he watched the proceedings through slitted eyes.

Nick joined them in Papa's study. "What do you suppose all that was about?" he asked.

"Witmore's last effort to secure Lily's hand," Papa said promptly. "Stupid fellow if ever I saw one. And that Laycock is even more stupid."

"Yet you wanted me to consider Revolting Reggie's offer of marriage," Lily said mildly.

"Did I?" Papa perched his spectacles on his nose. "Shows what a man can sink to when he's burdened with a particularly difficult daughter."

Lily noted Nick's stare at Oliver, and his subtle head motion toward the door, then Nick said, "Would you excuse us, please, Professor? And you, Lily? Oliver and I have some important business to attend." One of his rare smiles had what was no doubt its desired effect on Papa, who chuckled and nodded as the two men left the room.

"Are you happy?" Papa asked Lily.

"I couldn't be happier."

He regarded her over the tops of his spectacles. "A fine

fellow, Oliver. I knew it from the moment I met him. I'm glad you find him just as fine."

"I rather think you intended that I should," Lily said in as unconcerned a manner as she could muster. "In fact, I have wondered if you employed Oliver with the thought that you might like him to be your son-in-law."

Papa sat, opened a book, and said, "How is the wedding gown coming? Well, I hope."

She did not find comfort in the notion—no, the certainty—that her father had conspired to bring about her match to Oliver Worth.

In the early-afternoon hours, when Oliver didn't come to her as she might have expected, Lily had much time to consider what had passed between them. It hardly seemed credible that she had known Oliver only six weeks. She felt it could not be possible that he'd come into her life so recently.

This waiting was not at all her style.

Lily quitted her sitting room and went in search of him. The outdoors called to her. She'd seen Witless and his entourage depart. If she could locate Oliver, she'd suggest they go for a walk through the gardens, and perhaps even on the moors.

Oliver wasn't in his own rooms.

Where to start her search? She didn't want to ask the servants where he might be. Fribble ruled the household with fear. Any member of the staff would undoubtedly tell her that Lily was trying to find Oliver. And then Aunt Fribble might make some unpleasantness of that.

Lily set off for Nick Westmoreland's apartments. She heard the rumble of masculine voices from the other side of the door before she even drew close. Masculine voices raised in anger.

Reluctant to intrude on two old friends, she passed the suite and settled to wait on a carved wooden bench farther along the corridor. Opposite, a pretty room stood open and Lily recalled that her mother had once used it as a retreat where she went to read.

Lily tried, but failed, to remember her mother's face. The effort made her sad.

She waited a long time. So long she thought she should leave or be considered an eavesdropper when Oliver did come from his friend's rooms.

Knocking on the door would be the most natural thing to do.

There were endless excuses she could make for seeking Oliver at such a time.

She rose and approached, and raised a hand to knock.

"There's no point in this, Nick," she heard Oliver say. "We've wasted valuable time. You will not change my mind."

Nick's softer voice required Lily to lean closer to hear. "I will repeat," he said. "You are making a terrible mistake. Or you will be if you go through with this."

She gripped the doorjamb, and as she did so a movement made her look over her shoulder, in time to see the butler, Gambol, doing his best to quit her mother's old reading room and sneak away without being observed.

Lily deliberately turned her face from him. She felt sick and besieged—and confused.

"Oliver," Nick said. "Have you heard anything I've told you?"

"Every word. For longer than I've cared to listen. I will not be swayed in this. My mind is made up."

"Your mind is made up to throw your lot in with the eccentric collection in this house? Nothing will persuade you that within months you may be as mad as some of them already are?"

Sickness became weakness in Lily's limbs. She longed to sit down, and didn't trust her legs to bear her away.

"You forget I know you, Oliver Worth," Nick said. "You are my friend, my dearest friend, and I love you like the brother you've become to me. But I know your weaknesses."

Oliver said, "And I suppose you are about to remind me of them. Be quick about it, Nick. I've other matters to attend."

"Of course you do. Like continuing with this play in which you've taken the lead role. Never mind that it's obvious there are those who would do almost anything to stop you. It's dangerous here, Oliver. How many more unpleasant events will it require to convince you of that? Come away, man, before whoever is determined to be rid of you accomplishes something I shall regret, even if you don't. I cannot bear to lose you."

Lily turned her back to the wall beside the door and closed her eyes. She had to go, quickly.

"My mind is made up," Oliver said. "I remain at Blackmoor."

"Fool," Nick said, and Lily visualized him speaking through clenched teeth. "I thought you would abandon these grandiose notions, but you haven't, have you. And you will remain here and marry Lily Adler to achieve what you've always wanted."

"Which is?" There was menace in Oliver's voice.

"The kind of power that comes with all of this. The power of controlling an ancient estate. And you will do anything to get it. Including marrying a girl who is nice enough, but not anyone who would have caught your eye if she could not give you what you want."

"Have a care," Oliver said. "You go too far."

"Because I am honest? I'll take my chances. You will do all this to one day watch others fawn upon you. You will do it to be lord of the manor. The lord of Blackmoor Hall."

Chapter Twenty-four

Good friends were a prize beyond price, Lily thought. Even if one of them did have a particularly sanctimonious and annoying brother.

She looked at Rosemary, who looked back, then at Myrtle and, finally, at Eustace Godwin.

"I think we should make a proposition to the Senior Altar Society," Myrtle said.

Lily regarded her with interest. It was not usually Myrtle who thought of means to divert attention from the true endeavors of the Junior Altar Society.

"Do tell," Rosemary said.

Ensconced before the fireplace, dressed in what was clearly overly warm black serge and his customary leather gaiters, Eustace sniffed loudly enough to gain the attention of all.

"I have been thinking," he said, jutting his red lower lip. "Given the unfortunate tendencies I've observed in at least one of you, I must make a greater effort to take a hand in your moral guidance."

"Oh, Eustace!" Sounding quite unlike herself, Rosemary popped up from her seat. "Either make yourself clear, or be so good as to leave us to our toils. We are all too old to be subjected to lectures."

Lily realized her mouth had fallen open, but closed it at the sound of Myrtle's hands clapping together.

"I shall ignore your outburst," Eustace said. "All of you. But I will not be swayed. From now on I must insist upon being present with you for at least a part of your meetings."

Lily regarded the man's thin, fair hair, his pale eyes and wet mouth—and his protruding stomach—but decided her dislike of him had little to do with his unpleasant countenance. He was ponderous and self-serving. Obsequious. And ambitious.

"I should have preferred to speak with you alone, Lily," he said. "But since the household at Blackmoor has matters other than spiritual health in mind at the present, I am barely allowed entrance to the hall."

"Not so," Lily said hotly. "Why, I saw you there just this morning."

He colored slightly.

"And yesterday, also. In fact, you are there most days."

He cleared his throat and wriggled his snub nose. "Yes, well, your aunt is a most pious woman. She has been as troubled by this ridiculous marriage plan of yours as I have. And, since she has no other ally, she has come to me for solace. You are not grateful for her sacrifice in bringing you up, Lily. If you were, you would give her the respect of listening to the wisdom of her years."

The idea of Fribble bleating to Eustace angered Lily. She bit back the temptation to ask if her aunt had mentioned any disquiet over dallying with a man she continued to propose as a husband for her niece.

"This man you say you will marry is a stranger," Eustace said. "An *American*. What do you know of him? Nothing. You are besotted. The fact that a man with a smooth and flashy appearance shows an interest in you sweeps you off your feet. A more mature girl would understand that this is not the kind of man who would pursue her unless she was in the way of acquiring a fortune."

"Oh," Myrtle said faintly.

Rosemary's face had whitened. "Eustace, I am ashamed of you. Kindly leave us. We have much to accomplish. And you will not be welcome at our future meetings."

He showed no sign of remorse. "I will leave. But, since this is my house, I shall attend whatever I choose to attend here. And you will do well to think about what I've said, Lily. Look closer to home and to someone who has known and cared for you most of your life." With that he swept from the room.

The three friends waited until they heard the front door close behind him, then Rosemary and Myrtle rushed to the window to watch his progress through the gardens and into the churchyard on his way to St. Cedric's.

"Oh," Rosemary said. "I am so embarrassed."

"You are not to be embarrassed," Lily said promptly. "We are not responsible for the bad behavior of others."

"But what can have got into him? To make such awful statements?"

Lily put an arm around the other woman and led her back to her chair. "Eustace takes his responsibilities very seriously. Can we talk of other things, please? I sent word for the two of you to meet with me because I need you both. I am quite beside myself and cannot think what to do."

She gained immediate attention. Myrtle said, "Do tell, Lily. What's happened?"

Now she had brought the three of them together, and had begun to confide matters closest to her heart, Lily found she was unsure of what to say, or how much to reveal.

"Lily," Rosemary said. "Is it Oliver? Is something worrying you about Oliver?"

"No." Silly. She could not pretend and still hope to find solace.

"Good," Myrtle said, giggling suddenly. "You've news for us at last, haven't you?"

Lily frowned and said, "News? What kind of news?"

Myrtle plucked at the deep flounces at the knee of her skirts. "You know," she said coyly. "Rosemary and I are just dying to hear all about it. After all, neither of us has had the opportunity to report on the focus of our society with the benefit of firsthand observation."

"*Myrtle,*" Rosemary said. "We must not assume these things."

Myrtle was not to be subdued. "Of course we must assume them. Lily is engaged. Think of it, Rosemary, *engaged.* To one of them. Come along, Lily, do. What have you discovered about the mysterious parts?"

A rush of tears shocked Lily. She gulped, and fumbled in her reticule for a handkerchief.

"See what you've done, Myrtle?" Rosemary said. "Oh, Lily, dear. It's all right. Don't you say another word you don't feel like saying."

"The beast," Myrtle announced. "But we knew it. We knew that whatever this thing was that made them so different, it was capable of undoing the female. And this is the proof of it. Poor, poor Lily."

"It's not that," Lily said, wiping her eyes. "I love him, I do."

"I know you do," Rosemary said at once. "And there are bound to be areas of . . . adjustment?"

Areas of adjustment. Lily grew warm inside at the thought of some of the adjustments she'd already made to Oliver Worth.

"Tell us how we can help," Rosemary said.

Myrtle, who was inevitably slow to relinquish annoyance, said, "Bounder. We shall bare his mysteries to the world."

"Oh," Lily moaned. "You do not understand at all. He can't help it. At least, I don't think he can. He may not even know exactly the effect he's having on me. In fact, he doesn't know. You see, he's secretive. I *think* he's secretive. There are definitely things he has not revealed about himself."

"His mysteries," Myrtle said promptly.

"I'm almost certain he's keeping some parts of himself from me. And I wonder if it can be because he doesn't trust me."

"We're so glad you came to us," Rosemary said. She went to Lily and hugged her. "We're glad you know we are your friends who will always want to share your good times and your bad times—just as you will share ours."

"I love you both," Lily said. But she didn't know how to tell them exactly what troubled her, not completely.

"Couldn't it be part of the adjustment phase?" Rosemary asked. "For Oliver as well as for you? You are both coping with a new stage in life, one where you are responsible for the well-being of another."

"If men would acknowledge the burdens they carry, and be open in the matter, there would be far less need for women to suffer in trying to deal with the affair," Myrtle said.

"But perhaps they don't see those things as burdens," Rosemary suggested. "After all, they're born with them, so they may seem quite normal. What do you think, Lily?"

"I think you are remarkably astute, as usual. But I do think there may be a degree of shame that prevents them from complete openness."

"You may have expected too much of him, given his handicap," Myrtle said. "I say you teach him the power of trust by laying open the keys to his mysteries. Expose him and teach him to be accepting of the affliction for which he bears no responsibility. After all, he was born that way."

Lily wanted to say that, in most respects, she was exceedingly pleased with the way Oliver had been born, but thought better of it.

The Godwins' housekeeper tapped on the door and put her head into the room. "Miss Lily? There's someone here with a message for you from the Hall. He doesn't want to come in."

Lily got up at once and went into the foyer, where Leonard, one of the Blackmoor grooms, stood in the open doorway with his hat held in both hands.

"Leonard," she said. "Is something wrong?"

He looked awkward and shuffled his feet. "Why, no, Miss Adler. That is, I don't know. I were asked to tell ye something private." Stepping backward through the front door, he kept his eyes on Lily's face, and she followed him. He dropped his voice. "I were told to say you're needed at the Cathedral."

Lily waited for him to continue. When he didn't, she said, "The Cathedral, Leonard? That's all? The whole message?"

"In Salisbury, Miss Adler. Quick as ye can. That's what I were told."

"By whom?"

"The message come from the professor's man. Mr. Worth. You're to go to . . ." He scratched his forehead. "To St. Michael's Chapel. A matter of importance to your future. That's right. That's what it were. All right, then, Miss Adler?"

She nodded distractedly and glanced behind her into the hall of the rectory. Blessedly, the housekeeper had left. Rosemary and Myrtle were in the sitting room and should not be able to overhear from there.

It wasn't until Leonard had left the Rectory gardens that Lily realized she had no idea how she would get to Salisbury. She made move to call the groom back, but changed her mind. There was something about Leonard she didn't care for.

But she had to get to Salisbury. "A matter of importance to your future." Oliver wouldn't send such a message, and such instructions, if they weren't unavoidable.

With the excuse that she was required at home—and fervent promises that they would continue their discussion—Lily took her leave of Rosemary and Myrtle.

Salisbury wasn't far. Surely she could find someone going that way who would take her.

Closing the gate to the Rectory gardens, she walked directly into Leonard's very solid body. He stepped back, doffed his cap and bowed, and murmured profuse apologies.

"It was my fault," Lily said. "I was careless." She was about to bid him good day when she noted one of Papa's carriages on the opposite side of the narrow street.

"Ye all right, then, Miss Adler?" Leonard said.

"Yes. I need you to drive me to Salisbury."

"Aye, Miss Adler." He grinned. "O' course. What am I thinkin'. Y'need a ride there."

"Yes," she said, smiling with relief. "To the Cathedral."

"Aye. I'd say fortune's smiled on ye, miss. I might 'ave left already. Ye come along wi' me."

"Thank you," Lily said, triumphant. Really, fortune did smile if one kept one's wits about one.

The late-afternoon sun turned the Cathedral spire glistening white. As she had on every previous visit, Lily spared admiration for the beauty of the impressive building that had taken so many so long to complete. But deep foreboding soon smothered any other emotion.

What could possibly be desperate enough to cause Oliver to ask her to meet him here?

Leonard drove the coach past the entrance to Vestry Lane, and she remembered the day when she and Rosemary had come here with Oliver. Her life, hitherto so serene—abominably, boringly so—had become completely changed by Oliver Worth.

How much more daylight would there be?

Lily pressed closer to the window. She must return to Blackmoor before Papa became concerned at her absence.

She hadn't spoken with Oliver after the conversation she'd overheard. They hadn't as much as seen each other since Oliver and Nick left Papa's study.

That must be the reason Oliver wanted to see her. He must be unsettled by the things Nick had said. . . . She was making excuses for him without knowing the truth. Nick had announced that Oliver had always wanted to be "lord of the manor." Could it be that ambition was what drove him to want her?

The carriage passed through a stone gate into the Close

surrounding the Cathedral. They drove on a ways before the wheels slowed and ground to a halt. The springs sagged as Leonard jumped down and came to help her out.

"All right, then, Miss Adler? Wait 'ere for ye, then, shall I?" Leonard looked around. "I don't see no other coach."

"Yes," Lily said, absurdly grateful to know she had a way home. "Yes, Leonard. Thank you very much."

She entered the building by an entrance on the right side of the main face. Instantly she was enveloped by the scent of ancient holy incense, and more ancient stone—and dust in crevices, and the putrid dregs of water in urns that had held flowers.

Moving rapidly, disturbed at the feeling of being alone in a vast, sacred edifice with evening approaching, she made her way to the nave. A single figure in a black cassock, head bent, walked from the quire—at the opposite end of the nave—and slowly moved into the darker recesses of the Cathedral. Shortly another followed, and also disappeared.

Lily walked forward more slowly and heard the sound of her own breathing, the scuff of her own shoes. Dimming light through stained-glass windows spread muted patches of color high on massive, soaring pillars.

The sun was going down fast.

From a distance, possibly from the Chapter House, came a short exchange of male voices, then silence again.

Lily paused. The whole felt like a tabloid into which she'd intruded, and where she was invisible.

She was a silly goose. Papa had brought her here several times, and she remembered St. Michael's Chapel. Oliver would be waiting for her there.

A right turn between the nave and the facing rows of wooden pews in the quire and she saw the ornate screens that formed the outer wall of the chapel she sought.

Again she was aware of how loudly she breathed.

A bell sounded.

Lily pressed the palm of her right hand over her heart and closed her eyes. A very small bell. There were always bells in churches, for goodness' sake.

She reached the chapel and slipped inside. Candles glowed on an altar beautifully draped in richly embroidered tapestry.

Oliver wasn't there.

Her heart beat even harder, and louder. She could return to the coach at once. But he wouldn't have sent for her simply to cause her inconvenience.

Leonard might have given her the name of the wrong chapel, and the Cathedral housed many. In searching, she might miss Oliver. Trying to select another, more possible one was out of the question.

Turning to watch the entrance, she walked backward toward the altar. There was too little light, and the dimness frightened her.

Facing the altar again, she went to sink down on a kneeler and clasp her hands.

"You came."

She all but leaped to her feet. "Oliver!"

"Stay on your knees," he said in low tones. "And keep your voice down, please. Bow your head so that any who come this way will assume we are in prayer."

Lily did not care for intrigue—not intrigue of this variety—but she did as he instructed.

With measured steps, his boots clipped on stone. She

felt him draw near and looked around, and suffered another shock.

Oliver wore the brown habit of a monk, the çowl pulled forward to cover his face, his hands crossed and pressed inside the draping sleeves.

"What are you doing, Oliver? For goodness' sake, what on earth are you thinking? A monk's habit, why—"

"Hush!" The order was soft but insistent. "I beg of you to keep your voice down."

"Yes," she whispered. "You sound so strange. Not at all like yourself."

He went to his knees a few feet distant from her. "Listen to me. I have information, and it is my duty to pass it to you."

Lily peered at him. There was . . . "You are not Oliver, are you?" She began to rise. This was a stranger. "We have never met."

"That is immaterial. Stay on your knees, or rue your imprudent actions."

Slowly, she subsided again. "This day has been quite too much."

"No doubt. You do not know me. But I know someone who does. Someone who admires you greatly, and who has your interests at heart."

"Who?" Lily asked. "And why was it necessary to get me here through falsehood?"

"Because you do not hold my friend in high regard. I shall not discuss that matter further. Only know that what I have done is meant as a kindness. Oliver Worth is not what he would like you to believe he is."

"Oh, *really,* this is too much."

"Indeed, Miss Adler. It is very much too much. This

man Worth intends to use you. He would not marry you otherwise."

Anger stiffened Lily's back, and her nerves. "Did Lord Witmore send you?"

Silence.

"Did he? Speak up. Did Lord Witmore ask you to lure me here so that you could impart poisonous rumors about Oliver?"

"Absolutely not. I am not acquainted with Lord Witmore."

"Who, then?"

"I am not at liberty to share that information with you. But I will say that the person in question has worshiped you from afar for a long time. He knows you would never consider a suit on his part, but still feels it his duty to save you from a disastrous match."

"And to *save* me, he felt it necessary to submit me to this outrageousness?"

"He regrets that. He could think of no other way."

"But Leonard brought a message from Oliver."

"That is not my affair. Let me finish, please. This man, Worth, is an impostor. He is not who he says he is. If you marry him, you will not, in fact, be married at all."

Lily bowed her head. "Foolishness. I do not believe you."

"Call off the wedding. My friend begs you to call off the wedding—at least until you've taken the time to investigate Worth's background. We believe he had a mission here in England and that he thinks you can help him accomplish that mission."

"I—"

A clanging crash sealed Lily's lips. She jumped to her feet and whirled around. "What is it?"

Scuffling followed, and running footsteps—outside the chapel. The light had dimmed so that dust motes hovered in blue-gray swirls about each yellow candle flame.

"Remain," the cowled figure ordered. "Fear not. It may be that someone has listened to our conversation, but he'll be away now—and it's very unlikely to have been anyone who knows you. I'll check. Do not move from this spot or I can't be sure of your safety."

Lily took a step toward him. "Please let me come with you."

"You would impede me. Do as I ask. Now."

He walked swiftly from the chapel, and Lily heard him move down the nave.

The bell she'd heard before chimed again, and she flinched again.

Another set of footsteps sounded, but quickly faded.

Lily was left with only the beat of her heart, the pounding of blood in her ears, at her temples—and with perspiration on her palms.

The gold cross on the altar glimmered. She stared at it and prayed to be brave. And she did feel a little braver, but only a little.

If not Witless, then who had sent this so-called warning about Oliver?

Why would she believe a stranger who said he hadn't been sent by Witless? If he had sent the man, he'd tell him to deny it anyway.

But it could be someone else.

Beyond a window the sky was bruised puce and purple. Would Leonard wait? Would he come looking for her? Lily had never thought she would long so for the sight of Leonard's face.

She strained to listen for the sound of returning footsteps, but none came.

If the man intended to ensure her safety, would he have left her alone here? For so long?

Should she go?

Did they lock the Cathedral doors at night?

A great breath felt as if it might choke her. To spend a night here, alone, would surely kill her by fright.

The monk—or whoever he was—wasn't coming back.

Hesitantly at first, Lily went on tiptoe from the chapel. On the flagstones outside lay what must have made the frightful sound: a large brass candle branch, its candles scattered.

She searched in all directions but saw not a soul.

Lily ran. She dashed, taking as long steps as her legs, and the heaviness of her petticoats, would allow. And as she ran, she glanced repeatedly over her shoulder. Each monument and statue cast long, dark shadows over floor and pew.

A flittering thing brushed her cheek, and she shrieked.

A bat. The winged rodent soared upward into the cavernous recesses of the arches above.

Her throat wouldn't work anymore. Dry gasps hurt the roof of her mouth, and her tongue. How could a nave be so long?

Panting, she arrived at the door through which she'd entered and she burst into the air. Through the deepening dusk she saw the coach on the far side of the grassy yard, and almost sobbed with relief.

The air felt oppressive. Lily didn't care. Tearing her bonnet strings undone, she took the wretched thing off and let it trail from her fingers while she went across the grass. Finally she saw life. Two elderly people entering one of the houses that opened onto the Close.

She laughed, almost hysterically. So great was her relief that she felt tears on her cheeks.

"Leonard!" she cried, rushing through a gate and to the side of the coach. "Leonard?"

She looked up and grinned. Oh, she would never again think of him as other than a most useful man. Even if he did snooze on duty.

Climbing to a mounting step, she said, quite gently, "Leonard? I should like to return to Come Piddle now."

She gave his sleeve a small tug—and barely flattened herself to the wheel and box in time to avoid being crushed beneath his falling body.

Leonard met the stony grass verge with a dull thud, an awful, final thud.

He landed on his side, but didn't make a sound.

His eyes were open. Blood drizzled from his mouth and down his chin.

Leonard was dead.

Chapter Twenty-five

Damn them all. Oliver spurred on the gray he'd borrowed from the professor's stables and pounded into the outskirts of Salisbury.

Who in hell had presumed to send a message to Lily in his name? A possible answer presented itself, as it had at intervals all the way from Come Piddle, and it didn't please him. But Witmore wasn't a complete fool, was he? Surely he wouldn't do something so disastrous as to abduct Lily?

The gray, a game animal, galloped the way toward the Close, and thundered beneath an archway to that quadrangle of distinguished, gray stone homes.

Despite near darkness he had no difficulty picking out a lone conveyance—an Adler coach—apparently left unattended.

He looked toward the Cathedral and grimaced at the thought that Lily might be wandering somewhere inside.

Dismounting, he led the horse to the nearest gate and slung the reins over a post.

"Help me!" A cry, broken and low, and urgent.

Oliver spun in the direction from which it had come and gasped aloud. Huddled on the ground, with a man's head and shoulders cradled in her lap, was Lily.

"What the deuce—" He strode to her and crouched beside her. "Lily, dearest. What's happened here?"

"Oh, Oliver." Her voice held deep pain, but she didn't cry. "It's Leonard, Leonard who is—was—one of our grooms. I shouted for help, but no one heard me. He's dead!"

Oliver looked to the coach. He stood up, lighted, and removed a lantern to hold over the man. "God," he said softly. "He's dead, all right, poor devil."

"He must have suffered some terrible brain seizure," Lily said. "And he was so young."

Oliver noted the still-bright and frothy nature of the blood on the man's face and pulled his frock coat aside.

A muffled scream quickly died on Lily's lips, and he heard her rapid breathing take its place.

"So that's the way of it," he said grimly. "We shall have to summon a constable."

A knife had been driven into Leonard's side—all the way to the hilt.

"I would have done anything to save you from that," Oliver said, holding Lily before him on the gray as they rode toward home. "But I shall get to the bottom of it."

"Without Leonard, how shall we discover who really sent him? He said it was you."

Oliver whistled through his teeth and said, "I rather think that is why the fellow met an untimely end."

"I think so, too," said Lily. "Oliver, there is a terrifying plot afoot to stop our marriage."

"It will not succeed," he told her grimly.

Crammed into a space meant for one, Lily sat on Oliver's thighs—and other parts not at all discomforted by the process. Not discomforted, that was, unless one counted the resulting sensation of his breeches being too small.

"What will Papa say when we tell him what's happened?" Lily sounded plaintive.

"Which particular episode of what happened? Your deciding to run away to Salisbury without a word of warning?"

She squirmed to look at him. Oliver gritted his teeth and blessed the darkness.

"How dare you?" she said sharply. "You sent an urgent message requesting that I go at once to the Cathedral, and I went."

Attempting a mild, calming tone, he pointed out, "The message didn't come from me."

"No." She remained partially facing him. "So how did you know I'd gone there?"

"You think me a part of that deadly plot?"

"Answer me."

"You press me hard, my girl. I have already had a trying day. A very trying day. Finally I went in search of you to find some solace—or so I hoped. I tracked you to the Rectory, where that very nice Rosemary Godwin almost fainted at the sight of me. She said she'd heard you receive a message from me to go to Salisbury Cathedral and meet me there."

"She eavesdropped," Lily muttered. Then she gave a short laugh. "Rosemary has more spirit than I have credited her."

"So you are satisfied that I have no complicity in this?"

"Oh, Oliver, I am beside myself. Papa is such a gentle man. He will lament Leonard's death greatly, as do I. He will be convinced it was in some way his own fault for having sent him to Salisbury on an errand."

"Don't be too sure there ever was an errand," Oliver said.

They'd left the town and proceeded at a steady pace up a long hill bordered on each side by stands of dense and venerable beech trees. Oliver had noted them on his journey from Come Piddle.

"And the coach," Lily said. "Well, Papa being Papa, that will trouble him the least. He will understand that the constables didn't want us to take it until they're sure the murderer left no clue to his identity."

"Witmore is an ass," Oliver said. "An avaricious, jealous ass, unless I miss my mark. But I cannot credit that he would kill a man in cold blood—a servant. And if he did, then why? What possible purpose would that simple creature's death serve?"

With enough force to unbalance Oliver a little, Lily threw her arms around his neck and held him fiercely.

"Sweet one," he said, chuckling, and regaining his seat. "Such a tempestuous assault. A man might believe you have passionate feelings for him."

"A man might be right," she said against his coat. "But I am so afraid, Oliver. There is real evil here. We have felt it, but now we have seen it. That voice made threats. And there was the candle in your bed. I can't imagine why the one painting was stolen, unless it was intended that you would be accused of the theft. Then there was—"

"Yes, yes." He wished to steer her from any discussion of his room having been ransacked. He'd insisted nothing was missing. Admitting his untruth now was out of the question. "I have you, Lily. You're safe with me, my darling." He prayed he might be right.

"Poor Leonard. Could his death have been a warning to us?"

Oliver had entertained the same thought. "No, quite another matter, I'm sure." If he could, he would save her further anxiety. The sensation of her slight body layered against him loosed rushes of protective desire, and the urge to make love to her.

"*Damn* it." Thank the Lord for exceptional eyesight. "Some idiot farmer's dropped bales of hay on the road. Another few yards and our horse would have stumbled." Oliver peered around and murmured, "Or is this a ploy to ensnare us?"

He pulled on the reins and veered left onto the verge. Fortunately there'd been little rain of late and the earth was solid enough. He didn't want to waste a moment more than necessary in getting Lily home.

"Halt!" a voice shouted, a voice that cracked and scaled higher. *"Your money or your life."*

For Oliver, derision robbed the moment of its undoubtedly intended dire impact. But he reined in his mount.

"I've two pistols aimed at your heads—'eads—and I'm not—I ain't afeared ter use 'em. Dismount—orf yer 'orse, I says. Afore I blasts yer brains out."

"Don't be afraid," Oliver whispered to Lily. "You will come to no harm."

But he felt her violent shaking, and hatred for this inept highwayman swelled in his heart. He also felt disgust that he'd taken them directly into a trap.

"Orf yer 'orse, I says," thundered the thief, gaining confidence, and Oliver saw the creature at last. Oliver observed a tall man in a long, flapping frock coat. He wore a kerchief over his face, leaving only his eyes exposed beneath a ridiculous broad-brimmed hat that might have been worn by a preacher.

The man grabbed the reins of the gray, causing the animal to rear and whinny. "Orf, afore I drags you orf."

"Kindly allow me to calm the horse, my good man," Oliver said, taking measure of his assailant. "Then we'll be happy to follow your instructions."

The foolish creature found purchase on the bridle and yanked some more.

Finally Oliver managed to bring the horse under control. He sat quietly, holding Lily tightly against him. He felt the beat of her heart and rubbed the back of her neck.

"Orf!" the man shrieked. "Orf or I'll fill you with shot and kill you dead where you are. It's all the same t'me."

"Do as he says," Lily whispered to Oliver.

He did dismount then, and lift Lily to the ground beside him. "Very well, my man. Let's see what we have that will be of interest to you."

"I don't have anything," Lily said. "I have no jewels."

A situation he intended to right as soon as possible, Oliver thought. "A nice gold watch, perhaps?" he said. "And a purse with a guinea or two inside?"

The insinuation of a pistol barrel beneath his ribs startled Oliver. He stepped backward. The man followed.

"Oliver," Lily moaned. "Oh, Oliver give him whatever he wants. I do have an antique silver bottle I carry for luck. It was my mother's, and she used to keep crushed rose petals in it because she liked the smell. Do have it, sir. I assure you it will give you pleasure, and—"

"Silence! By the mouth of hell—how could any man stand a woman who babbled so?" The "highwayman" forgot his rude speech.

He did not forget to jab his second pistol into Oliver. "If you want—wants ter keep yer gentleman friend alive, lady, yer'll do wot I say. I've two pistols aimed at 'is innards. One little slip and e'll lose 'is appetite for Christmas dinners."

Lily's silence brought Oliver deep gratitude—and pride. No shrinking weakling, this sweet love of his.

"Lily," he said. "Stand a little away, please. Just while I complete my business with our friend."

The man laughed loudly and poked Oliver harder. "I'm the one who will decide what's to be done here." The voice was familiar now. "Come to my right side, please, Lily. And don't move."

Oliver heard Lily gasp, and saw her follow instructions.

"Good," the man said. "Now I'll do what must be done here and we'll be on our way."

"Good idea," Oliver said.

"I doubt you'll say so shortly. I doubt you'll say anything shortly. Lily. To my right and at a short distance where I can see you."

"It's . . . Sir Cecil, are you *mad*?" Outrage clipped Lily's words. "What do you mean by this prank? Stopping innocent people and threatening them with pistols. The very idea."

After a short silence, their abductor let out a frightful noise that perhaps resembled a fictional owl producing an egg. "Woo, woo, witty, woo!" he hollered. "Wit, wit, wahoo!"

"Oh, behave, do," Lily snapped as the sound died away. "You are a disgrace to yourself and to the state of manhood. Give me those ridiculous pistols now."

"I don't know who yer thinks I am." Sir Cecil Laycock—and Oliver was certain Lily was right in her identification—Sir Cecil made a poor attempt to regain his bogus identity. "I never saw yer afore. Either of yer. I'm goin' to shoot yer, matey, and take the lady. That's what I come for. Yer can keep yer watch and sovereigns fer them to bury yer with. The lady's worth a great deal more ter the buyer I've got."

"Well," Lily said. "Well, I never did. This is the very end. Sir Cecil, I am going to hit you over the head with this log."

The jabbing pistol barrels veered from Oliver's middle. "You put that down, you minx," Laycock said in his own voice entirely.

Oliver threw himself at the man, caught him around the knees, and crashed with him to the ground.

A suspiciously gleeful whoop erupted from Lily, and Oliver's face was promptly smothered in layers of silk skirts. He fought to clear the slippery material from his eyes.

"Take *that*!" he heard Lily announce as something thumped. "And *that*!"

Strangled cries issued from Laycock. "Stop it. You're hurting me. Ow ! Stop it, I say."

Oliver took a blow to the ear from Lily's stuffed reticule.

"You cur," she cried at Laycock. "Bounder. Fiddle, but I do detest a coward with no honor. Oliver, we must tie him up and bear him back to Come Piddle at once. Into the stocks with him. I shall mount guard myself, and sell rotten apples to be hurled at him. Of course, I'll give the money to the poor."

Oliver managed to extricate himself from beneath both Laycock's weight and Lily's, and to pin Laycock to the ground by one hand at the other's throat. Lily dragged the kerchief down. By the pale moonlight, unpleasantly familiar features were revealed.

Laycock moaned piteously.

"Now," Oliver said. "What have you to say for yourself?"

"Did you honestly think to kidnap me?" Lily asked, kneeling on the other side of the man from Oliver and peering downward. "Did Witless tell you to kidnap me?"

"Woo, woo, witty, woo!" Laycock wailed afresh.

"Aye, Sir Cecil," came a robust voice. "I'm on me way. Och, it's hard goin' when ye're tryin' to hop over cow cakes and ye canna' see where the beasties have bin."

Oliver met Lily's eyes across Laycock's prostrate body.

"The pistols, McLewd," Laycock bawled. "Get the pistols, you great, slow lout. What took you so long?"

Instantly Oliver was on his feet and casting about.

Too late.

"Would these be the ones, Sir Cecil? The ones wi' the silver handles? I think I saw them in Lord Witmore's—"

"Yes, they're the ones, you fool. Keep him away from me and give me the pistols."

To Oliver's utter amazement, the huge Scotsman pressed a pistol into his hand and settled a foot in the middle of Laycock's chest. "You'd best stay where ye are, Miss Adler," he said with surprising gentleness. "Is that the way ye wanted it, then, Sir Cecil? I'm to gi' the pistol t'him and keep ye away from him?"

"You dolt!" Laycock squirmed and slapped uselessly at a leg with the girth of a tabor. "I said give *me* the pistols, and keep *him* away."

"Och." Abruptly, McLewd withdrew a few feet. "Sorry. My mistake. Well, then, I suppose I'd best be on my way t'deal wi' Lord Witmore's affairs. He'll nae doubt be missin' me if I'm away too long."

"McLewd, don't leave me here."

"Och, ye've nae need o' a dolt like me. Mr. Worth and

Miss Adler will protect ye from any further threats, will ye not, Mr. Worth?"

"I will," Oliver agreed, smiling as McLewd walked into the trees and emerged with a sturdy mule. This he mounted. Holding his knees high to stop his feet from dragging the ground, he ambled away in the direction of Salisbury without another word.

"Come back!" Laycock sat on the dew-wet grass and blubbered. "Come back, I say! Come back or I'll—I'll do something really bad to you."

A full, bass voice singing about a "lassie wi' a yellow coatie" floated back, gradually growing fainter.

"So," Oliver said. "It's grown cold, Sir Cecil, and my fiancée will take a chill if I don't return her home shortly. We'd appreciate a speedy explanation for this inconvenience."

"Let me go," the man whined. "I didn't hurt you."

"Lily," Oliver said. "Don't move, please." He pointed the pistol McLewd had given him into the air, cocked it, and pulled the trigger. The explosion that followed proved that the weapon had been readied for business.

Lily let out a cry. "Oliver! He would have shot you. I was sure it was all some silly pretense."

"It wasn't. You did intend to kill me and take Lily, didn't you, Laycock?"

"No."

"You're a sniveling liar, aren't you, Laycock?"

"No."

"Very well. One ballock for the first lie. The other for the second." He gripped both of the man's thin wrists in one hand and shifted his weight.

"You wouldn't dare," Laycock said, his voice shaking.

Oliver shoved the pistol barrel into the other man's private parts.

A wild scream ensued. "I intended to kill you and take Lily."

"And you are a sniveling liar?" Oliver jabbed again, and was rewarded with another scream. "A sniveling liar, a cad, an opportunist who feeds off others as vultures feed off any ready carcass?"

"*Yes*. But it isn't my fault, I tell you."

"Really."

"If you give me a chance. Just a chance to make it away, is all I ask. Give me that chance and I'll tell you everything you want to know." He craned his neck to see Lily. "If you want to save her, you need to know."

Lily drew closer. "We don't need to know anything he has to say, Oliver. I say we do whatever you did to his bally—whatever those things down there are called—do it again. He needs his character built."

Despite his foul humor, and the extraordinary situation, Oliver grinned. "I rather agree with you, my love, but we may learn some very interesting things if we agree to his terms."

"He lies, yet he thinks we will keep our word."

Oliver didn't respond.

"Hmm," Lily said. "That's because we will. Let's listen and be rid of him. His are certainly mysteries I have no interest in pursuing."

Oliver decided not to wait for an explanation of that statement. "Very well, Laycock. Tell us something useful and we'll let you go. Start with how you knew you'd be able to accost us on this road."

"Yes, yes. Oh, yes, I will. Indeed, I will."

"Do it," Lily said. "And stop jabbering."

"Yes. I've been abused by the Beaumonts. And they abused my elder sister before me. Terrible, demeaning abuse. They ruined her. It is for her, only for her that I seek revenge."

This news meant nothing to Oliver, who waited quietly in hopes of expediting the process.

"I've been having Lily followed. I was told that fellow Leonard took her a message and that she subsequently went to Salisbury, to the Cathedral. I set out, too, hoping to take possession of her there, but I was slow in arriving—took a wrong turn—and when I did get there I saw Leonard atop the coach and no sign of Lily. Dash it all."

"Take possession of me?" Lily repeated the words incredulously. "Why on earth would you decide to do such a thing?"

"I'll explain."

"And why would you think *you* could manage such a thing? I'd have roused the countryside at the very sight of you."

"Go on," Oliver said, suppressing a chuckle.

"I hid, waiting for her to emerge. Then I saw the monk kill Leonard."

"The monk?" Lily gasped. "Oh, how could that be?"

"A monk," Laycock repeated. "He came from the Cathedral and approached the carriage. Then he simply stepped up beside Leonard, spoke into his ear, and stabbed him at the same time. It was all over so quickly, the murderer was slipping back into the Cathedral grounds before I really realized what had happened."

"You didn't go to Leonard's aid?" Lily said.

Laycock pulled his shoulders up to his ears. "No point. I could tell that. You came out only minutes afterward. Then you arrived, Worth, and I saw the way of it, so I set off back this way, meeting with that fool McLewd as we'd planned to do if necessary. He was to wait a short distance away while I accosted you, then help me with the rest. *Fool.*"

"And you made no attempt to pursue the murderer?" Oliver asked.

Laycock wriggled. "I was afraid to. Let me up, Worth."

"I think not," Oliver said. "Make your story brief. Then, if we believe you, you shall go—when it pleases us."

"My arms hurt," Laycock whined.

"Talk."

"The Beaumonts are a bad lot," Laycock said. "Hard. Uncompromising. Oh, not Reggie. He's weak as water. But his father, and grandfather."

Oliver saw Lily draw closer. Neither of them said anything.

"It was George who caused it all. Reggie's father. Started out as a great prank. And my dear sister was sucked in by George's promises of marriage. She's many years my senior, you understand. Bit doddery now. But, nevertheless—"

"Go on," Oliver said shortly.

"A great, dangerous prank. They accomplished a rather spectacular theft—or so I'm given to believe."

"You don't know?"

"I don't know what was stolen. I don't think anyone does anymore. But it must have been worth a great deal to cause so much trouble.

"Afterward, George was terrified of the consequences and he managed to blame the entire event on his older brother, Frederick. Poor devil was banished. Left England with nothing but his title, and no one heard from him again. Probably as weak and bloody as the rest of the Beaumonts."

The effort to restrain himself from strangling Laycock made Oliver's muscles ache. He hardly dared breathe. After so long, this creature was spewing the truth with no idea that his present captor was the son of that Frederick Beaumont, wronged so long ago.

"My sister distracted some sort of guards. Innocent enough, of course. You can imagine how it went."

Oliver said, "Yes, I can imagine."

"Yes, well, George—who inherited after Frederick was sent packing—George and a friend stole it. Whatever it was—or is—and then they waited for the ax to fall. But it never did. Or rather, when it did, it hit Frederick. George probably thought himself safe. But my sister would never tell me what was stolen, or exactly where it was hidden—except that George had it somewhere in the north wing at Blackmoor."

Letting out a long-held breath, Oliver said, "There must have been more to it. For a proud man to banish his eldest son, there had to be more."

"You're really hurting me," Laycock said.

"Answer me."

"There was more. But I only know bits of it. My sister said the old marquess swore everyone to silence because if the crime was discovered it would ruin the family name of the Beaumonts forever."

"And"—Oliver ordered what he would say carefully—"and this Frederick did nothing to defend himself?"

"No, stupid bastard. evidently good old Georgie boy, who had much more spirit, persuaded his brother to keep mum for the sake of the family. Freddie did just that and disappeared into the mist, as it were."

"That's a frightful story," Lily said. "How awful for poor Frederick. But what do Oliver and I have to do with any of this?"

"Watch yourself," Laycock said. "That's all I'm going to tell you."

The pistol barrel, poked into the man's throat, produced a gurgle. "Answer the lady," Oliver said.

"Obvious, isn't it?" Laycock croaked. "We had to get rid of you, Worth, so you couldn't marry Lily. If you did, you'd probably find a way to stop any of us from getting at the north wing. And it's there, I tell you. Somewhere."

"Yes, yes," Lily said. "Let the wretch go, Oliver. He is a terrible person."

"I'd like you to finish this story, Laycock," Oliver said. "What else?"

"Nothing, really." He squeaked when the pistol jabbed again. "We had to get Reggie married off to Lily. That way Blackmoor would eventually come to him anyway—and in the meantime we could come and go as we pleased. Nothing else would possess Reggie to marry the homely baggage, you must believe that."

His comment earned Laycock a blow that caused a loud snap. He yowled, and Oliver took some pleasure in the knowledge that the man's nose would be even more repugnant in the future.

"Let him go," Lily said quietly. "I'd like to return home."

Oliver fumed that she'd suffered yet another insult at the hands of these people. "Very well," he said, and stood, hauling Laycock up by the collar. "You will soon leave the area, do you understand?"

"You've broken my nose."

"*Do* you understand me?"

"I've said I do. And I will."

"*After* you follow my very explicit instructions, you will leave and never return. At that point I suggest you get out of England. If I ever see you again after that, what you've tried to do will be made public. I will let you go then because it will serve my purposes."

"Leave England?"

"Disappear," Oliver said, moving menacingly close. "Now. You are to return to Witmore and tell him you failed to abduct Lily."

"But—"

"Do it. Then, until I formulate what must be done to deal with Witmore, you will continue as if nothing has changed. I shall make certain that any betrayal on your part will only lead the authorities back to you. Do I make myself clear?"

"Clear," Laycock muttered. "I hope that fool, Witmore, rots."

Oliver was tempted to say he shared the sentiment. "Where's your mount?"

"Well back in the woods."

"Take it and return to Fell Manor. And have a care. I will carry out my threats if necessary."

Laycock scurried into the trees and returned after some time on the back of a horse. His last words to Oliver as he rode away toward Come Piddle were "May the devil take all Beaumonts."

With a bitter smile, Oliver gathered Lily to him. He'd just been told to go to hell—more or less. But he had his story, or a story that might well be the truth of it. He felt angry, and sad.

"So that's that," Lily said. "Something—who knows what?—hidden somewhere—who knows exactly where?—

and some wicked, greedy men. And a man who suffered because of a lie."

He grimaced in the darkness. Indeed, that was that. The woman in his arms had no idea that the man she spoke of had been his father. The time was fast approaching when everything must be made clear.

"Oliver," Lily said. "I'm grateful that you care for me. You make me forget I'm homely."

All anger fled, replaced by distress that she did not see herself as she was—on the outside as well as the inside. "It is I who am grateful, Lily. You are a lovely woman. Lovely inside and out. I look at you, and I cannot believe you have chosen me as your husband. I am the most fortunate of men."

She raised her face for his kiss, and returned it with pure ardor.

When they paused, she said, "Promise me something, Oliver?"

"Anything."

"Promise that because we trust each other we will never allow falsehood to come between us."

Chapter Twenty-six

At last their wedding day had arrived.

One of the elderly Misses Wiley—the sisters were twins and Lily couldn't tell them apart—but one of them played the church organ with many flourishes. These flourishes were famous in Come Piddle, for they were a means to cover up the multitude of mistakes made by whichever Miss Wiley happened to be playing.

"I'm very happy, my dear," Papa said. Papa had said the same thing many times since they'd arrived at St. Cedric's. "Oliver is the best of men."

Lily sighed. "He is." And she was quite terrified at the thought of processing through a church filled with every villager and every inhabitant of every home, from great house to small farm, for miles around.

"I hope you don't rue the day, my girl," Aunt Fribble said, but didn't meet Lily's eyes. "You could have brought great honor on your family, but you chose—"

"A much better man," Lily finished for her.

Papa said, "Hear, hear."

They waited in a small room at the back of the church, and even through the door they could hear the babble outside.

The music changed.

Conversation ceased.

Lily felt a hush as surely as had she sat among the wedding guests.

Myrtle Bumwallop's mother opened the door and whispered for Aunt Fribble to take her place by a side door so she wouldn't interrupt the proceedings.

"Hmph" was Aunt Fribble's response, but she did as she'd been asked.

"Are we ready?" the birdlike Mrs. Bumwallop asked, and when Lily nodded, the woman made a signal. "You look lovely, Lily. Off you go now."

Off she went, on Papa's steady arm. He rested his hand on top of hers and said, "I am so proud of you. I wish your mama could see you."

Lily swallowed with difficulty, and clutched the rose she carried tight against her stomach.

The organ music paused, and to Lily's extreme discomfort, the congregation rose to its feet as one and craned to see her. Then, with a great pounding of ominous notes—and a little push from Mrs. Bumwallop—Lily began her walk toward Oliver.

"They think themselves safe. They think I am confounded. Such a foolish mistake.

"She looks well enough, my little nemesis. Yes, it is you who are my real nemesis, Lily.

"So much fuss. So many gawkers. Such ceremony. And Oliver Worth the ardent, impatient groom. So handsome, they all agree in their silly whispers.

"Enjoy, Oliver and Lily—dear fools. Now I have nothing to lose and everything to gain. I must act almost at once, and I will.

"The next ceremony you attend together will be your funeral."

Grateful for Nick's strong presence at his side, Oliver braced his feet apart and willed stillness when he longed to go to meet her.

She was a small, straight-backed woman with a beloved face turned pink by the emotion of the moment. Her dress, white satin with a band around its high neck, fitted her slight body perfectly. Oliver relished the fantasy, the promise, of removing the satin and lace, the pearls, and making that body inexorably his own. He would like her to conceive a child this very night.

The thought shook him in its intensity.

The music faded, and the only sound was of restless onlookers and swishing satin. Tucked into the smooth loops of black hair over each of her ears was a bunch of tiny rosebuds. They were not as beautiful as Lily.

At the base of the banded collar, fitting exactly as Oliver had instructed the modiste to ensure, rested a necklace, a rope of diamonds. Their glitter reflected on the perfect skin of her face.

He had told her she would learn how he had come by the diamonds later—and he'd laughed when he said he didn't steal them.

But there would be time to deal with all that. Very deliberately he pushed aside the ongoing concern over the shocking events of the past few weeks.

"She is delightful," Nick murmured.

"More than that," Oliver said. "More than I can put into words."

As she drew slowly closer, he looked to her eyes and

she looked back, and so they remained, gazing, one at the other, until she stood beside him.

Together they faced Eustace Godwin, whose expression showed little pleasure in the proceedings.

The professor reached to pat Oliver's back, and to smile at him over Lily's head. *A good man,* Oliver thought. *If I could have chosen an alliance with any family in the world, I would have chosen this one.*

Godwin began his monotonous recitation of the marriage service. Lily looked up at Oliver and tried to smile, but the corners of her mouth quivered, and he brushed her lower lip with a knuckle.

The pompous clergyman harrumphed loudly and said, "If there be anyone who knows of any impediment to this marriage, let him speak now or forever hold his peace."

Oliver and Lily continued to look at each other. He drew strength from her, just as he knew she took the same from him. And she was almost his—forever.

Silence persisted until Oliver looked to Godwin and frowned.

The man slammed his Bible shut and pressed it to his chest. "I had hoped someone would take this task from me. In the absence of any such person, I must put forward that there is an impediment to this marriage."

Shocked conversation broke out in the church.

Oliver took both of Lily's hands in his and held them firmly. "It's not so," he said quietly.

"Silence," Godwin bellowed. "This man, Oliver Worth, seeks to marry Lily Adler. But Worth is not who he says he is. May God forgive me for not coming forward earlier, but I had prayed this onerous duty would be taken from me."

A hush fell.

"This man is not Oliver Worth, but Oliver Beaumont, Marquis of Blackmoor, the son of Frederick Beaumont, who was banished."

"Ah, victory!

"Saved by a man of God, no less. Look at the pious, jealous spider enjoying his meal.

"There will be no marriage.

"The game will proceed. Not for long, but long enough to allow my exquisite details to be employed.

"How sweet. I shall comfort the suffering almost-bride, commiserate with her father, lament at this revelation of the impostor's true identity.

"And then we shall progress a little farther, make my triumph a little more certain—and drive in the knife—again."

Lily could not take her eyes from his face. She felt her father walk behind her until he stood between them. Oliver held her hands so tightly, they hurt. That pain was the only feeling in her body.

"Why," she asked him.

He shook his head and looked to the rafters.

"Answer her, Oliver," Papa said. "And you will also be answering me."

"I was afraid," Oliver said at last. His gold eyes caught the light, and she couldn't stop herself from leaning a little closer. She felt as if he had wounded her. "I admit that at first I was guilty of subterfuge. That was when I wanted a way to come here, to the home that had been my father's and from which he was banished forever."

"You lied," she told him. If she relaxed a single muscle, she would collapse. Tears were impossible; her eyes burned with dry horror. "And you would have subjected me to a sham marriage."

Papa said, "Why would you do such a thing to Lily? She is—"

"She is extraordinary," Oliver said with passion. "She has become my life, and I will not live if I lose her."

"Why?" Lily asked.

He brought her white knuckles to his lips, and she didn't try to stop him from kissing them.

A sigh gusted around the church.

"I was afraid you would not accept me. But I did not lie about my name. I am Oliver Worth. My mother's maiden name was Worth. She was the last of her line, and my father took her name for his own—legally. Yes, he was Marquess of Blackmoor, but he never used the title. After what happened here, he preferred anonymity and rarely spoke of England at all."

"Did you think I would never discover the falsehood?"

His hands remained firm on hers. "I intended to tell you everything. But, Lily, I never expected to fall in love with you. You changed everything."

"I'm sorry for that."

"No! No, my love, you will kill me if you say that. You have taken the venom from my soul, the lust for revenge. I still yearn to discover the truth of what happened, but if I never do, but could have you at my side, I should be the happiest of men."

"Ah," Papa said. "How the ardent heart may blind the lover's eye. And you are meant to be lovers, my dear children."

"Please leave quietly," Eustace said loudly to the assembly. "There will be no wedding."

"Lily," Oliver said urgently bending to kiss her cheek.

"I am who I've said I am. I regret to have kept a secret from you. May I hope to be forgiven?"

Longing to embrace him, yet injured by his deceit, she could only allow him to nuzzle his cheek against hers. She closed her eyes and prayed for guidance, and for deliverance from the sickening anguish that drained her.

"Quickly and quietly," Eustace bellowed overbearingly.

Papa turned to the congregation and raised his arms. "Sit down, if you please, everyone. We will prevail upon your patience a while longer." He studied Lily seriously. "Tell me your decision. A word, and we leave at once. But if you love this man enough to marry him and resolve your difference, then do so with my blessing."

If she loved him enough? Oh, there would be difficult times ahead. Oliver Beaumont, Marquess of Blackmoor, had a great deal to explain. He had shaken her, broken her faith in him, but she loved Oliver.

Lily faced the Reverend Mr. Eustace Godwin and said in ringing tones, "The marquess bears the legal name of Oliver Worth."

Silence prevailed in St. Cedric's. All had heard her announcement.

She turned to the guests and asked, "Is there anyone else who can think of a reason to disrupt my wedding? And it does not count that I went through a marriage ceremony with Timothy Warren when we were ten."

A wave of laughter followed.

Lily looked to Eustace once more. "Kindly proceed."

In a most unsuitable manner, Oliver put an arm around her shoulders and rested his brow on hers. "Thank you, my darling."

She regarded him as innocently as she could, and said,

"Save your thanks. Our road will not be strewn with roses this day."

His frown hurt her, but she must be certain he learned that she would not tolerate further lies—and that she might need some time to adjust to the different circumstances in which she found herself.

"Are you sure?" Eustace whispered hoarsely. "He's lied to you."

"He has failed to tell me something," Lily said. "And I shall have more to say to you later, Eustacc Godwin. Now. Marry us, if you please. We can't spend all day at this."

With evident ill grace, Eustace resumed. Lily heard hardly a word and responded as she should respond, only upon being prompted, sometimes more than once.

". . . I pronounce you man and wife. Those whom God has joined together, let no man tear asunder."

Oliver turned her into his arms. She saw desire in his eyes, in the subtle lowering of his eyelids. He looked at her mouth and began to bring his lips toward hers.

Rather, she raised her averted face to receive his kiss on her cheek. His fingers dug into her upper arms. "I love you, Lily," he told her. "I adore you, my beautiful marchioness."

Stunned by the very idea of bearing such a title, she stared at him, then past his shoulder at Nicholas Westmoreland.

She sent Oliver's old friend a tight little smile, and Nick smiled back and said, "Let me be the first to congratulate the bride and groom."

"So be it.

"For the promise of a great inheritance, I married a

passionless woman. And I worked. God, how I worked for what should have become mine.

"I was a solid right hand for my wife's father. Only I could be trusted to stand at his side and never waver. I was a faithful husband until my wife died—that took a little longer to accomplish than I had planned. I am more practiced now.

"I, not Oliver, should have inherited Worth Shipping. It is mine, I say. It will be mine.

"There should only have been Oliver to dispose of, but this wretched obsession of his has doubled my task.

"Nevertheless, it will be simple enough effected. After all, what better time to surprise a man than in his marriage bed.

"That's right, Lily, smile bravely at me."

Chapter Twenty-seven

"I've only myself to blame," Oliver told Nick. "She's a strong woman. I should have told her the truth and allowed her to make up her mind how she felt about it."

"She'll get over it," Nick said. "After all, she's a marchioness now."

Oliver glanced at him. "I never had any intention of using my title. You know that."

"Perhaps not, but it seems to me you'll have a hard time denying it now it's known. At least here in England."

"We shall see about that."

"We shall have to see about a great many things."

Oliver didn't need to be reminded of the complications he faced. "I shall deal with what must be done. Worth Shipping will not suffer because I've married a wonderful woman."

"And caused the world to know you are a marquess, the son of a man banished for some secret crime everyone will now want to uncover."

"This is my wedding day," Oliver said, unwilling to face the truth so coldly at such a time. "I intend to take my bride on a honeymoon. On one of my ships, if she'd like that. I should enjoy showing her my home in Boston."

"Of course." Nick bowed formally. "And I'll be ready to assist you in any way that will be useful."

Oliver squeezed Nick's shoulder. "Thank you, old friend. Ah, here she comes."

Once she had her back to anyone who might be looking, Lily's stiff smile faded. "We should circulate, Oliver. At least for a short while."

"Your bride is anxious to be alone with you, Oliver." Nick laughed. "You are a fortunate man."

The blush produced by that comment made Oliver angry with Nick, but he said, "You must be tired, Lily."

"Indeed," she said, all cool reserve. "I have smiled and made empty conversation for most of the afternoon. I should be grateful to dispose of convention."

"Trouble approaches," Nick said, all but under his breath—and he wasn't talking about Lily's obvious ill humor. Lord Witmore and Lady Virtue arrived, seemingly breathless. With Sir Cecil Laycock hovering behind them, they smiled so broadly, Oliver wondered their faces didn't bleed. They smiled, and batted their eyelids, and bobbed curtsies, and swept bows.

With every gesture, they fawned.

Oliver met Laycock's eyes and understanding passed between them. Since the Salisbury debacle they had not communicated, but Oliver knew Laycock comprehended what was expected of him.

"*Cousin,*" Lady Virtue warbled. "I cannot believe our good fortune. After so long—and after not even knowing you exist—you are come home to us. We are ecstatic! Oh, what reminiscing we shall do. What parties we shall throw together. What balls! We are to become inseparable."

"Virtue's right," Lord Witmore said, shooting out a

hand. "Let us shake hands as cousins. Damned glad you're here, I can tell you. Now I can pass on the responsibility for filling a nursery to you, what?"

Oliver ignored the hand. "Thank you for congratulating Lily and me on our marriage."

"Oh, but we do," Virtue said, bobbing again and sending her flounced violet skirts, and a veritable forest of matching plumes in her hair, into a dizzying sway. Suddenly she threw her arms around Lily and cried, "I feel I have a sister at last."

Lily staggered under the woman's onslaught.

"Go easily on the little gel," Witmore said. "You'll knock her down, Virtue. Congratulations, Worth—er, Oliver. Damned clever of you to pull it off. You've got to admit you've made quite a coup. Marry the little female and assure yourself of getting the family estates back in your pocket. Bit of a jump from being Professor Adler's secretary, what? But we're dashed glad you're here. Shoulder-to-shoulder. Family loyalty's the thing. I'll show you the ropes. We'll run the estate together."

Oliver saw no point in explaining his true circumstances to the man, or the fact that he neither needed nor would tolerate any interference in his life from his unwanted relations. "Thank you both," he said. "Now, if you'll excuse us. Nick, we'll speak in the morning?"

The Fell Manor troupe continued to hover.

"Perhaps," Nick said with a knowing smile. "One cannot predict exactly what condition you'll be in, in the morning."

Professor Adler, with a scowling Eustace Godwin in tow, prevented any reply Oliver might have made.

The professor looked with adoration upon his daughter, and, Oliver noted gratefully, with only slightly less pleasure at himself. "Eustace wanted a word," Professor Adler said. "I've told him neither of you are about bearing grudges, but I don't think he believes me."

Lily crossed an arm over her middle and fingered the diamonds Oliver had given her. She cast Eustace an inscrutable look.

"Well," the professor said, "I'd best pop along and make sure our guests are enjoying themselves at my expense, eh?" He laughed at his own little joke and withdrew, gathering Witmore, Lady Virtue, and Sir Cecil with him as he went.

"Unfortunate business," Eustace Godwin said, elevating his nose. "I was jealous of you, er, Lord Blackmoor."

Totally unaccustomed to the title, Oliver took an instant to compose himself. "Is that an apology?"

"Not enough, I know," Godwin continued. "Unforgivable behavior during the ceremony."

"Very few things are unforgivable, Eustace," Lily said. "I forgive you."

The effort pained him, but Oliver echoed with "Forgiven and forgotten. But how did you know?"

The clergyman's eyes slid away. "Certain evidence came into my possession."

Oliver all but accused the man of being the one to search his rooms, but collected himself in time. "What evidence?"

"I have heard enough of this for one evening," Lily said. "Thank you for your apology, Eustace. We'll speak again."

The dismissal was clear. Godwin bowed and backed away at once.

"Queer cove," Nick remarked.

"Yes," Oliver agreed. "Good afternoon to you, Nick."

He managed to capture Lily's hand and lead her through the ballroom that had been opened in the east wing and made opulently festive for the occasion. Guests sat at long tables the length of the room. A string quartet played on a raised dais. Oliver was tempted to insist upon dancing with Lily, but had sense enough not to further pursue disaster.

They negotiated a path between laden tables, and glittering guests too engrossed in their own affairs to notice that the reason for the celebration was about to depart.

Oliver paused, lifted a goblet, and tapped it repeatedly with a spoon until silence gradually fell.

"Thank you for helping my wife and me celebrate our joy in this occasion. Please forgive us if we leave you now."

A chorus of ribald remarks went up, and Oliver signaled to be heard again. "I have a small surprise for the ladies. My gift to each of you to remember this day." He beckoned several flunkies forward. "One for every lady present."

Gasps soon echoed through the gilt and green ballroom with its massive crystal chandeliers

Blue velvet boxes were opened to reveal beds of white satin. Nestled in the satin were gold pendants in the shape of stars, with a cinnamon diamond at the center of each.

Lily bowed her head, and Oliver couldn't see her face.

"Stars have a special meaning to us," Oliver said, his throat constricting. "We bid you goodbye. Enjoy yourselves."

Lily had left the details of their post-wedding arrangements to Oliver, but wasn't surprised when their path took them toward his rooms.

"Alone at last," he murmured. "I have dreamed of this."

"I doubt you have dreamed with any accuracy, sir." All could not be so easily brushed aside, not by any means.

He settled a hand at her waist and, when she attempted to pull away, Oliver swept her up and carried her.

"Put me down," she told him through her teeth. "Learn the rules of appropriateness. This isn't appropriate."

"It's perfectly appropriate. I'm carrying my bride to our chambers, where we will be alone for the first time in our married life."

The thrill she felt could not be quelled, but she would fight it valiantly and crush it if she could. Her husband had a great deal to explain before . . . She crossed her arms, stared at the walls they passed, and assumed a dour expression.

Oliver carried her into his rooms and set her down. She remained standing with her arms still folded.

His sigh had no power to move her. "Lily, will you allow me to take you to my bed?"

Her belly tightened, but she averted her face. "It is still daylight."

"Ah," he said softly. "But what does it matter? We are man and wife, my love, and the days and the nights are ours. I should like to remove your beautiful gown and see you before me by sunlight."

Lily pushed her train behind her and paced toward the fire that had been lighted. A decanter of wine and two crystal goblets glittered on a silver tray atop a low table. She poured wine to the brim of one glass and drank it down quickly, gasping at the unfamiliar warmth that rushed through her.

"Lily?"

She poured another glass.

Oliver intercepted it on the way to her mouth and gently took it from her fingers. "My poor sweetheart. How I have wronged you by my silence. But I cannot allow you to become foxed so that you may tolerate me."

Lily's mouth felt odd. "I have never been foxed, sir. And I never shall be foxed. It isn't ladylike."

"If you persist in guzzling wine like that, you most certainly will be foxed." He held her in one arm and took several swallows of the wine himself before setting the glass down. "There are many things I have to teach you."

She wrinkled her nose. "About what?"

"Making love. What else? I've waited for this, for the time when I could use all of your body, and have you use all of mine."

"I thought we'd already used them."

The amusement she saw in his eyes didn't please Lily. He said, "Trust me, sweets, there is so much more. So many ways. I want to watch your pretty breasts grow flushed, and your nipples harden. I—"

"Oliver!" She squirmed; she couldn't help it.

"Indeed. And I want to hear you call my name many times."

He raised her chin and kissed her, the taste of wine on his mouth mingling with the taste on hers. He played, sucking her upper lip between his teeth, nibbling, rocking her head from side to side, licking the soft, moist skin inside her mouth.

She should not allow him to so easily distract her.

With the very tips of his fingers he caressed the sides of her face, her ears, her jaw and neck, and he bent to kiss the sensitive spot beneath her ear.

Lily squeezed her eyes shut and kept her arms at her sides. The warmth in her veins had progressed to a slight tingling on her skin, but then, perhaps the tingling had nothing to do with the wine.

"Relent, dearest," Oliver murmured. "I will make my transgressions up to you."

Lily stepped backward and wagged a finger at him. She had to gulp and fight to breathe normally. "I insist," she said, and swallowed. "I insist that all is clear between us before . . . well, before."

He nodded solemnly. "We could speak of this in bed."

Shaking her head, she backed farther away. "Oh, no, sir. I have experienced your speaking of things in bed before. It has been my observation that a great deal is accomplished, very little of it being conversation."

His wounded expression didn't move her.

"We shall remove our clothes and touch each other," Lily said. "Then one thing will lead to another and you will no doubt manage to make me quite forget any question I intended to ask you."

He worked his jaw, then said, "What a perfectly wonderful thought. Let's begin at once."

"You did not want to love me."

Oliver didn't look away. "No, I didn't. But I do love you. And I'm glad I do."

"You lied when you told my father you were a man of letters seeking employment."

"I didn't put it precisely like that."

"More or less?"

He frowned. "Yes."

"And you lied."

"Yes."

"And when you pretended you were a stranger to this house, you lied."

"I was a stranger to this house."

"But you knew of it. You were not a stranger to its existence, as you led us to believe."

"That is correct."

Lily went to the table where the wine stood and took several large swallows from the glass Oliver had set down. She found the ensuing warmth most gratifying. In fact, amazingly, it emboldened her.

She stood straight and said, "By omission you lied about that."

"Yes." He looked glum.

"Did the kind people who took you in after your parents' death bring you up to fear God?"

Oliver said, "I fail to see the reason for the question."

"God-fearing people abhor falsehood. Didn't those good people teach you to be truthful?"

His face grew decidedly red. "There were no people who took me in."

Lily opened her mouth to respond, but swept up the wineglass again instead. Another mouthful of the delicious red wine warmed her to her toes. And it made her much more certain of what had to be done here.

"You were not adopted by an English couple?"

"No."

"You said you were."

"I know."

"When did your parents die?"

"God," he muttered. "My mother died some years since. My father—Frederick Beaumont Worth—passed away a year ago."

"You lied."

"Well—"

"You *lied*."

"*Yes,* damn it. I lied."

Lily stumbled a little and made her way to plop into a chair. She carried the wineglass carefully in both hands. "Men were deceivers ever," she said, feeling doleful.

"What?"

"Shakespeare. *Much Ado about Nothing.* So true. So very true."

"I never set out to deceive you. I became trapped by my own foolishness. But it is over now and I am the luckiest of men."

"Hmm," she said into her glass. "You may change your mind about that. There are those who are quick to say I am not only plain, but possessed of a shrew's tongue."

"You are not plain. And I like your tongue."

"Hmm." This wine was really fine. "I suppose Nick was never married to your sister. I suppose you never had a sister."

"He certainly was. And I certainly did." Oliver appeared offended. "I wouldn't lie about such a thing."

"Good. So he knew about your scheme to insinuate yourself here?"

"Yes."

"And I suppose that's why he decided to study the design of sacred buildings in Salisbury."

There was a lengthy pause before Oliver said, "No."

"Oh, it was chance?"

"Nick isn't an architect."

"But you both intimated—"

"I know! I *lied*!" He poured himself a glass of wine and drained it in one long swallow. "I have been a wretch, and I do not deserve you."

"No, you don't. What was Nick really doing in Salisbury?"

"Staying close to me so we could be in touch over business matters."

"What business?"

He sat in a chair facing her and rested his eyes on the heels of his hands. "Worth Shipping," he said indistinctly. "I own Worth Shipping. Clipper ships. Most successful line in the world. Inherited it from my father. Nick's worked in the business for years. He's my right hand. I would trust him with my life."

"You never said"—he seemed a little blurry at his edges—"you didn't tell us anything about that."

"How could I, Lily? I was mired in my own subterfuge."

"You're rich, aren't you?"

"Yes."

"Very rich?"

"Exceedingly so."

"Which is why you could give such extravagant gifts to all the female guests. And this to me." She touched the necklace.

"Yes."

"You lied."

"Yes, I lied, goddammit!"

"Oliver. You will not blaspheme in front of me."

"No. Sorry."

"We have a great deal to overcome."

He fell back in his chair. "So it would seem, but I am a tenacious man. Could we go to bed?"

"Might not be safe."

"I beg your pardon."

She smiled, pleased with her own sense of humor in such trying times. "I might set upon you when you're in a moment of weakness."

"I'm terrified."

"This is not a joke, Oliver. In that church I made an emotional decision. I love you and I want you. I wanted to be married to you, and now I am. But I cannot be certain I haven't made a great mistake, can I?"

"Yes. Oh, yes, Lily."

His intensity made him even more irresistible. "So you say now. But perhaps it would be best if we postponed entering into—"

"No! If you're going to suggest we wait to pursue our married life together, the answer is, emphatically, *no*."

"You mean you will force me?" She did not feel so brave as she sounded.

"I would never force you," Oliver said, his lips drawn tight. "But what would be gained by such a wait? Only a lifetime will prove our faith. I give my life to you willingly and trust you will treat it kindly. And I ask you to do the same for me. I will falter sometimes. And I will make more mistakes. But from this day forth you will know everything there is to know about me."

He made it so hard to resist him. "I think I had decided you should be punished." How foolish that sounded. "Oh, Oliver, I can't remain angry with you. But I don't think we should let our guards down anyway. We still don't know for certain who made those threats. Or who killed poor Leonard."

"Witmore," Oliver said promptly. "And I'm going to find a way to prove it. But not, my dear wife, until I have had my way with you. Nick is making sure my *cousin* doesn't make any unfortunate moves in the meantime."

"I still can't imagine how Witless got in here to search your things."

"He managed. He could easily have entered by the north wing and come from that direction."

"I wonder what he hoped to find."

"The family seal must have been good enough. Gave him the proof he wanted. That and . . . Yes, well."

Lily sat up straight. "The family seal, and . . . ?"

"My father's engraved watch and signet ring," Oliver said, scowling. "I didn't want to leave them behind in Boston."

"And they were stolen that night?"

"Yes."

"You said nothing was stolen."

He glared into the fire.

"You lied."

"Oh, for . . . Yes, Lily, I lied. But that was then. This is now."

She must not laugh at his downcast countenance. "Yes. This is now. Take off your clothes, please."

His head whipped around and he raised his eyebrows. "Did you just ask what I think you asked?"

Lily pushed to the back of her chair, settled her feet on a stool, and rested her head. Her mind was somewhat light-feeling anyway. "Would you like to make me a happy woman?"

"You know I would."

"Good. Then kindly remove your clothes. That would make me very happy."

"I'm damned if I'm going to . . . Oh, why not. You titillate me, witch." He removed his coat and let it fall, untied his cravat and pulled it off. "This is beyond all. You cannot be serious." He laughed, but Lily thought the laughter sounded uncomfortable.

"I'm perfectly serious. Your body gives me absolutely

delicious sensations. And, since I believe in equality in all things, I see no reason why I shouldn't want to have you take off your clothes just as much as you want me to take off mine."

His serious expression suggested she'd given him reason for deep thought. "I suppose you're right, but you're a deuced unusual female."

"Am I?" The thought pleased her. "It isn't true that it's wrong for a woman to enjoy the Act, is it?"

His evident discomfort shouldn't satisfy her so, but it did. It was small enough punishment for his transgressions. He said, "You are so direct. But I can only believe that a woman who gains pleasure from her husband's attentions is bound to return pleasure. That cannot be wrong. Do I have to continue undressing?"

She laughed and wriggled deeper in the chair. "Next your shirt."

He kept his eyes on her face while he unbuttoned his shirt and pulled it free of his trousers.

"You are so big, Oliver," she told him. "I don't think many men are as big as you. When I look at your shoulders and chest—and your arms—I feel funny inside. I want to be naked in your arms."

"Lily, you are destroying me. Come, let us go to bed."

"Oh, no. Not yet. I'm enjoying feeling funny far too much. Now your trousers."

"Lily?"

"I have a particular reason for wanting to inspect you in your entirety."

"*Inspect* me?"

"Your trousers, sir."

With narrowed eyes and gritted teeth, Oliver unfastened that garment and stripped naked in a few economical movements. "There." With feet braced apart and his hands on his hips, he stood before her. The room glowed in the firelight.

Oliver glowed in the firelight.

The dark hair on his chest tapered where it ran downward. It glistened. Similar hair peppered his strong, hard-muscled legs.

Lily took a breath that didn't expand her lungs at all. The funny feeling had become a raging thing, and she wondered if Oliver could actually see how she squirmed.

And she was wet.

There.

"Well?" Oliver said, in a voice very unlike his own.

Lily collected herself somewhat and sat upright again. She leaned forward and concentrated on *That*. It certainly had extraordinary upward mobility, although, once upward, it appeared to fix where it was.

Oliver said, "Well?" again.

"Well," Lily murmured. "Well, indeed." Scooting to the edge of her seat, she took an even closer look. It sprang from a bed of dense hair as dark as the rest of the hair on his body. The tip shone somewhat, as if moist, in fact . . . Cautiously, she reached to touch it with a fingertip.

"*Lily!* I have to have you."

"Hush," she told him. "It's wet."

"Oh, my God."

"Blasphemy is—"

"I was praying, not blaspheming."

Shiny, wet, and rather ruddy. Lily tilted her head to look beneath.

"I don't believe this," Oliver said. "But you've got my full attention, wife. Oh, yes, my turn comes next."

Quickly, Lily cupped the pendulous sack she'd discovered. She cupped and weighted it, and squeezed slightly. And she whipped her hand away before Oliver could catch it.

"No, no," she said as he made a move toward her. "A strong man is a patient man. Now, tell me. Are those your ballocks?"

"Saints preserve me," he moaned.

"Oliver?"

"Yes. And it is most unsuitable for you to speak so."

"Hmm. Just two of them."

"What?" He bent, hands on knees, and looked into her face. "Did you just ask me—"

"If you have just two ballocks. Yes."

"That's correct. Two. Is there anything else you'd like to know?"

She began to count on her fingers.

"What on earth are you doing?"

"Remembering how you threatened to punish Sir Cecil for his falsehoods and counting all the lies you've told me. You don't have enough ballocks."

They laughed at her little joke for a long time, but she'd accomplished what she could not have expected: Oliver had never felt the degree of arousal he felt now.

Lily didn't resist when he pulled her from the chair and spun her around. But she did when he all but ripped her dress off.

"Oliver, my gown!"

"We're married now. You don't need a wedding gown anymore." He struggled with the stays, managed to unlace and remove them, and when she was left in her chemise, pulled her with him into the bedroom.

"What shall I wear back to my rooms?" she asked breathlessly.

"Goose," he told her. "There will no longer be your rooms and my rooms. Only our rooms. Don't you think I arranged for things to be brought here for you?"

"I am—throbbing, Oliver. It is extraordinary."

He pulled the chemise over her head, and her drawers around her ankles. Confronted with the sight of her rosy breasts, the flare of her hips, and the hair at the apex of her legs, Oliver began to lose control.

Taking her by the waist, he hoisted her to the bed. She overbalanced and turned to grab the covers, with the result that he was presented with a view of her perfect bottom and shapely legs encased in white silk stockings.

When she wiggled to right herself, Oliver held her where she was, facedown. "Stay, love. Stay. There are so many ways for us to love."

She grew quite still.

Oliver stroked her buttocks, kissed them, placed small nipping kisses that brought cries of arousal from her. He took off her stockings, licking the back of each leg from thigh to heel while she squealed.

And then he feathered the sides of her breasts with the tips of his fingers and smiled at her moans. Pushing beneath, he held the firm flesh and closed his eyes to fill himself with the sensations she aroused in him.

"Come, love," he said, flipping her to her back, and kissing her hard on the lips.

She caught at his hair and tugged.

Oliver layered himself against her and slowly drew downward, running his lips and tongue over every inch of her skin. The centers of her pink nipples were puckered and hard, and when he flipped them with his tongue her body arched from the bed.

He gauged how far he could take her so soon. And he felt her trust, and her readiness for whatever he offered her.

He offered Lily his mouth at the entrance to her body and smiled with triumph when she cried out and sought to press even closer.

The strong strokes of his tongue, a pattern of things to come, sent her arms flailing against the mattress. She clung to the bedcover until her hips tossed with the spasms of her release.

Oliver could not wait for her to calm. He leaned to whisper in her ear, "Will you allow me my way in this? Whatever way I choose?"

"Anything, Oliver," she murmured.

He turned her to her stomach once more and layered himself over her.

But it was Lily who led the way.

Chapter Twenty-eight

Rain on the windows awakened Lily. The draperies hadn't been drawn, and the sound of heavy drops was unmuffled. She was warm, but pulled the bed-covers up to her nose.

She was naked.

Naked and in the arms of someone else—who was also naked.

Oliver.

Lightning crackled in the distance. A soft rumble of thunder came some seconds later.

Lily concentrated on sensations, on how it felt to have her head resting on Oliver's shoulder, her cheek nestled against his chest.

He held her to his side, her hip against his, her leg against his. The side of her foot rested on his shin—his slightly hair-rough shin. She smiled, just a little. A happy smile. They were so differently made, so perfectly differently made.

Very carefully, Lily turned toward him until her breast pressed his hard flesh. Her nipple tingled. With tentative strokes she smoothed the skin over his ribs, and then the hair on his chest.

Lily raised her head to look at his face. At the same

moment lightning flashed again, closer this time. Blue-white light shot through the casement and across the bed in a flickering swath.

Oliver looked down into her eyes.

She was startled. "You're awake."

"So are you. Awake and busy, madam. Ever the curious creature, aren't you?"

"Mmm."

Thunder burst with vicious force and, a moment later, the rain became a torrent.

"I felt you awaken," Oliver said. "Like a young animal uncurling—and feeling about." He laughed.

Lily made circles on his belly. "An inquiring mind is a good thing. And there is much about you to discover. I was wondering, Oliver. I understood it to be usual for husbands and wives to wear nightclothes."

"We are not usual."

"No, I suppose not. I'd also heard that it's usual for husbands and wives to occupy separate bedrooms. After . . . Well, when they aren't actually . . . engaged in the Act?"

"We are not usual."

"Oh!" She poked him till he captured her hand. "Is that all you can say? That we are not usual?"

"I prefer to sleep naked, and since I have a wife I adore, I choose to sleep with her. All the time. Now, are you tired?"

"Tired? Why do you ask?"

Without warning, he pulled her to lie on top of him and set about stroking her back from neck, to bottom, and all points between. He took particular pleasure in tickling the sides of her breasts, then captured her hands behind her back when she tried to stop him.

"Torturer," she said, raising her shoulders to glare down at him.

Promptly, he tweaked a nipple and she writhed.

Again the lightning hit, this time with a ripping sound that parted the sky with white veins beyond the windows. Thunder shook the Hall.

Oliver rolled her to her back and leaned over her, kissed her slowly, thoroughly, while the roar outside slowly faded.

Hammering followed.

Lily's eyes opened and she grew still.

The pounding she heard wasn't part of the storm, but someone thumping the sitting-room door. She pushed on Oliver's shoulders until he raised his head. "The door," she said. "There's someone knocking—urgently."

"No. It's the storm." He grew still. "The deuce. It is someone at the door. This had better be important, or someone's head will roll for interrupting us at such a time. Stay here, my darling."

"Don't leave me."

"I'm not leaving you, Lily. I'm answering the door. Whoever's banging isn't going away until they get a response."

He climbed from bed and lit a lamp before pulling on trousers and going into the sitting room.

The knocking sounded again, even louder.

Lily slid from bed and located the gown and robe that had been left for her. Slipping into them, she tiptoed across the room.

"Damn it, man," she heard Oliver say. "What can you mean by this?"

"Let me in." Nick's voice. "We've a pretty pickle on our hands. Shut the door behind me. And lock it."

Lily wrapped the robe tightly about her and tied its belt. She longed to go into the sitting room, but thought it more prudent to obey Oliver's wishes, at least this once.

She heard the key turn in the lock of the sitting-room door, then Oliver said, "Out with it, Nick. What's happened?"

"That fool Witmore's gone mad. As the festivities progressed, he and that jade sister of his grew more and more drunk. Finally the female had to be dispatched home. Laycock had the sense to go with her. But Witmore refused to leave."

Lily's heart beat a little faster.

"Surely there were enough able-bodied men to subdue one drunken idiot," Oliver said.

"There were. They did, or so we all thought. He passed out cold. But now he's gone and we're not sure where he is—except he's probably somewhere in the house."

"With luck he's at the bottom of the lake," Oliver said.

"He's in this house, I tell you. And before he got away from the man who tried to stop him, he declared he intended to kill you and Lily. He said if he couldn't have her, neither should you."

Oliver laughed, a disturbing sound. "And you're afraid he'll come here? Let him come. I've a score or two to settle anyway."

"Fair enough," Nick said. "Look, I know this is damnable timing. Return to your wife. I've a pistol, and I'll stand guard."

Oliver lowered his voice, but Lily could still hear every word. "Let's speak softer, Nick. I don't want her frightened. She'll fall asleep again and we'll watch together till first light, then find the bastard."

"Fair enough. Too bad you've finished the nuptial wine. I could use a measure of something."

"Have a brandy," Oliver said. "Sit down and I'll get you one."

"Thank you. You're remarkably spry. How goes the wedding night?"

Lily blushed and strained to hear, but Oliver didn't answer.

"Forgive me, old chap," Nick said. "Out of order, am I? You never used to mind discussing your conquests."

"Lily isn't a conquest," Oliver said. Crystal clinking crystal sounded. "She is my wife. She—ahh!"

The cry was short and stopped abruptly. Glass shattered.

Oliver's cry.

Lily threw open the bedroom door and rushed into the sitting room. With remnants of a broken goblet glittering beside one outstretched hand, Oliver lay facedown on the carpet.

"He fell," Nick said. "He just cried out and fell down." He went to a knee beside his friend.

"Oliver." Lily ran to him. "Oliver!"

"He's out," Nick told her. "I think he hit his head on that table as he went down."

"Fetch someone. I'll stay with him, but be quick, Nick. What can have happened? He hasn't done this before, has he?"

"No."

There was blood behind Oliver's right ear. "He's cut himself," she said, dabbing the wound with the hem of her robe. "Glass must have flown. Oh, do be quick."

"No."

"He may be very ill." She looked up and drew back.

Nick's green eyes stared into hers, unblinking, hard. "What is it?" she asked.

She hadn't seen his right hand until then. He raised it and revealed the pistol he held.

"Please get up," Nick said. "And step away from Oliver."

Except to cover as much of Oliver as she could with her own body, Lily didn't move.

The short, sharp kick to her thigh from Nick's boot stole her breath.

"Get up, or I'll shoot him now." To make his point more clear, he leveled the weapon at Oliver's head. "Do as I ask and I may be able to get what I want and save you both."

"I'm not a fool," Lily snapped. "You've gone too far to draw back. I don't know what you want from this, but you would not have treated Oliver so if you wished to keep his friendship."

Nick snorted. "Friendship? Friendship with a man who stole everything that should have been mine? My God, woman, don't talk drivel."

Nothing was ever hopeless. From her earliest years, Papa had taught her that clear consideration could provide a solution to any problem.

Papa had not had a man pointing a gun at her husband in mind.

Nick inclined his head. "You're quite fetching in a way." He grabbed her so quickly, she had no time to react. "Quite fetching." With little effort he pulled her up.

The balance was between inflicting whatever damage she could to him and accepting inevitable disaster, or pretending cooperation in hope of seeing some means of escape.

Lily smiled at Nick and prayed he didn't hear her throat click shut.

His eyes narrowed to slits. He looked at Oliver's unmoving form and drew down the corners of his mouth. "I've dreamed of this moment for a long time. I'd thought it would be longer in coming, but he forced my hand by coming here. By marrying you. He had to die for that."

Aghast, Lily stared at her husband. He didn't move. The cut behind his ear had stopped bleeding. Streaks of blood congealed on his hand where the goblet had broken.

"I know where to hit a man," Nick said, his nostrils flaring. "He won't move again."

"You're wrong."

"I married his pathetic sister, you know. Anne. A sickly thing. Then she died. So sad." His glance let her know he felt no pity for his dead wife. "When Frederick died, the business should have been mine. I worked. I was the one who stood at his side while his son played. For seven years I gave him my life. Then Oliver—wonderful Oliver—decided to show interest, and my position became his."

"Oliver is very grateful for all you've done. He's told me so."

"Grateful? How touching. I didn't want his gratitude, I wanted what I deserved. Now I shall have it. In the event of his death, his estate comes to me."

Lily could only stare at him.

"Too bad I couldn't divert him from marrying you. You could have been saved. But he did marry you, and now you must also die."

"Let me go." She tried to pull away. "Let me go to Oliver. And get out. Or I'll scream and bring people running to find you."

He tipped back his head and laughed. "Your scream would bring people running to the bridal suite? Hardly, my dear. It would simply be taken as part of the night's proceedings."

"Kill us, and Oliver's estate would not pass to you. You are not my heir."

He twisted her arm until she gasped. "Oh, yes it will. In the absence of children, it will come to me."

"You'll be charged with murder."

"Lord Witmore will be charged with murder. He was easily enough drugged. He's in the corridor. He'll be found with your bodies, and with this pistol in his hand."

Lily's leg made contact with a table, and she put a hand back to steady herself—and closed her fingers around a brass beetle Oliver used as a paperweight.

"I have wondered what Oliver saw in you," Nick said. "I might as well find out. After all, a little fun and games would be quite in keeping with Witmore's expected behavior."

Acid burned her throat. She mustn't panic, or any chance would be lost.

Nick caught the neck of her robe and gown and ripped them to the hem.

Inside, Lily shook with fear, and with loathing, but she stood straight and looked into Nicholas Westmoreland's face. With the barrel of the pistol, he flipped her tattered nightclothes aside and took his time studying her.

His finger was on the trigger of the pistol. One small twitch and he would blast her open.

"Correct," he said softly. "I see you understand that it would be unwise to resist me."

He knew exactly what she'd thought. The realization shook her. "I've already said I'm no fool."

"You could always try enticing me. Any sensible woman would be wise enough to offer me some inducement to spare her."

"Then I am not a sensible woman. I do not believe you would do other than find more pleasure from my pleading, then kill me anyway. I will not debase myself. My husband would not want me to do that."

He wrapped his left arm around Lily, trapping both of her hands at her sides. Please God he wouldn't realize she held the beetle.

With the pistol, he tipped up her chin. His mouth covered hers with suffocating force. He parted her lips and reached his tongue deep into her mouth.

The shreds of composure to which she clung frayed, bit by bit. He devoured her, caught her against him so that she felt what she never wished to feel from any man but her husband.

Nick raised his head. "You are sweet enough, I'll give you that. To taste. No woman is sweet otherwise."

Revulsion all but overcame her. If she lost her head she would sacrifice Oliver as well as herself. "Kiss me!" She spat the words. "Kiss me, Nick. I want you. Oh, I want you."

When his face was above hers again, she saw how lust had maddened him. He took short breaths, and veins at his temples stood out. "I believe you do," he murmured. "Oliver primed the pump, hmm. Well, why not?"

He made to loosen his trousers, frowning at the awkwardness of the task, and he released her to finish the job.

And Lily brought the many-legged brass beetle up. With every ounce of strength and hate in her being, she struck the side of his head. He screamed, and threw up an arm. She hit him again, on the brow this time, and watched with mixed horror and satisfaction as blood flowed from jagged wounds.

"*Bitch,*" he roared, flinging her aside. She crashed into the ebony table and fell to the floor. Objects from the table's surface rained around her.

Bellowing, Nick stood astride her body. She stared up into a face streaked with blood. He pointed the gun, but turned aside to wipe his eyes.

Lily swung at his leg.

"Enough," Nick said. He stood on her arm and she dropped the beetle. "You are wrong to cross me. Anne crossed me. I had to punish her, too."

She closed her eyes and waited. Pain numbed her arm, but she would not cry. A whining sound grew in her brain.

Then another sound. Different. Air shifted over her all-but-nude body.

"I'm going to *kill* you, Nick." *Oliver's voice.*

She sobbed.

Weight, Nick's suffocating weight slammed on top of her—and Oliver's. Then they rolled sideways until she lay unmolested.

"Oliver!" Lily scrambled to her hands and knees. "Oliver!"

The two men were locked together, turning, over and over, fists seeking, and finding their marks with sickening impacts.

Oliver wasn't dead. *He wasn't dead.* Tears of joy blurred her vision. She rose to her feet and wrapped the tattered remnants of her clothes around her, tying them together with the belt of her robe.

"Stop it," she cried.

Nick's face was all blood now, and Oliver's. On his back beneath Nick, Oliver heaved the other man up and threw him. A lacquered chest tipped and fell. The hasp broke and the lid flew open, spewing papers and books.

"I'm going to kill you," Nick shouted, swiping blood from his face with hands that also bled. "Both of you. I will have what's mine."

He made to fall upon Oliver again, but Oliver rolled away and leaped to his feet.

Then Lily saw the pistol beneath a chair where it must have slid in the scuffle. Oliver threw himself upon Nick and fastened his hands around his neck.

Gurgling rose from Nick's throat.

Lily rushed to retrieve the gun.

With a clenched fist, Nick drove at Oliver's windpipe. Horrified, Lily watched him lose his grip and grab for his own throat. Gasping, he fought for breath.

She held the pistol in both hands and used her thumbs to cock it.

Nicholas Westmoreland rose and advanced on her.

"One more step and I shoot you," she told him.

He stopped and said, "Give it to me. Come along. We both know you won't use it. Give it to me."

"Don't do it, Lily," Oliver managed to say.

Nick took another step toward her, and Lily peered along the pistol barrel. "I have your nose in my sights, sir," she said. "I believe your brain is close behind that spot."

With a mighty crash, the door opened. Or rather, the door broke from its hinges and flew across the room to land on an armchair.

Nick swung around in time to see—absolutely nothing but the apparently empty hall, and the leather-and-brass elephant against the far wall.

Oliver was on his back, bringing him down, before he

could recover. And Lily promptly sat astride his thighs, the pistol poked between his legs. "Move and there'll be no need for anyone to consider your mysteries further," she said, giving an extra shove and thrilling to the sound of his moans.

"Have at ye!" Bellowing, swinging a knobby club above his head, McLewd exploded into the room. "It's all over for ye, laddie. Ye're about t'meet your maker."

Peering around Oliver, Lily said, "McLewd? What are you doing here?"

Holding the club aloft, he pushed back his shock of red hair and came closer, bending to see the spectacle more clearly. "Gambol," he said. "Get in here, ye daft creature. Ye made me wait too long. They've kilt him a'ready."

"Not quite," Oliver said. "Would you mind assisting—"

"Not dead yet?" McLewd said. "Och, I'll get the right o'it. Move aside, Lord Blackmoor."

Gambol crept hesitantly into the room. "Forgive me, my lord. I do have my troubles with getting around quickly enough these days. I'd thought Mr. Westmoreland would take a little longer getting here. He has Lord Witmore tied up outside, you know. I believe he intended to blame—"

"We dinna need a bloody dissertation from ye, Gambol," McLewd said, and took Nick by the hair. He hauled the semi-unconscious man along the floor. "See t'the comfort o' his lordship and his lady, while I deal wi' this."

"Um, a constable, I think, McLewd," Oliver said, turning to gather Lily in his arms. "Killing Mr. Westmoreland would be—"

"Too good fer him. Aye, ye're right, laddie. I mean, your lordship. I'll deal wi' it. He kilt Leonard, y'know. Saw that wi' my own eyes. An' him dressed like a man o' God t'do it. Rot he will. I'll see to it. That fool Laycock dinna make things easier wi' his plans t'find whatever it is they've bin lookin' fer and not findin' fer years. Gambol will tell ye the way o' it. We'd a problem or two gettin' things straight or we'd ha' saved ye this. But we kept an eye on ye. Didn't want to risk having him find a way to wriggle out o' his crimes. All's well now. I'll deal wi' Lord Witmore, too."

"Thank you, McLewd," Oliver said.

Lily was speechless while the Scotsman left with Nick thrown over his shoulder.

Gambol wrung his hands. "I wasn't completely sure at first, you see. And I certainly didn't want to make a dreadful mistake."

Oliver and Lily helped each other up and staggered to fall onto a couch. "Perhaps you could explain all this tomorrow?" Oliver suggested.

"Well, my lord, if it pleases you, McLewd would have my liver and lights—excuse the expression, his, not mine—but he would if I didn't dispose of this now."

Oliver nodded and pushed Lily's hair from her face. "I'm so sorry, my darling."

"I'm all right if you're all right," she told him.

"I though you were . . . well, I though you were who you are," Gambol said querulously. "You see, I was here in your father's time. When he was sent away. A nicer young gentleman you'd never want to meet. Not like master George, who was troublesome. We—that's the staff—always believed Master George had done whatever was done and blamed Master Frederick. But we had no proof. And there never was any proof, except that after the death of his father—who had been Master George—the present Lord Witmore spent so much time searching the north wing. That's why McLewd was persuaded to leave the

Hall and go to work at Fell Manor. So he could keep a watch on things there, you see."

The length of the speech rendered the old man breathless. Lily and Oliver waited patiently for him to resume.

"McLewd's sister suffered at the hands of Lord Witmore, you see, and the simple solution McLewd at first thought of didn't quite deal with all our concerns. So we joined forces and bided our time. We waited, and then you came back. I couldn't believe it. I knew you almost at once. I had to take down Master Frederick's picture because I was afraid someone else would notice the likeness. And then I observed Lord Witmore coming from these rooms when you were out. I had to make sure there was nothing here that might arouse suspicion. I'll return your possessions, of course."

"Thank you, Gambol," Oliver said. "Thank you very much. My wife and I will never be able to fully repay you."

"Hmm, well, there's nothing to repay, my lord. I am sorry about the other."

Lily looked at him. "The other?"

"I shouldn't have gone to Mr. Godwin. I only thought I ought to make certain it was all right for me to remove the painting and your things, my lord. Just until it was safe to return them. I didn't want a theft on my soul."

"Think nothing of it," Oliver said, and Lily was almost certain she felt him chuckle. "Get along to bed with you. We'll speak in the morning. And close the door behind you, please."

Gambol bowed even lower and backed away. On the threshold he frowned and looked around.

"What is it?" Oliver asked.

"The door, my lord. I'm very sorry, but I can't close it. It isn't here anymore."

Chapter Twenty-nine

If his head didn't ache as if an animal had attempted to tear it in two, his incredibly brave wife's laughter might amuse him more.

Oliver leaned back on the couch, closed his eyes, and pretended to doze. At least McLewd had been persuaded to execute a hasty rehanging of the door, and the professor and Fribble, whose shocked visit had been unavoidable, had gone.

"You aren't asleep," Lily said, snorting in her efforts to control mirth. "You are tetchy, though, dearest. Be truthful, now. You're annoyed with me."

"I certainly am not annoyed with you."

"Aha!" Triumph dramatized the word. "But you are awake. And you look frightful, Oliver. Fie, I wonder if you'll ever be less than monstrous again."

He regarded her through slitted eyes. "I am recovering from a blow to the head, madam."

"Then I shall administer a proven cure." She kissed his brow many times—softly—and leaned on the back of the couch. "Of course, I find this sudden reduction of your beauty perfectly acceptable. I shall love you regardless, perhaps even more so. After all, as a plain person myself, I am more than comfortable in the company of another just—no, almost as plain."

Oliver gave her his entire attention. "That, madam, had best be the last time I hear you make a similar remark about yourself. There is no woman in England—no, in the world—who is more lovely than my wife. She has an ugly tongue, but a beautiful form.

"Her only problem is that she grew up in the company of blind numskulls who insisted upon forcing their misinformed opinions on her. Now, if she would just be quiet and allow an injured man peace, she might be considered perfect."

Lily wound one of her unbound curls through her fingers. "Hmm, hmm, hmm. We have suffered together, husband."

"And survived together—thanks to the undeniable truth that I am married to a tiger of a creature."

Her smile disappeared. "The days to come will not be easy. You will mourn the loss of your friend."

"He was never my friend," Oliver said. He made to push a hand through his hair, looked at the bandages Fribble had applied, and changed his mind.

Lily settled herself on an arm of the couch. "You believed Nick was your best friend. And you will grieve the loss, Oliver. But you will not be alone."

He smiled at her and moved closer. "I shall never be alone again. We'll deal with matters here. Then I intend to take you to Boston on one of my ships. Should you like that?"

She leaned toward him, her expression contemplative. "A sea journey with the man I love? Aboard one of his fast and famous ships? To America, to Boston? Oh, Oliver, I'm not sure a woman should be expected to tolerate such boring possibilities."

He made a grab for her, but she was too quick and leaped away. "I want you to go to bed," she said.

Oliver gave her his best lascivious grin. "You're insatiable."

"And you're a sick man," she said severely. "With a pain in the head, you tell me. Rest is what you must have."

"My head is vastly improved." He rose to his feet. "I have a few cuts and bruises. And so, wife, do you. Shall we allow them to interfere with our pleasures?"

Lily came into his arms. They both bore bruises, not all of which were visible. But the professor, who had been summoned and whose outraged reaction had stilled every other tongue, had sagely informed them that they must heal each other, and heal alone for as long as they needed to be alone. With that he had shepherded all others away with him. Now that Nick was in custody, the business of dealing with legal and other unpleasant issues could wait.

"I hope I shall eventually stop wondering what crime caused my father's banishment," Oliver said. "The injustice cuts me, but if it must be so that I remain ignorant, it must be so."

Lily rubbed his back through the clean, white cotton shirt he wore. Her warm hands made him shudder with awareness of her. She had donned a demure pink nightgown and robe, but her face remained unnaturally pale.

"I cannot sleep," he told her. "And I am sane enough to accept that other options might prove more painful than we'd find desirable."

"Oh." She tilted her head and smiled up at him. "Perhaps we would find that other sensations can divert us from the pain."

"Perhaps we would." He pulled her face to his chest

and rested his chin atop her head. "The storm is past. Two hours at most and the dawn will break."

"I think I'd like a walk," Lily said. "If you could, that is. Perhaps to the north wing. We might take another look there and—"

"There's nothing to be found, my love. We must accept it. *I* must accept it."

"Yes." Her eyes clouded.

Hurriedly Oliver said, "But a walk would please me. Especially since we will obviously not sleep easily."

Hand in hand, they made their way to the bridge and the north wing.

In the center of the bridge, they paused. The faintest silvery underbelly cradled the dying night sky.

"Fickle storm," Lily said, leaning against Oliver. "All noisy rage, then it creeps away."

"And leaves the world clean," he told her. "And gives me a few stars."

"Only you?"

"Yes, only me. They are for me because the sight of you beneath them stuns me yet again."

"Fiddle," Lily said. "It's cold."

Oliver led her into the north wing and smiled to note that his father's portrait had been replaced. "Papa posed in the music room here," he said. "Leaning on the very piano you play."

Lily studied the painting closely. "Indeed. How odd to think of his fingers on the very same keys." Without further discussion, Lily went directly to the staircase and they descended to the lowest floor.

"Lily—"

"I *like* it here, Oliver," she said, interrupting him fiercely. "And so should you. Forget about Witless. Your grandparents had their apartments here. And your father obviously spent happy times in these rooms."

He made no response. Inevitably their path led to the exotic room that had been his uncle's final human sanctuary.

"Well!" Lily plunked her hands on her hips and turned a circle. "Can you believe it? That wretched cousin of yours has managed to be here yet again."

Oliver righted the skin-covered chair and sat down to survey evidence of a hurried, and careless, search. This time there had been no attempt to disguise the intrusion.

"He pulled up the floorboards," Lily said, pointing to several gaping spaces in the floor. "And he's taken the furniture apart. Oh, Oliver, such destruction. How *dare* he?"

"Let's not forget our culprit could have been Laycock. Although I don't think he has the courage to risk enraging me."

Lily gathered bedcovers from the floor and heaped them on top of the mattress. "He shall not come here again."

"No," Oliver said, beyond anger now. "No, I doubt he will. We'll make certain your father sees what's happened here. That will take care of the issue."

"The chest." Lily started picking up the tiny drawers that had been torn out and thrown down. "This is madness. For years that dreadful man has taken advantage of my father's good nature. What could possibly make him do this now?"

"Put those down," Oliver told her. "Come here. I need to hold you."

She came to him, a drawer in each hand, but would not allow him to pull her onto his lap. "He has even torn down the bed curtains, Oliver. Ooh, I must discuss this with Rosemary and Myrtle."

Interest overcame exhaustion and Oliver sat up straight. "Really? Why would you do that?"

Rather than return his gaze, she walked a complete circle around the bed that had been pulled away from the wall.

"Lily? Answer me."

"We have made a habit of discussing human peculiarities. Such as obsessive behaviors." She studied him then as if evaluating his response to her announcement.

He only shrugged.

Lily set down the drawers. She pulled loose the last few fastenings that held a trailing bed curtain, and covered her head when the canopy swayed.

One bedpost creaked, giving way beneath the mattress.

"Lily!" Oliver shot to his feet and grabbed her, swept her from her feet, and deposited her at a safe distance. "That fool Witmore has destroyed everything here. Come, let's return to more pleasant surroundings. Later I shall suggest to your father that this room be cleared. It would be for the best."

His wife had grown still, her gray eyes fixed, her lips parted. Color mounted in her cheeks.

"My darling?" Concerned, Oliver touched her brow. "You need to rest. You have been through far too much."

"No," she whispered. "Oh, it cannot be."

"It's all right," he told her. "Sleep is what we both need."

"Oliver." Her fingers gouged him through his shirt. "Oh, Oliver, look."

He did look, and saw nothing other than a room in violent disarray.

Lily pulled away from him and approached the bed. She pointed to the top of the golden canopy, now madly tilted and visible in its entirety for the first time.

"I'm . . ." He joined her. "It isn't."

She swallowed loudly and said, "It *is*," in a croaky voice.

"No. I refuse to believe it." But he removed the severed carving that had crowned the bed. Beneath it glittered . . . He could not even *think* the words that identified what they had found.

With cautious reverence, Lily retrieved what had been revealed and held it in both hands. "It is, isn't it?" she said, panting a little. "And the canopy decoration was molded to cover it exactly. Who would ever think to look beneath a crown for another— Oh, Oliver, that's exactly what it is."

"Yes. Unbelievable. There all the time."

Lily stroked it. "A clever hiding place. All but in the open. It's been looked at a million times."

"How could they . . . Laycock's sister diverted the guards, isn't that what he said?"

"Yes," Lily said. "And once George and his friends had it, it wasn't fun or adventurous anymore. It was dangerous. They must have feared death if they were discovered. For treason, I should imagine. They must have been too terrified to even try to return it."

"Outrageous," Oliver murmured.

"The Queen?"

Oliver nodded and said, "The Queen indeed. The Coronation?"

"What did they put on her head? Could this be a copy?"

Oliver looked closely and shook his head. "I know enough about jewels to recognize the real thing. Two large drop pearls. Presented to Queen Elizabeth I by Catherine de Medici and set as these are? They certainly fit the description." He felt sick. "And the Stuart Sapphire? And the sapphire taken from the finger of Edward the Confessor's finger when Henry II moved his remains to Westminster?"

"And the Black Prince's spinal," Lily said. "No. No, it can't be. The Coronation took place, Oliver."

He put an arm around Lily's shoulders and led her to the chair. There he sat down and pulled her into his lap. On her knees rested what had unjustly brought about his father's disinheritance.

"Not a word has ever been spoken of this by the royal family or anyone else who must have known." Lily ran her fingertips over hundreds of closely set diamonds. "And the theft was kept so secret by your grandfather and your uncle that not even your father or Witless ever found out. Witless was certain there was something very valuable, but not what it was. Everyone decided Witless was searching for some sort of treasure. Servants usually know everything, but they didn't this time. Good heavens, Oliver, the knowledge died with George.

"The authorities must have feared a public outcry at such stupid carelessness. An uprising, even. But there was the Coronation. What did the Queen wear?"

"A fake," Oliver told her.

"And now? When there are State occasions—"

"The same fake. Our task is to decide how to put the real thing back. Anonymously. At least no one will be on guard, as they must have been right after George took it. Maybe they even suspected him, and that's why he never tried to return it himself."

With a gusty sigh, Lily wriggled free and returned to

the bed. She considered finding out how it might feel to wear a queen's hat, just for a moment, but replaced the shimmering nuisance instead, and covered it with its molded casket.

"We will have to decide on the simplest method of ridding ourselves of that, dearest," Oliver pointed out.

Lily cast her gaze to the ceiling and said, "I know." She returned to his lap and commenced to unbutton his shirt. "All I can say is . . . fiddle. What a nuisance."

And with that, she kissed her husband again, and again—and again.

Author's Note

Some years ago a quantity of papers came into my possession. Among them I discovered some extraordinary information about a family named Beaumont, otherwise known as the lords of Blackmoor in Come Piddle, Hampshire, England.

There is a reference to the discovery of an item I dare not name precisely. It must be sufficient for me to state that this item had caused great upheaval in the family until Oliver, Marquis of Blackmoor in 1848, and his wife, Lily, contrived to return it to its rightful place. Apparently there was no subsequent mention of its having been missing—at least not in any public manner.

Another note mentions that the Earl of Witmore, cousin to Oliver, married a certain Mrs. Fribble and that the two were considered very suited to each other.

A Mr. Nicholas Westmoreland contracted a fever in jail and died before he could stand trial for crimes not detailed, although this reader surmised they must have been grave—perhaps the gravest.

I should explain that the papers came into my possession through my connection to the Worth family of Boston, and via a female descendant. In fact, I am a distant relative of those Worths and it was in my own great-

great-grandmother's journal that I found reference to the findings of "The Society for the Exposure and Examination of Mysterious Male Parts."

The members of the society were listed as Lily Adler, Rosemary Godwin, and Myrtle Bumwallop. And, in light of their times, their advanced analytical powers continue to amaze me. It seems that careful examination of what they termed "male mysteries" revealed some uncontrovertible evidence: The female mind is made so differently from that of the malc that the latter is assured of remaining a mystery to the former—and the former to the latter.

Stella Cameron
Frog Crossing
Nether Piddle

Please turn the page
for a bonus excerpt
from Stella Cameron's
December 1997 release
Wait for Me
a new romance
coming from Warner Books
in stores November 1997

CHAPTER 1

Ballyfog, Scotland, 1837

"Humility reduces a female to butter every time, old man. A fellow must be humble. Go to the girl, hat in hand, heart on sleeve, soul in the eye, adoration in every word—"

"Gray."

Gray Falconer blinked several times and frowned at his friend Max Rossmara. "What?"

"The girl in question is Minerva Arbuckle?"

"You know it is. *She* is. That's why we're here. This is her home. Her parents' home." He felt exasperated.

"Quite. And Minerva is the very female you have rhapsodized all the way home from the West Indies? She who is most unlike any other woman? A sweet creature, but with a will of her own, and a strong head, and a fierce temper when aroused? The same Minerva Arbuckle who is ahead of her time, determined, and who will never allow another to persuade her of her own mind?"

Max had only grown more apt to annoy in the years since their meeting at Eton.

Just in time to save Gray from searching out another response, Mrs. Hatch, the Arbuckles' plump, phlegmatic housekeeper, appeared in the foyer of Willieknock Lodge where she'd left them—without a civil word—before going in search of her mistress.

"Well, Mrs. Hatch," Gray said, bestowing one of the smiles famous for shaking any female's reserve. "You left us so quickly I hadn't the time to tell you how very fine you're looking."

"I've the gout," Mrs. Hatch responded, sniffling, and hobbled to prove her point. "Hersel' says ye're to wait in the garden room. Daft, I call it. *Garden room.* Hoity-toity. Cold in there, too. No better than ye deserve, though. Disturbin' folks at such an hour." She turned away and shuffled past the foot of the no-nonsense mahogany staircase that divided an oppressive entry hall hung with so many paintings of nudes that the dark burgundy-colored wallpaper might not be noticed at all.

"I told you we shouldn't be making calls so late in the day," Max said. He paused to study a painting of a recumbent raven-haired damsel of impressive proportions and said, "I say, Gray, look at these—"

"Yes," Gray said quickly. "Mr. Arbuckle is Mr. Porteous Arbuckle."

"Really?" Clearly Max failed to make any connection between Min's father and the paintings.

"The celebrated painter," Gray clarified. A man could be forgiven a small, judicious exaggeration. After all, Mr. Arbuckle *had* done the paintings.

"Does he paint anything other than nudes?"—Max cleared his throat—"I mean, I don't recall if he paints anything other than nudes."

"Doesna'," Mrs. Hatch said, leading the way from the hall, through a corridor lined with more tributes to billowing white flesh, toward a door fashioned of stained-glass panels. "Ye wouldna' get me takin' my clothes off the way those hussies do. All in the name o' art." She made a scoffing noise. "I wouldna' no matter how much the master begged."

Gray met Max's eyes, managed not to smile, and entered the garden room he remembered so well from the many hours he'd spent at Willieknock Lodge before leaving for the Falconer sugar plantations in the West Indies.

"That's that, then," Mrs. Hatch said when she'd deposited

them amid raised, brick-lined beds devoid of anything but unlikely holly bushes and the bare stalks of plants too fragile to stand the bone-chilling cold inside the glass walls and dome of the room. "Hersel' will be here when she's primped enough. Daft." Mrs. Hatch left with a mighty swishing of her black skirts.

Light in the garden room was low. Snow fell softly from a black sky onto the glass overhead and nestled in here-and-gone puffs against the windows.

"Damn cold," Max muttered, shifting his wide shoulders inside a heavy coat of a similar black cloth as Gray's caped cloak. "I say we should have gone directly to Drumblade. You'll have much to share with your uncle, and you could have come here at an appropriate hour in the morning."

"Minerva would never have forgiven me had I wasted another moment in coming to her." The anticipation of seeing her caused warmth enough to shut out the night chill.

"You'd do well to tell her it all, then, Gray. The whole truth."

"Hush," Gray said, glancing over his shoulder. "I told you we must keep everything between us until I discover more." Max didn't know *everything*, but Gray had considered it wise to hold his own counsel on some details of his abduction at sea on his way home to England, and his subsequent detainment on a primitive island held by a murderous pirate band.

"They intended to kill you," Max said, undeterred by Gray's exhortation to be cautious. "There could be no other explanation."

"Possibly." Gray had his own theories about the cutthroats' plans for his fate, but knew he must not reveal them yet. "I thank God that I was picked up from that pathetic raft."

"And I thank God for the amazing coincidence that put me aboard that ship. I wasn't to have sailed in her at all."

They'd marveled many times at the chance that had placed

Max aboard the very vessel that came upon Gray's exhausted body.

"Max, bear with me. I know it's your way to have everything out in the open, but I know what I'm about here." He knew that his captors had been paid for their efforts, and that they'd been expected to kill him. He'd heard them in the dark of hot nights, drunk and planning to turn "Lord Ice-eyes," as they called him, into a bigger fortune than any they'd ever dreamed of before. They referred to his enemy as: "Mr. No-name," and laughed while they congratulated themselves on outwitting that gentleman and causing him to keep them supplied with "fat boons," in exchange for their repeatedly broken promises to kill Gray.

"Of course it'll be the way you want it," Max said. "But I'd have thought you'd be chafing to see Drumblade. It's your home, man, and you almost bid it goodbye."

"I almost bid Min goodbye. My house and lands are dear to me, but not as dear as Minerva Arbuckle."

Heavy, hurrying footsteps approached and Janet Arbuckle, Minerva's mother, entered. A large lady with blue eyes and a great many blond ringlets bouncing about her ears, she rushed at Gray with outstretched arms. "My dear Mr. Falconer, our joy knows no bounds. We are beside ourselves with ecstasy."

Gray kept his teeth together and his lips parted and took Mrs. Arbuckle's plump hands in his. "Ecstasy," he murmured. "I hope you are well."

"Oh, I've been far from well." She averted her face and bowed her head. "How could I be well while my dearest Minerva pined for you? How could I be other than *destroyed* when she has barely eaten a decent meal since she began to watch for you with less and less hope that you would ever return?"

"How indeed?" Max asked, his green eyes solemn. "Any

woman awaiting Gray Falconer's return for long would be bound to fade away entirely."

Janet Arbuckle shot Gray's friend a suspicious glance. "And you are, sir?"

"Max Rossmara," Gray said hurriedly. "An old friend. He's also by way of being a neighbor."

Mrs. Arbuckle had already lost interest in Max. "Ahem." She produced a lace handkerchief and flapped it before her full but pretty face. "I do wonder if it mightn't be kinder to have you come back in the morning. Just to give me time to prepare Minerva."

Gray frowned and swung his cape back from his shoulders. "I doubt Minerva would be amused to discover I'd visited and gone away without seeing her." He propped a foot on the edge of a brick wall and rested a forearm on his thigh. The pose should assure Mrs. Arbuckle that he had no intention of going anywhere very soon.

Mrs. Arbuckle made a twittery noise, not unlike the canary Gray had once given Min. "Well, I'm sure you aren't to be dissuaded. Gentlemen can be *so* forceful." She smiled coyly. "But then, isn't that what we ladies find so irresistible?"

Max coughed and turned to stare through the glass into snow-dotted darkness.

"Surely Min's been told I'm here," Gray said.

"Oh"—the lady raised plump shoulders shown off by an inappropriately frilly, low cut dress in peach-colored silk—"she'll be along very soon, I'm sure."

More footsteps sounded in the corridor and Gray stood up. His palms were suddenly damp.

A familiar high, soaring to even higher laugh reached them, and Gray closed his eyes for a moment, anticipating the arrival of Porteous Arbuckle. Even the thought of the man made nerves in Gray's jaw twitch and fixed his spine until it ached. That his wonderful Minerva was the product of such a couple would always bemuse him.

"What's this, then?" Porteous demanded, all but capering into view. "Hatch said I'd best come and deal with things. I said I pay *her* to deal with things, but she just walked away. *Walked away.*" He laughed again, slapping his knees through a paint-splotched blue smock.

"Mr. Arbuckle," Mrs. Arbuckle said severely. "We have visitors. Very *welcome* visitors, I may add." She went to her husband's side.

"I can't see anyone of importance," the man said, peering at Gray. "Who is this, then, m'dear?"

"Mr. Arbuckle," that gentleman's lady said, and delivered a kick to his skinny shin without making any attempt at disguising the blow. When he shrieked and hopped about, she caught him by the voluminous sleeve of his smock and jerked him back beside her. The top of his head, in a huge, floppy blue beret, reached her chin. "Gray Falconer has returned from his travels. Praise be, when we all thought something dreadful had happened to him. We are grateful that was not the case, aren't we, Mr. Arbuckle?"

Gray watched the man closely. Never deceived by the idiotic act, Gray regarded the other as almost certainly dangerous, but he could not risk giving his suspicions away. Given warning, Arbuckle might find a way to conceal the connections Gray was certain he had, and the treacherous steps he'd taken to rid himself of the man he'd never wanted as a son-in-law. Porteous Arbuckle didn't want any son-in-law at all.

How would Minerva regard Gray if he unmasked her father as a would-be murderer?

Later, Gray thought, he must deal with that question later, and that's why every move must be cautiously made.

"Mr. Arbuckle," Mrs. Arbuckle said again, treading on her husband's toe this time. When he howled, she shook her head

until her ringlets flapped. "Do stop giving vent to your artistic temperament, my dear. Gray Falconer has returned."

Arbuckle stood quite still and looked at Gray. "Who?"

"*Gray Falconer.* He's your daughter's fiancé."

"My daughter doesn't have a fiancé. She's a spinster. Going to remain a spinster. Not the marrying kind. Who's that?" He pointed rudely at Max.

"Mr. Max Rossmara," Mrs. Arbuckle said. "He's a friend of Gray's."

"And who is he when he's not a friend of . . . whatever his name is?"

Max turned back from the windows, his color suspiciously high. His dark red hair glinted in the subdued light. "I'm estate commissioner to the Marquess of Stonehaven at Castle Kirkcaldy."

"Never heard of either of them."

"I'm sure not," Max said, deeply polite. "Dunkeld way. Somewhat beyond. Gray and I met at Eton and we haven't seen much of each other since."

"Fortunate for you, I should say," Arbuckle announced and earned himself a pinch to the cheek. He clapped a hand over his face and said, "Dunkeld way? *Dunkeld* way. No wonder I haven't heard of you, or it, or him, or whatever. You're a foreigner."

A foreigner? Dunkeld couldn't be more than thirty miles distant. Ballyfog lay between that village and Edinburgh.

Gray gave his attention to Mrs. Arbuckle once more. "What do you suppose is keeping Minerva?"

"The silliness," she said, with another exuberant shake of the head. "She'll give all that up now you're back."

"Good night to you," Porteous said. "Nice of you to pay your respects. Do have a safe trip to . . . wherever. Let yourself out, will you?" Abandoning his jerky movements, he drew his slight stature up and strutted from the room without looking back.

Mrs. Arbuckle wound her handkerchief between her fingers and leaned forward from the waist. "Excuse Mr. Arbuckle. He hasn't been well. I'd better go to him."

Afraid he would be forced to leave without seeing Minerva, Gray said, "Please do take care of your husband. If you'd just direct me, I'll find Minerva. Is she busy with her piano?"

"Um, nooo."

"Her own painting, then. I always said she'd inherited some of her father's brilliance in that direction." Actually Minerva was an excellent water-colorist.

"Nooo," Mrs. Arbuckle said. "Gray, I really do think tomorrow might be preferable."

He allowed his desperation to show. "I need to see her. Surely you can understand my fervor to do so."

Another coy smile was his reward. "Of course. I'm not so old that I forget how these things are. I shall send you to her, but you must promise me you'll make allowances for the time she's spent awaiting your return. She's—*changed.* Somewhat changed. Quite changed."

"Really?"

"Yes, she"—Mrs. Arbuckle blinked rapidly—"she's the dear girl you left but with a few minor, mmm, idiosyncrasies. Yes, that's what they are. Developed to help mask her desperate concern for you."

"I see."

"I'm sure you will. The third floor. She's taken it over and spends all of her time up there with her cousins."

Morag and Fergus Drummond, twins orphaned by the deaths of Janet Arbuckle's brother and his wife, had lived with the Arbuckles since their early teens. "Thank you," Gray said. "Don't let me take up any more of your time. You've already been more than kind."

"No more kind than I should be. Oh, this is wonderful. Oh, how *wonderful*."

"Thank you," Gray said again.

Mrs. Arbuckle turned away, then turned back, a frown puckering her brow. "Now you won't forget what I said? You must be patient with Minerva. Whatever she says, don't believe a word of it. She doesn't mean it."

Gray tried but failed to avoid Max's eyes. Max raised his arched brows.

"You know how difficult she can be," Mrs. Arbuckle continued. "And she only becomes more so. In fact, she's positively infuriating sometimes. Frequently. Almost all the time."

"Don't worry." Gray was worried—just a little worried. "Leave her in my hands."

"Yes, yes, I'll do that. That's what I'll do. Leave her in your hands. Oh, yes, in your hands . . ." The lady's voice continued to a meaningless babble that faded as she got farther from the garden room.

"Right," Gray said. "The third floor. Big closed rooms are all I remember. Didn't think anyone went up there."

"Apparently the infuriating Minerva Arbuckle goes there now," Max said in deceptively even tones. "Are you still convinced she's going to turn to butter the moment she sets eyes on you?"

"Utterly convinced."

"Why?"

He considered. "It's best to be blunt at times like this."

Max crossed his arms. "Times like this?"

"When dealing with matters of the heart, and the head, and the soul, and the—"

"Quite. You be blunt, then, Gray."

"Min worships me." There was the slightest disquiet lurking amid the conviction, but it was nothing worth consideration. "She has worshipped me from the moment we met. And when I had to leave for the West Indies, she promised she'd be waiting for me when I returned."

Max made a humming noise, of which Gray was not at all fond, before announcing, "She promised she'd be waiting for you when you returned."

"Yes." Irritation made itself felt.

"When you returned a year after you left."

Rossmara could be a *damnably* irritating fellow. *"Yes."*

"But you're three years late."